> "...the sensation of depth is overwhelming. And the darkness is immortal."
> —Carl Sagan

PLEASE STAND BY .... TOM ENGLISH   3

SPECIAL FEATURES
  WE'LL KNOW WHEN WE GET THERE, WE'LL TELL YOU WHEN WE GET BACK:
  DESTINATION MOON SEVEN DECADES LATER
  .... JUSTIN HUMPHREYS   34
  REVISITING SPACE:1999 .... GREGORY L. NORRIS   169

STORIES
  SIX FRIGHTENED MEN .... ROBERT SILVERBERG   13
  SLOW BURN .... HENRY STILL   21
  THE SKY PEOPLE .... GREGORY L. NORRIS   43
  BRIGHTSIDE CROSSING .... ALAN E. NOURSE   57
  BELOW THE SURFACE .... VONNIE WINSLOW CRIST   71
  SATELLITE OF DEATH .... RANDALL GARRETT   93
  I, ROCKET .... RAY BRADBURY   99
  ROCKET SUMMER .... RAY BRADBURY   109
  MORGUE SHIP .... RAY BRADBURY   117
  HANGING VINES .... JAMES DORR   139
  THE ROCKETEERS HAVE SHAGGY EARS .... KEITH BENNETT   144
  SEA LEGS .... FRANK QUATTROCCHI   187
  MINUTEMEN .... KURT NEWTON   211
  DUEL ON SYRTIS .... POUL ANDERSON   213
  TEST ROCKET .... JACK DOUGLAS   225

DEPARTMENTS
  THREAT WATCH .... MATT COWAN   124

COMICS
  THE LAST STAR WARDEN .... JASON J. McCUISTON   83
  SPACE ANGEL .... ALEX TOTH   227

COVER: EARLE K. BERGEY (THRILLING WONDER), AFTER DESTINATION MOON
INTERIOR ILLUSTRATIONS: ALLEN KOSZOWSKI, ED EMSHWILLER & OTHERS

EDITOR AND PUBLISHER: TOM ENGLISH

Black Infinity: Rocketships and Spacesuits (Issue #8, Winter/Spring 2022) is published by Rocket Science Books, an imprint of Dead Letter Press. *Black Infinity: Rocketships and Spacesuits* is copyright © Tom English and Dead Letter Press, PO Box 134, New Kent, VA 23124-0134. All rights reserved, including the right to reproduce this book, or portions thereof, in any form including but not limited to electronic and print media, without written permission from the publisher. *Black Infinity* is published semi-annually.

www.DeadLetterPress.com   www.BlackInfinityMagazine.com   ISBN-13: 978-1732434493

The Romance of Rocketships*

DECADES AGO, WHILE THE UNITED STATES AND RUSSIA WERE RACING TO REACH THE MOON AND BEYOND, SPACESUITS WERE HIP, AND ROCKETSHIPS WERE ALL THE RAGE.

Science was finally catching up to science fiction—and vice versa. Throughout the 1950s and '60s, images of spaceships blasted across the covers of scores of SF digests. The pulp-paper pages of these cheap magazines routinely featured stories of bubble-helmeted adventurers braving alien worlds across the cold seas of interstellar space.

In the film industry, just when the popularity of mad scientists and more traditional monsters was waning, savvy movie producers caught a glimpse of a cash-cow constellation in the starry night sky. Cinematic trips to the moon and Mars began to fill matinees and double-bills. And by the late '50s, toy rockets and space helmets were glutting the shelves of department stores such as Macy's and Gimbels.

Cars were being designed with futuristic fins and bumpers with bullet-shaped ornamentation. Amusement parks often featured rocketship rides. And in a few places, there were even diners built to look like spaceships.

* As to which is correct, "rocket ship" or "rocketship": the editor has taken his cue from the title of the 1950 movie *Rocketship X-M*. And, too, if "spaceship" can be a single word, then why not *rocketship*?

BLACK INFINITY • 3

For the science fiction enthusiast, the world had become a pretty cool place. All eyes were raised to the heavens, as people from all walks of life hoped in the future and dreamed of far-off worlds.

Space travel wasn't new to post-WWII science fiction literature. The motif can be traced back as far as German astronomer Johannes Kepler's 1634 essay *Somnium* ("The Dream"), in which a man is spirited to the moon by a demon. The French playwright Cyrano de Bergerac tried to approach the subject in a slightly more scientific manner: in his satirical novel *L'autre monde* (*The Other World*), published posthumously in 1657, the protagonist straps three rows of rockets to his back in an attempt to leave Earth. Many of the earliest fictional modes of space travel that followed are equally as absurd.

In Edgar Allan Poe's 1835 tale "The Unparalleled Adventure of One Hans Pfaall," a journey to the moon is accomplished in a balloon. In Jules Verne's *From the Earth to the Moon* (1865), a vessel is fired from a huge cannon, a method depicted in the 1936 movie *Things to Come*—based on H. G. Wells' 1933

novel *The Shape of Things to Come*. And speaking of Wells, in his 1901 novel *The First Men in the Moon*, an antigravity coating called Cavorite is used to lift a spherical ship to the moon.

During the early twentieth century, many pulp SF authors had the good sense to be vague about their fictional methods of propulsion, giving free reign to Frank R. Paul and other pulp cover artists, who depicted space vehicles in a variety of geometric shapes, including spheres and cylinders. But after the U.S. inventor Dr. Robert H. Goddard launched

---

Previous page: (top) the 1959 Cadillac Eldorado, complete with rocket fins and jet-blast taillights; (bottom) Collier's Magazine ran a popular series on the future of space travel from 1952 to early 1954.

Left: Claude Shepperson's illustration of Cavor's sphere from the first hardcover edition of H. G. Wells' *The First Men in the Moon*, published by George Newnes in 1901.

Above: Along Route 66 in Wilmington, Illinois, the 24-foot-tall Gemini Giant greets customers to The Launching Pad Restaurant. The statue dates to 1960 when the restaurant first opened as Dairy Delite. (It was renamed The Launching Pad in 1965.)

the first liquid-fuel rocket in 1926, rocket science continued to advance—quickly, thanks to Nazi Germany's war efforts—and SF would generally keep pace with it.

The German rocket-research pioneer Hermann Oberth successfully launched several rockets in 1931. He was aided in his research by two young assistants, Wernher Von Braun and Willy Ley. Ley emigrated to the US in 1935, where he published numerous articles and books on rocketry and space travel, and became a noted science consultant for several magazines, books, and movie productions.

Clockwise from top: Dr. Robert Goddard prepares to launch the first liquid-fueled rocket on March 16, 1926; Wernher von Braun with the first stage engines of the Saturn V rocket; German artist Kurt Röschl's depiction of the classic 1952 Ferry Rocket developed by Wernher von Braun.

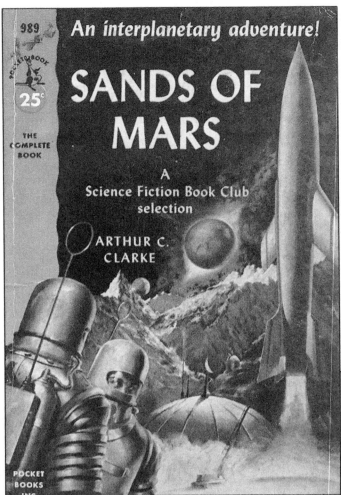

After WWII and throughout the development of rocket science in the 1950s and '60s, several SF writers including Arthur C. Clarke and Robert A. Heinlein, became huge advocates of space travel. Clarke had earlier published the essay "We Can Rocket to the Moon—*Now!*" in the Summer 1939 issue of *Tales of Wonder*, and produced several fine space exploration novels grounded in the technology of his day, such as *The Sands of Mars* and *Prelude to Space* (both published in 1951), and most famously, *2001: A Space Odyssey* (1968).

Ray Bradbury, on the other hand, mostly downplayed hard science in his own fiction, concentrating instead on the romance of rocketships. In such stories as "I, Rocket" ('44) and "Rocket Summer" ('47), he helped to create a deep yearning for space exploration. (Three of his excellent stories are featured in this issue.)

Wernher von Braun remained in Germany. After the German economy crashed, and Oberth's rocket project was abandoned, von Braun joined a military project that would eventually develop the V-2 rockets that rained massive destruction upon Great Britain for several months near the end of World War II.

Within months of Germany's surrender, von Braun and his team were transplanted to the United States to work on a project that would eventually lead to the launch of the Jupiter rocket carrying the USA's first space satellite in 1958, and finally, the Saturn V rocket that in 1969 would put the first man on the moon.

Robert A. Heinlein published several space adventures firmly rooted in rocket science, one of the earliest being *Rocket Ship Galileo*, in 1947. Heinlein's novel served as the source material for producer George Pal's influential and highly successful 1950 movie *Destination Moon*, the first cinematic attempt to realistically depict space travel. With a script cowritten by Heinlein, *Destination Moon* captivated moviegoers and inspired a decade of space adventure films, including Pal's *When Worlds Collide* (1951), *Riders to the Stars* (1954), *Conquest of Space* (1955; based on the book by Willy Ley and artist Chesley Bonestell), and *It! The Terror from Beyond Space* ('58), all of which feature space travel via rocketships. (Don't miss this issue's retrospective of *Destination Moon* by author and film historian Justin Humphreys, Curator of the George Pal Estate.)

Following is a mostly complete list of the dozens of rocketship and spacesuit movies that helped to make life in the 1950s and '60s an almost constant interstellar adventure. A few may be obscure, but many readers will fondly remember several of these films—the good, the bad, and the downright ugly.

Awe-inspiring special effects from George Pal's 1955 production of *Conquest of Space*, based on the book by Willy Ley and artist Chesley Bonestell.

Ouch!
Le voyage dans la lune, 1902

THE GRANDDADDY OF ALL SPACE FILMS is French filmmaker Georges Méliès' thirteen-minute 1902 silent short, *Le voyage dans la lune*, (U.S. title: *A Trip to the Moon*), loosely based on the novels *From the Earth to the Moon* by Jules Verne (1865) and *First Men in the Moon* by H. G. Wells (1901), and featuring a bullet-shaped ship fired to the moon from a giant cannon. As crazy as the idea sounds, this launch method was repeated in director William Cameron Menzies' 1936 production of Wells' *Things to Come* (based on *The Shape of Things to Come*, 1933).

Fritz Lang, the director of *Metropolis,* is credited with producing the first serious spaceship film, *Frau im Mond* (U.S. title: *Woman in the Moon*). The 1929 silent German movie features a multi-stage rocket, but Lang's attempt to be scientifically accurate crashes once the ship reaches the moon and its passengers step onto the airless surface without spacesuits.

Cinematic space travel during the 1930s was limited to the movie serials *Flash Gordon* ('36), *Flash Gordon's Trip to Mars* ('38) and *Buck Rogers* ('39). In 1940, *Flash Gordon Conquers the Universe* concluded Buster Crabbe's reign at the box office as America's favorite interstellar hero.

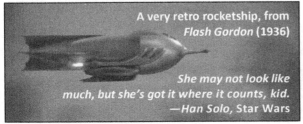

A very retro rocketship, from *Flash Gordon* (1936)

She may not look like much, but she's got it where it counts, kid.
—Han Solo, *Star Wars*

A ROCKET MEN PRIMER

IN 1949, REPUBLIC PICTURES released *King of the Rocket Men*, the first of three serials featuring a guy wearing a jetpack and bullet-shaped helmet. Tristram Coffin played the eponymous hero in *King*, but for each succeeding movie serial, Republic rebooted the rocket man, renaming the hero and hiring a different actor to play the part. The only thing connecting all three productions were director Fred C. Brannon and the recycling the rocket suit. In the second serial, *Radar Men from the Moon* (1952), George Wallace stars as Commando Cody. The third serial, *Zombies of the Stratosphere* (also '52), features Judd Holdren as Larry Martin, with Leonard Nimoy popping up as a zombie. (Holdren had roles in numerous SF productions, most notably playing Captain Video in the movie version of the popular TV show.)

King of the Rocket Men was edited as the 1951 feature film *Lost Planet Airmen*. *Radar Men from the Moon* was edited as the 1966 TV movie *Retik the Moon Menace*.

Judd Holdren also played the rocket man in *Commando Cody: Sky Marshall of the Universe,* originally produced as a 12-episode television series, but initially shown in 1953 as a "serial"—minus the cliff-hanger chapter endings characteristic of true movie serials. The series finally made it to the tube, airing on NBC in 1955.

Illustrator Dave Stevens (1955–2008) paid homage to the Rocket Men films with his retro comics character the Rocketeer. Stevens' character in turn made it into the movies, in Walt Disneys' *The Rocketeer* (1991).

The year 1950 ushered in the age of the "spacesuit film," beginning with *Rocketship X-M*, a cheap but enjoyable "quickie" rushed into production to take advantage of the publicity George Pal's more ambitious *Destination Moon* was receiving. *Rocketship*, directed by Kurt Neumann (*The Fly*), managed to beat Pal's landmark film to theaters by a few weeks. Regardless, the success of both movies launched a film genre that all but dominated SF cinema throughout the 1950s and '60s:

1951: *Flight to Mars* (pure pulp SF, seemingly ripped from the pages of *Planet Stories*); and *When Worlds Collide* (another Pal classic).

CONTINUED AFTER NEXT PAGE

Above: The Space Ark, from Pal's *When Worlds Collide* (1951)
Right (with apologies to Elton John): "I'm a Rocket Man"

1953: Pal's invasion classic *War of the Worlds*; Hammer's *Spaceways*; *Abbot and Costello Go to Mars*; and *Cat-Women of the Moon*, in which beautiful, oversexed alien women have a thing for rather plain-looking spacemen from Earth. Corny stuff to begin with, but even worse when remade in 1958 as *Missile to the Moon*, and further recycled in '56 as *Fire Maidens from Outer Space*—quite possibly the worst SF movie ever made—and again in '58 as *Queen of Outer Space*. (Oh, and watch out; there's a giant rubber spider in many of these flicks.)

Missile to the Moon (1958)

1954: *Riders to the Stars*, a low-budget Ivan Tors film written by Curt Siodmak that strives for realism.

1955: Conquest of Space, George Pal's second attempt to present space travel in a scientifically accurate manner; *This Island Earth*, the Star Wars of its day; and *Satellite in the Sky*, a gorgeous but talky UK production.

1956: *On the Threshold of Space*, in which test pilots train for space travel; and *World Without End*, a cheesy movie set on a post-nuclear war Earth, complete with beautiful women, angry mutants and ... a giant rubber spider.

1957: *Road to the Stars* (Russian)

1958: *War of the Satellites*, directed by Roger Corman; *The Lost Missile*; and *It: The Terror from Beyond Space*. (This suspenseful space-monster movie takes place on a rocketship traveling back to Earth, and is forerunner of Ridley Scott's 1979 film *Alien*. (Check out Matt Cowan's coverage of this and other flicks in this issue's Threat Watch.)

1959: *The Angry Red Planet*, directed by Ib Melchior; *Have Rocket—Will Travel*, a Three Stooges satire, complete with a giant spider; the SF horror *First Man into Space*; *Battle in Outer Space* (a Japanese film with good special effects); *Destination Space*, an unsold TV pilot that lost out to the superior show *Men into Space*; and *Battle Beyond the Sun*, Corman's butchered version of the Soviet film *Nebo Zovyot*, aka *The Sky Calls* ('59).

1960: *The Silent Star,* the original German film edited to create *First Spaceship on Venus*. Both versions are ahead of their time, depicting an international, interracial ship crew with a robot; *12 to the Moon*; and *Assignment: Outer Space*, by Italian director Antonio Margheriti.

Faith Domergue in the clutches of a Metaluna Mutant, in *This Island Earth* (1955)

1961: *Battle of the Worlds*; More Spaghetti Sci-fi by Margheriti, who made four similar films released in 1966 and '67: *Wild, Wild Planet; War of the Planets; War Between the Planets;* and *Snow Devils.*

1962: *Journey to the Seventh Planet;* Gorath (Japanese); *and Planeta Bur* (aka *Planet of Storms*), another Soviet film Roger Corman chopped up to create *Voyage to the Prehistoric Planet* ('65) and *Voyage to the Planet of Prehistoric Women* ('68). A similarly titled movie, *Women of the Prehistoric Planet,* was released in 1966. Although not related to the Corman films, it's just as bad, if not worse. (And don't expect to see any prehistoric women in *WotPP,* unless you can track down the uncut, international version. But take heart, there IS a giant rubber spider.)

1963: *Ikarie XB-1* (*Icarus XB-1*), an overlooked Czechoslovakian masterpiece based on a Stanislaw Lem novel. This *color* film was heavily edited and dubbed to create American-International's black-and-white release *Voyage to the End of the Universe* (1964).

1964: Director Byron Haskin's cult classic *Robinson Crusoe on Mars;* and *First Men in the Moon* (based on the H. G. Wells novel, with special effects by Ray Harryhausen.

SPAGHETTI SCI-FI SIMPLIFIED

FREQUENTLY CREDITED in the U.S. as Anthony Dawson, versatile and prolific Italian filmmaker Antonio Margheriti either wrote, directed, produced, or created makeups and special effects in nearly every movie genre, from spaghetti westerns to sword and sandal epics to gothic horror movies such as *Castle of Blood,* in 1964, and *The Long Hair of Death,* in 1965, both of which starred Barbara Steele.

In 1965, MGM contracted Margheriti to produce four television movies about the adventures of space station Gamma One. Margheriti had already directed two SF films, *Assignment: Outer Space,* in 1960, and *Battle of the Worlds,* with Claude Rains in 1961, and he recycled many of the models, props, and design elements from those earlier films, including the ships and space helmets. And by shooting the MGM movies together, using the same sets, actors, and stock effects footage, Margheriti managed to produce and direct—in under four months—four shared-universe films about the United Democracy Space Center and its string of Gamma space stations. Three of the films were scripted by Ivan Reiner, the fourth by Batman comics co-creator Bill Finger.

MGM was impressed with the finished movies and decided to release them theatrically, beginning with *The Wild, Wild Planet,* in early 1966. *War of the Planets* and the similarly—and hence, confusingly—titled *War Between the Planets* quickly followed, both in 1966. *Snow Devils* premiered in 1967. The movies performed well at the box office, and Reiner, who had also coproduced the films, was eager to do another Gamma spacestation movie. So an unofficial fifth film in the series was made, *The Green Slime* (1968), scripted by Reiner and Finger.

Although helmed by Japanese director Kinji Fukasakku, the film retains the Spaghetti Sci-fi look and feel of Margheriti's work. The only connection Slime has to the initial films, however, is a similarly designed space station, this time designated Gamma Three. (Margheriti returned to SF in 1983, directing the cult classic *Yor: The Hunter from the Future.*

1965: *Mutiny in Outer Space* (fungus on a space station); *Planet of the Vampires,* from Italian director Mario Bava; *Space Flight IC-1* (British); *The Wizard of Mars; Space Probe Taurus;* and *Invasion of Astro-Monster* (Toho Kaiju).

BLACK INFINITY • 11

1966: *Queen of Blood*, another ravenous "alien running wild on a space ship" movie made using footage from two Soviet films, *Mechte Navstrechu* (1963), aka *A Dream Come True*, and *Nebo Zovyot* (1959), previously edited as *Battle Beyond the Sun*.

1967: *Countdown*, with James Caan; and *Mission Stardust*, an Italian Perry Rhodan film.

1968: *Mission Mars*, with Darren McGavin; the original *Planet of the Apes*, with Charlton Heston; *Barbarella*, based on the French comic strip by Jean-Claude Forest; *The Green Slime*; and the classic *2001: A Space Odyssey*.

1969: *Marooned*, with Gregory Peck and Gene Hackman; and Gerry Anderson's *Journey to the Far Side of the Sun*, aka *Doppelgänger*.

GROWING UP IN THE 1950s and '60s was a grand time for anyone who's ever dreamed of traveling to the stars. The newsstands were well stocked with SF magazines and paperbacks depicting the majesty of spaceships and alien worlds; movies and television brought these pulp tales to vivid life; and rocketship designs and imagery could be seen just about everywhere, reaching up and shining bright—not unlike those who hoped, and continue to hope, in the future.

The rest, as they say, is history.

But one has to wonder: What happened to the world's enthusiasm for space travel? Why was humankind content with simply landing on the moon? Why did we stop reaching for the stars?

How on Earth did we ever lose touch with the romance of rocketships?

Tom English
New Kent, VA

Previous page: *Assignment: Outer Space*

Above and below: *2001: A Space Odyssey*; *Journey to the Far Side of the Sun*; and Rocket Raccoon (Marvel Studios)

HEY! YOU WANNA STOP REPEATIN' MY FRICKIN' NAME NOW?

SIX FRIGHTENED MEN

ROBERT SILVERBERG

ART BY ALLEN KOSZOWSKI

YOU PUT YOUR LIFE ON THE LINE WHEN YOU JOIN THE EXPLORATORY WING OF THE SPACE CORPS. They tell you that when you sign up. The way they told it to me, it went like this:

"You'll be out there on alien worlds where no human being has ever set foot—worlds which may or may not have been inhabited by hostile alien creatures. You take your life in your hands every time you make a planetfall out there. Still interested?"

"That's old stuff," I said. "You don't think I'd join up if it was an old ladies' tea party, do you?"

Which was how I happened to be crouching behind a fantastically-sculptured spiraling rock out on the yellow wind-blasted desert of Pollux V, huddling there with the fierce sweep of sand against my faceplate, looking at the monster that barred my path.

The thing was at least sixty feet tall and all eyes and mouth. The mouth yawned, showing yellow daggers a foot long. As for the eyes—well, they burned with the cold luminosity of an intelligent and inimical being.

I didn't know what the thing was. One minute I'd been examining an interesting rock formation, a second later I was hiding behind it, watching the ravening thing that had appeared out of nowhere.

Other members of the expedition were sprawled here and there on the desert too. I could see Max Feld, our paleontologist, curled in a tight plump little ball under an outcropping of weathered limestone, and there was Roy Laurence, the biochemist, flat on his stomach peering at the thing incredulously.

Back behind me were three others—Don Forster, Leo Mickens, Clyde Hamner. That made six. The two remaining members of the team, Medic Howard Graves and Anthropologist Lyman Donaldson, were back at the ship. We always left a shift of two back there in case of trouble.

And trouble had sure struck now!

I saw Laurence swivel in the sand and stare goggle-eyed at me. His lips moved, and over my helmet radio came: "What the hell is it, Phil? Where'd it come from?"

I'm a morphologist; I'm supposed to know things like that. But I could only shrug and say, "A thing like that could only come from the pits of Hell. I've never seen anything like it before."

I HADN'T. We had been fine-combing the broad windswept plain in front of the ship, looking for archaeological remains. The planet was uninhabited, or so we thought after running a quick check—but Max Feld had discovered relics of a dead race, an exciting find, and we had all fanned out to help him in his search for more.

We had been heading toward a flat mountain wall that rose abruptly from the desert about a mile from the ship when—from nowhere—the creature appeared, towering above the desert like a dinosaur dropped from the skies.

But no dinosaur ever looked like this one. Sixty feet high, its skin a loathsome gray-green quivering jelly with thick hairy cilia projecting, its vat-like mouth gaping toothily, its cold, hard eyes flicking back and forth, searching for us as we flattened ourselves out of sight, it was an utterly ghastly being. Evolution had gone wild on this planet.

And we were cut off from the ship, hemmed between the mountain wall and the creature.

"What are we going to do?" Clyde Hamner whispered. "He's going to smell us out pretty soon."

As he spoke, the monster began to move—*flowing*, it seemed, like some vast protozoan.

"I'm going to blast it," I said, as it oozed closer to us. Cautiously, I lifted my Webley from its shoulder-holster, turned the beam to *Full*, began to squeeze the firing-stud.

A bright white-hot beam of force leaped from the nozzle and speared the creature's eye. It howled, seemed to leap in the air, thrashed around—

And changed.

It became a boiling mass of amorphous protoplasm, writhing and billowing on the sand. I fired again into the mass—again and again, and the alien creature continued to shift its form. I was cold with horror, but I kept up the firing. My bolts seemed to be absorbed into the fluid mass without effect, but at least I had halted the oozing advance.

It reached one final hideous stage: a giant mouth, opening before us like the gate of hell. A mouth, nothing more. It yawned in front of us—

Then advanced.

I felt noxious vapors shoot out, bathing my thermosuit, and I saw a gargling larynx feet across. I fired, again and again, into the monster's throat.

My companions were firing too. We seemed to have halted the thing's advance. It paused some twenty feet from us, a wall of mouth.

Then it disappeared.

It blinked out of sight the way it had come—instantaneously. For a moment I didn't realize what had happened, and fired three useless charges into the space where the monster had been.

"It's gone," Hamner exclaimed.

My hands were trembling—me, who had stood up to Venusian mudworms without a whimper, who had fought the giant fleas of Rigel IX. I was shaking all over. Sweat was running down my entire body, and the wiper of my faceplate was going crazy trying to blot my forehead.

Then I heard dull groans coming from up ahead. One final grunt, then silence. They had been coming from Max Feld.

Looking around cautiously, I rose to my feet. There was no sign of the creature. I ran to where Max lay.

The plump paleontologist was sprawled flat in the sand, face down. I bent, yanked him over, peered in his facemask. His eyes were open, staring—and lifeless.

IT WASN'T TILL WE GOT BACK to the ship that we could open his spacesuit and confirm what I thought I saw on his face.

Doc Graves pronounced it finally: "He's dead. Heart attack. What the devil did you *see* out there, anyway?"

Quickly I described it. When I was finished the medic shivered. "Lord! No wonder Max had an attack What a nightmare!"

Donaldson, the anthropologist, appeared from somewhere in the back of the ship. Seeing Max's body, he said, "What happened?"

"We were attacked on the desert. Max was the only casualty. The thing didn't touch us— it just stood there and changed shape. Max must have died of fright."

Donaldson scowled. He was a wry, taciturn individual with a coldness about him that I didn't like. I could pretty much guess what he would say. No expression of grief, or anything like that.

"It's going to look bad for you, Doc, when it's discovered we had a man with a weak heart in the crew."

The medic stiffened. "I checked Max's heart before we left. It was as good as anyone's. But the shock of seeing that thing—"

"Yeah," Don Forster said angrily. "You'd have been shivering in your boots too if that thing had popped out of nowhere right over *your* left shoulder."

"Keep your remarks to yourself, Forster. I signed on for the Exploratory Team with the same understanding any of you did—that we were going into alien, uncharted worlds and could expect to meet up with anything. Anything at all. Fright's a mere emotional reaction. Adults—as you supposedly are—should be able to control it."

I felt like hitting him, but I restrained myself. That ordeal out on the desert had left me drained, nerves raw and shaken. I shrugged and looked away.

"Well?" Hamner said. "What do we do? Go home?"

It was said half as a joke, but I saw from the look on young Leo Mickens' face that he was perfectly willing to take the suggestion seriously and get off Pollux V as fast as he could.

To forestall any trouble, I said, "It's a tempting idea. But I don't think it would look good on our records."

"You're right," Hamner agreed. "We stay. We stay until we know what that thing is, where it came from, and how we can lick it."

WE STAYED. We spent the rest of that day aboard ship, having called off the day's explorations in memory of Max. The bright orb of Pollux set about 2000 ship time, and the sky was filled with a glorious sight: a horde of moons whirling above. The moons of Pollux V were incredible.

There were *one hundred* of them, ranging in size from a hunk of rock the size of Mars' Deimos to one massive high-albedo satellite almost a thousand miles in diameter. They marched across the sky in stately order, filling the Polluxian night with brightness.

Only we didn't feel much sense of wonder. We buried Max in a crude grave, laid him to rest under the light of a hundred moons, and then withdrew to the ship to consider our problem.

"Where'd it come from?" Doc Graves asked.

"Nowhere," I said. "Just nowhere. One second it wasn't there, next second it was. It vanished the same way."

"How could that be?" Donaldson asked. "Matter doesn't work that way; it's flatly impossible."

Holding myself in check, I said, "Maybe so, Donaldson. But the thing was *there*."

"How do you know?" the anthropologist persisted, sneering a little. "You sure it wasn't a mass illusion of some kind?"

"Damn you," Forster shouted, "*You* weren't there. We were—and we saw it. *Max* saw it. Ask *Max* if it was there!"

Evenly, Donaldson said, "On the basis of your description, I'm convinced it must have been an illusion. I'm willing to go out there and have a look first thing in the morning—either alone or with any of you, if you can work up the courage. Fair enough?"

"Fair enough," I said. "I'll go with you."

THE NEXT MORNING, we left the ship, clad in thermosuits, armed to the teeth—at least I was. I carried a subforce gun and a neural disruptor; Donaldson scornfully packed only the prescribed blaster.

We crossed the flat plain together, without speaking. I led the way, looking back nervously every few paces, but there was nothing behind me but Donaldson. We made a complete reconnaissance of the area, picked up a few interesting outlying fossils—Donaldson thought they might be relics of the dead race of Pollux V—and reached the bare face of the mountain without any difficulties.

"Well?" Donaldson asked sneeringly. "Where's your monster this time? He afraid of me?"

"So it didn't show up," I snapped. "That doesn't prove anything. For all we know it might jump us on the way back to the ship."

"So it might. But I doubt it. For one thing, I've been checking footprints in the sand. I've counted six tracks—one each for you, Feld, Hamner, Laurence, Forster, and Mickens. Unfortunately, that doesn't leave any for your monster. There's no sign of him anywhere."

I was a little startled by that. I glanced around. "You're right," I admitted, frowning. Licking dry lips, I said, "There ought to be some trace—unless the wind's covered it."

"The wind hasn't fully covered the traces of you six yet," Donaldson pointed out with obstinate logic. "Why should it obliterate only those of your nemesis?"

I scowled, but said nothing. Donaldson was right again—but I still found it hard to convince myself that what we had seen was only an illusion.

On the way back to the ship, I formulated all sorts of theories to explain the creature. It was a monster out of subspace, generated by etheric force; it was a radiation-creature without tangible physical body; it was—

I had half a dozen conjectures, each as unlikely as the next. But we returned to the ship safely, without any trouble whatever. I was sure of one thing: the creature was real, no matter what hell-void had spawned it.

WHEN WE RETURNED, I saw the tense faces of the men in the ship ease.

"All right," Donaldson said. "We've both been out there and come back. I say we ought to investigate this place fully. There's been a high-level civilization here at one time, and—"

"Suppose it's this monster that killed off that civilization?" Forster suggested.

"Then it's our duty to investigate it," I had to say. "Even at the cost of our lives." Here I agreed with Donaldson; monster or no, it was our job to fathom the secrets of this dead world.

We agreed to explore in twos, rather than risk the customary complement of six all at once. Two men would go out; five remain within, three of them space-suited and ready to leave the ship to answer any emergency call.

Mickens and Forster drew the first assignment. They suited up and left. Tensely, we proceeded about our shipside duties, cataloguing information from our previous stops, performing routine tasks, busying ourselves desperately in unimportant work to take our minds off the men who were out on that desert together.

An hour later, Forster returned. Alone.

His face was pale, his eyes bulging, and almost before he stepped from the airlock we knew what must have happened.

"Where's Mickens?" I asked, breaking the terrible hush in the cabin.

"Dead," he said hollowly. "We—we got to the mountain, and—God, it was awful!"

He sank down in an acceleration cradle and started to sob. Doc Graves fumbled at his belt, drew out a neurotab, forced it between the boy's quivering lips. He calmed; color returned to his face.

"Tell us about it," Hamner urged gently.

"We reached the back end of the plain, and Leo suggested we try the mountain. He thought he saw a sort of cave somewhere back in there, and wanted to have a look. We had to go over that sharp rock shelf to get in there.

"So we started to scale the cliff. We were about a hundred feet up, and going along a path maybe four feet wide, when—when—" He shuddered, then forced himself to go on. "The monster appeared. It popped out of nowhere right in front of Leo. He was taken by surprise and toppled over the edge. I managed to hang on."

"Were you attacked?" I asked.

"No. It vanished, right after Leo fell off. I went down to look at him. His facemask had broken. I left him there."

I glanced around at the tight-jawed, hard faces of my crew-mates. No one said a word—but we all knew the job that faced us now. We couldn't leave Pollux V until we'd discovered the nature of the beast that menaced us—even if it cost us our lives. We couldn't go back to Earth and send some other guys in to do the job. That wasn't the way the Exploratory Wing operated. We had a tradition to uphold.

WE DREW LOTS, and Hamner and Donaldson went out there to recover Mickens' body. They encountered no hazards, and brought young Mickens' shattered body back. We buried it next to Max's. The monster had taken a toll of two already, without actually touching either.

It was almost like some evil plan unfolding to wipe us out one by one. I didn't like it—but I didn't have anything too concrete to base it on, not till the fifth day.

I was teamed with Donaldson again, and I felt strangely confident about our safety. So far the monster had yet to materialize any time Donaldson was out on the plain. That fact had been in the back of my mind for quite a while. It was the only clue I had.

We prowled over the plain, which by now had been pretty well fine-toothed, and then I suggested we try the cave where Mickens had met his fate.

"I don't like the idea," Donaldson said, eyeing the narrow shelf of rock we would have to walk across. "You remember what happened to Mickens, and—"

I laughed harshly. "Don't tell me you're beginning to believe in this monster of ours?"

"Of course not. Mickens simply had an attack of vertigo and toppled off; Forster's active imagination supplied the monster. But that shelf looks treacherous. I'd just as soon not go up there."

"You're not talking like an Exploratory Wing man, Donaldson. But it's okay with me if you want to wait down here. That cave might be a goldmine of artifacts. We ought at least to have a look."

His hard face dropped within his mask. "No—I couldn't let you go alone. You win," he said. "Let's try the cave."

We began the climb—and it was, I saw, a deadly road. It narrowed dizzyingly—and while the drop was only a hundred feet, which a man could survive if he landed right, spacesuits weren't made to take falls of that sort. And without a suit, a man was instantly dead on this methane-ammonia atmosphere world.

We were about ten feet out on the ledge, I in the lead and Donaldson behind me, when I heard him gasp.

"Great God! There it is!"

I felt him lurch against me in sudden terror, nearly heaving me into the abyss, but somehow I steadied myself, dropped to my knees, hung on. I turned.

He had avoided a fall too. But I saw no monster.

"Where is it?" I asked.

"It came out of the air right next to me—just popped out of the void and vanished again. I saw it, though." His voice was hoarse. "I apologize for everything I've said. The thing is real. If it weren't for your sure footing we'd both have gone the way Mickens did."

He seemed almost hysterical. There was no sign of the monster, but I wasn't going to take any chances out on this ribbon of rock with a hysterical man.

"Let's go back," I said. "We'll try to get to the cave some other time."

"All right," Donaldson said, shaken. We turned and inched our way back along the shelf to safety, and half-ran to the sanctuary of the ship.

But once we were inside and I was thinking clearly again, I began to sprout some suspicions.

I reasoned it out very carefully. Every time Donaldson had gone out previously, the monster had failed to show. There wasn't another man aboard ship who hadn't had some encounter with the thing. And some of them were remarking about Donaldson's apparent luck.

So this time we're out on the shelf, and the monster *does* show up—but Donaldson's the only one who sees him, after staunchly denying its existence all along. It seemed to me that it might only have been pretense, that he had faked seeing the monster for some reason of his own.

I didn't know what that could be. But I had some ideas. Donaldson, after all, had been a member of the first party to explore Pollux V, the day before the exploration that killed Max. I had remained on the ship while that group had been out.

Suppose, I thought, Donaldson had found something on that first trip, something that he hadn't bothered to tell the rest of us about. Something he might want badly enough to kill all of us for.

It was pretty farfetched, but it was worth a try. I decided to explore Donaldson's cabin.

Ordinarily we respected privacy to an extreme degree aboard the ship. I had never been in Donaldson's cabin before—he never invited anyone in, and naturally I never went uninvited. But this was a special case, I felt.

The door was locked, but it's not hard to coerce a magneplate into opening if you know how they work. Donaldson was in the ship's lab and I hoped he'd stay out of my way till I had a good look around.

The room was just like any of ours, filled with the usual things—a shelf of reference books, a file of musictapes, some minifilms, other things to help to pass away the long hours between planets. It seemed neat, precise, uncluttered, just as Donaldson himself was crisp and reserved.

I moved around the room very carefully, looking for anything out of the ordinary. And then I found it.

It was a black box, nothing more, about four inches square. It was sitting on one of his shelves. Just a bare black box, a little cube of metal—but *what* metal!

Beyond the blackness was a strange

unearthly shimmer, an eye-teasing pattern of shifting molecules within the metal itself. The box had a sleek, alien appearance. I knew it hadn't been in the cabin when we left Earth.

With a sudden rush of excitement, I realized my mad guess had been right. Donaldson *had* found something and kept news of it back from the rest of us. And perhaps it was linked to the deaths of Max Feld and Leo Mickens.

Cautiously I reached out to examine the box. I lifted it. It was oddly heavy, and strange to the touch.

But no sooner did I have it in my hands when the door opened behind me. Donaldson had come back.

"What are you doing with that?" he shouted.

"I—"

He crossed the cabin at top speed and seized the box from my hands. And suddenly the monster appeared.

It materialized right in the cabin, between Donaldson and me, its vast bulk pressing against the walls. I felt its noisome breath on me, sensed its evil reek.

"Donaldson!"

But Donaldson was no longer there. I was alone in the cabin with the creature.

I backed away into the far corner, my mouth working in terror. I tried to call for help, but couldn't get a word out. And the beast squirmed and changed like a vast amoeba, writhing and twisting from one grey oily shape to another.

I sank to the floor, numb with horror—and then realized that the monster wasn't approaching.

It was just staying there, making faces at me.

Making faces. Like a bogeyman.

It was trying to scare me to death. That was how Max Feld had died, that was how Leo Mickens had died.

But I wasn't going to die that way.

I rose and confronted the thing. It just remained in the middle of the cabin, blotting everything out behind it, stretching from wall to wall and floor to ceiling, changing from one hell-shape to another and hoping I'd curl up and die.

I stepped forward.

Cautiously I touched the monster's writhing surface. It was like touching a cloud. I sank right in.

The monster changed, took the dragon form again—much smaller, of course, to fit the cabin. Teeth gnashed the air before my nose—but didn't bite into my throat as they promised to do. Nervelessly I stood my ground.

Then I waded into the heart of the monster, right into its middle with the grey oiliness billowing out all around me. There seemed to be nothing material, nothing to grapple hold of. It was like fighting a dream.

But then I hit something solid. My groping hands closed around warm flesh. I started to squeeze.

I had a throat. A living core of flesh within the monster? It might be. I constricted my fingers, dug them in, heard strangled gasps coming from further in. I couldn't see, but I hung on.

Then a human voice said, "Damn you—you're choking me!" And the monster thinned.

Through the diminishing smoke of the dream-creature, I saw Donaldson, and I was clutching his throat. He still held the black box in his hand, but it was slipping from his grasp, slipping....

He dropped it. It clattered to the floor and I kicked it far across the cabin.

The monster vanished completely.

IT WAS JUST THE TWO OF US, there in the cabin. I heard fists pounding on the door from outside, but I ignored them. This was between me and Donaldson.

"What is that thing?" I asked, facing him, tugging at his throat. I shook him. "Where'd you find that hell-thing?"

"Wouldn't you like to know?" he wheezed.

My fingers tightened. Suddenly he drew up his foot and lashed out at my stomach. I let go of his throat and fell back, the wind knocked out of me. As I staggered backward, he darted for the fallen box, but I recovered and brought my foot down hard on his outstretched hand.

He snarled in pain. I felt his other fist crash into my stomach again. I was almost numb, sick, ready to curl up in a knot and close my eyes. But I forced myself to suck in breath and hit him.

His head snapped back. I hit him again, and he reeled soggily. His neat, precise lips swelled into a bloody mass. His fists moved hazily; I blackened one of his eyes, and he groaned and slumped. Fury was in my fists; I was avenging the honor of the Exploratory Wing against the one man who had broken its oaths.

"Enough ... enough...."

But I hit him again and again, till he sagged to the floor. I picked up the black metal box, fondled it in my hands. Then, tentatively, I threw a thought at it.

Monster.

The monster appeared in all its ugliness.

Vanish.

It vanished.

"That's how it works, isn't it?" I said. "It's a thought projector. That monster never existed outside your own mind, Donaldson."

"Don't hit me again," he whined. I didn't. He was beneath contempt.

I threw open the door and saw the other crewmen huddled outside, their faces pale.

"It's all over," I said. "Here's your monster."

I held out the black box.

WE HELD COURT on Donaldson that night, and he made a full confession. That first day, he had stumbled over an alien treasure in the cave beyond the hill—that, and the thought-converter. The idea came to him that perhaps, as sole survivor of the expedition, he could turn some of the treasure to his own uses.

So he utilized the thought-converter in a campaign to pick us off one by one without aiming suspicion at himself. Only his clumsy way of pretending to see the creature himself had given him away; else he might have killed us all.

Our rulebook gave no guide on what to do about him—but we reached a decision easily enough.

When we left Pollux V, taking with us samples of the treasure, and other specimens of the long-dead race (including the thought-converter) we left Donaldson behind, on the bare, lifeless planet, with about a week's supply of food and air.

No one ever learned of his treachery. We listed him as a casualty, along with Max and Leo, when we returned to Earth. The Exploratory Wing had too noble a name to tarnish by revealing what Donaldson had done ... and none of us will ever speak the truth. The Wing means too much to us for that.

And I think they're going to award him a posthumous medal.... 👽 👽 👽

"Five Frightened Men" first appeared in the June 1957 issue of Imagination. *Although originally credited to Randall Garrett, Robert Silverberg has confirmed that he wrote the story.*

American author and editor Robert Silverberg started writing in his early teens. In 1956, at the age of twenty-one, he won his first Hugo Award, for Most Promising New Writer, beating out finalists Harlan Ellison and Frank Herbert. Silverberg wrote prolifically, under several pseudonyms, including Gordon Aghill, Alexander Blade, Richard Greer, Calvin Knox, and Clyde Mitchell. Occasionally he collaborated with Randall Garrett, usually as Robert Randall. He was soon generating about a quarter of a million words a month in a variety of genres. In the August 1956 issue of Fantastic, *Silverberg set a personal record, contributing four of the six stories in that issue—plus an essay. His voluminous output diminished during the '60s, with Silverberg producing what Algis Budrys described in 1968 as "deeply detailed, highly educated, beautifully figured books." Silverberg continued to be honored, earning three more Hugos and six Nebulas, among other awards. Perhaps the greatest work of this SFWA Grand Master is his celebrated fantasy novel* Lord Valentine's Castle.

SLOW BURN

BY HENRY STILL

ILLUSTRATION BY KELLY FREAS

"TELL 'EM TO LOOK SHARP, BERT. THIS PICK-UP'S GOT TO BE GOOD." Kevin Morrow gulped the last of his coffee and felt its bitter acid gurgle around his stomach. He stared moodily through the plastic port where the spangled skirt of stars glittered against the black satin of endless night and a familiar curve of the space station swung ponderously around its hub.

Four space-suited tugmen floated languidly outside the rim. Beyond them the gleaming black and white moonship tugged gently at her mooring lines, as though anxious to be off.

Bert Alexander radioed quiet instructions to the tugmen.

"Why the hell couldn't he stay down there and mind his own business?" Kevin growled. "McKelvie's been after our hide ever since we got the appropriation, and now this." He slapped the flimsy radio-gram.

He looked up as the control room hatch opened. Jones came in from the astronomy section.

"Morning, commander," he said. "You guys had breakfast yet? Mess closes in 30 minutes." Kevin shook his head.

"We're not hungry," Bert filled in.

"You think you've got nerves?" Jones chuckled. "I just looked in on Mark. He's sleeping like a baby. You wouldn't think the biggest day of his life is three hours away."

"McKelvie's coming up to kibitz," Morrow said.

"McKelvie!"

"The one and only," Bert said. "Here, read all about it."

He handed over the morning facsimile torn off the machine when the station hurtled over New England at 18,000 miles an hour. The upper half of the sheet bore a picture of the white-maned senator. Clearly etched on his face were the lines of too many half-rigged elections, too many compromises.

Beneath the picture were quotes from his speech the night before.

"As chairman of your congressional watch-dog committee," the senator had said, "I'll see that there's no more waste and corruption on this space project. For three years they've been building a rocket—the moon rocket, they call it—out there at the space station.

"I haven't seen that rocket," the senator had continued. "All I've seen is five billion of your tax dollars flying into the vacuum of space. They tell me a man named Mark Kramer is going to fly out in that rocket and circle the moon.

"But he will fail," McKelvie had promised. "If God had intended man to fly to the moon, he would have given us wings to do it. Tomorrow I shall fly out to this space station, even at the risk of my life. I'll report the waste and corruption out there, and I'll report the failure of the moon rocket."

Jones crumpled the paper and aimed at the waste basket.

"Pardon me while I vomit," he said.

"We've been there," Kevin sighed deeply. "I suppose Max Gordon will be happy."

"He'll wear a hole in his tongue on Mc-Kelvie's boots," Bert said bitterly.

"Is it that bad?"

"How else would he get a first-class spaceman's badge?" Morrow said. "He can't add two and two. But if stool pigeons had wings, he'd fly like a jet. We can't move up here without McKelvie knowing and howling about it.

"Don't worry," Jones said, "If the moon rocket makes it, public opinion will take care of the senator."

"If he doesn't take care of us first," Kevin said darkly. "He'll be aboard in 15 minutes."

DAWN TOUCHED the High Sierras as the station whirled in from the Pacific, 500 miles high.

"Bert. Get me a radar fix on White Sands."

Morrow huddled over the small computer, feeding in radar information as it came from his assistant.

"Rocket away!" Blared a radio speaker on the bulkhead. The same message carried to the four space-suited tugmen floating beyond the rim of the wheel, linked with life-lines.

Jones watched interestedly out the port.

"There she is!" he yelled.

Sunlight caught the ascending rocket, held it in a splash of light. The intercept technique was routine now, a matter of timing, but for a moment Kevin succumbed to the frightening optical illusion that the rocket was approaching apex far below the station. Then, slowly, the slender cylinder matched velocity and pulled into the orbit, then crept to its destination.

With deceptive ease, the four human tugs attached magnetic shoes and guided the projectile into the space station hub with short, expert blasts of heavy rocket pistols.

"Take over Bert," Morrow directed, "I guess I'm the official greeter." He hurried out of the control room, through a short connecting tube and emerged floating in the central space surrounding the hub where artificial gravity fell to zero. Air pressure was normal to transfer passengers without spacesuits.

The connecting lock clanked open. The rocket pilot stepped out.

"He got sick," the pilot whispered to Kevin. "I swabbed him off, but he's hoppin' mad."

The senator's mop of white hair appeared in the port. Kevin braced to absorb a tirade, but McKelvie's deep scowl changed to an expression of bliss as he floated weightless into the tiny room.

"Why, this is wonderful!" he sputtered. He waved his arms like a bird and kicked experimentally with a foot.

"Grab him!" Kevin shouted. "He's gone happy with it."

The pilot was too late. McKelvie's body sailed gracefully through the air and his head smacked the bulkhead. His eyes glazed in a frozen expression of carefree happiness.

Kevin swore. "Now he'll accuse us of a plot against his life. Help me get him to sick bay."

The two men guided the weightless form into a tube connecting with the outer ring. As they pushed outward, McKelvie's weight increased until they carried him the last 50 feet into the dispensary compartment.

Max Gordon burst wild-eyed into the room.

"What have you done to the senator?" he shouted. "Why didn't you tell me he was coming up?" Morrow made sure McKelvie was receiving full medical attention before he turned to the junior officer.

"He went space happy and bumped his head," Kevin said curtly, "and there was no more reason to notify you than the rest of the crew." He walked away. Gordon bent solicitously over his unconscious patron.

Kevin found Anderson in the passageway.

"I ordered them to start fueling Moonbeam," Bert said.

"Good. Is Mark awake?"

"Eating breakfast. The psycho's giving him a clinical chat."

"I wish it were over." Morrow brushed back his hair.

"You've really got the jitters, huh chief?"

Morrow turned angrily and then tried to laugh.

"I'd sell my job for a nickel right now, Bert. This will be touch and go, without having the worst enemy of space flight aboard. If this ship fails, it's more than a rocket or the death of a man. It'll set the whole program back 50 years."

"I know," Bert answered, "but he'll make it."

Footsteps sounded in the tube outside the cabin. Mark Kramer walked in.

"Hi, chief," he grinned, "*Moonbeam* ready to go?"

"The techs are out now and fuel's aboard. How about you? Shouldn't you get some rest?"

"That's all I've had since they shipped me out here." Kramer laughed. "It'll be a snap. After all, I'll never make over two gees and pick up 7000 mph to leave you guys behind. Then I play ring around the rosy, take a look at Luna's off side and come home. Just like that."

"Just like that," Kevin whispered meditatively. The moon rocket, floating there outside the station's rim was ugly, designed never to touch a planet's atmosphere, but it was the most beautiful thing man had ever built, assembled in space from individual fragments boosted laboriously from the Earth's surface.

Another clatter of footsteps approached the hatch. Max Gordon entered and stood at attention as Senator McKelvie made a dignified entrance. The senator wore an adhesive patch on his high forehead. He turned to Kramer.

"Young man," he rumbled, "are you the fool risking your life in that—that thing out there? You must know it'll never reach the moon. I know it'll never—"

Kramer's face paled slightly and he moved swiftly between the two men. Without using force, he backed the senator and Gordon through the hatch and slammed it behind him. Anger was a knot of green snakes in his belly.

"I want to talk to that pilot," McKelvie said belligerently.

"I'm sorry, senator. The best psychiatrists on Earth worked eight months to condition Kramer for this flight. He must not be emotionally disturbed. You can't talk to him."

"You forbid...?" McKelvie exploded, but Morrow intercepted smoothly.

"Gordon. I'm sure the senator would like a tour of the station. Will you escort him?"

McKelvie's face reddened and Max opened his mouth to object.

"Gordon!" Morrow said sharply. Max closed his mouth and guided the grumbling congressman up the tube.

"TWENTY MINUTES to blastoff," Bert reported.

"Right," Kevin acknowledged absently. He studied taped data moving in by radio facsimile from the mammoth electronic computer on Earth.

"Our orbit's true," he said with satisfaction and wiped a sweaty palm on his trousers. "Get the time check, Bert." Beeps from the Naval Observatory synchronized with the space station chronometer.

"Alert Kramer."

"He's leaving the airlock now," Bert said. From the intercom, Morrow listened to periodic reports from crew members as McKelvie and Gordon progressed in their tour.

"Mr. Morrow?"

"Right."

"This is Adams in Section M. The senator and Gordon have been in the line chamber for 10 minutes."

"Boot 'em out," Kevin said crisply. "Blast-off in 15 minutes."

"That machinery controls the safety lines," Bert said.

Kevin looked up with a puzzled frown, but turned back to watch Kramer creeping along a mooring line to the moon ship. A group of tugmen helped the spacesuited figure into the rocket, dogged shut the hatch and cleared back to the station rim.

"Station to Kramer," on the radio, "are you ready?"

"All set," came the steady voice, "give me the word."

"All right. Five minutes." Kevin turned to the intercom. "Release safety lines."

In the weightlessness of space the cables retained their normal rigid line from the rim of the station to the rocket. They had been under no strain. Their shape would not change until they were reeled in.

"Two minutes," Morrow warned. Tension grew as Anderson began the slow second count. The hatch opened. McKelvie and Gordon entered the control room. No one noticed it.

"Five ... four ... three ... two ... one...."

A gout of white fire jabbed from the stern of the rocket. Slowly the ship moved forward.

Morrow watched tensely, hands gripping a safety rail.

Then his face froze in a mask of disbelief and horror.

"The lines!" he shouted. "The safety lines fouled!"

He fell sprawling as the space station lurched heavily, tipped upward like a giant platter under the inexorable pull of the moon rocket.

Kevin scrambled back to the viewport, the shriek of tortured metal in his ears. Horror-stricken, he saw the taut cables that had failed to release. Then a huge section of nylon, aluminum and rubber ripped out of the station wall, was visible a second in the rocket glare, and vanished.

Escaping air whistled through the crippled structure. Pressure dropped alarmingly before the series of automatic airlocks clattered reassuringly shut.

Kevin's hand was bleeding. He staggered with the frightening new motion of the space station. Gordon and the senator had collapsed against a bulkhead. McKelvie's pale face twisted with fear and amazement. Blood streaked down the pink curve of his forehead.

Individual station reports trickled through the intercom. Miraculously, the bulk of the station had escaped damage.

"Line chamber's gone," Adams reported. "Other bulkheads holding, but something must have jammed the line machines. They ripped right out."

"Get repair crews in to patch leaks," Morrow shouted. He turned frantically to the radio. "Station to *Moonbeam*. Kramer! Are you all right?"

He waited an agonizing minute, then a scratchy voice came through.

"Kramer, here. What the hell happened? Something gave me a terrific yaw, but the gyro pulled me back on course. Fuel consumption high. Otherwise I'm okay."

"You ripped out part of the station," Kevin yelled. "You're towing extra mass. Release the safety lines if you can."

The faint answer came back, garbled by static.

Another disaster halted a new try to reach him.

With a howling rumble, the massive gyroscope case in the bulkhead split open. The heavy wheel, spinning at 20,000 revolutions per minute, slowly and majestically crawled out of its gimbals; the gyroscope that stabilized the entire structure remained in its plane of revolution, but ripped out of its moorings when the station was forcibly tilted.

Spinning like a giant top, the gyro walked slowly across the deck. McKelvie and Gordon scrambled out of its way.

"It'll go through!" Bert shouted. Kevin leaped to a chest of emergency patches.

The wheel ripped through the magnesium shell like a knife in soft cheese. A gaping rent opened to the raw emptiness of space, but Morrow was there with the patch. Before decompression could explode the four creatures of blood and bone, the patch slapped in place, sealed by the remaining air pressure.

Trembling violently, Kevin staggered to a chair and collapsed. Silence rang in his ears. Anderson gripped the edge of a table to keep from falling. Kevin turned slowly to McKelvie and Gordon.

"Come here," he said tonelessly.

"Now see here, young man—" the senator blustered.

"I said come here!"

The two men obeyed. The commander's voice held a new edge of steel.

"You were the last to leave the line control room," he said. *"Did you touch that machinery?"*

Gordon's face was the color of paste. His mouth worked like a suffocating fish. McKelvie recovered his bluster.

"I'm a United States senator," he stuttered, "I'll not be threatened...."

"I'm not threatening you," Kevin said, "but if you fouled that machinery to assure your prediction about the rocket, I'll see that you hang. Do you realize that gyroscope was the only control we had over the motion of this space station? Whatever it does now is the result of the moon rocket's pull. We may not live to see that rocket again."

As though verifying Morrow's words, the lights dimmed momentarily and returned to normal brilliance. A frightened voice came from the squawkbox.

"Hey, chief! This is power control. We've lost the sun!"

Anderson looked out the port, studied the slowly wheeling stars.

"Mother of God," he breathed. "We're flopping ... like a flapjack over a stove."

And the power mirrors were on only one face of the space station, mirrors that collected the sun's radiation and converted it to power. Now they were collecting nothing but the twinkling of the stars.

The vital light would return as the station continued its new, awkward rotation, but would the intermittent exposure be sufficient to sustain power?

"Shut down everything but emergency equipment," Morrow directed. "When we get back on the sun, soak every bit of juice you can into those batteries." He turned to Gordon and McKelvie. "Won't it be interesting if we freeze to death, or suffocate when the air machines stop?"

Worry replaced anger as he turned abruptly away from them.

"We've got a lot of work to do, Bert," he

said crisply. "See if you can get White Sands."

"It's over the horizon, I'll try South Africa." Anderson worked with the voice radio but static obliterated reception. "Here comes a Morse transmission," he said at last. Morrow read slowly, as tape fed out of the translator:

"Radar shows moon rocket in proper trajectory. Where are you?"

The first impulse was to dash to the viewport and peer out. But that would be no help in determining position.

"Radar, Bert," he whispered.

Anderson vernieried in the scope, measuring true distance to Earth's surface. He read the figure, swore violently, and readjusted the instrument.

"It can't be," he muttered at last. "This says we're 865 miles out."

"365 miles outside our orbit?" Morrow said calmly. "I was afraid of that. That tug from the *Moonbeam* not only cartwheeled us, it yanked us out." He snatched a sheet of graph paper out of a desk drawer and penciled a point.

"Give me a reading every 10 seconds."

Points began to connect in a curve.

And the curve was something new.

"Get Jones from astronomy," Kevin said at last. "He can help us plot and maybe predict."

When the astronomer arrived minutes later, the space station was 1700 miles above the Earth, still shearing into space on an ascending curve.

"Get a quick look at this, Jones," Kevin spoke rapidly. "See if you can tell where it will be two hours from now."

The astronomer studied the curve intently as it continued to grow under Kevin's pencil.

"It may be an outward spiral," he said haltingly, "or it could be a ... parabola."

"No!" Bert protested. "That would throw us into space. We couldn't—"

"We couldn't get back," Kevin finished grimly. "There'd better be an alternative."

"It could be an ellipse," Jones said.

"It must be an ellipse," Bert said eagerly. "The *Moonbeam* couldn't have given us 7000 mph velocity."

Abruptly the lights went out.

The radar scope faded from green to black. Morrow swore a string of violent oaths, realizing in the same instant that anger was useless when the power mirrors lost the sun.

He bellowed into the intercom, but the speaker was dead. Already Bert was racing down the tube to the power compartment. Minutes later, the intercom dial flickered red. Morrow yelled again.

"You've got to keep power to this radar set for the next half hour. Everything else can stop, even the air machines, but *we've got to find out where we're going.*"

The space station turned again. Power resumed and Kevin picked up the plot.

"We're 6000 miles out!" he breathed.

"But it's flattening," Jones cried. "The curve's flattening!" Bert loped back into the control room. Jones snatched the pencil from his superior.

"Here," he said quickly, "I can see it now. Here's the curve. It's an ellipse all right."

"It'll carry us out 9600 miles," Bert gasped. "No one's ever been out that far."

"All right," Morrow said. "That crisis is past. The next question is where are we when we come back on nadir. Bert, tell the crew what's going on. Jones, you can help me. We've got to pick up White Sands and get a fuel rocket up here to push."

"Good Lord, look at that!" Jones breathed. He stared out the port. The Earth, a dazzling huge globe filling most of the heavens, swam slowly past the plastic window. It was the first time they had been able to see more than a convex segment of oceans and continents. Kevin looked, soberly, and turned to the radio.

The power did not fail in the next crazy rotation of the station.

"There's the West Coast." Kevin pointed. "In a few minutes I can get White Sands, I hope."

Jones had taken over the radar plot. At last his pencil reached a peak and the curve started down. The station had reached the limit of its wild plunge into space.

"Good," Kevin muttered. "See if you can extrapolate that curve and get us an approximation where we'll cut in over the other side." The astronomer figured rapidly and abstractedly.

"May I remind you young man," McKelvie's voice boomed, "you have a United States senator aboard. If anything happens—"

"If anything happens, it happens to all of us," Kevin answered coldly. "When you're ready to tell me what *did* happen, I'm ready to listen."

Silence.

"White Sands, this is Station I. Come in please."

Kevin tried to keep his voice calm, but the lives of 90 men rode on it, on his ability to project his words through the crazy hash of static lacing this part of space from the multitude of radio stars. A power rocket with extra fuel was the only instrument that could return the space station to its normal orbit.

That rocket must come from White Sands.

White Sands did not answer.

He tried again, turned as an exclamation of dismay burst from the astronomer. Morrow bent to look at the plotting board.

Jones had sketched a circle of the Earth, placing it in the heart of the ellipse the space station was drawing around it.

From 9600 miles out, the line curved down and down, and down....

But it did not meet the point where the station had departed from its orbit 500 miles above Earth's surface.

The line came down and around to kiss the Earth—almost.

"I hope it's wrong," Jones said huskily. "If I'm right, we'll come in 87 miles above the surface."

"It can't!" Morrow shouted in frustration. "We'll hit stratosphere. It'll burn us—just long enough so we'll feel the agony before we die."

Jones rechecked his figures and shook his head. The line was still the same. Each 10 seconds it was supported by a new radar range. The astronomer's lightning fingers worked out a new problem.

"We have about 75 minutes to do something about it," he said. "We'll be over the Atlantic or England when it happens."

"Station I, this is...."

The beautiful, wonderful voice burst loud and clear from the radio and then vanished in a blurb of static.

"Oh God!" Kevin breathed. It was a prayer.

"We hear you," he shouted, procedure gone with the desperate need to communicate with home. "Come in White Sands. Please come in!"

Faintly now the voice blurred in and out, lost altogether for vital moments: "...your plot. Altiac computer ... your orbit ... rocket on standby ... as you pass."

"Yes!" Kevin shouted, gripping the short wave set with white fingers, trying to project his words into the microphone, across the dwindling thousands of miles of space. "Yes. Send the rocket!"

"Can they do it?" Jones asked. "The rocket, I mean."

"I don't know," Kevin said. "They're all preset, mass produced now, and fuel is adjusted to come into the old orbit. They can be rigged, I think, if there's enough time."

THE COAST OF CALIFORNIA loomed below them now, a brown fringe holding back the dazzling flood of the Pacific. They were 3000 miles above the Earth, dropping sharply on the down leg of the ellipse.

At their present speed, the station appeared to be plunging directly at the Earth. The globe was frighteningly larger each time it wobbled across the viewport.

"Shall I call away the tugmen?" Bert asked tensely.

"I can't ask them to do it," Kevin said. "With this crazy orbit, it's too dangerous. I'm going out."

He slipped into his space gear.

"I'm going with you," Bert said. Kevin smiled his gratitude.

In the airlock the men armed themselves with three heavy rocket pistols each. Morrow ordered other tugmen into suits for standby.

"I wish I could do this alone, Bert," he said soberly. "But I'm glad you're coming along. If we miss, there won't be a second chance."

They knew approximately when they would pass over the rocket launching base, but this time it would be different. The space station would pass at 750 miles altitude and with a new velocity. No one could be sure the feeder rocket would make it. Unless maximum fuel had been adjusted carefully, it might orbit out of reach below them. Rescue fuel would take the place of a pilot.

ANDERSON AND MORROW floated clear of the huge wheel, turning lazily in the deceptive luxury of zero gravity. The familiar sensation of exhilaration threatened to wipe out the urgency they must bring to bear on their lone chance for survival. They could see the jagged hole where the *Moonbeam* had yanked out a section of the structure.

An unintelligible buzz of voice murmured in the radios. Unconsciously Kevin tried to squeeze the earphones against his ears, but his heavily-gloved hands met only the rigid globe of his helmet.

"You get it, Bert?"

"No."

"This is Jones," a new voice loud and clear. "Earth says 15 seconds to blastoff."

"Rocket away!"

Like a tiny, clear bell the words emerged from static. Bert and Kevin gyrated their bodies so they could stare directly at the passing panorama of Earth below. They had seen it hundreds of times, but now 250 more miles of altitude gave the illusion they were studying a familiar landmark through the small end of a telescope.

"There it is!" Bert shouted.

A pinpoint of flame, that was it, with no apparent motion as it rose almost vertically toward them.

Then a black dot in an infinitesimal circle of flame—the rocket silhouetted against its own fire ... as big as a dime ... as big as a dollar....

...as big as a basketball, the circle of flame soared up toward them.

"It's still firing!" Kevin yelled. "It'll overshoot us."

As he spoke, the fire died, but the tiny bar of the rocket, black against the luminous surface of Earth, crawled rapidly up into their sector of starlit blackness. Then it was above Earth's horizon, nearly to the space station's orbit, crawling slowly along, almost to them— a beautiful long cylinder of metal, symbol of home and a civilization sending power to help them to safety.

Hope flashed through Kevin's mind that he was wrong, that the giant computer and the careful hands of technicians had matched the ship to their orbit after all.

But he was right. It passed them, angling slowly upward not 50 yards away.

Instantly the two men rode the rocket blast of their pistols to the nose of the huge projectile. But it carried velocity imparted by rockets that had fired a fraction of a minute too long.

Clinging to the metal with magnetic shoes, Morrow and Anderson pressed the triggers of the pistols, held them down, trying to push the cylinder down and back.

Bert's heavy breathing rasped in the radio as he unconsciously used the futile force of his muscles in the agonizing effort to move the ship.

Their pistols gave out almost simultaneously. Both reached for another. Thin streams of propulsive gas altered the course of the rocket, slightly, but the space station was smaller now, angling imperceptibly away and down as the rocket pressed outward into a new, higher orbit.

The rocket pistols were not enough.

"Get the hell back here!" Jones' voice blared in their ears. "You can't do it. You're 20 miles away now and angling up. Don't be dead heroes!" The last words were high and frantic.

"We've got to!" Morrow answered. "There's no other way."

"We can't do the impossible, Chief," Bert gasped.

A group of tiny figures broke away from the rim of the space station. The tugmen were coming to help.

Then Kevin grasped the hideous truth. There were not enough rocket pistols to bring the men to the full ship and return *with any reserve to guide the projectile.*

"Get back!" he shouted. "Save the pistols. We're coming in."

Behind them their only chance for life continued serenely upward into a new orbit. There, 900 miles above the earth, it would revolve forever with more fuel in its tanks than it needed.

Fuel that would have saved the lives of 90 desperate men.

By leaving it, Morrow and Anderson had bought perhaps 30 more minutes of life before the space station became a huge meteor riding its fiery path to death in the the upper reaches of the atmosphere.

Both suffered the guilt of enormous betrayal. The fact that they could have done no more did not erase it.

Frantically, Kevin flipped over in his mind the possible tools that still could be brought to bear to lift the space station above its flaming destruction. But his tools were the stone axe of a primitive man trying to hack his way out of a forest fire.

EAGER HANDS pulled them back into the station. For a moment there were the reassuring sounds as their helmets were unscrewed. Then the familiar smells and shape of the structure that had been home for so long. Now that haven was about to destroy itself.

Then Morrow remembered the Earth rocket that had brought Senator McKelvie to the great white sausage in space.

That rocket still contained a small quantity of fuel.

If fired at the precise moment, that fuel, anchored with the rocket in the hub socket, might be enough to lift the entire station.

He shouted instructions and men raced to obey. Kevin, himself, raced into the nearest tube. There was no sound, but ahead of him the hatch was open to the discharge chamber. He leaped into the zero-gravity room.

McKelvie was crawling through the connecting port into the feeder rocket. Kevin sprawled headlong into Gordon. The recoil threw them apart, but Gordon recovered balance first.

He had a gun.

"Get back," he snarled. "We're going down." He laughed sharply, near hysteria. "We're going down to tell the world how you fried—through error and mismanagement."

"You messed up those lines," Kevin said. It didn't matter now. He only hoped to hold Gordon long enough for diversionary help to come out of the tube.

"Yes," Gordon leered. "We fixed the lines. The senator wasn't sure we should, but I helped him over his squeamishness, and now we'll crack the whip when we get back home."

"You won't make it," Kevin said. "We're still more than 600 miles high. The glide pattern in that rocket is built to take you down from 500 miles."

McKelvie's head appeared in the hatch. He was desperately afraid.

"You said you could fly this thing, Gordon. Can you?"

Max nodded his head rapidly, like a schoolboy asked to recite a lesson he has not studied.

Kevin was against the bulkhead. Now he pushed himself slowly forward.

"Stay back or I'll shoot?" Gordon screamed. Instead, he leaped backward through the hatch.

Hampered by his original slow motion, Kevin could not move faster until he reached another solid surface.

The hatch slammed shut before his grasping fingers touched it.

A wrenching tug jostled the space station structure. The rocket was gone, and with it the power that might have saved all of them.

Morrow ran again. He had not stopped running since the beginning of this nightmare.

He tumbled over Bert and Jones in the tube. They scrambled after him back to the control room. The three men watched through the port.

"If he doesn't hit the atmosphere too quick, too hard...." Kevin whispered. His fists were clenched. He felt no malice at this moment. He did not wish them death. There was no sound in the radio. The plummeting projectile was a tiny black dot, vanishing below and behind them.

When the end came, it was a mote of orange red, then a dazzling smear of white fire as the rocket ripped into the atmosphere at nearly 20,000 miles an hour.

"They're dead!" Jones voice choked with disbelief. Kevin nodded, but it was a flashing thing that lost meaning for him in the same instant. He knew that unless a miracle happened, ninety men in his command would meet the same fate.

LIKE A PERPETUAL MOTION machine, his brain kept reaching for something that could save his space station, his own people, the iron-nerved spacemen who knew they were near death but kept their vital posts, waiting for him to find a way.

Stories do not end unhappily—that thought kept cluttering his brain—a muddy optimism blanking out vital things that might be done.

"What's the altitude, Jones?"

"520 now. Leveling a bit."

"Enough?" It was a stupid question and Kevin knew it. Jones shook his head.

"We might be lucky," he said. "We'll hit it about 97 miles up. The top isn't a smooth surface, it billows and dips. But," he added, almost a whisper, "we'll penetrate to about 80 miles before...."

"How much time?" Kevin asked sharply. A tiny chain of hope linked feebly.

"About 22 minutes."

"Bert, order all hands into spacesuits—emergency!"

While the order was being carried out, Kevin summoned the tugmen.

"How many loaded pistols do we have?"

"Six," the chief answered.

"All right. Get this quick. Anchor yourselves inside the hub. Aim those pistols at the Earth and fire until they're exhausted."

The chief stared incredulously.

"I know it's crazy," Kevin snapped. "It's not enough, but if it alters our orbit 50 feet, it'll help." The tugmen ran out. Bert, Kevin and Jones scrambled into spacesuits. Morrow called for reports.

"All hands," he intoned steadily, "open all ports. Repeat. Open all ports. Do not question. Follow directions closely."

Ten seconds later, a whoosh of escaping air signaled obedience.

"Now!" Kevin shouted, "grab every loose object within reach. Throw it at the Earth. Desks, books, tools, anything. Throw them down with every ounce of strength you've got!"

It was insane. Everything was insane. It couldn't possibly be enough.... But space around the hurtling station blossomed with every conceivable flying object that man has ever taken with him to a lonely outpost. A pair of shoes went tumbling into darkness, and behind it the plastic framed photograph of someone's wife and children.

Jones knew his superior had not gone berserk. He bent anxiously over the radar scope.

It was not a matter of jettisoning weight. Every action has an equal reaction, and the force each man gave to a thrown object was as effective in its diminutive way as the exhaust from a rocket.

"Read it!" Morrow shouted. "Read it!"

"265 miles," Jones cried. "I need more readings to tell if it helped."

There was no sound in the radio circuit, save that of 90 men breathing, waiting to hear 90 death sentences. Jones' heavily-gloved hands moved the pencil clumsily over the graph paper. He drew a tangent to a new curve.

"It helped," he said tonelessly, "We'll go in at 100 miles, penetrate to 90...."

"Not enough," Kevin said. "Close all ports. Repeat. Close all ports!"

An unheard sigh breathed through the mammoth, complex doughnut as automatic machinery gave new breath to airless spaces.

It might never be needed again to sustain human life. But the presence of air delivered one final hope to Morrow's frantic brain.

"Two three oh miles," Jones said.

"Air control," Kevin barked into the mike, "how much pressure can you get in fifteen minutes?"

"Air control, aye," came the answer, and a pause while the chief calculated. "About 50 pounds with everything on the line."

"Get it on! And hang on to your hats," Kevin yelled.

The station dropped another 30 miles, slanting in sharply toward the planet's envelope of gas that could sustain life—or take it away. Morrow turned to Anderson.

"Bert. There are four tubes leading into the hub. Get men and open the outer airlocks. Then stand by the four inner locks. When I give the signal, open those locks, fast. You may have to pull to help the machinery—you'll be fighting three times normal air pressure."

Bert ran out. Nothing now but to wait. Five minutes passed. Ten.

"We're at 135 miles," Jones said.

Far below the Earth wheeled by, its apparent motion exaggerated as the space station swooped lower.

"120 miles."

Kevin's throat was parched, his lips dry. Increasing air pressure squeezed the space-suit tighter around his flesh. A horror of claustrophobia gripped him and he knew every man was suffering the same torture.

"110 miles."

"Almost there," Bert breathed, unaware that his words were audible.

Then a new force gripped them, at first the touch of a caressing finger tip dragging back, ever so slightly. Kevin staggered as inertia tugged him forward.

"We're in the air!" he shouted. "Bert. Stand by the airlocks!"

"Airlocks ready!"

The finger was a hand, now, a huge hand of tenuous gases, pressing, pressing, but the station still ripped through its death medium at a staggering 20,000 miles an hour.

Jones pointed. Morrow's eyes followed his indicating finger to the thermocouple dial.

The dial said 100°F. While he watched, it moved to 105, quickly to 110°.

FIVE SECONDS MORE. A blinding pain of tension stabbed Kevin behind the eyes. But through the flashing colors of agony, he counted, slowly, deliberately....

"Now!" he shouted. "Open airlocks, Bert. *Now!*"

Air rushed out through the converging spokes of the great wheel, poured out under tremendous pressure, into the open cup of the space station hub, and there the force of three atmospheres spurted into space through the mammoth improvised rocket nozzle.

Kevin felt the motion. Every man of the crew felt the surge as the intricate mass of metal and nylon leaped upward.

That was all.

Morrow watched the temperature gauge. It climbed to 135°, to 140° ... 145 ... 150....

"The temperature is at 150 degrees," he announced huskily over the radio circuit. "If it goes higher, there's nothing we can do."

The needle quivered at 151, moved to 152, and held....

Two minutes, three....

The needle stepped back, one degree.

"We're moving out," Kevin whispered. "We're moving out!"

The cheer, then, was a ringing, deafening roar in the earphones. Jones thumped Kevin madly on the back and leaped in a grotesque dance of joy.

MORROW LEANED BACK in the control chair,

pressed tired fingers to his temples. He could not remember when he had slept.

The first rocket from White Sands had brought power to adjust the orbit. This one was on the mark.

The next three brought the Senate investigating committee.

But that didn't matter, really. Kevin was happy, and he was waiting.

The control room door banged open. Mark Kramer's grin was like a flash of warm sunlight.

"Hi, commander," he said, "wait'll you see the marvelous pictures I got."

Outside, the *Moonbeam* rode gently at anchor, tethered with new safety lines.

"Slow Burn" first appeared in the October 1955 issue of Worlds of If Science Fiction, *and featured an illustration by Frank Kelly Freas.*

Before he abandoned the genre, author and longtime newspaperman Henry Still (1920– ?) published close to a dozen science fiction stories during the mid-1950s, mostly in Fantastic, Worlds of IF, *and* Amazing Stories *magazines. In 1956, he was a Hugo Award finalist for "Most Promising New Author"—along with Harlan Ellison, Robert Silverberg, and Frank Herbert. (Silverberg won, by the way.) Henry Still later became a public relations manager for the aerospace company Northrup Ventura (now Northrup Grumman).*

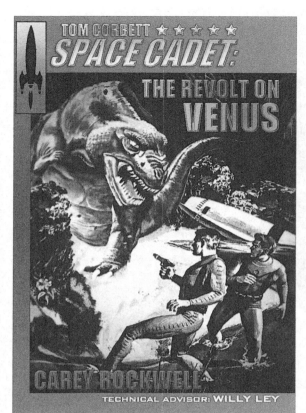

NOW AVAILABLE

TOM CORBETT, SPACE CADET:
THE REVOLT ON VENUS
BOOK 5 IN THE SERIES

On term break from Space Academy, Tom Corbett and Roger Manning accompany their pal Astro to his native planet Venus for a well-deserved rest. There the cadets plan to hunt the biggest game in the star system, but their vacation is soon interrupted when the intrepid crew of the *Polaris* stumble across a secret plot to overthrow the Solar Alliance.

Lost in the Venusian Jungle, unable to contact the Solar Guard, separated from their ship and each other, the hunters have now become the hunted: caught between the heavily armed forces of a would-be tyrant mad for power… and the tyrannosaurus Astro wounded years earlier—thirty tons of terror mad for revenge.

$8.00 ♦ ISBN: 978-0-9966936-6-0

TOM CORBETT, SPACE CADET:
TREACHERY IN OUTER SPACE
BOOK 6 IN THE SERIES

Why has Roger Manning suddenly gone dark? Can his pal Tom Corbett really be dead? What caused the strange trouble on Titan—and how is it connected to a rocket race in outer space?

These are but a few of the mysteries confounding Captain Steve Strong and the big Venusian engineer, Astro, as the Solar Guard races against time to save the mining colony on Saturn's largest satellite. At stake are the lives of hundreds of men, women and children; the future of the intrepid *Polaris* crew; and quite possibly the fate of the entire star system.

$8.00 ♦ ISBN: 978-1-7324344-0-0

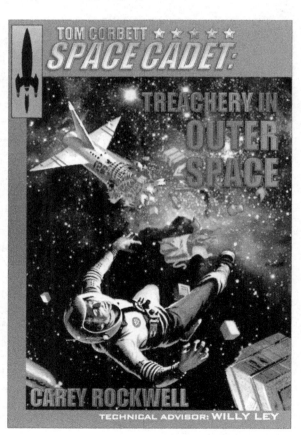

WE'LL KNOW WHEN WE GET THERE, WE'LL TELL YOU WHEN WE GET BACK: DESTINATION MOON SEVEN DECADES LATER

BY JUSTIN HUMPHREYS

21ST CENTURY VIEWERS FREQUENTLY DON'T KNOW WHAT TO MAKE OF *DESTINATION MOON*. A dull condescension might set in—they dismiss it as a "creaker," an artifact from the dawn of the Space Age. To generations of viewers weaned on $200 million spectacles—many of whom were born long after the first *real* moon landing—the film's documentary-like depiction of a lunar voyage might seem downright quaint.

In reality, with *Destination Moon*, producer George Pal took American science fiction cinema a quantum leap forward. It ignited the 1950s science fiction film boom, and, in so doing, jumpstarted the most profitable and popular film genre of the last seventy years. What modern viewers so often miss is that *Destination Moon* made the mega-blockbusters that followed it *possible*.

Not only was *Destination Moon* the first realistic depiction of a Moon voyage in an American film—at a time when people dismissed space travel as *Flash Gordon*-esque nonsense—but shot in Technicolor, no less. Rarest of rarities in his own era, Pal frequently employed top-notch science fiction and fantasy specialists to write his scripts, rather than screenwriters tone-deaf to the genre—*Destination Moon*'s co-author was SF giant Robert Heinlein. Heinlein and Pal, along with the great astronomical artist Chesley Bonestell, among others, strove to make *Destination Moon* as scientifically plausible and mature as possible, eschewing pulp SF cliches like sexy moon maidens and ravening space creatures. In 1949, the very idea of SF films for adults

DESTINATION MOON and all associated images copyright WADE WILLIAMS

was a seismic cultural shift, and Pal was ably guiding that transition. To fully appreciate the film so many decades later, it's critical for viewers to put themselves in the context of its time. It was made for audiences unused to thoughtful, well-made SF cinema and whose expectations, knowledge, and standards were entirely different from our own. And the film's impact in its own era was incalculable.

Destination Moon's basic premise is simple: an intrepid team led by a scientist and an industrialist are determined to travel to the Moon. Frustrated by massive bureaucratic hassles—and also likely enemy sabotage—

they seek private funding. They successfully prepare their rocket, the *Luna*, and narrowly manage to launch it before government agents can shut them down. The rest of the film presents their voyage—its dangers, near-fatal hardships, their lunar exploration, and their return.

To make the film's basic story accessible to the widest possible audience, its plot works essentially like a Warner Bros. soldiers-on-a-mission story, right down to the presence of a wisecracking (and unfunny, and unnecessary) Brooklynite, a clear descendent of similar World War II-movie comic relief types. The film's title even echoes Warners' *Destination Tokyo*. To further simplify rocketry concepts for pre-NASA audiences, Pal worked in an educational short on space travel starring Woody Woodpecker, animated by his dear friend, Walter Lantz.

Woody Woodpecker learns about rocket science, in an educational short animated by Walter Lantz.

A brief digression for those unfamiliar with Pal and his career: Pal initially made a name for himself in Europe and Hollywood directing a series of very musical and colorful stop-motion featurettes. Intent on graduating to feature film production, Pal began developing full-length projects. In the late 1940s, he struck a deal for his first two full-length productions with Eagle-Lion Studios. For these films, Pal carried over some of his animation staff, including editor Duke Goldstone and animator Stuart O'Brien, who did some very brief stop-motion animation for *Destination Moon*. Pal's new collaborators like composer Leith Stevens and art director Ernst Fegte also contribute notably to Pal's initial features, as did cinematographer Lionel "Curly" Lindon.

Destination Moon was Pal's second full-length production after *The Great Rupert*, an

Pal's amazing animated squirrel star tidies his attic home—by tossing out money stashed away by a miserly landlord, in THE GREAT RUPERT.

innocuous, family-friendly Christmas movie starring Jimmy Durante and an animated dancing squirrel; both it and *Destination Moon* were directed by Irving Pichel, an actor-turned-director whose extensive acting credits include playing the servant of *Dracula's Daughter* and whose directorial work included co-directing the excellent *The Most Dangerous Game* and *She*.

But arguably the most critical member of *Destination Moon*'s artistic team was artist Chesley Bonestell. Not only did Bonestell undoubtedly rank among the most important and seminal astronomical artists of the 20th century, but was also a skilled matte painter whose work appeared in masterpieces like *Citizen Kane*. In his stunning paintings for *Collier's* and other magazines and in his 1949 book (with Willy Ley) *The Conquest of Space*, Bonestell vividly realized visions of spaceflight and other worlds and, in so doing, made space travel not only highly plausible to his readers, but left them feeling like they had *been*. Pal was infusing *Destination Moon* cinematically

Industrialist Jim Barnes (John Archer) and Dr. Charles Cargraves (Warner Anderson); Cargraves: "By the grace of God, and in the name of the United States of America, I take possession of this planet on behalf of, and for the benefit of, all mankind."

with this same spirit: Pal didn't see the film as science fiction, but as a "documentary of the near future." Bonestell, Pal, and the rest of the *Destination Moon* crew admirably represented the best of the mid-century American spirit: a can-do/make-do attitude of unswerving dedication to reaching the moon.

Although Bonestell strove for scientific accuracy, Pal, Pichel, and art director Ernst Fegte deliberately altered their moon's surface, giving it the look of a caked river bed. They had practical reasons: they felt that the cracks added visual interest and, more importantly, they could use them to create forced perspective to make their moonscape set look much vaster. To enhance that particular illusion, little people in smaller spacesuits were used in the background in several shots.

Pal and company's efforts paid off handsomely, particularly Bonestell's. Critic Bob Stephens lauded Bonestell's moonscape matte painting, deeming it "The greatest alien landscape in movie history. Parts of it seem to glow from within, and the reinforcement of Stevens' eerie music makes it even more of an otherworldly marvel. The vast mountain range bathed in Earthlight and the fractured desolate plains are so remarkable I've often told people that Bonestell's moon is better than God's."

Bonestell imbued *Destination Moon* and other early Pal features with a reality and sheer aesthetic beauty that American SF films had so often previously lacked. "Probably no other living artist could have done those pictures," Pal told the press in 1950. "Mr. Bonestell is as mathematically conscientious as an astronomer or a physicist. He takes no artist's license and refuses to compromise with fact. His gifts, plus the art direction of Ernst Fegte, make the perfect team for this type of picture."

The film's sleek *Luna* rocketship epitomized early 1950s visions of spacecraft. Likewise, the bellows-jointed spacesuits reflected the general concepts of the era, and those costumes became a staple of '50s SF movies, appearing in *Flight to Mars* and others, even popping up in other media like the cover of Les Baxter's *Space Escapade* album. (Pal personally kept several of the spacesuits, which were incinerated in his 1961 Bel Air housefire.)

Pal often said throughout his working life in Hollywood that special effects were as big a star as any actor or actress. This was particularly true of his initial modestly-budgeted features, whose leads were very capable actors but not (at the time) big names. *Destination Moon*'s F/X were critical to its success, and Pal put them in Lee Zavitz's capable hands. Zavitz's many previous on-screen miracles included masterminding the titular tropical storm in John Ford's *The Hurricane* and engineering the burning of Atlanta for *Gone With the Wind.*

One aspect of *Destination Moon* that is still vividly apparent is how beautifully it captures the eerie, awe-inspiring grandeur of space. An enthusiastic music-lover, Pal took great pains with his films' scores, frequently sitting-in on his composers' recording sessions. His work, including his animated featurettes, shows an innate knack for meshing onscreen imagery with music. A prime example is the initial pan over the lunar surface in *Destination Moon*, set to Leith Stevens' outstanding score, which presents an extraordinary and eloquent vision of the unexplored cosmos' vastness and mystery. Outside of Jerry Goldsmith's *Star Trek: The Motion Picture* soundtrack, few SF scores have so poetically conveyed that very genuine sense of wonder.

Destination Moon's unusual nature helped win it a publicity blitz in magazines and elsewhere, including a fascinating tour of its set on the local L.A. show "City at Night." Infamously, producer Robert Lippert rode on the coattails of this overall buzz and

The crew take a walk across the surface of *Luna* to repair frozen equipment.

Two examples of publications involved in *DM*'s publicity blitz.

hastily assembled a competitor in the space film sweepstakes, *Rocketship X-M*, which was in theaters before *Destination Moon*. For the remainder of Pal's career, he would carefully safeguard his projects to avoid such claim-jumping.

Destination Moon and *The Great Rupert* were cross-collateralized, meaning if one lost money, the other's profits would be used to defray those box-office losses. *The Great Rupert* was predicted to be Pal's hit, with *Destination Moon* generally deemed a risky gamble. The reverse proved to be true: *Rupert* performed only mildly well, while *Destination Moon* hit big and changed world cinema. Decades later, Heinlein still publicly chastised Eagle-Lion for using *The Great Rupert* to keep from having to fork over any well-earned royalties on *Destination Moon* to him, Pal, or anyone else. Nonetheless, *Destination Moon* established Pal as Hollywood's preeminent fantasist of the '50s, and the film received two Academy Award nominations, winning for Best Special Effects. Pal's movies would go on to win many more.

In hindsight, the impact of *Destination Moon* and Pal's subsequent SF hits *When Worlds Collide*, *Conquest of Space*, and *The Time Machine* was vast. In 2018, when director James Cameron interviewed Steven Spielberg for his series, *James Cameron's Story of Science Fiction*, Cameron praised Spielberg as a cinematic visionary. Spielberg replied, "Well, there's always a guy ahead of all of us. There's a whole bunch of guys ahead of me. George Pal, Stanley Kubrick, Willis O'Brien." Notably, Spielberg named Pal first.

"...The first time I really felt suspense [at the movies]," Spielberg told Cameron, "was I was very young and saw a movie, and it was a reissue, called *Destination Moon*. Another

40 • **DESTINATION MOON**

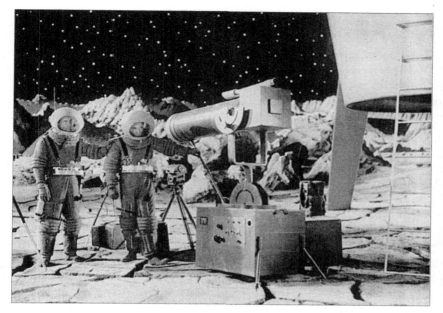

George Pal film. When that first moon voyage lands and they can't get off the moon unless they take several tons of weight out of the ship itself, I remember as a kid not being able to sit still ... I didn't realize suspense starts at the stomach. And it goes up to the throat. And then it comes out as a scream."

Visual effects giant Douglas Trumbull has said that he and Stanley Kubrick were inspired by Chesley Bonestell's work to give the moonscape in *2001: A Space Odyssey* a deliberately inaccurate rocky surface, a la *Destination Moon*. In spite of these testimonials, *Destination Moon* isn't as widely-known as Pal's *When Worlds Collide* or *The War of the Worlds*, partly because it lacks their blood and thunder. It and Pal's *Conquest of Space* were both relatively straightforward depictions of space travel devoid of apocalyptic catastrophes or monsters. *Destination Moon* also isn't strikingly visually futuristic like *Forbidden Planet*, and it isn't entertainingly ridiculous like, say, *Missile to the Moon*. *Destination Moon*'s innate sobriety of approach won it respect during its initial release, but decades of real spaceflight have diminished its ability to grab modern viewers.

Along with millions of others, Pal and Bonestell were overjoyed when the first moon landing in 1969 proved their cinematic prophecy true. But perhaps the most delicious irony of Pal's visionary abilities is the realization of privatized space travel. When Pal's film debuted and for many decades thereafter, unimaginative critics blithely scoffed at the idea of private interests bankrolling spaceflight. Now, Elon Musk's SpaceX and Richard Branson's Virgin Galactic have proved these smug windbags wrong.

Early in *Destination Moon*, a potential investor asks the project's leader, Barnes,

The crew hurriedly jettison tons of equipment in an attempt to escape the moon and return to Earth.

what the payoff is when they reach the moon. "We'll Know When We Get There, We'll Tell You When We Get Back." Always decades ahead of the curve, George Pal knew why we were going all along. It just took the world a while to catch up with him.

JUSTIN HUMPHREYS *is a writer, film historian, consultant and curator. He has published three books, including the Rondo Award-winning* The Dr. Phibes Companion. *Humphreys is currently completing George Pal's authorized biography,* George Pal: Man of Tomorrow, *with the Pal family's full cooperation. Humphreys has also been the curator of Pal's estate since 2011 and often acts as the family's representative at various events. He frequently appears on-camera and in audio commentaries for video labels like The Criterion Collection, Paramount, Arrow, Imprint, Mill Creek, and Scream Factory, among others. His most recent commentary is* Flight to Mars *(Film Detective). He also regularly appears on various podcasts.*

Humphreys specializes in curating, cataloging, and brokering entertainment memorabilia—particularly props and costumes—and rare books. While working at Bonhams Auctions, he handled countless Hollywood treasures, including cataloging large portions of the estates of Natalie Wood, Maureen O'Hara, Charlton Heston, Tod Browning, and Harper Goff, as well as many of Rudolph Valentino's personal effects. In 2017, Humphreys cataloged the original Robby the Robot from Forbidden Planet, *which sold for $5.3 million, setting a World Record for the most expensive movie prop to ever sell at auction. For more information about Humphreys' George Pal biography, follow him at the book's only authorized Facebook page:*

www.facebook.com/GeorgePalManOfTomorrowOfficialPage

THE SKY PEOPLE

BY GREGORY L. NORRIS

ART BY ALLEN KOSZOWSKI

ERIC THIRTEEN DONNED THE UNIFORM WITH PRIDE. HE STOOD BEFORE THE MIRROR IN THE TIGHT PRESS OF HIS QUARTERS ON CENTAUR STATION, buttoning the BDU shirt with its familiar dark camouflage that honored a void full of constellations and nudged his gaze up to the new addition—the pair of "Virtus ad astra" silver stars on the collar that identified him as station commander. His next breath came with difficulty.

Valor to the stars. The first, his inner voice reminded. *You're the first Number to command a frontline defense installation as big as Centaur.*

Heat tickled Eric's belly. He swallowed down the emotion before it could rise higher. Hubris was foolish, he already agreed. As though to remind him of this fact, while he fastened the top button of his shirt the station sounded its sharp alert. The warning lights altered from their white standby color to the blood red of imminent danger.

"Incoming enemy contacts spotted at Orbital Five-Five-Nine," called Levring over the station's intercom. His new second-in-command added, "This is not a drill. I repeat, *this is not a drill*. All defense teams move into position!"

Eric reached for the wall terminal. "This is the commander."

"Sir," Levring said. "Two of their capitol ships raced in past Mars at top speed. We detected their deceleration."

Too bad those Klavalk didn't spiral out of control and smash into Deimos or Phobos, he thought. "Have you alerted the other Watchdogs?"

"Minotaur, Cerberus, and Cyclops Stations have all gone on alert. Our forces report readiness to engage the enemy."

"Launch Bayonets," Eric ordered, and how strange it felt to not be one of the pilots about to blast away from Centaur to meet their adversaries in space. "Raise the station's defense batteries."

"All silos and cannons at ready, Sir," Levring said.

Eric nodded. "On my way."

One last glance in the mirror, and Eric exited the commander's quarters. The new day would test the uniform and the Number wearing it, he sensed. Just how much would be revealed in the seconds and hours ahead. While marching at a brisk pace through the main artery that connected Centaur Station's living area with the Bayonet hangar, the weapons section, and the command deck, his mind traveled back. Klaxons shrieked in warning, the soundtrack aiding his memory. The launch. The sensation he always equated with falling directly following separation from the hangar's anchor. Then the freedom after he turned the fighter jet away from the satellite and the blue mother planet it and the other Watchdogs guarded over. He'd aimed the Bayonet's nose straight at the incoming Klavalk juggernaut's bridge and had fired the killing shot, a single Bayonet alone against one of their heavy capitol warships.

Here was his reward.

The station woke around him, baring its teeth.

"First squadron of Bayonets ready to launch," Levring announced over the intercom.

Eric entered Centaur Command in time to hear that the second wing was on its way. A dozen other Earth Defense Corps uniforms manned the key stations. As Eric neared Levring, the safety shutters rolled into place over the command deck's space windows. The tactical display showed the pair of enemy warships streaking toward Earth with the tails of comets and the fangs of hungry predators as they attempted to decelerate from breakneck speeds.

"Targeting solutions acquired," said Lieutenant Basinelle. "Station's cannons on automated track. Missiles aimed and ready to fire!"

It was all textbook—a script that had been rehearsed dozens of times here and throughout the Watchdog line in high orbit above the Earth. Only something didn't quite match. Eric Thirteen first sensed it in the prickle crawling over his flesh, warning him like an organic version of the alarm klaxon.

"Sir—!" Basinelle said only to then go silent as she swiped buttons on the control board.

"Speak to me, Baz," Eric urged more than commanded. "Those two Klavalk ships—"

The warning broadcast over his skin was given form a second later. Eric tipped a look at the screen in time to see both comets wink out of existence, seemingly devoured by a roiling storm cloud there one instant, gone the next.

"What the hell just happened?" Levring posed aloud. "Lieutenant, where are those two enemy ships?"

"The debris cloud, did you see it?" Eric asked. "Did those ships decelerate out of control and collide?"

"Wouldn't that be poetic and fitting," Levring said.

The screen, broadcasting imagery in real-time relayed by Centaur Station's eyes-in-the-skies, only showed empty space.

"We're not detecting any debris or power readings from damaged engines, Commander," Basinelle said.

Eric wandered closer to the screen. "Is it possible they powered back up again to full speed for a crash dive at us?"

Basinelle checked instruments and shook her head. "There's no indication of those ships anywhere out there."

Levring radioed to the two wings of Bayonets, the station's vanguard. "All fighters maintain formation and standby. Hold for Centaur Station."

"Holding, Centaur Station," the lead pilot of the first squadron acknowledged.

Eric silently placed the voice—Calvin Ten, another Number in a key role regarding the operation of his Watchdog command and the defense of the Earth.

His people went through the playbook again—some scanning space between Centaur Station and the last contact with the Klavalk. Fighters held their staggered-wing form-ups. *His* people—that concept still felt somewhat uncomfortable unlike the uniform that fit him to perfection like second skin.

Then the crawling phantom chill returned, and Eric sensed the danger on its heels.

He whirled toward Basinelle right as she detected the anomaly moving in from a dozen kilometers off the station's starboard defenses.

"Sir, energy surge detected—coming at us on collision course!"

The maelstrom appeared on the screens tracking Centaur's orbit and her fighters. The massive black cloud was identical to that which had engulfed the two Klavalk warships. It raced across the distance, growing in scope as it neared.

"*Identify,*" Levring barked above the reawakened din of alarm bells.

Basinelle thawed from her temporary paralysis and activated the station's scanners. "We're detecting powerful particles within the disturbance—tachyon-based!"

"Get our fighters back on Centaur," Eric said.

Even as he issued the order, he doubted there was time. Tachyons traveled faster than the speed of light, and the storm cloud was almost on top of them.

Energy whipped around the command deck, tickling skin and traveling deeper. He sensed it in his molars, his marrow, before it invaded that place Numbers weren't supposed to have but Eric Thirteen believed he did—his soul. Then everything around him lit up with a blinding lightning flash. The cacophony of voices from pilots and command personnel along with the counterpoint of station alarms crackled out, and he felt nothing.

HE RETURNED from oblivion, his left cheek intimate with the floor. Eric tasted blood. He licked the inside of his mouth on instinct and recorded the place where the soft meat had struck a tooth. The jab of pain helped him focus.

His next breath filled with the acrid smell of burned circuitry. A haze of oily smoke drifted through Centaur Command. Eric's numbed hearing caught up to the rest of his senses a few seconds later. Alarm bells continued to bleat, their speed slowed down. The red lights flashed at the periphery. He stood straight on his feet and instantly felt the wrongness through the treads of his uniform boots.

The station's inertia was off, its orbit failing. Eric cast a look around the command deck and saw that all of his people were still down, as were the instruments tracking every detail of their purpose, including the massive satellite's course around the Earth.

Eric hurried over to Levring. His Executive Officer was stunned but alive.

Tachyons, he recalled while helping Levring out of the fog—particles capable of traveling faster than the speed of light. There was no telling how badly they'd scrambled the station and its personnel.

"I'm okay," Levring said despite the pallor of his face.

In short order, the rest of the command staff recovered.

"The station's orbit is off," Eric said. "Get those systems up and reporting in so we know where we stand!"

Basinelle initiated a restart of key controls.

"What about our pilots?" Eric asked, directing the question to Levring.

His second-in-command activated the radio. "Centaur Command to all Bayonets, do you copy?"

Dead air answered. The floor beneath Eric's soles lurched, and his stomach followed.

"*Baz*," he shouted. "Orbital status?"

Systems came alive. A dozen displays reactivated, one showing the status of their fighter fleet as well as the station's current trajectory.

And Eric Thirteen, recently promoted to Commander of Centaur Station, saw the problem. They were no longer *in* orbit.

"My God," Levring got out before his instincts cut in. "Brunson," he barked toward one of the operatives. "Get us stabilized! Fire steering rockets one and three!"

"Aye, Sir!"

The view on their Bayonets showed a similar nightmare glimpse. Most of their fighters were out of formation and adrift in a chaotic spiral.

While scrambling to reestablish radio contact with their pilots, Brunson asked, "Where's the Earth?"

Eric Thirteen glanced up. "What?"

The image of Centaur Station righting itself thanks to the added boost from its steering rockets pulled back to show the view at their six. The familiar blue and silver orb of the mother planet was gone. In its place was a dense cluster of unfamiliar stars.

"Sir, I'm not detecting any EDC beacons—Cerberus, Cyclops, Minotaur … nothing from any of our moon bases or EDC Command," Basinelle said. "But I am receiving multiple target contacts at close range to the station."

Even as he absorbed this latest unbelievable intelligence, Eric nodded, the order given without words. Basinelle activated the station's eyes, and the results were broadcast in an expanded view from just beyond Centaur Station and the paralyzed fleet of Bayonet fighters. In ones and twos, the other spacecraft appeared, a dozen at first, then two, finally three before Eric stopped counting. He recognized the pair of Klavalk enemy warships. Some of the constructs within the zone surrounding the space station didn't resemble spaceships in configuration and appeared to have been grown rather than manufactured. One sleek, arrow-shaped craft reminded him more of a submarine than a vessel designed for space travel. Only the colossus drifting at a pitched angle fifty kilometers to their port was larger than Centaur Station.

"It's like a graveyard of spaceships," Levring said, his eyes trained without blinking at the imagery.

"Only we know for a fact that we're not aboard a ghost ship, and neither is the enemy," Eric said. "I'm willing to wager those other spaceships are in the same predicament we are."

The radio crackled. Calvin Ten checked in ahead of the other pilots.

"What the hell hit us?" Calvin asked.

"We'll get back to you on that," Levring said.

"Centaur Command, are you seeing what we are?"

Eric took the radio. "Captain, maintain your defensive formation around Centaur until we have a better understanding of what happened, where we are, and who's at the wheel over on those other ships."

"Aye, Commander," Calvin said.

"There are still two Klavalk warships within striking range of the satellite," Eric said.

"No need to remind us, Sir," Calvin fired back.

"Good."

"*Virtus ad astra*," Calvin said.

Eric turned to face the image of the pile-up and its many different representatives. Doing so allowed him to focus on something other than the fact they were no longer in orbit around Earth and that he couldn't place any of the stars or constellations.

"That tachyon surge," Eric said. "It was the same one that engulfed the two Klavalk ships. It wasn't some random space storm."

"Is that a theory?" Levring asked, punctuating the statement with a humorless chuckle.

"We were taken just like them—and those other spaceships," Eric continued. "Have you determined our exact location yet?"

"Negative, Sir—none of the stars match known charts. Cross-referencing long-range database now," Basinelle said.

The radio chirped. Another prompt followed.

"We're being hailed by one of those alien ships," Levring said.

"Answer," said Eric.

Levring opened the channel. A high-pitched shrill poured out, sharp of the ear and sounding angry in its delivery. Levring cut the call. Another came through, the language guttural, equally untranslatable apart from its panicked timbre. Six more general messages crowded in after that.

"*Help us!*" one voice cried out. "Please, we are dying!"

The voice, genderless in sound, originated from the vessel Eric had mentally compared to a submarine. The screen zeroed in to show the arrow-shaped hull spiraling out of control between an asymmetrical, organic craft and the pair of Klavalk warships.

Eric reached for the radio. "Alien vessel, this is Commander Eric Thirteen of the Earth Defense Corps Watchdog Satellite Centaur Station. Do you understand my words?"

"Yes, Commander," the genderless voice answered.

"State the nature of your emergency."

"This craft, *The Heart of Uhmev*, is a seafaring vessel. We are losing life support and unable to maintain our position. Please help us, Centaur Station!"

TEN BAYONETS surrounded the out of control Uhmev sea vessel, attaching onto its hull one at a time and spaced out evenly. The fighters from Earth activated steering rockets in a coordinated pattern, which stopped the pitch and roll of their rescue target. From there, the Bayonets labored to return to Centaur Station's hangar deck, the prize in tow.

Eric watched from the command deck, standing between Basinelle and Levring. The rescue mission required their focus while others searched the starmap for clues as to their position, and the station's greatest minds and computers worked out solutions to get them back where they belonged.

"On final approach," Calvin Ten called over the radio.

The fit would be tight but manageable. Along with their defensive status, the Watchdogs had been designed to double as repair depots for the EDC's frigate fleet. The Uhmev submarine approximated the size of the EDC's main mobile strike vessels. Its mass would be felt, but Eric guessed Centaur Station could handle it and still put up a hell of a fight if required.

The Bayonets inched the alien craft in past the hangar doors. The doors trundled shut, and Eric left to greet their new guests.

THE SIGHT WAS SPECTACULAR—*The Heart of Uhmev* positioned between supports, the ten Bayonets having detached and returned to their launch anchors, and the row of armed station security guards holding a line between the alien construct and Eric.

Eric moved forward and then through the line. As he did so, an aperture in the submarine's hull irised open. From that airlock, a localized cloud of blue-white vapor drifted out, and within the oblong bubble was a creature unlike any he'd seen. Its graceful movements reminded Eric of undersea plant life swaying in the tides. It showed no obvious head—not as he knew the term. Eric wondered if the creature was a form of intelligent plant life on a scale that could construct submarines and invent such sophisticated technologies as localized atmosphere chambers.

"Commander Thirteen," the delegate asked.

Eric nodded. "You speak our language?"

"No, Commander," the alien said. "We speak *all* languages through a version of what you would consider surface telepathy. We communicate with all other forms of life on

Uhmev in this manner, down to the most basic of our planet's species."

"Can you communicate with the other ships and people out there?"

"Yes," the Uhmev said.

"Good. What do I call you?"

"Uhmev. We of Uhmev are all Uhmev."

"Uhmev, come with me to my center of operations—we could use your help in understanding those other people and, hopefully, what happened to all of us so we can effect a return to our home world."

Uhmev followed Eric through the guards.

"Commander," the alien delegate said. "You should know that we sent our call for help to every ship out there. Your space station was the only one who responded."

THEY STEPPED THROUGH the security doors and into the nerve center of Centaur Station. Uhmev kept close to Eric as all eyes focused upon them. Contact with aliens was no new wonder—the Klavalk and their attacks had removed scales from eyes a decade-plus earlier. But to the command crew, the universe grew bigger in scope with the arrival of the Uhmev delegate.

"My executive officer, Stan Levring. Tactical officer Sofia Basinelle. Officer Ken Brunson," Eric said.

"I offer you greetings and thanks from Uhmev herself, mother of all we are."

Eric motioned for Uhmev to join Levring. "Uhmev will help translate all of that alien chatter."

Levring nodded and put the radio on open channel directed at the spaceships and crews gathered in the area surrounding the satellite.

"To all who listen, hear me, please. I am broadcasting from the Earth Defense Corps satellite Centaur Station," Uhmev said.

The message went out to the small and large, the streamlined and asymmetrical, to potential friends and enemies alike.

"We propose an exchange of information and mutual cooperation in the face of the present crisis that has brought us all to this sector of space. We—"

The message was still being broadcast when space lit with another tachyon surge, and the real enemy showed its face.

THE RIFT OPENED, a massive black storm cloud roiling with tachyon emissions. Centaur Station trembled, requiring quick action from Brunson at the steering rocket controls to keep the satellite from listing to port.

A hundred and eleven k distant, the maelstrom unfurled.

"Put up visual," Eric ordered. "Scan the region for any and all power readings."

Basinelle did as ordered. Even at the distance, it was clear that this version of the event that had transported them from Earth orbit to space unknown was vaster and more powerful in scope. Instead of devouring the nearest of the spaceships clustered around the storm front, the cloud discharged something huge. It floated out, not quite circular but close enough to resemble an orb. Grooves pitted and sliced across the orb's surface—what Eric guessed were shuttered gun emplacements right before the first opened and took aim at the Klavalk warships.

The opening salvo of energy tore out of the emplacement as dark lightning, striking and stunning the nearest warship. Watching, horrified, Eric held his breath as the second shot punched through the warship's hull, wiping it from their tactical screens and existence.

A breathless silence settled over the command deck. In those tense seconds, Eric Thirteen faced the circular orb and, with certainty, he sensed it staring back—not only at him, at Centaur Station, but all of the vessels of the alien fleet captured and taken against their will.

He also sensed it gloating.

It had destroyed a Klavalk warship in two shots. In the last of those stunned seconds, the orb fired again, this time striking the second Klavalk cruiser. The next would deliver the kill.

Two shots. Eric had slain a Klavalk battleship with *one*, his inner voice reminded. He thawed. "Mister Levring, target that new contact. Fire before it takes out the Klavalk!"

"Sir?" Levring asked.

Eric whirled on his second-in-command. "I said *fire!*"

Levring moved into action. "Lieutenant Basinelle, you heard the Commander. Fire!"

Centaur Station's cannons unleashed their full fury. The plasma beams soared out, slicing between the stunned onlookers still recovering from the shock of the situation, raced over the dorsal armor of the paralyzed Klavalk warship, and impacted against the massive orb, knocking it off kilter enough that its kill-shot went wide.

"That got their attention—and everyone else's," said Levring.

The next moment tolled with the weight of an eternity. Then the orb's guns retargeted, and its next paralytic shot took aim at Centaur Station. The blast pulsed through bulkheads and defensive shielding, flesh and soul. Eric sensed his consciousness being eclipsed but willed it to stay present and frosty. He mostly succeeded.

Around him, the command staff and Uhmev succumbed. Eric gripped the edge of the nearest workstation, fought against the sting, and tasted blood. The shadows pulled back. Struggling to remain upright, he rounded the control board, stepping past Basinelle's prone body, and fired the satellite's main armaments again. The cannons lashed out, striking target.

This time, Centaur Station wasn't alone.

Joining in, the asymmetrical spacecraft that appeared to have been grown rather than built, along with the largest vessel, unleashed the savagery of their weapons. Streamers of colorful light-energy streaked out, impacting against the enemy contact. From the cut of his struggling vision, Eric saw their Bayonets giving chase, firing as well.

"Don't stop hammering away, pilots!" Calvin Ten called over the radio. "*Virtus ad astra!*"

A dozen Bayonet pilots shouted the familiar battle cry as more of the vessels added to their defense, their guns creating a blinding instant that seared its afterimage into Eric's vision. The gallop of his own heart struck him like tribal drumbeats, the music of war.

The satellite's scanners ran in constant sweeps as the show of resistance reached its crescendo. The alien construct lashed out, delivering more of its paralyzing stings. By that point, Eric's palsy was gone, and he trained the station's warheads on the enemy.

"Missile launchers engaged," the male computer voice answered. "You have overridden the countdown."

"*Fire!*" Eric shouted.

Five high-speed projectiles streaked forth, accompanied by another barrage from Centaur Station's cannons. The salvo raced past the stalled Klavalk battleship, zeroed in on target, and erupted across the orb's outer armor, releasing powerful mushrooms of flame, smoke, and another substance that caught fire before the vacuum of space smothered the conflagration.

In the wake of the barrage, the orb drew back. From the periphery, Eric saw his people recovering. The Uhmev delegate stood, their atmosphere bubble smoothing out around them. Something alien blasted over the radio, deep and infused with pain. Another glance at the screen revealed the orb withdrawing into the vortex of fresh tachyon storm clouds.

"It's retreating," Levring said.

"Keep firing," Eric said, his voice commanding not only in Centaur's nerve center but also over the radio to all who listened.

The satellite continued to fire, as did every vessel able to.

The damaged orb vanished back into the folds of the rupture in space. Centaur Station's scanners tracked, and the Uhmev delegate listened.

"Contact gone," said Basinelle.

"Continue monitoring," Eric said. He straightened, shook out the last of the venom in his system, and studied the screen. "Damage report."

Calls came in from throughout the station.

"Commander," Uhmev said above the chatter.

Eric faced them.

"The enemy construct," Uhmev said.

"Yes?"

"It wasn't merely one of their ships. It's one of *them*."

"Alive?" Levring asked.

"Not as we know life, but yes, a living entity. And as it departed, the life form spoke, and we listened. We believe we understand its motives and why we are here."

UHMEV'S MESSAGE was again broadcast to the survivors of the sneak attack. Spacecraft huddled around Centaur Station, their guns displayed to mirror the satellite's in readiness should the aggressors return. In a steady stream, smaller support craft shuttled delegates over to Centaur for a meeting to be held in the conference room, which could accommodate one hundred humans. The Quahalos, creatures from the asymmetrical ship, in their bulky organic version of spacesuits, struggled through door openings and were too wide for chairs. Even so, they made do.

There were bipeds like the Brindlosians, who wore form-fitting black that looked to be more like second skin than uniform, the Vrinn from the massive battleship, and a race of exoskeletals called the Umbrians. One triped race exited the hangar under security escort: the Klavalk.

Eric Thirteen faced the Klavalk captain, Leus Drogen. Drogen nodded and met Eric's gaze without blinking.

"For the purpose of this meeting, I suggest a ceasefire from our former hostilities," Eric said, his voice translated to all of the delegates thanks to Uhmev's help but meant only for Drogen.

"Commander Thirteen, you put your station in the line of enemy fire to defend us," Drogen said. "We view your actions with a seriousness of purpose. You have my word that we will honor the ceasefire."

"Good," Eric said.

He maintained his gaze, not diverting it until Drogen blinked first. With that small but vital victory earned, he moved to the dais at the head of the conference table, where Uhmev stood. Looking out at the diverse representatives of cultures and life forms threatened to overwhelm him. But there were already enough forces in the surrounding universe trying to knock his legs from beneath him. Clearing his throat, Eric addressed the gathering.

"We have all been abducted from familiar space and taken here," he said.

He thumbed a button on the lectern. The screen of the terminal on the conference table lit, showing the Milky Way Galaxy. Orion's Arm was highlighted near its shoulder, some 3,000-plus light years from Sol. Those forces were back, seeking to knock him off his feet and punch him in the gut.

There's no way Centaur Station can cross that distance on its own—we need their help!

He cleared his throat. "Based upon intelligence collected during the battle, we believe the construct that attacked us was, in effect, a living creature representative of the force responsible for our abductions."

Words, screeches, chirps, and gasps sounded around the chamber.

"*Alive,* Commander?" asked Zersha, the captain of the Vrinn juggernaut.

A handsome woman with short silver-purple hair, Eric greeted Zersha's gaze, again without blinking. "Yes. Our Uhmev friends sensed that what appeared to be a machine of war was, in reality, sentient. They translated its broadcast before the entity slipped back through the puncture in space. Uhmev?"

The alien delegate took point. "It said, 'Test complete. Second analysis of resistance strengths tabulated. Threat level minimal.'"

More chatter undulated among the representatives.

Eric again assumed the lead. "Based upon that translation, we have concluded the reason we've all been brought here is to gage our combined strengths. We represent all of the significant planets and powers throughout this region of our galaxy, in what we call Orion's Arm."

"So this is some kind of first wave for an invasion?" asked Drogen.

"At least the groundwork for one," Eric answered.

"Who are these living machines, and were do they originate?" asked Zersha.

Eric thumbed the button on the podium. The screen's image altered, showing scans recorded by Centaur Station during the assault. Calculations accompanied. The glimpse past the threshold of the tear in space was like staring down a deep, dark well. A bottomless pit. The center of Hell.

"Where-?" this came from Drogen.

"We're not entirely sure," Eric said. "The energy readings are not consistent with our galaxy or even our universe. They come from somewhere *other* that is very far from here."

Silence shrouded the conference room. Eric rightly guessed his legs weren't the only ones threatening to give out; his the only gut filled with magma.

After what seemed a long spell, Zersha spoke. "Commander, the enemy's paralyzing sting. In your report, you reference a kind of natural resistance in yourself and certain members of your team."

"It isn't a natural resistance," Eric said. Explaining felt like disrobing. "I and twenty-nine others among my people are Numbers—manufactured versions of earlier individuals. *Clones*, if you prefer. We Numbers appear to have some immunity to the energy discharges —or they're less effective on our physiology, according to my Chief Medical Officer."

"Then you Numbers are alone in that ability," Zersha said. "Which is a slight advantage."

Eric nodded.

Drogen waved a hand and stood, the scuffle of his three soles over the floor sharp, jarring. "While we cower here sharing tales, the enemy could be out there waiting to test us again! I suggest we join forces to stage a counteroffensive that sends them back to whatever dark realm spawned them forever!"

Eric raised his hands in the hope of quelling the outbursts that followed the Klavalk delegate's statement. "Please, let us not move blindly into action until we know more."

Drogen eyed him, this time not bothering to hide his contempt. "More talk. More endless talk from Earth—no wonder these enemies from the abyss have acted in this manner, considering the din of your miserable voices!"

Suddenly, Eric didn't know what to say. Drogen leered his way before motioning to his adjutant. The two stormed out of the room under cover of EDC armed escort, the cadence of their bootfalls somehow rising over the cacophony of alien voices.

In groups, the delegates departed Centaur Station, and none of what Eric hoped to accomplish materialized.

Less than an hour later, the fleet fractured, and the first of the races made a run at escape.

"It's the Ereb," said Basinelle. "They've powered up their engines. Accelerating toward Orbital Seven-Seven-Two."

The direction of their home world, some untold distance of light years away, thought Eric.

"Contact them. Ask them to hold," Eric said.

Levring moved to make the call, only to stop. "Sir!"

Eric looked toward the screen. A maelstrom formed directly in the path of the fleeing star vessel. From the folds of ruptured space, another living metal giant appeared. It fired two shots—one to incapacitate, the next to destroy. The Ereb spaceship vanished in a cloud of smoke and debris, gone from the starmap less than a minute after making its run toward open space.

The enemy orb drew back and disappeared before any of the nearest vessels could mount rescue or defense.

"So much for the next test," Eric said. "This confirms it. They won't let us just leave. We're all trapped in a killing jar."

"DON'T DO THIS, COMMANDER," Levring said.

Eric finished fastening the seals of his flight suit. The helmet in his hand suddenly weighted more like a boulder. "Keep Bayonets at the ready and guns raised in case the enemy returns."

"Which enemy?" Levring challenged.

Eric set a gloved hand on his XO's shoulder. "From the time I took command of Centaur, you've treated me with respect."

"That's because you've earned it, Commander—mine, the crew's, and everyone back on Earth."

"You've treated me as more than a Number."

"You are," Levring said.

Eric flashed his spare smile. "I have no intention of falling into Klavalk clutches. But if things turn ugly, it's up to you to stop those demons and get our people home."

Levring nodded. "Virtus ad astra."

Eric released him, donned the helmet, and climbed into the Bayonet's cockpit, a place he'd known intimately before taking command of Centaur Station. The body didn't forget, and his hadn't. While running through his preflight checklist, it struck Eric that he was going on automatic, his gloved fingers flipping switches in sequence, the space fighter an extension of his spacesuit, his psyche, his *soul*. The Bayonet came alive around him, reminding him of its readiness, its sleekness, its bite.

"Centaur Station Command to Bayonet 13," Brunson called over the radio. "You're cleared for takeoff."

"Thanks, Centaur Command," Eric said.

He gripped the flight controls. The Bayonet's engines kicked in, sending them off the launch anchor and through the open space shutter. Eric flew away from Centaur Station, aware of the massive satellite at his six thanks to the image projected onto the view screen by the aft camera.

Its design wasn't particularly elegant, but at that moment the Watchdog was the most beautiful sight he'd ever glimpsed. Centaur was proof of home far from Earth. More than that, he realized it *was* home.

The formations of dozens of alien vessels clustered around the satellite drew his focus away from the image of Centaur Station.

The lone Bayonet, so insignificant compared to the Vrinn colossus or most of the alien armada, continued forward. Eric steeled himself against the overwhelming odds that threatened to crush him. In his mind's eye, he was back at Orbital Three-One-One, a lone pilot, an insignificant Number at the controls of a Bayonet, facing off against an entire Klavalk warship. He'd navigated through a blind spot in its defenses and took aim at its command deck. In the breathless second that followed, he unleashed the killing shot, ramming it into the warship's face and down its throat. The Klavalk behemoth came apart as secondary explosions gutted it from within. He'd almost not made it out of the conflagration intact, his Bayonet scorched in the blast and barely spaceworthy. He'd returned to Centaur Station to fanfare, promotion, and hubris—the only Number to command one of the Watchdogs.

Eric blinked. Drogen's Klavalk warship loomed ahead of him on high alert, its guns drawn. There'd be no sneaking up this time. Not that he intended to.

"Captain Drogen, this is Commander Eric Thirteen from the Earth Defense Corps' Centaur Station. I request permission to come aboard your ship to discuss your plan."

Two of the powerful deck turrets swiveled up and locked onto target. The Bayonet's alarms screamed in warning. Seconds passed, each heavy with the promise of death. But the warship didn't open fire, and as though the tense wait was intentional, the cannons released their lock and lowered.

Drogen's voice responded. "Commander Thirteen, do come on board so that I might hear your human voice blather on yet one more time."

HE LANDED IN the warship's hangar, touching down on the deck, which bore the same tarnished patina of all Klavalk ships. The moment Eric removed his helmet and stepped free of the Bayonet, Klavalk soldiers surrounded him and muscled him down to his knees under the threat of drawn weapons.

Drogen and his adjutant clomped along the deck to the procession. Like the delay in releasing their targeting lock, Drogen let him stew on his knees for a few additional seconds before offering a silent tip of his pointed chin with its pair of feeler-whiskers, signaling the guards to fall back.

Eric stood. The air smelled of metal and of Klavalk, a briny odor he associated with the ocean.

"Do you hear that, Commander?" Drogen asked, indicating the cavernous interior of the hangar deck.

Apart from the tick of the dormant Bayonet, the surrounding space was quiet.

"No," Eric said.

"Precisely. Which is how we Klavalk like it. Even here, so far from all that is familiar, you Earthers continue broadcasting, talking —endlessly *talking!*"

Eric checked the seals on his spacesuit gloves for no other reason than to give his hands something to do. "This is the third time you've referenced our voices, Captain."

Drogen fixed him with a look. "The Music of the Cosmos was always quiet before, and that's how we loved it. Until one day, it filled with billions of voices, all talking, all screaming, and the melody was lost ... because of *you.*"

Eric narrowed his gaze. "The war between Earth and Klavalk—it's all been about noise pollution?"

"Your primitive broadcasts have robbed us of something we held close to our hearts, Commander."

"Why didn't you-?"

"*Talk?* And make you talk more?"

Drogen's expression hardened. Eric absorbed the truth, and it filled his stomach with imaginary rocks. "I am so very sorry, Captain." Then, choking down a dry swallow, he faced the alien with the same focus he had once an entire Klavalk warship. "But if you can force yourself to hear more human words, I'm here to tell you that I think you're right."

"Right?" Drogen said.

"The enemy won't let us leave. They'll pick us off one at a time—unless we take the offensive. Bring the fight to them. Show them we won't sit idle while they finalize their invasion of our home space."

Drogen tipped a glance at his adjutant. Then his gaze returned to Eric. "What do you suggest?"

Eric risked a smile. "We give them a black eye. One so big they crawl back to whatever hopeless realm they call home and stay there."

Another spell of long seconds ensued. "You might find this a curious statement, Commander Thirteen," Drogen said. "But I'm listening."

THE COMMANDER'S BAYONET exited Drogen's warship ahead of the Klavalk delegation and, for the second time, a meeting of the races convened in Centaur Station's conference room. With Drogen at one side and Uhmev on the other, Eric Thirteen took to the podium.

"We face a war on three fronts," Eric addressed the gathering. "The immediate, closest being that we've been herded and kept here and will not be permitted to leave—at least not alive. The other is the greater threat to our home planets and our civilizations if the enemy concludes its tests and attacks. And last, there is a war front of distance. We are all far from our origins, many—*most*—without the means to return. But in order to win those two other fronts, we must first prove victorious on the first. We must show these aggressors from another realm that they picked the wrong people to confront."

Zersha stood. "Yes, Commander Thirteen. The Vrinn stand with you!"

"As do the Brindlos!"

"And the Quahalos!"

Within seconds of the first declaration, every delegate was standing and pledging support for the plan. Eric wondered if the cacophony of voices further hacked off Drogen or fueled his faith in the rally. Eric raised his hands and called for silence. The delegates quieted.

"Commander, we are powerless against their paralyzing weapon save for a small handful of your people," said Zersha.

All the emotion drained from Eric's face. "Captain Zersha, if it's one truth the universe has revealed, it's that a handful of Numbers can get the job done. Any job required."

IN QUICK, ORDERLY FASHION, Eric's people evacuated the station. Bayonets containing pilots and crew sped away from the satellite and were received aboard the Vrinn colossus. The fighters from Earth cradled *The Heart of Uhmev* with them.

Zersha's image appeared on the screen. Eric and the alien captain faced one another.

"Your people will be as safe as possible here, Commander," she said.

Eric nodded. He trusted her. "If we don't come back from the abyss, it's up to you to warn Earth and return my people to home soil, Captain."

"You have my word," Zersha promised. "And my thanks. In fact, the thanks of the entire Vrinn Procure for what you are about to do in all of our interests."

Eric nodded. "Hang in as long as you can—and save some room for one more passenger, just in case."

Zersha nodded and the link closed.

"*Showtime*," he whispered to the empty nerve center.

Centaur Station pulsed with energy as the steering rockets powered up, sending the satellite forward in maneuvers its designers hadn't imagined. But like the Numbers, Eric knew Centaur could handle it. The station could do whatever was needed above and beyond its original purpose. The same pride at taking out the Klavalk warship filled him, and Eric welcomed it.

"*Virtus ad astra*," Eric said. "Centaur Station, prove us right!"

Centaur surged forward. And as she did, a dozen other spacecraft including Drogen's Klavalk warship took up a line behind its superstructure. As the edge of the killing jar neared, Eric activated the satellite's weapons. Cannons armed and took aim. The points of warheads appeared as shutters rolled aside. The wait for a response from the enemy didn't take long.

Space churned, splitting open in a violent display of tachyons and dust clouds. The massive orb appeared beyond the horizon. The first stinging shot lashed out. Eric dodged it and, wasting no time, pushed the satellite's engine assembly up to full speed. He opened fire with all of Centaur Station's armaments. Powerful streamers of weapon's fire and a salvo of ten warheads tore out, all zeroing in on target. A massive fireworks display erupted within the fabric of that other realm. The orb fell back, and Centaur pressed its attack. Another salvo lashed out, the projectiles complimented by more cannon fire.

The punch hammered the enemy construct. More bio-substance poured from its wounds, enough to confirm the accuracy of the assault. Spiraling out of control, the orb came apart in a spectacular display even greater than the attack that had sealed its demise.

When space cleared enough for Eric to see, the screen showed that Centaur Station had charged beyond the rip in space. More than via scanners, Eric felt it, sensed the change, the darkness that now surrounded him. He focused on the screen broadcasting what the station's eyes saw. Desolation spread before him, a realm with no planets, no stars. Nothing.

"What-?" he posed aloud.

The answer came in a warning not from ahead but below as the station's lower cameras detected movement. The screen adjusted, filling for as far as could be seen with the nightmare image, that of the enemy's true face.

It spread across a vast distance, at least a hundred kilometers that he could tell. The construct was composed of many other constructs, all identical, all linked together in a way that suggested a kind of galaxy spiral pattern. Then Eric remembered the construct was alive. What he'd destroyed in the attack was but a single cell in the nightmare's identity.

And the creature was on the move toward him.

He slowed the station's charge, activated steering rockets in sequence, and rotated the angle of attack. The darkness surrounding Centaur Station thickened. It was the creature. Its malevolence radiated in tangible waves. He heard its thoughts as clearly as if translated by the Uhmev.

You have been judged and found of no significant threat to me, it said.

Eric Thirteen, Commander of Centaur Station, re-gripped the firing controls. "Come for our homes and you'll regret it!" Then, flipping the switch, he put out the call to the others. "Break and attack!"

Centaur Station opened fire. The dozen alien ships flying in formation behind the satellite jumped forth and joined in, and, from the rupture's horizon, the Vrinn and every other capable ship added to the counter-attack.

Warheads and particle blasts streaked down, paling in scope to the nightmare rising up to greet them. But then the impacts against its exterior drew its version of blood, and the creature's wounds expanded across its mass. Centaur continuously fired, until its arsenal was emptied, and the last of its stings delivered.

The satellite's cannons maintained their attack, as did the armada. The darkness filled with smoke, with blood. The nightmare ceased its upward charge and sank.

"Commander Thirteen," Drogen called. "The rift is closing behind us!"

Eric aimed the cameras back up. True to the Klavalk's claim, the rupture was sealing.

"All fleet ships, make for our side of the tear!" Eric barked. "Break off your attack and speed to the other side without delay!"

"What about you, Centaur Station?" Drogen asked.

"I won't be far behind!"

The armada split, turned, and raced away. Eric cast a look at the injured, bleeding monstrosity barely visible now beyond all the blood and smoke.

"Remember my warning," he called over the radio. "We will fight back!"

Then he powered Centaur up to full speed and made for the rip in space.

One minute from the horizon, the computer's male voice warned that the exit point had sealed down to a size too small for the satellite to cross.

"Commander," Levring called from the Vrinn giant's bridge. "Get out of there! Centaur's done the job!"

Eric looked around the command deck. A mix of pride and loss welled within him, paralyzing him in a way the enemy's sting hadn't managed. Shaking it off, he ran.

And ran.

The rupture in space tightened, escape almost not there. Centaur Station slammed into what remained of the horizon at full speed. Right before the fourth of the Watchdog satellites blasted apart, a single Bayonet exited through the hangar ahead of the detonation, soaring into normal space where the armada waited.

ERIC, LEVRING, BASINELLE, and Brunson gathered together in the Vrinn version of a mess hall. They raised goblets filled with water and toasted.

"To Centaur Station—for all she gave to us and our neighbors in space," Eric said.

"Here, here," said Levring.

"Virtus ad astra," they all said, chiming

their goblets together. When glasses lowered, Captain Zersha joined them.

"We're ready to depart, Commander," Zersha said.

Eric nodded. "Thank you, Captain."

"First stop, the Uhmev home world," Zersha said.

In clusters and alone, the fleet split, going in separate directions. The Vrinn used their engine's field to take along the Klavalk and ten other vessels headed the same way. The going would be fraught with danger and long, but it had begun.

They were headed home.

AFTER THE FIRST faster-than-light jump, Drogen invited Eric back to his warship. They sat together, and the old melodies of space played, haunting and beautiful from that time before human radio chatter polluted the spacewaves.

"Stunning, isn't it?"

Eric nodded but didn't speak out of respect and understanding.

"We're still a long way from Klavalk and Earth," Drogen said.

Eric grinned. "Who's the verbose one now?"

"Please, allow me to finish. When we return and report in to our superiors, I intend to suggest we continue the ceasefire. Even with all your noise, the universe is better off with Earth people in it, my friend."

THEY REACHED THEIR first destination, and the Bayonets stationed in the Vrinn hangar escorted *The Heart of Uhmev* down to the planet's turquoise waters. It was only one of many goodbyes—and many skies—between there and Earth.

"The Sky People" debuts in this issue of Black Infinity. *Art by Allen Koszowski.*

Raised on a healthy diet of creature double features and classic SF TV, Gregory L. Norris writes regularly for numerous short story anthologies, national magazines, novels, and the occasional episode for TV or film. Gregory novelized

the NBC Made-for-TV classic by Gerry Anderson, The Day After Tomorrow: Into Infinity *(as well as a sequel and a forthcoming third entry into the franchise for Anderson Entertainment in the U.K.), a movie he watched as an eleven-year-old sitting cross-legged on the living room floor of the enchanted cottage where he grew up. Gregory won HM in the 2016 Roswell Awards in Short SF Writing. He once worked as a screenwriter on two episodes of Paramount's* Star Trek: Voyager. *Kate Mulgrew,* Voyager's *"Captain Janeway," blurbed his book of short stories and novellas,* The Fierce and Unforgiving Muse, *stating, "In my seven years on* Voyager, *I don't think I've met a writer more capable of writing such a book—and writing it so beautifully."*

In late 2019, Gregory sold an option on his modern Noir feature film screenplay, Amandine, *to the new Hollywood production company Snarkhunter LLC, owned by actor Dan Lench, a devotee of Gregory's writing. In late 2020,* Snarkhunter *optioned Gregory's tetralogy Horror film based upon four of his short stories,* Ride Along. *That same month, his short story "Water Whispers" (originally appearing in the anthology 20,000 Leagues Remembered), was nominated for the Pushcart Prize.*

Gregory lives and writes at Xanadu, a century-old house perched on a hill in New Hampshire's North Country with spectacular mountain views, with his rescue cat and emerald-eyed muse.

Read his fond remembrance of Space: 1999, *also featured in this issue, and follow his further literary adventures at:*

www.gregorylnorris.blogspot.com

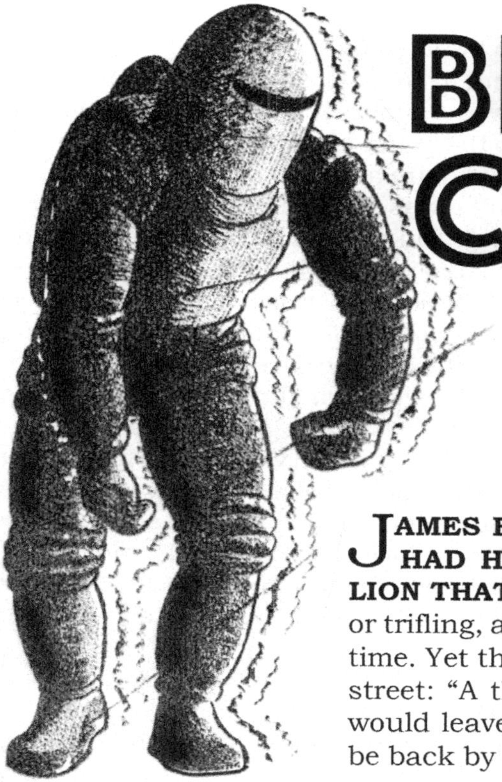

BRIGHTSIDE CROSSING

BY ALAN E. NOURSE
ART BY MEL HUNTER

JAMES BARON WAS NOT PLEASED TO HEAR THAT HE HAD HAD A VISITOR WHEN HE REACHED THE RED LION THAT EVENING. He had no stomach for mysteries, vast or trifling, and there were pressing things to think about at this time. Yet the doorman had flagged him as he came in from the street: "A thousand pardons, Mr. Baron. The gentleman—he would leave no name. He said you'd want to see him. He will be back by eight."

Now Baron drummed his fingers on the table top, staring about the quiet lounge. Street trade was discouraged at the Red Lion, gently but persuasively; the patrons were few in number. Across to the right was a group that Baron knew vaguely—Andean climbers, or at least two of them were. Over near the door he recognized old Balmer, who had mapped the first passage to the core of Vulcan Crater on Venus. Baron returned his smile with a nod. Then he settled back and waited impatiently for the intruder who demanded his time without justifying it.

Presently a small, grizzled man crossed the room and sat down at Baron's table. He was short and wiry. His face held no key to his age—he might have been thirty or a thousand —but he looked weary and immensely ugly. His cheeks and forehead were twisted and brown, with scars that were still healing.

The stranger said, "I'm glad you waited. I've heard you're planning to attempt the Brightside."

Baron stared at the man for a moment. "I see you can read telecasts," he said coldly. "The news was correct. We are going to make a Brightside Crossing."

"At perihelion?"

"Of course. When else?"

The grizzled man searched Baron's face for a moment without expression. Then he said slowly, "No, I'm afraid you're not going to make the Crossing."

"Say, who are you, if you don't mind?" Baron demanded.

"The name is Claney," said the stranger.

There was a silence. Then: "Claney? *Peter* Claney?"

"That's right."

Baron's eyes were wide with excitement, all trace of anger gone. "Great balls of fire, man—*where have you been hiding?* We've been trying to contact you for months!"

"I know. I was hoping you'd quit looking and chuck the whole idea."

"*Quit looking!*" Baron bent forward over

BLACK INFINITY • 57

the table. "My friend, we'd given up hope, but we've never quit looking. Here, have a drink. There's so much you can tell us." His fingers were trembling.

Peter Claney shook his head. "I can't tell you anything you want to hear."

"But you've *got* to. You're the only man on Earth who's attempted a Brightside Crossing and lived through it! And the story you cleared for the news—it was nothing. We need *details*. Where did your equipment fall down? Where did you miscalculate? What were the trouble spots?" Baron jabbed a finger at Claney's face. "That, for instance—epithelioma? Why? What was wrong with your glass? Your filters? We've got to know those things. If you can tell us, we can make it across where your attempt failed—"

"You want to know why we failed?" asked Claney.

"Of course we want to know. We *have* to know."

"It's simple. We failed because it can't be done. We couldn't do it and neither can you. No human beings will ever cross the Brightside alive, not if they try for centuries."

"Nonsense," Baron declared. "We will."

Claney shrugged. "I was there. I know what I'm saying. You can blame the equipment or the men—there were flaws in both quarters—but we just didn't know what we were fighting. It was the *planet* that whipped us, that and the *Sun*. They'll whip you, too, if you try it."

"Never," said Baron.

"Let me tell you," Peter Claney said.

I'D BEEN INTERESTED in the Brightside for almost as long as I can remember (Claney said). I guess I was about ten when Wyatt and Carpenter made the last attempt—that was in 2082, I think. I followed the news stories like a tri-V serial and then I was heartbroken when they just disappeared.

I know now that they were a pair of idiots, starting off without proper equipment, with practically no knowledge of surface conditions, without any charts—they couldn't have made a hundred miles—but I didn't know that then and it was a terrible tragedy. After that, I followed Sanderson's work in the Twilight Lab up there and began to get Brightside into my blood, sure as death.

But it was Mikuta's idea to attempt a Crossing. Did you ever know Tom Mikuta? I don't suppose you did. No, not Japanese—Polish-American. He was a major in the Interplanetary Service for some years and hung onto the title after he gave up his commission.

He was with Armstrong on Mars during his Service days, did a good deal of the original mapping and surveying for the Colony there. I first met him on Venus; we spent five years together up there doing some of the nastiest exploring since the Matto Grasso. Then he made the attempt on Vulcan Crater that paved the way for Balmer a few years later.

I'd always liked the Major—he was big and quiet and cool, the sort of guy who always had things figured a little further ahead than anyone else and always knew what to do in a tight place. Too many men in this game are all nerve and luck, with no judgment. The Major had both. He also had the kind of personality that could take a crew of wild men and make them work like a well-oiled machine across a thousand miles of Venus jungle. I liked him and I trusted him.

He contacted me in New York and he was very casual at first. We spent an evening here at the Red Lion, talking about old times; he told me about the Vulcan business, and how he'd been out to see Sanderson and the Twilight Lab on Mercury, and how he preferred a hot trek to a cold one any day of the year—and then he wanted to know what I'd been doing since Venus and what my plans were.

"No particular plans," I told him. "Why?"

He looked me over. "How much do you weigh, Peter?"

I told him one-thirty-five.

"That much!" he said. "Well, there can't be much fat on you, at any rate. How do you take heat?"

"You should know," I said. "Venus was no icebox."

"No, I mean *real* heat."

Then I began to get it. "You're planning a trip."

"That's right. A hot trip." He grinned at me. "Might be dangerous, too."

"What trip?"

"Brightside of Mercury," the Major said.

I whistled cautiously. "At aphelion?"

He threw his head back. "Why try a Crossing at aphelion? What have you done then? Four thousand miles of butcherous heat, just to have some joker come along, use your data and drum you out of the glory by crossing at perihelion forty-four days later? No, thanks. I want the Brightside without any nonsense about it." He leaned across to me eagerly. "I want to make a Crossing at perihelion and I want to cross on the surface. If a man can do that, he's got Mercury. Until then, *nobody's* got Mercury. I want Mercury—but I'll need help getting it."

I'd thought of it a thousand times and never dared consider it. Nobody had, since Wyatt and Carpenter disappeared. Mercury turns on its axis in the same time that it wheels around the Sun, which means that the Brightside is always facing in. That makes the Brightside of Mercury at perihelion the hottest place in the Solar System, with one single exception: the surface of the Sun itself.

It would be a hellish trek. Only a few men had ever learned just *how* hellish, and they never came back to tell about it. It was a real hell's Crossing, but someday, I thought, somebody would cross it.

I wanted to be along.

THE TWILIGHT LAB, near the northern pole of Mercury, was the obvious jumping-off place. The setup there wasn't very extensive—a rocket landing, the labs and quarters for Sanderson's crew sunk deep into the crust, and the tower that housed the Solar 'scope that Sanderson had built up there ten years before.

Twilight Lab wasn't particularly interested in the Brightside, of course—the Sun was Sanderson's baby and he'd picked Mercury as the closest chunk of rock to the Sun that could hold his observatory. He'd chosen a good location, too. On Mercury, the Brightside temperature hits 770°F at perihelion and the Darkside runs pretty constant at -410°F. No permanent installation with a human crew could survive at either extreme. But with Mercury's wobble, the twilight zone between Brightside and Darkside offers something closer to survival temperatures.

Sanderson built the Lab up near the pole, where the zone is about five miles wide, so the temperature only varies 50 to 60 degrees with the libration. The Solar 'scope could take that much change and they'd get good clear observation of the Sun for about seventy out of the eighty-eight days it takes the planet to wheel around.

The Major was counting on Sanderson knowing something about Mercury as well as the Sun when we camped at the Lab to make final preparations.

Sanderson did. He thought we'd lost our minds and he said so, but he gave us all the help he could. He spent a week briefing Jack Stone, the third member of our party, who had arrived with the supplies and equipment a few days earlier. Poor Jack met us at the rocket landing almost bawling, Sanderson had given him such a gloomy picture of what Brightside was like.

Stone was a youngster—hardly twenty-five, I'd say—but he'd been with the Major at Vulcan and had begged to join this trek. I had a funny feeling that Jack really didn't care for exploring too much, but he thought Mikuta was God, followed him around like a puppy.

It didn't matter to me as long as he knew what he was getting in for. You don't go asking people in this game why they do it—they're liable to get awfully uneasy and none of them can ever give you an answer that makes sense. Anyway, Stone had borrowed three men from the Lab, and had the supplies and equipment all lined up when we got there, ready to check and test.

We dug right in. With plenty of funds—tri-V money and some government cash the Major had talked his way around—our equipment was new and good. Mikuta had done the designing and testing himself, with a big assist from Sanderson. We had four Bugs, three of them the light pillow-tire models, with special lead-cooled cut-in engines when the heat set in, and one heavy-duty tractor model for pulling the sledges.

The Major went over them like a kid at the circus. Then he said, "Have you heard anything from McIvers?"

"Who's he?" Stone wanted to know.

"He'll be joining us. He's a good man—got quite a name for climbing, back home." The Major turned to me. "You've probably heard of him."

I'd heard plenty of stories about Ted McIvers and I wasn't too happy to hear that he was joining us. "Kind of a daredevil, isn't he?"

"Maybe. He's lucky and skillful. Where do you draw the line? We'll need plenty of both."

"Have you ever worked with him?" I asked.

"No. Are you worried?"

"Not exactly. But Brightside is no place to count on luck."

The Major laughed. "I don't think we need to worry about McIvers. We understood each other when I talked up the trip to him and we're going to need each other too much to do any fooling around." He turned back to the supply list. "Meanwhile, let's get this stuff listed and packed. We'll need to cut weight sharply and our time is short. Sanderson says we should leave in three days."

Two days later, McIvers hadn't arrived. The Major didn't say much about it. Stone was getting edgy and so was I. We spent the second day studying charts of the Brightside, such as they were. The best available were pretty poor, taken from so far out that the detail dissolved into blurs on blow-up. They showed the biggest ranges of peaks and craters and faults, and that was all. Still, we could use them to plan a broad outline of our course.

"This range here," the Major said as we crowded around the board, "is largely inactive, according to Sanderson. But these to the south and west *could* be active. Seismograph tracings suggest a lot of activity in that region, getting worse down toward the equator—not only volcanic, but sub-surface shifting."

Stone nodded. "Sanderson told me there was probably constant surface activity."

The Major shrugged. "Well, it's treacherous, there's no doubt of it. But the only way to avoid it is to travel over the Pole, which would lose us days and offer us no guarantee of less activity to the west. Now, we might avoid some if we could find a pass through this range and cut sharp east—"

It seemed that the more we considered the problem, the further we got from a solution. We knew there were active volcanoes on the Brightside—even on the Darkside, though surface activity there was pretty much slowed down and localized.

But there were problems of atmosphere on Brightside, as well. There was an atmosphere and a constant atmospheric flow from Brightside to Darkside. Not much—the lighter gases had reached escape velocity and disappeared from Brightside millennia ago—but there was CO_2 and nitrogen, and traces of other heavier gases. There was also an abundance of sulfur vapor, as well as carbon disulfide and sulfur dioxide.

The atmospheric tide moved toward the Darkside, where it condensed, carrying enough volcanic ash with it for Sanderson to estimate the depth and nature of the surface upheavals on Brightside from his samplings. The trick was to find a passage that avoided those upheavals as far as possible. But in the final analysis, we were barely scraping the surface. The only way we would find out what was happening *where* was to be there.

Finally, on the third day, McIvers blew in on a freight rocket from Venus. He'd missed the ship that the Major and I had taken by a few hours, and had conned his way to Venus in hopes of getting a hop from there. He didn't seem too upset about it, as though this were his usual way of doing things and he couldn't see why everyone should get so excited.

He was a tall, rangy man with long, wavy hair prematurely gray, and the sort of eyes that looked like a climber's—half-closed, sleepy, almost indolent, but capable of abrupt alertness. And he never stood still; he was always moving, always doing something with his hands, or talking, or pacing about.

Evidently the Major decided not to press the issue of his arrival. There was still work to do, and an hour later we were running the final tests on the pressure suits. That evening, Stone and McIvers were thick as thieves, and everything was set for an early departure after we got some rest.

"AND THAT," said Baron, finishing his drink and signaling the waiter for another pair, "was your first big mistake."

Peter Claney raised his eyebrows.

"McIvers?"

"Of course."

Claney shrugged, glanced at the small quiet tables around them. "There are lots of bizarre personalities around a place like this, and some of the best wouldn't seem to be the most reliable at first glance. Anyway, personality problems weren't our big problem right then. *Equipment* worried us first and *route* next."

Baron nodded in agreement. "What kind of suits did you have?"

"The best insulating suits ever made," said Claney. "Each one had an inner lining of a fiberglass modification, to avoid the clumsiness of asbestos, and carried the refrigerating unit and oxygen storage which we recharged from the sledges every eight hours. Outer layer carried a monomolecular chrome reflecting surface that made us glitter like Christmas trees. And we had a half-inch dead-air space under positive pressure between the two layers. Warning thermocouples, of course—at 770 degrees, it wouldn't take much time to fry us to cinders if the suits failed somewhere."

"How about the Bugs?"

"They were insulated, too, but we weren't counting on them too much for protection."

"You weren't!" Baron exclaimed. "Why not?"

"We'd be in and out of them too much. They gave us mobility and storage, but we knew we'd have to do a lot of forward work on foot." Claney smiled bitterly. "Which meant that we had an inch of fiberglass and a half-inch of dead air between us and a surface temperature where lead flowed like water and zinc was almost at melting point and the pools of sulfur in the shadows were boiling like oatmeal over a campfire."

Baron licked his lips. His fingers stroked the cool, wet glass as he set it down on the tablecloth.

"Go on," he said tautly. "You started on schedule?"

"Oh, yes," said Claney, "we started on schedule, all right. We just didn't quite end on schedule, that was all. But I'm getting to that."

He settled back in his chair and continued.

WE JUMPED OFF from Twilight on a course due southeast with thirty days to make it to the Center of Brightside. If we could cross an average of seventy miles a day, we could hit Center exactly at perihelion, the point of Mercury's closest approach to the Sun—which made Center the hottest part of the planet at the hottest it ever gets.

The Sun was already huge and yellow over the horizon when we started, twice the size it appears on Earth. Every day that Sun would grow bigger and whiter, and every day the surface would get hotter. But once we reached Center, the job was only half done—we would still have to travel another two thousand miles to the opposite twilight zone. Sanderson was to meet us on the other side in the Laboratory's scout ship, approximately sixty days from the time we jumped off.

That was the plan, in outline. It was up to us to cross those seventy miles a day, no matter how hot it became, no matter what terrain we had to cross. Detours would be dangerous and time-consuming. Delays could cost us our lives. We all knew that.

The Major briefed us on details an hour before we left. "Peter, you'll take the lead Bug, the small one we stripped down for you. Stone and I will flank you on either side, giving you a hundred-yard lead. McIvers, you'll have the job of dragging the sledges, so we'll have to direct your course pretty closely. Peter's job is to pick the passage at any given point. If there's any doubt of safe passage, we'll all explore ahead on foot before we risk the Bugs. Got that?"

McIvers and Stone exchanged glances. McIvers said: "Jack and I were planning to change around. We figured he could take the sledges. That would give me a little more mobility."

The Major looked up sharply at Stone. "Do you buy that, Jack?"

Stone shrugged.

"I don't mind. Mac wanted—"

McIvers made an impatient gesture with his hands. "It doesn't matter. I just feel better when I'm on the move. Does it make any difference?"

"I guess it doesn't," said the Major. "Then you'll flank Peter along with me. Right?"

"Sure, sure." McIvers pulled at his lower lip. "Who's going to do the advance scouting?"

"It sounds like I am," I cut in. "We want to keep the lead Bug light as possible."

Mikuta nodded. "That's right. Peter's Bug is stripped down to the frame and wheels."

McIvers shook his head. "No, I mean the *advance* work. You need somebody out ahead —four or five miles, at least—to pick up the big flaws and active surface changes, don't you?" He stared at the Major. "I mean, how can we tell what sort of a hole we may be moving into, unless we have a scout up ahead?"

"That's what we have the charts for," the Major said sharply.

"Charts! I'm talking about *detail* work. We don't need to worry about the major topography. It's the little faults you can't see on the pictures that can kill us." He tossed the charts down excitedly. "Look, let me take a Bug out

ahead and work reconnaissance, keep five, maybe ten miles ahead of the column. I can stay on good solid ground, of course, but scan the area closely and radio back to Peter where to avoid the flaws. Then—"

"No dice," the Major broke in.

"But why not? We could save ourselves days!"

"I don't care what we could save. We stay together. When we get to the Center, I want live men along with me. That means we stay within easy sight of each other at all times. Any climber knows that everybody is safer in a party than one man alone—any time, any place."

McIvers stared at him, his cheeks an angry red. Finally he gave a sullen nod. "Okay. If you say so."

"Well, I say so and I mean it. I don't want any fancy stuff. We're going to hit Center together, and finish the Crossing together. Got that?"

McIvers nodded. Mikuta then looked at Stone and me and we nodded, too.

"All right," he said slowly. "Now that we've got it straight, let's go."

• • •

IT WAS HOT. If I forget everything else about that trek, I'll never forget that huge yellow Sun glaring down, without a break, hotter and hotter with every mile. We knew that the first few days would be the easiest and we were rested and fresh when we started down the long, ragged gorge southeast of the Twilight Lab.

I moved out first; back over my shoulder, I could see the Major and McIvers crawling out behind me, their pillow tires taking the rugged floor of the gorge smoothly. Behind them, Stone dragged the sledges.

Even at only 30 percent Earth gravity they were a strain on the big tractor, until the ski-blades bit into the fluffy volcanic ash blanketing the valley. We even had a path to follow for the first twenty miles.

I kept my eyes pasted to the big polaroid binocs, picking out the track the early research teams had made out into the edge of Brightside. But in a couple of hours we rumbled past Sanderson's little outpost observatory and the tracks stopped. We were in virgin territory and already the Sun was beginning to bite.

We didn't *feel* the heat so much those first days out. We *saw* it. The refrig units kept

our skins at a nice comfortable seventy-five degrees Fahrenheit inside our suits, but our eyes watched that glaring Sun and the baked yellow rocks going past, and some nerve pathways got twisted up, somehow. We poured sweat as if we were in a superheated furnace.

We drove eight hours and slept five. When a sleep period came due, we pulled the Bugs together into a square, threw up a light aluminum sun-shield and lay out in the dust and rocks. The sun-shield cut the temperature down sixty or seventy degrees, for whatever help that was. And then we ate from the forward sledge—sucking through tubes—protein, carbohydrates, bulk gelatin, vitamins.

The Major measured water out with an iron hand, because we'd have drunk ourselves into nephritis in a week otherwise. We were constantly, unceasingly thirsty. Ask the physiologists and psychiatrists why—they can give you have a dozen interesting reasons—but all we knew, or cared about, was that it happened to be so.

We didn't sleep the first few stops, as a consequence. Our eyes burned in spite of the filters and we had roaring headaches, but we couldn't sleep them off. We sat around looking at each other. Then McIvers would say how good a beer would taste, and off we'd go. We'd have murdered our grandmothers for one ice-cold bottle of beer.

After a few driving periods, I began to get my bearings at the wheel. We were moving down into desolation that made Earth's old Death Valley look like a Japanese rose garden. Huge sun-baked cracks opened up in the floor of the gorge, with black cliffs jutting up on either side; the air was filled with a barely visible yellowish mist of sulfur and sulfurous gases.

It was a hot, barren hole, no place for any man to go, but the challenge was so powerful you could almost feel it. No one had ever crossed this land before and escaped. Those who had tried it had been cruelly punished, but the land was still there, so it had to be crossed. Not the easy way. It had to be crossed the hardest way possible: overland, through anything the land could throw up to us, at the most difficult time possible.

Yet we knew that even the land might have been conquered before, except for that Sun. We'd fought absolute cold before and won. We'd never fought heat like this and won. The only worse heat in the Solar System was the surface of the Sun itself.

Brightside was worth trying for. We would get it or it would get us. That was the bargain.

I learned a lot about Mercury those first few driving periods. The gorge petered out after a hundred miles and we moved onto the slope of a range of ragged craters that ran south and east. This range had shown no activity since the first landing on Mercury forty years before, but beyond it there were active cones. Yellow fumes rose from the craters constantly; their sides were shrouded with heavy ash.

We couldn't detect a wind, but we knew there was a hot, sulfurous breeze sweeping in great continental tides across the face of the planet. Not enough for erosion, though. The craters rose up out of jagged gorges, huge towering spears of rock and rubble. Below were the vast yellow flatlands, smoking and hissing from the gases beneath the crust. Over everything was gray dust—silicates and salts, pumice and limestone and granite ash, filling crevices and declivities—offering a soft, treacherous surface for the Bug's pillow tires.

I learned to read the ground, to tell a covered fault by the sag of the dust; I learned to spot a passable crack, and tell it from an impassable cut. Time after time the Bugs ground to a halt while we explored a passage on foot, tied together with light copper cable, digging, advancing, digging some more, until we were sure the surface would carry the machines. It was cruel work; we slept in exhaustion. But it went smoothly, at first.

Too smoothly, it seemed to me, and the others seemed to think so, too.

McIvers' restlessness was beginning to grate on our nerves. He talked too much, while we were resting or while we were driving; wisecracks, witticisms, unfunny jokes that wore thin with repetition. He took to making side trips from the route now and then, never far, but a little further each time.

Jack Stone reacted quite the opposite; he grew quieter with each stop, more reserved and apprehensive. I didn't like it, but I figured that it would pass off after a while. I was apprehensive enough myself; I just managed to hide it better.

And every mile the Sun got bigger and whiter and higher in the sky and hotter. Without our ultraviolet screens and glare filters we would have been blinded; as it was our eyes ached constantly and the skin on our faces itched and tingled at the end of an eight-hour trek.

But it took one of those side trips of McIvers' to deliver the penultimate blow to our already fraying nerves. He had driven down a side-branch of a long canyon running off west of our route and was almost out of sight in a cloud of ash when we heard a sharp cry through our earphones.

I wheeled my Bug around with my heart in my throat and spotted him through the binocs, waving frantically from the top of his machine. The Major and I took off, lumbering down the gulch after him as fast as the Bugs could go, with a thousand horrible pictures racing through our minds....

We found him standing stock-still, pointing down the gorge and, for once, he didn't have anything to say. It was the wreck of a Bug; an old-fashioned half-track model of the sort that hadn't been in use for years. It was wedged tight in a cut in the rock, an axle broken, its casing split wide open up the middle, half-buried in a rock slide. A dozen feet away were two insulated suits with white bones gleaming through the fiberglass helmets.

This was as far as Wyatt and Carpenter had gotten on *their* Brightside Crossing.

ON THE FIFTH DRIVING PERIOD OUT, the terrain began to change. It looked the same, but every now and then it *felt* different. On two occasions I felt my wheels spin, with a howl of protest from my engine. Then, quite suddenly, the Bug gave a lurch; I gunned my motor and nothing happened.

I could see the dull gray stuff seeping up around the hubs, thick and tenacious, splattering around in steaming gobs as the wheels spun. I knew what had happened the moment the wheels gave and, a few minutes later, they chained me to the tractor and dragged me back out of the mire. It looked for all the world like thick gray mud, but it was a pit of molten lead, steaming under a soft layer of concealing ash.

I picked my way more cautiously then. We were getting into an area of recent surface activity; the surface was really treacherous. I caught myself wishing that the Major had okayed McIvers' scheme for an advanced scout; more dangerous for the individual, maybe, but I was driving blind now and I didn't like it.

One error in judgment could sink us all, but I wasn't thinking much about the others. I was worried about *me*, plenty worried. I kept thinking, better McIvers should go than me. It wasn't healthy thinking and I knew it, but I couldn't get the thought out of my mind.

It was a grueling eight hours and we slept poorly. Back in the Bug again, we moved still more slowly—edging out on a broad flat plateau, dodging a network of gaping surface cracks—winding back and forth in an effort to keep the machines on solid rock. I couldn't see far ahead, because of the yellow haze rising from the cracks, so I was almost on top of it when I saw a sharp cut ahead where the surface dropped six feet beyond a deep crack.

I let out a shout to halt the others; then I edged my Bug forward, peering at the cleft. It was deep and wide. I moved fifty yards to the left, then back to the right.

There was only one place that looked like a possible crossing; a long, narrow ledge of gray stuff that lay down across a section of the fault like a ramp. Even as I watched it, I could feel the surface crust under the Bug trembling and saw the ledge shift over a few feet.

The Major's voice sounded in my ears. "How about it, Peter?"

"I don't know. This crust is on roller skates," I called back.

"How about that ledge?"

I hesitated. "I'm scared of it, Major. Let's backtrack and try to find a way around."

There was a roar of disgust in my earphones and McIvers' Bug suddenly lurched forward. It rolled down past me, picked up speed, with McIvers hunched behind the wheel like a race driver. He was heading past me straight for the gray ledge.

My shout caught in my throat; I heard the Major take a huge breath and roar: "Mac! *stop that thing*, you fool!" and then McIvers' Bug was out on the ledge, lumbering across like a juggernaut.

The ledge jolted as the tires struck it; for a horrible moment, it seemed to be sliding out from under the machine. And then the Bug was across in a cloud of dust, and I heard McIvers' voice in my ears, shouting in glee. "Come on, you slowpokes. It'll hold you!"

Something unprintable came through the earphones as the Major drew up alongside me and moved his Bug out on the ledge slowly and over to the other side. Then he said, "Take it slow, Peter. Then give Jack a hand with the sledges." His voice sounded tight as a wire.

Ten minutes later, we were on the other side of the cleft. The Major checked the whole column; then he turned on McIvers angrily. "One more trick like that," he said, "and I'll strap you to a rock and leave you. Do you understand me? *One more time*—"

McIvers' voice was heavy with protest. "Good Lord, if we leave it up to Claney, he'll have us out here forever! Any blind fool could see that that ledge would hold."

"*I* saw it moving," I shot back at him.

"All right, all right, so you've got good eyes. Why all the fuss? We got across, didn't we? But I say we've got to have a little nerve and use it once in a while if we're ever going to get across this lousy hotbox."

"We need to use a little judgment, too," the Major snapped. "All right, let's roll. But if you think I was joking, you just try me out once." He let it soak in for a minute. Then he geared his Bug on around to my flank again.

At the stopover, the incident wasn't mentioned again, but the Major drew me aside just as I was settling down for sleep. "Peter, I'm worried," he said slowly.

"McIvers? Don't worry. He's not as reckless as he seems—just impatient. We *are* over a hundred miles behind schedule and we're moving awfully slow. We only made forty miles this last drive."

The Major shook his head. "I don't mean McIvers. I mean the kid."

"Jack? What about him?"

"Take a look."

Stone was shaking. He was over near the tractor—away from the rest of us—and he was lying on his back, but he wasn't asleep. His whole body was shaking, convulsively. I saw him grip an outcropping of rock hard.

I walked over and sat down beside him. "Get your water all right?" I said.

He didn't answer. He just kept on shaking.

"Hey, boy," I said. "What's the trouble?"

"It's hot," he said, choking out the words.

"Sure it's hot, but don't let it throw you. We're in really good shape."

"*We're not*," he snapped. "We're in rotten shape, if you ask me. *We're not going to make it*, do you know that? That crazy fool's going to kill us for sure—" All of a sudden, he was bawling like a baby. "I'm scared—I shouldn't be here—I'm *scared*. What am I trying to prove by coming out here, for God's sake? I'm some kind of hero or something? I tell you I'm scared—"

"Look," I said. "Mikuta's scared, *I'm* scared. So what? We'll make it, don't worry. And nobody's trying to be a hero."

"Nobody but Hero Stone," he said bitterly.

He shook himself and gave a tight little laugh. "Some hero, eh?"

"We'll make it," I said.

"Sure," he said finally. "Sorry. I'll be okay."

I rolled over, but waited until he was good and quiet. Then I tried to sleep, but I didn't sleep too well. I kept thinking about that ledge. I'd known from the look of it what it was; a zinc slough of the sort Sanderson had warned us about, a wide sheet of almost pure zinc that had been thrown up white-hot from below, quite recently, just waiting for oxygen or sulfur to rot it through.

I knew enough about zinc to know that at these temperatures it gets brittle as glass. Take a chance like McIvers had taken and the whole sheet could snap like a dry pine board. And it wasn't McIvers' fault that it hadn't.

FIVE HOURS LATER, we were back at the wheel. We were hardly moving at all. The ragged surface was almost impassable—great jutting rocks peppered the plateau; ledges crumbled the moment my tires touched them; long, open canyons turned into lead-mires or sulfur pits.

A dozen times I climbed out of the Bug to prod out an uncertain area with my boots and pikestaff. Whenever I did, McIvers piled out behind me, running ahead like a schoolboy at the fair, then climbing back again red-faced and panting, while we moved the machines ahead another mile or two.

Time was pressing us now and McIvers wouldn't let me forget it. We had made only about three hundred twenty miles in six driving periods, so we were about a hundred miles or even more behind schedule.

"We're not going to make it," McIvers would complain angrily. "That Sun's going to be out to aphelion by the time we hit the Center—"

"Sorry, but I can't take it any faster," I told him. I was getting good and mad. I knew what he wanted, but didn't dare let him have it. I was scared enough pushing the Bug out on those ledges, even knowing that at least *I* was making the decisions. Put him in the lead and we wouldn't last for eight hours. Our nerves wouldn't take it, at any rate, even if the machines would.

Jack Stone looked up from the aluminum chart sheets. "Another hundred miles and we should hit a good stretch," he said. "Maybe we can make up distance there for a couple of days."

The Major agreed, but McIvers couldn't hold his impatience. He kept staring up at the Sun as if he had a personal grudge against it and stamped back and forth under the sunshield. "That'll be just fine," he said. "*If* we ever get that far, that is."

We dropped it there, but the Major stopped me as we climbed aboard for the next run. "That guy's going to blow wide open if we don't move faster, Peter. I don't want him in the lead, no matter what happens. He's right though, about the need to make better time. Keep your head, but crowd your luck a little, okay?"

"I'll try," I said. It was asking the impossible and Mikuta knew it. We were on a long downward slope that shifted and buckled all around us, as though there were a molten underlay beneath the crust; the slope was broken by huge crevasses, partly covered with dust and zinc sheeting, like a vast glacier of stone and metal. The outside temperature registered 547°F and getting hotter. It was no place to start rushing ahead.

I tried it anyway. I took half a dozen shaky passages, edging slowly out on flat zinc ledges, then toppling over and across. It seemed easy for a while and we made progress. We hit an even stretch and raced ahead. And then I quickly jumped on my brakes and jerked the Bug to a halt in a cloud of dust.

I'd gone too far. We were out on a wide, flat sheet of gray stuff, apparently solid—until I'd suddenly caught sight of the crevasse beneath in the corner of my eye. It was an overhanging shell that trembled under me as I stopped.

McIvers' voice was in my ear. "What's the trouble now, Claney?"

"Move back!" I shouted. "It can't hold us!"

"Looks solid enough from here."

"You want to argue about it? It's too thin, it'll snap. Move back!"

I started edging back down the ledge. I heard McIvers swear; then I saw his Bug start to creep *outward* on the shelf. Not fast or reckless, this time, but slowly, churning up dust in a gentle cloud behind him.

I just stared and felt the blood rush to my head. It seemed so hot I could hardly breathe as he edged out beyond me, further and further—

I think I felt it snap before I saw it. My own machine gave a sickening lurch and a long black crack appeared across the shelf—and widened. Then the ledge began to upend. I heard a scream as McIvers' Bug rose up and up and then crashed down into the crevasse in a thundering slide of rock and shattered metal.

I just stared for a full minute, I think. I couldn't move until I heard Jack Stone groan and the Major shouting, "Claney! I couldn't see—what *happened*?"

"It snapped on him, that's what happened," I roared. I gunned my motor, edged forward toward the fresh broken edge of the shelf. The crevasse gaped; I couldn't see any sign of the machine. Dust was still billowing up blindingly from below.

We stood staring down, the three of us. I caught a glimpse of Jack Stone's face through his helmet. It wasn't pretty.

"Well," said the Major heavily, "that's that."

"I guess so." I felt the way Stone looked.

"Wait," said Stone. "I heard something."

He had. It was a cry in the earphones—faint, but unmistakable.

"Mac!" The Major called. "Mac, can you hear me?"

"Yeah, yeah. I can hear you." The voice

68 • BRIGHTSIDE CROSSING

was very weak.

"Are you all right?"

"I don't know. Broken leg, I think. It's—hot." There was a long pause. Then: "I think my cooler's gone out."

The Major shot me a glance, then turned to Stone. "Get a cable from the second sledge fast. He'll fry alive if we don't get him out of there. Peter, I need you to lower me. Use the tractor winch."

I lowered him; he stayed down only a few moments. When I hauled him up, his face was drawn. "Still alive," he panted. "He won't be very long, though." He hesitated for just an instant. "We've got to make a try."

"I don't like this ledge," I said. "It's moved twice since I got out. Why not back off and lower him a cable?"

"No good. The Bug is smashed and he's inside it. We'll need torches and I'll need one of you to help." He looked at me and then gave Stone a long look. "Peter, you'd better come."

"Wait," said Stone. His face was very white. "Let me go down with you."

"Peter is lighter."

"I'm not so heavy. Let me go down."

"Okay, if that's the way you want it." The Major tossed him a torch. "Peter, check these hitches and lower us slowly. If you see any kind of trouble, *anything*, cast yourself free and back off this thing, do you understand? This whole ledge may go."

I nodded. "Good luck."

They went over the ledge. I let the cable down bit by bit until it hit two hundred feet and slacked off.

"How does it look?" I shouted.

"Bad," said the Major. "We'll have to work fast. This whole side of the crevasse is ready to crumble. Down a little more."

Minutes passed without a sound. I tried to relax, but I couldn't. Then I felt the ground

BLACK INFINITY • 69

shift, and the tractor lurched to the side.

The Major shouted, "*It's going, Peter—pull back!*" and I threw the tractor into reverse, jerked the controls as the tractor rumbled off the shelf. The cable snapped, coiled up in front like a broken clock spring. The whole surface under me was shaking wildly now; ash rose in huge gray clouds. Then, with a roar, the whole shelf lurched and slid sideways. It teetered on the edge for seconds before it crashed into the crevasse, tearing the side wall down with it in a mammoth slide. I jerked the tractor to a halt as the dust and flame billowed up.

They were gone—all three of them, McIvers and the Major and Jack Stone—buried under a thousand tons of rock and zinc and molten lead. There wasn't any danger of anybody ever finding their bones.

PETER CLANEY leaned back, finishing his drink, rubbing his scarred face as he looked across at Baron.

Slowly, Baron's grip relaxed on the chair arm. "*You* got back," he said.

Claney nodded. "I got back, sure. I had the tractor and the sledges. I had seven days to drive back under that yellow Sun. I had plenty of time to think."

"You took the wrong man along," Baron said. "That was your mistake. Without him you would have made it."

"Never." Claney shook his head. "That's what I was thinking the first day or so—that it was *McIvers'* fault, that *he* was to blame. But that isn't true. He was wild, reckless, and had lots of nerve."

"But his judgment was bad!"

"It couldn't have been sounder. We had to keep to our schedule even if it killed us, because it would positively kill us if we didn't."

"But a man like that—"

"A man like McIvers was necessary. Can't you see that? It was the Sun that beat us, that surface. Perhaps we were licked the very day we started." Claney leaned across the table, his eyes pleading. "We didn't realize that, but it was *true*. There are places that men can't go, conditions men can't tolerate. The others had to die to learn that. I was lucky, I came back. But I'm trying to tell you what I found out—that *nobody* will ever make a Brightside Crossing."

"We will," said Baron. "It won't be a picnic, but we'll make it."

"But suppose you do," said Claney, suddenly. "Suppose I'm all wrong, suppose you *do* make it. Then what? *What comes next?*"

"The Sun," said Baron.

Claney nodded slowly. "Yes. That would be it, wouldn't it?" He laughed. "Goodbye, Baron. Jolly talk and all that. Thanks for listening."

Baron caught his wrist as he started to rise. "Just one question more, Claney. Why did you come here?"

"To try to talk you out of killing yourself," said Claney.

"You're a liar," said Baron.

Claney stared down at him for a long moment. Then he crumpled in the chair. There was defeat in his pale blue eyes and something else.

"Well?"

Peter Claney spread his hands, a helpless gesture. "When do you leave, Baron? I want you to take me along."

👽👽👽

"Brightside Crossing" *first appeared in the January 1956 issue of* Galaxy. *The story was a finalist for the Hugo Award.*

Alan E. Nourse was an American physician and author of nonfiction books about medical science, as well as SF (often focusing on medicine or paranormal phenomena in relation to the application of electronics). He initially wrote to help pay for his medical education, but after completing his internship and practicing for five years, Nourse chose to exclusively pursue his writing career. His 1974 novel The Bladerunner *was optioned for film adaptation but no movie was ever produced from the book. Ridley Scott did use the title—which he purchased—for his '82 neo-noir flick* Blade Runner *(based on Philip K. Dick's novel* Do Androids Dream of Electric Sheep?*). So, Nourse may well hold the record for receiving the highest per-word rate in the history of SF.*

BELOW THE SURFACE
BY VONNIE WINSLOW CRIST

"Why Tau Ceti-e?" groaned Rhea Grey. She hated visiting underwater habitat sites. She preferred open skies above her. But on some planets, research needed to be done beneath the surface.

"Why?" asked Edgar, her companion since childhood.

Rhea smiled. Though many would consider Edgar a pet, Rhea knew the raven was a sentient being with emotions and intelligence equal to that of a twelve- or thirteen-year-old human. She also knew that countless times over the years, his loyalty and raven logic had helped get them out of a tight spot.

"Because it's been five days since the archaeological research team on Tau Ceti-e sent the mandatory daily check-in signal to the starship *Morella*." If she was being honest, Rhea wasn't sure she was answering herself or Edgar.

"Then, we check on them," said the raven.

Again, Rhea smiled at Edgar. His limited vocabulary lent a bluntness to his comments. And often, that bluntness was just what she needed to snap herself out of self-pity, apathy, or just plain laziness.

"Yup, let's pinpoint their location," she said while entering the Beta Archaeological Team's TC-e Groundsite coordinates into the shuttle *Eulalie*'s control pad.

"Arrival in forty-three minutes," stated the shuttle's metallic voice.

"Gives us enough time to grab lunch." She

wanted to add, *above water*, but belaboring the whole underwater thing seemed whiny.

"Meat?" asked Edgar.

"Yeah, we have got jerky for you." Rhea swore the raven smiled when she assured him he would have something better than a protein bar to munch on. "You're spoiled," she said before rummaging in the food chest.

"Spoiled," agreed Edgar as he ruffled his feathers and watched Rhea unwrap a stick of jerky.

IN EXACTLY THE ESTIMATED TIME, the *Eulalie* reached the small island near TC-e's equator which served as the off-planet landing and launch pad, mini-submarine dock and storage venue, and communication relay site for Beta Team's underwater habitat.

"Are you secure, Rhea?" asked the shuttle.

She knew the ship deliberately left the raven out of the safety reminder. Though shuttle computers were supposed to be nothing-but-the-facts artificial intelligence, *Eulalie* didn't like Edgar. Perhaps it was because the bird sometimes mimicked its voice, or maybe it was the feathers he shed in its interior, or it could even have been a touch of jealousy. Whatever the cause, the shuttle did its best to ignore the raven's existence.

"Edgar and I are belted in." Which was only a half-truth when it came to Edgar. Rhea had jury-rigged a harness attached to the standard seat belt and shoulder strap that prevented the raven from being tossed about during landings, takeoffs, and rough sailing. She had endured many punny remarks and much teasing from the other starship *Morella* shuttle pilots during the harness' construction. But it was in a spirit of fun. They all liked Edgar, and would have designed safety equipment for him themselves if she had asked.

After a slight pause, *Eulalie* announced, "Commencing touchdown."

Had it been anything but a routine landing, Rhea would have overridden the ship's computer and landed the shuttle herself, but this landing site and safety-check were no-brainers. She expected to find Beta Team in fine shape. Often research teams became so involved in their work that check-in protocols fell to the wayside. TC-e's team was likely no different.

Per their usual routine, *Eulalie* scanned the surrounding terrain for hostiles while Rhea inspected the contents of her knapsack. She removed several weapons. Tau Ceti-e's underwater research was funded by a conglomerate which espoused peaceful interactions with all alien species and worlds. She was forbidden to take any weapon into their site.

"Doesn't seem smart to me to be vulnerable," she said as she slid a gun from her belt. Rhea hesitated, then removed knives from one sleeve and her left boot.

Edgar perched on the locked-down all-terrain rover's fender watching her. "Right boot?" he asked.

"No one will notice," she replied with a shrug of her shoulders. "The best weapon is the one you have but don't need. Better to be reprimanded for rule-breaking than be captured or killed."

The raven clicked his beak in agreement before tapping on the all-terrain vehicle beneath his feet. "Take rover?"

"Nope. Habitat is underwater."

The raven croaked several times in a raucous voice.

She laughed. Whenever the bird resorted to raven-speak, she suspected he was complaining or cursing. Maybe both.

"You can stay with *Eulalie* if you would prefer."

Before the shuttle could point out all the reasons that the raven remaining onboard was a terrible idea, Edgar ruffled his feathers, stomped one of his clawed feet, and said, "We go together."

"Then, we are off," she said as he flew to her shoulder. "*Eulalie*, lock up and stay here until we return."

"As you wish," replied the shuttle. And though computers were supposed to be emotionless, Rhea could have sworn the shuttle sounded relieved that the bird would be leaving, too.

Rhea entered the small, utilitarian structure which served as the above surface facility for Beta Team's underwater habitat. TC-e Groundsite was unmanned. This was not unusual for a planet which appeared to have no land-based sentients or apex predators. The communication relay system, air circulation and power units, water pumps, and other equipment seemed to be functioning at optimal levels. It was looking more and more like Beta Team was so involved in their research that they had forgotten to check in with the starship *Morella*.

But Captain Parry *never* forgot any of the personnel working at remote research facilities, excavation camps, and archaeological digs. If every twenty-four hours they didn't confirm with the *Morella* that things at their site were copacetic and equipment operational, he notified a shuttle pilot to ready for deployment. After seventy-two hours, a shuttle was sent to confirm the site was functioning normally. Captain Parry's motto was: *Better to check on a distracted team than collect the remains of a dead one.*

"Let's find our ride," said Rhea as she strolled through the plasti-glass tunnel and into the facility's submarine bay. There were seven docks labeled with the colors of the spectrum, but only Indigo had a mini-sub locked in place.

"Looks like the *Indigo* is waiting for us, Edgar."

"Where are others?"

"Probably at the Underwater Station. With nearly two dozen people assigned to USTC-e, I am betting the rest of the subs are docked beneath the waves."

Rhea paused before climbing into the *Indigo*. She hated being underwater. In an attempt to hide her uneasiness, she whistled a few bars of a maritime tune while slapping her thigh.

Edgar tilted his head and peered at her. After stretching his wings and shifting his position on her shoulder, he mimicked her whistle, then muttered, "So, under ocean we go."

She nodded. Before she could lose courage, Rhea opened the door in the rear of the vehicle, placed her knapsack on the vessel, climbed aboard with Edgar on her shoulder, and closed the door behind her. A glance at the control screens and instrument panel confirmed, that like the *Eulalie*, this mini-sub's computer could launch, navigate, and dock without human assistance.

"*Indigo*," began Rhea, "your mothership, the *Morella*, sent me, Rhea Grey, to check on Beta Team." She repeated a series of numbers and letters which had been provided by Captain Parry, then said, "Activate and obey my commands."

The *Indigo* flickered to life. "Rhea Grey, I await your orders," said the mini-sub.

"Great." Rhea sat in the pilot's seat and set Edgar on the co-pilot's seat. "This is Edgar the raven, my associate. He is well-trained and welcomed aboard ships of air, space, and sea."

"Noted." Whatever else the computer may have been thinking—and since *Indigo* was of the same A.I. class as *Eulalie*, it was thinking something—the sub chose not to add an opinion as to whether the bird was actually welcome onboard.

"Find them," squawked Edgar.

"Soon," she replied. "*Indigo*, are your sister subs at Underwater Station TC-e?"

"*Red, Orange, Yellow, Green, Blue*, and *Violet* are either docked at USTC-e or deployed to the ruins."

"Are they still communicating with you?" asked Rhea. If the answer was *yes*, she might be able to sort out the "missing-in-action" status without actually having to go underwater.

"No. All communications stopped five days ago, which is why I was unable to send all-is-well messages to the starship *Morella*. I cannot diagnose the problem from TC-e Groundsite. Perhaps, when we are closer, I can collect sufficient data to hypothesize the cause of Beta Team's silence."

"Let's hope you are able to do so. I'm not a fan of underwater habitats. The sooner we re-establish communications and I can return to my shuttle, the better."

Indigo offered no response, but Rhea suspected as a mini-sub, it was not only designed to be submerged in water, but relished its time in aquatic environs.

"Set sail for USTC-e," she ordered.

"Complying," responded *Indigo* as it sank below the waterline and moved toward open ocean.

THE PILOTS' SEATS where Rhea and Edgar sat were at the front of the mini-sub and surrounded on three sides by a thick plasti-glass bubble. As the *Indigo* sailed through the shimmering waters of Tau Ceti-e, they were witness and audience to the sights and sounds of the planet's sea.

Being a shuttle pilot and survivalist, not an aquatic biologist, botanist, or alien species specialist, Rhea decided to just enjoy the wonders of the planet, while trying not to think about being hundreds of meters below breathable air. Edgar's lack of chatter seemed to indicate he had also decided to make the best of things and quietly observe the watery world around them.

In this part of the TC-e ocean, long strands of filmy kelp-like plants covered most of the rocky seafloor. Swimming among the pastel-hued plants were schools of sea dwellers. Though the creatures ranged from smaller than a guppy to larger than a beluga, all the life forms appeared to have multiple fins, tentacles, tails, and feathery fingers which allowed them to travel gracefully through water.

Rhea noticed that most of the animal species she spotted had protruding needle-like teeth and several eyes at the ends of willowy eye stalks. And all of the creatures and plants visible from the *Indigo* were bioluminescent—an evolutionary feature well-suited to survival on a mostly saltwater planet. No degree in a bio-science was needed to surmise self-generated light would be an aid in navigation, communication, finding food, and locating potential mates in even the deepest parts of the Tau Ceti-e seas.

As Rhea and Edgar watched, the glowing stripes and blotches of color covering the swaying plants and swimming creatures blinked on and off in a series of repeating patterns. This living light show was accompanied by rhythmic gurgling, whistling, piping, and pinging.

After a few minutes of the serenade, Rhea yawned, then rubbed her eyes. She barely flinched when a group of aquatic humanoids swam in front of the *Indigo*, then attached themselves by dozens of suckers to the plasti-glass. Their expressionless black eyes stared at Edgar and her. Their mouths pressed against the glass with lips open. The light from the interior of the mini-sub revealed several rows of shark-like teeth and a fringed tongue which coiled and uncoiled like a millipede inside each mouth. Next, the water people pressed their translucent bodies against the glass and rainbows of pulsating lights filled the cockpit. The volume of the gurgling, whistling, piping, and pinging increased.

"It's so beautiful," Rhea murmured. "So beautiful…"

"Rhea! Do not look. Rhea!" shouted Edgar as he fluttered in front of her face.

"Move," whispered Rhea, "and shush. I'm trying to hear…"

Edgar croaked several phrases in raven and continued to flap his wings in front of her. Then, he screeched, "Bagpipes! *Indigo* play bagpipes."

"What song would you like to hear?" asked the sub.

"Scotland," he said between squawks.

"*Scotland the Brave*?" queried *Indigo*.

"Yes. That song." Edgar was now hopping up and down on Rhea's lap, flapping his wings, and lightly pinching her arm with his beak. Rhea felt like she was in a trance. Soon, Edgar's nips became strong enough to cause bruises. Somewhere in a corner of her mind, she understood if he nipped her any harder, he would draw blood.

As the wail of great pipes bellowing out *Scotland the Brave* filled the mini-sub, she slowly became more aware of her surroundings. Rhea studied the beings on the other side of the plasti-glass. There was no mistaking the horror on the flat, fish-eyed faces of the humanoids. Their glowing stripes and spots flared as red as the sunset, then they released their grip on the mini-sub's cockpit bubble. The pod quickly swam about five meters away, but continued to keep pace with the *Indigo*.

"Edgar, what is that noise?" asked Rhea, feeling slightly sick to her stomach. "I can barely think. *Indigo*..."

"Stop!" Edgar grabbed her sleeve with a foot. "Let bagpipes play. Water people were putting you to sleep."

She frowned, then squeezed the bridge of her nose. "Their lights and sounds were hypnotizing me." She tried to lean to the side and see where the aquatic humanoids were now located.

"No!" Edgar continued to flap his wings and obscure her view. "Do not look at the lights."

"Right." Rhea searched the contents of her knapsack, pulled out a pair of military-style glare glasses, and put them on. "Let's see if these will help."

Keeping his eyes focused on her face, the raven stopped flapping his wings and allowed Rhea to view the merfolk.

"These help, but it would not take much for me to be lulled into a stupor again." She stroked Edgar's soft back. "Good job, partner. It was brilliant to play bagpipes. Their sound not only drowned out the merfolk, but drove them further away."

Edgar pressed close to Rhea, then looked again into her eyes. "Others had no raven."

"Nope. Which means, we can assume Beta Team are sitting in the habitat or one of the mini-subs staring at flashing lights and listening to the songs of the merfolk."

"Water people," observed Edgar, "try to kill Rhea."

"We don't know that. They might be just trying to communicate. Even warning us of danger." She glanced at the displays on the control panel in front of her. "How much longer to Underwater Station TC-e, *Indigo*?"

"Seven minutes."

"I don't think I can listen to another verse of *Scotland the Brave*." She sighed and tried to think of other bagpipe songs which the mini-sub could play instead. "*Indigo*, play *Auld Lang Syne,* followed by *Amazing Grace,* then *The Bonnie Banks of Loch Lomond.*"

"As you wish. Do you want me to repeat the four selections after I have played them through?"

"Yes."

"*Indigo* help you?" suggested Edgar.

"Maybe. *Indigo*, the sounds and lights of the merfolk cause me to drift into a daze. I need to block or alter them in order to remain alert. Can you do that?"

After about two seconds of silence, the mini-sub said, "I cannot alter the view out of the cockpit nor can I add another layer of metal to my exterior. The plasti-glass is already polarized, shatterproof, and corrosion resistant."

"Thanks. It was worth asking." She rubbed her forehead. "I guess bagpipes and glare glasses are my only protection."

"And Edgar," added the raven.

"And Edgar." She scratched the bird's neck.

"Wait." As her mind cleared, Rhea considered another strategy. "*Indigo*, analyze the lights and sounds coming from the aquatic humanoids and compare them to known languages. Let's see if we can ask them to stop."

"Proceeding as ordered," replied the mini-sub as Beta Team's underwater habitat came into view.

The research facility was enormous. Lowered complete and fully operational into Tau Ceti-e's ocean by a hulking transport spaceship, the structure included both research and lab levels in addition to recreational and living areas. Designed to maximize the twenty-three member Beta Team's underwater experience, every room had a minimum of one transparent plasti-glass wall—except sleeping quarters and bathrooms. Though its designers had spared no expense to make the underwater station as organic in appearance as possible, the metal pilings driven into bedrock which anchored the facility to Tau Ceti-e were a dead giveaway. USTC-e was not of this planet and not of this sea.

"Look! Water people!" squawked Edgar.

"*Indigo*, can we safely enter Underwater Station TC-e?" asked Rhea as she surveyed the throng of merfolk attached to the glass of the facility. Nearly every available centimeter of clear plasti-glass was covered by a flickering aquatic humanoid.

"A scan indicates the mini-sub access tubes are clear. The humanoids are clustered on the plasti-glass walls and windows."

"Then, proceed into the access tubes." Rhea observed a few of the merfolk turn their faces to watch the *Indigo*, and wondered what the creatures were thinking. "Any results on the language of the aquatic humanoids' vocalizations and light patterns?"

"Nothing yet, Rhea Grey."

TUBE NAVIGATED, seawater drained away, and the *Indigo* transferred into a shallow-water, docking area filled with breathable air, Rhea finally felt a degree of safety. "Turn down the volume on the music," she told *Indigo*.

"I still cannot communicate with Underwater Station TC-e," said the mini-sub after obeying Rhea's order.

"How is that possible?"

"The computers could have been deactivated by the crew."

"Water people want to kill humans," said Edgar. "They told crew to turn off computer."

"You are jumping to conclusions," she told the raven. "If the merfolk wanted Beta Team dead, why not tell them to turn off their air supply systems instead?"

"Lure more humans," responded Edgar as he looked out the cockpit at the empty mini-sub docks. "Where subs?"

"Deployed," answered *Indigo*.

Rhea frowned. She needed to remain mentally sharp, but one mini-sub's sound system would be inadequate for the whole station. "*Indigo*, can I access the station's computers from here?"

"Yes. There is an emergency port located behind the silver panel two bays to my left."

"Great! What do I need to do?"

"The whole station must be shut down using the appropriate numeric code. Next, after waiting three minutes, a restart password and different code need to be entered. Then, the system will reboot."

"Oxygen? Water?" queried Edgar.

"No additional breathable air will be generated by Underwater Station TC-e during shutdown-reboot, but there should be sufficient oxygen for one human and one avian. Water will gradually enter the access tubes, but drowning levels will not be reached before reboot is complete."

"No drowning," suggested the raven.

"Agreed." This scenario was right out of Rhea's nightmares, but there was no backing out now. "Can I return to the *Indigo* after rebooting has begun?"

"No, Rhea Grey. You must press the Drain Docking Bay icon after reboot is complete. *Then*, you may re-enter *Indigo*."

"Fine. What is the shutdown code?"

Silence.

Rhea supposed the *Indigo* was considering the security risk-threat ratio. Finally, the mini-sub rattled off a string of about thirty numerals and mathematical symbols.

"Whoa! There is no way I can memorize all of those, then enter them correctly into the port. Edgar, I need you to listen to *Indigo*, then repeat exactly what she says to me."

In response, the raven nodded, then repeated the code sequence exactly as it had been spoken by *Indigo*—including using the sub's voice.

"Correct," said the mini-sub.

Rhea thought she noted a surprised tone to the comment, though with A.I.s you could never be certain. "Let's go, Edgar," she said as the *Indigo* opened its rear door. With the raven on her shoulder, she stepped onto the dock, walked to the panel two bays to the left, turned the brads holding the panel in place, and accessed the emergency computer port.

"Now, repeat the shutdown code slowly," she told Edgar.

He did as she asked, then flew back to the *Indigo*, went inside, and waited for the mini-sub to tell him the password and reboot code. After three minutes, the mini-sub complied, and the raven flew back to Rhea's shoulder. Edgar repeated the password and began the reboot code.

"Slower!" said Rhea. "It takes me a few seconds to switch keypads and find the symbols."

Again, Edgar repeated the password and code. This time, he paused periodically to make sure numbers and symbols were entered before moving on to the next sequence.

The raven perched on her shoulder as the water level rose. Soon, her feet and lower legs were wet. Still, the Underwater Station TC-e's computers were not rebooted. When the water level reached her waist, Rhea started to doubt the wisdom of this plan. Years ago, a fortune speaker on her home world had told her she would die by drowning. Though she was not the superstitious sort, the foretelling spooked her. At this moment, it appeared the prognostication might be true.

"We drown?" asked Edgar. There was no denying the sadness in his voice.

She looked into the eyes of her best friend. "Maybe, but at least…"

"Terminal ready!" croaked the raven as she saw the various icons reflected by his pupils.

"Yes!" Rhea shouted as she pressed the Drain Docking Bay icon. "Fly to the *Indigo*. I will be right behind you."

Edgar soared into the diminishing air and swooped through the mini-sub's entrance. Rhea swam to the mini-sub, climbed up its side using the handholds and footholds molded into its exterior, and slid into the sub's interior.

"Close and lock rear entrance," she shouted. It was an unnecessary order. The *Indigo* had begun lowering the door as soon as she was aboard.

"Can you talk with Underwater Station TC-e now?"

"Yes," replied the sub. "Beta Team attempted to communicate with the aquatic humanoids when they first appeared near an underwater city's ruins about a kilometer from here. One mini-sub after another failed to return or respond to communication requests from Underwater Station TC-e. Finally, with no remaining subs to deploy, members of Beta Team were ready to send an SOS message to the starship *Morella*. But humanoids appeared at this location, and shortly thereafter, the crew deactivated the computers."

Edgar stopped preening his feathers. "Water people want humans dead," he said.

"Maybe you are right, but our job is not to determine the motives or goals of the aquatic humanoids. Our job is to secure Underwater Station TC-e and retrieve Beta Team if they are in danger."

"They are in danger," said the *Indigo*. "The Underwater Station TC-e computer has checked the life-sign monitors of the members of Beta Team. All of them are dehydrated, malnourished, and covered in their own excrement. In addition, those in the mini-subs are running out of oxygen."

"Don't the mini-subs maintain breathable air, even if its occupants are comatose?" To Rhea, this seemed like it should be a standard emergency feature.

"Not if the subs have been ordered to shut down," said *Indigo* in a matter-of-fact voice.

"Can you or Underwater Station TC-e recall the mini-subs?" Again, to Rhea this seemed to be a must-have feature in case of an emergency situation.

"*Red*, *Yellow*, *Green*, and *Violet* have already been ordered to return to the Underwater Structure. *Orange* and *Blue* are unresponsive."

Suddenly, the situation seemed critical. Rhea said, "*Indigo*, relay to the starship *Morella* we are evacuating Underwater Station TC-e. Ask them to send a medical shuttle."

"Done," replied the mini-sub.

"Let me speak with Underwater Station TC-e."

Indigo obliged.

"Underwater Station Tau Ceti-e, this is Rhea Grey of the starship *Morella*. I'm assuming command of this facility until help arrives." Rhea recited the same series of numbers and letters she had given to the *Indigo* earlier. "I order you to play bagpipe music throughout the station. *Indigo* will share the playlist. Also, send that command to the missing mini-subs."

"Implementing your order, Rhea Grey," said the underwater station.

"Any response from the aquatic humanoids?"

"Yes," answered Underwater Station TC-e. "They are disengaging."

"Edgar," began Rhea, "the docking bay is dry enough for me to enter the station. With the help of the Underwater Station TC-e computer, I will locate the members of Beta Team who are still here and prepare them for evacuation. Four mini-subs containing other team members are on their way back the station. I'm hoping to use those subs in addition to the *Indigo* to transport Beta Team back to TC-e Groundsite."

"Get out of water fast," agreed the raven.

"Yes." She paused, wondering about the enormity of what she was about to do. "Edgar, someone needs to go with the *Indigo* and tow the remaining two subs back here. Will you do it?"

"Yes," responded Edgar. "Tell *Indigo* to obey."

"Okay." This was a first—putting the lives of several humans solely in the hands—well, the claws—of a raven. "*Indigo*, I order you to obey Edgar the raven. Turn on interior monitors so I can keep abreast of the situation."

Without hesitation, the *Indigo* said, "I will do as you command."

"Great! Underwater Station TC-e's computer and I will be monitoring you two. See you both shortly."

USING THE Underwater Station TC-e's life-support system, Rhea was able to find eleven Beta Team members in the underwater station's public areas. Before she rescued them she wanted to see how Edgar was doing.

She sat at a terminal and pulled up the video stream from the cockpit of the *Indigo*. "Edgar, what's going on?"

The raven looked into the camera and shook his shiny, black head. "*Indigo* scanned *Blue* and *Orange*. No life on subs. We try to drag subs back."

"*Indigo*, you detected no life-signs on either vessel?"

"No life-signs," replied the mini-sub. "They are both covered with humanoids. Neither can be towed into the docking bay until the TC-e water creatures are removed. Also, playing bagpipe music no longer deters the humanoids."

As if to confirm the situation, Rhea saw two merfolk clinging to the *Indigo*'s cockpit plasti-glass bubble to the right of the raven.

"That means I will soon be in trouble here."

"Change music," suggested Edgar.

"What?"

"Screaming, loud instruments."

"Yes!" said Rhea. A quick search of music history yielded a new playlist. "Underwater Station TC-e and all mini-subs, play the most popular songs of Black Sabbath, Metallica, Iron Maiden, Megadeth, and Judas Priest."

As Ozzie Osborn's voice filled the *Indigo*, Rhea saw the merfolk fling themselves from the plasti-glass. There was no telling how long heavy metal music would hold off the creatures, so she needed to act fast.

"*Indigo*, abandon *Blue* and *Orange*. Return at top speed to the station. All other mini-subs enter the docking bay and prepare for additional passengers."

While waiting for the subs, Rhea loaded the comatose Beta Team members one by one onto a cart and pushed them to the elevator, rode down to the docking bay, and dumped them on the platform. As soon as the mini-subs arrived, she push-pulled the crew onto one sub or the other. When the *Indigo* finally arrived, Edgar flew to her shoulder and rubbed his bill against her neck.

"More crew?" he asked.

"Two more on level six. Then we can head for land."

"Must hurry. Water people want to kill Rhea and Edgar."

"I am beginning to think you are right," she replied as they rode the elevator up to level six."

One of the two remaining Beta Team members seemed slightly alert. Thankfully, he was a large man and able to help Rhea maneuver the other person onto the cargo cart before climbing onto the cart himself. When they reached the submarine bay, he helped her load the last team member onto the *Violet* before climbing in. Rhea boarded the *Indigo* with Edgar on her shoulder and ordered the subs to close their doors and depart for Tau Ceti-e Groundsite.

"Underwater Station TC-e, once all five subs are clear of the access tubes, lock-down the station."

"Understood," said the underwater facility's computer.

"*Indigo*, send regular location updates to the starship *Morella*," ordered Rhea. She wasn't certain how far gone the research team members were, but hoped the requested medical shuttle arrived quickly. Though Rhea had basic first aid training, any medical treatment beyond that would require additional personnel and equipment.

"Crew need water," said Edgar.

"I know," replied Rhea. "I am hoping the crew begins to come out of their stupors, because I do not have enough intravenous equipment and fluid bags on the *Eulalie* to handle this many semiconscious people."

"Look!" croaked the raven. "Water people coming."

Rhea saw hundreds of the merfolk pursuing the two subs slightly ahead of the *Indigo*. She imagined behind them and the other slower mini-subs hundreds of additional aquatic humanoids swam.

"Increase speed," she told the *Indigo*. "And relay that order to your sister subs."

"Order complied with," said the mini-sub.

"Are you equipped with any weapons?" she asked the *Indigo*. Hoping that someone in a shadowy corner of the controlling conglomerate's oversight committee had the sense to hide at least one weapon on Tau Ceti-e.

"No. Nor is TC-e Groundsite fitted with any weaponry," replied the sub.

"Banjos," said Edgar.

"What?" For a split second, she thought the raven had succumbed to stress.

"Need new music. Use banjos."

"Okay, it is worth a try," said Rhea, relieved to know her partner was still thinking clearly. "*Indigo*, find music with multiple, fast picking banjo players. As soon as a selection is found, switch to banjo music and relay the new playlist to the other subs."

Moments later, the *Indigo* was filled with the plinks and strums of banjos. A look out the cockpit window showed the merfolk backing away from the other mini-subs.

"They are just going to adjust again—probably even more quickly than before."

"City sounds?" suggested Edgar.

"Brilliant!"

Edgar stretched his wings and opened his bill slightly. Rhea thought he looked like he was smiling.

"*Indigo*, just prior to docking at TC-e Groundsite, switch to urban noises—horns honking, brakes squealing, jack hammers, engines revving.... And relay your audio to the other subs."

"As you wish," replied the *Indigo* before stating, "there is a warning alarm in case of fire or other danger at Tau Ceti-e Groundsite."

"Great! After we have arrived at Groundsite and the Beta Team members are unloaded and removed from the dock area, I need you to activate the alarms. Then, send an order to each of the mini-subs to broadcast a different playlist: bagpipes for *Red*, heavy metal for *Yellow*, banjo for *Green*, and urban noise for *Violet*."

"What should I play?"

"Owl screeches," interjected Edgar.

"Not a bad idea." Rhea had been trying to think of another sound which would be alien to the merfolk. Since she hadn't seen any birds when the *Eulalie* arrived, and avians certainly could not survive underwater, any bird call would be disturbing to them. "Mix in the sound of migrating geese and eagles, too," she added.

THEY ARRIVED at TC-e Groundsite just as the merfolk began to draw close again. The noise of a congested city at rush hour suddenly blared in and from the mini-subs. As soon as the subs docked, they popped open their doors.

Rhea climbed out of the *Indigo* and she patted its hull. "Thanks. We could not have gotten here without your help."

"I was only adhering to my programming," replied the mini-sub A.I., though Rhea would have sworn that *Indigo*'s computer sounded pleased with itself.

With nineteen stupefied Beta Team members to get off of the subs and into the Groundsite's primary building, Rhea didn't take the time to respond. Instead, she sent Edgar to check in *Red*, *Yellow*, and *Green* for anyone who might be able to help their teammates off the subs. Meanwhile, she climbed aboard the *Violet* and was greeted by the man who had helped her at the underwater station. He was already standing, and in the process of lifting an older woman to her feet.

"We need to get everyone off the subs and into the main part of the facility before the aquatic humanoids enter the docking bay," she explained. "Can you help with that?"

"I will get the people off the *Violet*," he assured her. "You see to the others."

"Counting you, there are six people onboard the *Violet*?"

"Yes," he answered. "Then, if you are still unloading the other subs, I'll come back and help."

"Thanks," Rhea called over her shoulder as she hurried toward the *Green*.

"No help *Green*," croaked Edgar as he flew to her shoulder. "Help on *Red*. No help *Yellow*."

"Okay," she said as she continued down the platform to the first bay. "Who is awake in the *Red*?" Rhea called as they neared the *Red*.

"Lakita," came the response as a muscular woman with close-cropped hair stuck her head out of the *Red*'s door.

"I need you to get everyone from your sub into the main facility as soon as possible. Can you do that?"

"No problem. There are five of us. I can easily make four trips," Lakita assured Rhea.

"Hurry," said Edgar.

"Yes, hurry," repeated Rhea as she began to assist the remaining eight Beta Team members from *Yellow* and *Green*.

WITH LAKITA IN CHARGE of getting everyone who was mobile to the tarmac where the *Eulalie* was parked, the man from level six of the underwater station and Rhea returned to the *Yellow* for the last team member. Edgar flew back with them and did a quick check to make sure Beta Team was out of the subs.

"My name is Jamie," said the man as he and Rhea lifted the last team member, an unconscious woman. "I appreciate what—"

Whatever he meant to say next was lost as the water beneath and beside the mini-subs erupted in a mass of shimmering lights and squirming tentacles, fins, and tails.

"*Indigo*, alarms!" shouted Rhea as she did her best to walk backwards while holding the limp woman's ankles.

But the change in sound was too late for Jamie. Several translucent tentacles covered in gold and purple bioluminescent splotches wrapped around his lower legs. A hero until the end, before the aquatic humanoids yanked him into the water, Jamie lowered his hands, then released his grip on the unconscious team member.

Suddenly, a terrible cacophony of alarms, bagpipes, heavy metal, banjo music, urban noises, and bird calls blasted from the mini-subs and Tau Ceti-e Groundsite. The merfolk vanished—taking Jamie with them. Retaining her hold on the woman's ankles, Rhea pulled her to the plasti-glass tube. With the last of her strength, Rhea dragged her toward TC-e Groundsite's entrance.

Edgar helped by grabbing the woman's hair with his claws. He did his best to prevent her head from flopping around. As they neared the door to the outside, he asked, "Dead?"

"I don't think so." Before she could elaborate, Rhea saw hundreds of merfolk were crawling up onto the beach on either side of the TC-e Groundsite facility. She had assumed the species was solely aquatic. It had never crossed her mind that the merfolk were able to breathe air.

The raven noticed the mass of merfolk crawling toward them, too. After several seconds of loud raven-speak, he said, "Water people want to kill Edgar and Rhea."

"You are right!" she answered, ignoring Edgar's additional squawks.

Rhea tapped her communication neck piece. "*Eulalie*, I am bringing eighteen survivors with me. Can you accommodate that number safely?"

"If we use the rover as additional seating it is possible," responded Eulalie.

"Then, open up and let everyone on board. Edgar and I are not there yet, but close by."

"Door open," said the shuttle.

As they dragged the woman toward the *Eulalie*, Rhea thought about Jamie. She wondered why the urban noises failed to deter the merfolk. Then, it hit her like a ton of plasti-steel. When Underwater Station TC-e was lowered by a transport spaceship and installed, there would have been similar sounds. City and construction noises were not strange enough. If only she had thought about that sooner, then maybe Jamie would still be alive.

"We die?" asked Edgar.

"What?" Rhea had been thinking about the past instead of focusing on the now—a mistake in her line of work. The merfolk, their rows of shark teeth wet and glistening, were within three meters of them. Without weapons or backup, Edgar and she could either drop the woman and race to the shuttle, or continue to drag her and all three of them would perish.

"Leave her," said Rhea, "and fly to *Eulalie*."

She released her grip on the woman's ankles, turned, and ran as if her life depended on speed. And it did.

Though the raven could easily have beaten Rhea to the shuttle, they entered the *Eulalie* at the same time. She tried not to think about the slurping and crunching sounds she had heard as they raced away from the unconscious Beta Team member, but she knew they would haunt her.

"Close and lock the door. Lift-off as soon as possible," ordered Rhea as she stepped inside the shuttle.

"Destination?" asked the *Eulalie*.

"The starship *Morella* unless we receive different orders."

"Stinks," said Edgar.

"They can't help it," whispered Rhea. Though she had to agree. After sitting in their own excrement for days and not practicing normal hygiene, the seventeen remaining members of Beta Team were an odoriferous bunch.

"Tau Ceti-e humanoids are attached to *Eulalie*," said the shuttle. "Interstellar League protocol prohibits takeoff."

This time, Rhea did not rely on the raven. She plucked an annoying sound from her childhood. "Blast the sound of fingernails on a chalkboard at them until they release their suckers," she told the shuttle.

As the screech of fingernails screamed from the shuttle's speakers, Edgar squawked several phrases of raven-speak, the people onboard the *Eulalie* groaned and covered their ears, the merfolk let go of the shuttle, and *Eulalie* lifted into the air.

"Now quiet?" asked the raven.

"Yes," said Rhea. "*Eulalie*, turn off the noise."

After the shuttle stopped broadcasting the fingernail scraping sounds, the conscious members of Beta Team uncovered their ears. Rhea was certain if she handed out water containers, they would be able to re-hydrate themselves. But a half a dozen people were still unconscious and needed IVs.

"Edgar, let's *quietly* attend to these people," she said to her partner as she opened the supply cabinet.

Though she did not say it out loud, Rhea decided when Edgar and she returned to the *Morella*, they deserved a few weeks of rest. Music-free, noise-free, no-life-and-death-decisions, above-the-water rest.

👽👽👽

"Below the Surface" first appeared in Deep Space *(Vol. 1), 2019, published in Australia by Black Hare Press.*

Vonnie Winslow Crist, SFWA, HWA, is author of Dragon Rain, Beneath Raven's Wing, The Enchanted Dagger, Owl Light, The Greener Forest, Murder on Marawa Prime, *and other books. Her fiction appears in* Amazing Stories, Cirsova Magazine, Lost Signals: A Terran Republic Anthology, Black Infinity, Planetary Anthology Series: Neptune, Storming Area 51, Worlds, Galactic Goddesses, Insignia 2021: Best Asian Speculative Fiction, *and elsewhere.*

Believing the world is still filled with mystery, magic, and miracles, Vonnie strives to celebrate the power of myth in her fiction. For more information:
http://www.vonniewinslowcrist.com

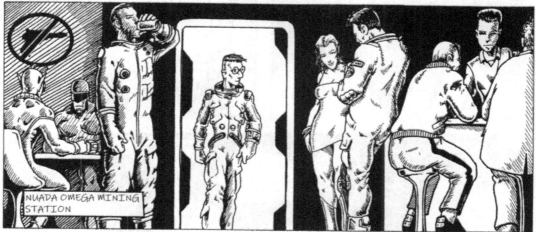

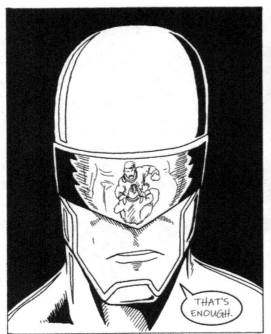

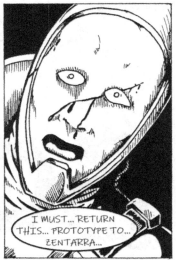

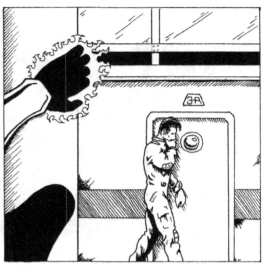

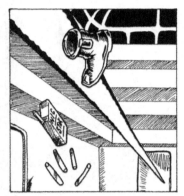

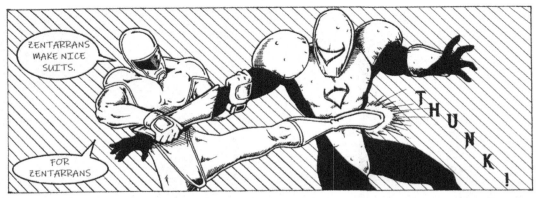

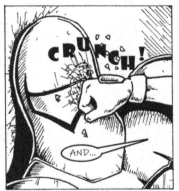

THE LAST STAR WARDEN

"A rare and refreshing level of pure pulpy fun."
~ Gregory L. Norris, Author of the Gerry Anderson's Into Infinity novels

VOLUME 1

NOW AVAILABLE!
PAPERBACK AND KINDLE

NOVELLA

STARTING ON VELLA
OCTOBER 8, 2021

VOLUME II

PUBLISHING
NOVEMBER 1, 2021

Written and Illustrated by
JASON J. MCCUISTON
Author of Project Notebook

For more details and to order, visit Dark Owl Publishing
www.darkowlpublishing.com

FIRST THREE ISSUES STILL AVAILABLE!

Purchase online at Amazon, Walmart, or BN.com—or order through your local bookstore.

Strange science, weird worlds, hostile aliens, renegade robots ... and the cold vacuum of space.

200 oversized pages packed with exciting stories, articles and art by some of the best writers of yesterday, today and tomorrow.

Black Infinity: Deadly Planets (#1)
ISBN: 978-0996693677

Black Infinity: Blobs, Globs, Slime and Spores (#2) ISBN: 978-0996693684

Black Infinity: Body Snatchers (#3)
ISBN: 978-1732434424

SATELLITE OF DEATH

By RANDALL GARRETT

Art by JG

THERE WERE FIVE ABOARD THE ORBITING WHEEL IN THE SKY—AN AMERICAN, A RUSSIAN, A FRENCHMAN, AN ENGLISHMAN, AN INDIAN. Their job was to keep watch—over each other. The Wheel held enough fission-fusion bombs to blast all of Earth but the five watchdogs saw to it that those bombs remained stored, a potential threat and no more to aggressors below.

And then Gregson and Lal discovered the alien spaceship moored outside Supplementary Airlock One.

It looked like no spaceship they had ever set eyes on before. Gregson, the American, said, "You see that thing out there?"

The Indian, Lal, nodded and rubbed his aquiline nose reflectively. "I see it—but what is it?"

"Spaceship of some kind," said Gregson. "Damndest-looking spaceship I've ever seen, though. Looks like it's moored near the airlock. Wonder if we have visitors?"

He peered at the ship. It had little in common with the un-streamlined dumbbells Earth used for spaceflight; it was slim and tapering, with no visible rocket orifices; it was made of some strange iridescent metal that glimmered in the moonlight.

"Let's investigate," Gregson said.

"We should call the others," said Lal. "All five should be on hand."

"You're right." Gregson touched his belt-stud, giving the signal that called all five crewmen to hand. They appeared quickly—Lasseux, Beveridge, Golovunoff. Silently, Gregson pointed through the view-plate at the newcomer.

After a long look Beveridge shook his head. "That didn't come from Earth," the

Englishman said. "Not unless they've developed an entirely new drive principle. And look at the design...."

"That's an alien spaceship, all right," Lasseux said.

"From the stars," added Golovunoff. A cold chill seemed to sweep through the space satellite as he spoke the words.

Quietly Gregson said, "We'd better go out there and see what's inside. Since Lal and I saw the ship first, we'll be the ones to go look."

"No," said Golovunoff. "I wish to go also."

"I'd rather like to get first look too," said Beveridge.

"I think we'd all better go," Lasseux suggested. "The station can operate without us for a while. And we'll never agree on who's to go, eh?"

FIVE FIGURES in spacesuits clustered about the alien ship. At close range its iridescent skin looked otherworldly and vaguely frightening, gleaming purple and green and dull-bronze by moonlight. A quartz window gave a view of the ship's interior.

"I don't see anyone in there," said Gregson. "You?"

"Looks empty to me," commented Beveridge.

"Empty! Impossible!" said Lasseux vehemently. "Empty spaceships do not pilot themselves across the void to Earth. Empty spaceships do not complicatedly moor themselves outside a space satellite's airlock. Empty spaceships...."

"That's enough, Lasseux," growled the Russian. "Whether it makes sense or no, that spaceship's empty."

"Let's find the hatch," suggested Lal. "Perhaps there's someone injured inside, out of the line of sight."

The five Earthmen covered the surface of the ship, looking for an exterior hatch control. Beveridge found it first—a narrow lever extruding a few inches from the skin of the alien vessel. He called to the others, then yanked down on the lever. The hatch pivoted back, opening into an airlock.

There was the usual moment of Alphonse-Gaston as the five crewmen jockeyed for position, none willing to let any of the others get ahead of him on anything. Then Lasseux slipped through and into the alien spaceship, followed by Gregson and Beveridge almost simultaneously, and then Golovunoff and Lal.

The ship *was* empty.

There was not the slightest sign of life. The five men roamed through the vessel, noting the utterly alien control panel, the strange furnishings, the peculiar fixtures and appurtenances. But the ship was void of life.

Finally they returned to the Wheel and, puzzled, discussed the situation.

"It makes no sense," objected Lasseux. The small Frenchman was plainly obsessed with the inconsistency of the thing. "The ship crosses the interstellar void ... alone? Can remote control extend so far?"

"Looks like it did," said Gregson.

"Impossible!" Lasseux sputtered.

"In any case," said Beveridge, "we have a prize—a gift from the stars. An alien spaceship, free and without strings of any kind. We should notify Earth of our find."

"Do you suppose," said Lal, "that the pilot of that ship may be around yet?"

"Huh?" From Gregson and Beveridge at the same time.

"What I mean is, suppose that pilot is not like you and me—suppose, that is, that he is invisible? Perhaps he is still aboard his ship, and we passed over him unknowing? Or perhaps he has come right in here with us and listens to our very words?"

Gregson shuddered. "You've got a wild imagination, Lal. But we have enough problems on our hands without worrying about ghosts from outer space."

"I said not ghosts—"

"Enough," boomed Golovunoff. "We can continue this silly quarrel indefinitely. Let us assume, since we see no one and nothing aboard the ship, that it arrived empty. And therefore that it is ours for study."

"Do empty ships moor themselves to airlock hatches?" asked the Frenchman sarcastically. "I tell you, Lal's right—there must have been intelligence guiding that ship!"

Gregson shook his head. "No. Listen to me, will you? We built this satellite station jointly, as a global watch-station. But does that mean that everything the satellite discovers is to be shared equally?"

"Of course," said Beveridge.

"Then how do we divide that spaceship into five equal parts? Whose country gets it?"

There was a moment's silence. Then Lal said, "We'll turn it over to the United Nations. They can let all nations examine it freely."

For once there was general agreement. "Good idea," Gregson said approvingly, and then the five went back to their tasks aboard the satellite.

THE SATELLITE had been in space less than a year. The development of spaceflight had put an end to the possibility of war on Earth by bringing into being a watchdog for the uneasy planet.

Put a satellite in the sky. Arm it with enough fission-fusion bombs to blast any country to flinders. Man it with a squad chosen from the leading countries of the world and let them keep watch over one another. Any threat of aggression on the mother planet could easily be squashed by the more potent threat of blazing vengeance from the skies. The satellite was the guardian of the world's peace.

The five men chosen to be the first crew were almost ideal for the job—sensitive, intelligent men, skilled in the techniques of spaceflight, loyal to the countries of their birth. There wouldn't be any chance of collusion among them, of a conspiracy against one country or against Earth itself, as some feared.

Their tasks for the hours immediately after the discovery of the strange spaceship were mostly routine; Lal dictated a comprehensive report on the spaceship and beamed it to United Nations Headquarters on Earth, while Beveridge and Golovunoff, space-suited, filmed the alien ship from every conceivable angle, inside and out. Lasseux and Gregson tended to the workings of the satellite, overseeing the cybernetic governors which had the actual responsibility of operating the big wheel in the sky.

Lasseux was cook that night, according to the strict rotation that had been set up. The men ate a strange meal; their spirits seemed oddly dampened by the spaceship that had so unpredictably come into their midst. Lal's words preyed on them despite themselves. Suppose there had been an invisible alien aboard that ship? Suppose he lurked aboard the wheel this very moment?

"Suppose," said Beveridge suddenly, "that alien ship was an invasion scout."

"What's that?" Gregson asked.

"What I mean is, the advance guard of an invasion force. The alien finds the satellite and, being telepathic, parks here a while to see what's going on." He giggled self-consciously. "I'm speaking imaginatively, of course. The alien moors here and reads our minds; finds out we have a load of bombs here that can blow up the works down there. So he comes drifting out of the ship and takes over someone of us here. When no one else is looking—*poof!*—Earth is destroyed like that!" Again Beveridge giggled.

Gregson looked at him sourly. "You better leave those crazy magazines alone, Beveridge."

But Lasseux interjected, "We should devote careful attention to what he has said. There may be a grain of truth in it. After all, *who moored the spaceship*?"

A moment's silence. Then the Russian said, "Assuming one of us is an alien—not that I believe Beveridge's fanciful story—how would we know? Until Earth is destroyed, that is?"

"That's just it," said Lal gloomily. "We. *wouldn't* know. Not until it was too late."

WHAT BEGAN AS Beveridge's dinner-table joke soon became an earnestly held belief. Perhaps it was the strain of life aboard the satellite, 10,000 miles above the Earth's surface. Perhaps the tensions of a year's isolation from the rest of humanity were taking their toll. But, from a dinner-table jest, the concept soon became a source of serious discussion. And tension.

Tension wrapped cold fingers around them as the days passed. They agreed to operate in teams, never to let one out of another's sight, always to keep constant watch ... for there was no way of telling which of them harbored in his body or his mind Earth's potential destroyer.

Two days passed this way, and a third. Then Lal went for a walk in space—without a suit.

"He cracked," Gregson said, staring at the Indian's corpse. "This crazy alien business—it just broke him apart."

"Yes," Lasseux said moodily. "The tension ... the looking and spying ... he couldn't take it anymore. Our first casualty. But not the last, I fear."

Beveridge and Gregson brought Lal's body in—it was orbiting around the Wheel—and a brief funeral service was conducted. The Indian's body was fed to the atomic converters that ran the station and consumed in an instant's blaze of light.

Lasseux radioed Earth and gave them a full account of the tragedy. He was told that a replacement for Lal would be on his way within a week or two.

"Now there are just four of us," he said, turning from the radio. "It will make keeping watch easier. I will team with Golovunoff for the rest of the day; you two English-speakers can work together."

They did. It was a cold, cheerless day. The little Indian had added an exotic spark to the group that was missing now and the tragic nature of his death dampened everyone's spirits.

Then Beveridge suggested, "Perhaps Lal was the one carrying the alien. When he discovered the truth he ran out into space, killing himself and the alien...?"

"No," Gregson said. "Why would he wait so long? Lal was the type to do such a thing the moment he found out. Besides, the alien wouldn't be bothered by space if it has no body."

"Damn; you're right. Just trying to cheer things, old man. Just trying...."

Suddenly the sound of a pistol-shot echoed through the chambers of the space satellite. The crewmen always carried pistols as safeguards against one another.

"You hear that?" Gregson said.

Beveridge nodded.

Moments later Lasseux came running into the chamber, muttering excitedly and incoherently to himself in French. He carried a smoking gun in his hand. Gregson and Beveridge immediately drew but Lasseux raised his other hand and dropped the gun.

"Calm yourself!" Gregson ordered, shaking Lasseux roughly. "Calm down! What happened!"

The flow of French finally ceased. Lasseux made a visible effort to master himself and said. "Golovunoff—the Russian—*he* was the alien!"

"What?"

"I saw him change shape," Lasseux gasped. "He seemed to waver for a moment when he thought I wasn't looking. The edges of his body blurred. It was awful! Then he saw me—and I shot him!"

"Is he dead?"

"Yes! Yes! I sealed off the chamber, so the alien couldn't escape if it's still alive." Lasseux was trembling violently. Beveridge and Gregson, pale, stared at him.

"Two men dead," Gregson said. "And we don't know if we've killed the creature yet. Or if there really is a creature," he added more silently to himself.

Then—"Great God! *Lasseux!*"

Gregson gaped. The Frenchman was ... *wavering*. It was the only way to describe it. He seemed to be blurring and shifting mistily, but only for an instant.

An instant was long enough. Gregson had his gun out and pumped three shots into

Lasseux's body. The Frenchman looked incredulously at him a moment, then crumpled.

Gregson took four steps back and let the gun drop from his nerveless fingers. "It was a trick," he said in a half-whisper. "He killed the Russian and made up the story about him—but he couldn't control his own wavering! Lucky thing I got him first, wasn't it?" He turned to Beveridge for confirmation, but the Englishman was gazing at him sternly, coldly, almost angrily.

"He *was* wavering, wasn't he?" Gregson asked. "You saw it too—that sort of blurring?" The American knotted his hands tensely. "Well, now the alien's dead—unless it's taken a new host. You don't think that's possible, do you, Beveridge? I mean, if you shoot the body it's in, can it hop to the next person like that? Do you think…?"

"Yes," said the Englishman. "I think so."

He was wavering.

But *he* held the gun.

Gregson yelled once and charged madly toward Beveridge. The bullet caught him in mid-run and sent him spinning back toward the crumpled corpse of Lasseux. Coldly, Beveridge fired twice more, then stopped wavering.

Ten minutes later, the rain of bombs began to shower down on Earth.

👽 👽 👽

"Satellite of Death" first appeared in the December 1957 issue of Imagination Stories.

American author Randall Garrett (Gordon Randall Phillip David Garrett, 1927–1987) was an incredibly prolific contributor to such vintage science fiction magazines as Amazing Stories, Astounding, Fantastic, Imagination, *and* Infinity, *to name a few, under a variety of pseudonyms that included Gerald Vance, S. M. Tenneshaw, Ivar Jorgensen, Alexander Blade, and Robert Randall (in collaboration with Robert Silverberg).*

An incorrigible punster and cutup, Garrett was a favorite guest at SF conventions, befriending numerous fans and delighting them with his antics. He was posthumously honored in 1999 with a Sidewise Award for Alternate History, for his Lord Darcy fantasy series.

R is for Rocket.
S is for Space.
B is for...
Bradbury!

B³

ART BY ALLEN K

I, ROCKET

Ray Bradbury

Art by Virgil Finlay

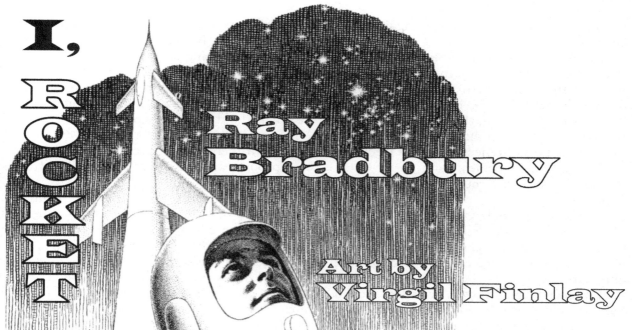

AT THE RATE THINGS ARE COMING AND GOING it'll take a few hundred years to break me down into rust and corrosion. Maybe longer. In the meantime, I'll have many days and nights to think it all over. You can't stop atoms from revolving and humming their life-orbits inside metal. That's how metal lives its own special life. That's how metal thinks.

Where I lie is a barren, pebbled plateau, touched here and there with pale weedy growths, a few hunched trees coming up out of planetoid rock.

There's a wind comes over the plateau every morning. There's rain comes in the twilight, and silence comes down even closer in the night. That's my whole life now, lying here with my jets twisted and my fore-plates bashed.

Somehow I feel I haven't fulfilled my destiny *in toto*. A rocket ship isn't built to lie on a hard gray plateau in the wind and rain—alone. After those trips through space it's almost too much to believe, that the rest of my days will be wasted here—

But while I'm rusting and wondering, I can think it all over. How I came to be here, how I came to be built....

I'VE TAKEN THEM ALL in their time, the crew; seen them wounded, crushed by centrifuge, or shattered by space-bombs; and once or twice I've had my rear-jets pounded off in a double-fisted foray: there's hardly a plate in my hull hasn't been welded again and again, not a chronometer in my control console hasn't been blasted and replaced.

But the hardest thing of all was replacing the men inside me. The little guys who ran around with greasy faces, yelling and fighting for air, and getting their guts frozen to their peritoneum every time I swung into an unexpected arc during the days when free gravity was experimental.

The little guys were hard to find, harder to replace after a particularly violent thrust between worlds. I loved the little guys, the little guys loved me. They kept me shining like a nickel moon, nursed me, petted me, and beat me when I deserved it.

From the very first I wanted to be of some help in the wild excursions from Earth to Deimos-Phobos coordinate Bases, the war moons held by Earth to strike against the Martians.

My birth-period, and the Base where I was integrated, skeleton, skin and innards, went through the usual birth-pains. It is a dim portion in my memory, but when the final hull was melted to me, the last rungway and console fitted to my hulk, the awareness was there. A metal awareness. The free electrical atom flow of metal come aware.

I could think and could tell nobody that I thought.

I was a war rocket. Fore and aft they placed their space-artillery nozzles, and weighted me with scarlet ammunition. I began to feel my purpose, expectantly, perhaps a bit impatiently.

I wasn't really alive yet. I was like a child half out of the womb, but not yet breathing or making any sound or making any movement. I was waiting for the slap on the back to give me strength and directed purpose.

"Hurry it up, hurry it up! Skip!" directed the munitions-lieutenant, standing by my opened airlocks that day so many years ago. Sunlight baked my metal as men hustled in and out with small rubber-tired trucks bearing the tetron space explosives. "We've got a war to meet!" cried the lieutenant.

The men hurried.

There was some fancy bit of business about a christening going on simultaneously with this scurrying about in my cargo cubicles. Some mayor from some city crashed a bottle of foaming liquor on my prow. A few reporters flicked their cameras and a small crowd put up their hands, waved them a fraction and put them down again, as if they realized how stupid it really was, wasting that fine champagne.

IT WAS THEN AND THERE I saw the captain, Metal bless him, for the first time. He came running across the field. The Master of my Fate, the Captain of my Soul. I liked him right off. He was short and whipped out of wrinkled hard brown leather, with green, implacable diamond eyes set in that hard leather, and a slit of white uneven teeth to show to anybody who disobeyed. He stomped into the airlock and set his clipping boots down and I knew I had my master. Small tight knuckle bones and wrists told that, and the way he made fists and the quick, smooth manner in which he cracked out the orders of the day:

"Snap it!" he said. "Get rid of that damned mayor out there! Clear apron! Seal the locks, clamp ports and we'll push the hell out of here!"

Yes, I liked him. His name was Lamb; ironic for a man lacking lamblike qualities. Captain Lamb, who threw his voice around inside me and made me like the steel edge to it. It was a voice like silk-covered brass knucks. It flowed like water, but burned like acid.

They rapped me tight. They expelled the mayor and his splintered champagne bottle, which by now seemed childish. Sirens shouted across the base apron. The crew did things to my alimentary canal. Twenty-seven of them.

Captain Lamb shouted.

That was the slap on the back that brought me my first breath, my first sound, my first movement. Lamb pounded me into living.

I threw out wings of fire and powder and air. The captain was yelling, snuggled in his crash-hammock, zippered up to his sharp chin; men were swaying, sweating in all their suspensory control hammocks. Quite suddenly I wasn't just metal lying in the sun anymore. I was the damnedest biggest bird that ever sang into the sky. Maybe my voice wasn't anything but thunder, but it was still singing to me. I sang loud and I sang long.

This was the first time I had been outside the hangar and the base to see the world.

I was surprised to find that it was round.

AS ADOLESCENCE IS TO MAN, his days from thirteen to eighteen when overnight his viewpoints are radically reformed, so it was with my first plunge into space. Life was thrown at me in one solid piece. All of the life I would ever know was given to me without apprenticeship, suckling or consideration. I had growing pains.

There were stresses, forces attacking me from all sides simultaneously, feelings, impressions I had never considered possible. The solid understandable gravity of Earth was suddenly taken away and the competition of space gravities each tried their luck with me.

The moon, and after the moon a thousand dark meteors crashing by, silent. Tides of space itself, indescribable, and the urge of stars and planets. And then a thing called momentum when my jets were cut and I moved without breathing or trying to move.

Captain Lamb sat in the control room, cracking his knuckles. "She's a good ship. A fine ship. We'll pound the holy marrow out of those Martians."

The young man by the name of Conrad sat beside the captain at the duo-control. "We'd better," he said anxiously. "There's a girl waiting in York Port for us to come back."

The captain scowled. "Both of you? You *and* Hillary?"

Conrad laughed. "The two of us. Both on the same war-rocket, going to the fray. At least I can keep my eye on that drunkard this way. I'll know he's not down in York Port scudding along on my acceleration...."

Captain Lamb usually said all his words quick, fast, like lines of mercury. "Space is a funny place to talk about love. Funny place to talk about anything. It's like laughing out loud in a big cathedral, or trying to make a waltz out of a hymn."

"Lo, the sentimentalist," remarked Conrad.

Lamb jerked. He scowled at himself, "Lo, the damned fool," he said, and got up to measure the control room with his little strides.

They were part of me. Lamb, Conrad and the crew. Like blood pulsing in the arteries of a warm body, like leucocytes and bacteria and the fluid that sustains them—air—locomoting through my chambers into my heart, my driving engines, feeding my livened appetites, never knowing that they were only units of energy like corpuscles giving a greater mass— myself—nourishment, life, and drive.

Like any body—there were microbes. Destroying elements. Disease, as well as the sentinel leucocytes.

We had one job to do. I knew of this. To fend off the ever increasing attacks against earth's Phobos-Deimos citadels. I felt tension spreading, growing as each day went by. There was too much cigarette smoking, lip biting, swearing among the crew-members. Big things lay ahead.

THE MICROBES within my body were in a small dosage; but virulent because they moved free, unchecked, unsuspected. Their names were Anton Larian and Leigh Belloc. I refer to them as bacteria simply because, like microscopic forms in a large body, their function was to poison and destroy me. And the best way to render me inactive would be the destruction of part of my red-blood. That meant Captain Lamb. Or part of his technical war-staff. Larian and Belloc planned for their poisoning, quietly, carefully.

Self-preservation is an eternal, all-encompassing thing. You find it in metal as you find it in amoebas; you find it in metal as you find it in men. My body would be attacked. From outside I feared nothing. From inside I was uncertain. Coming from an unexpected quarter that attack might kill me so very soon after my birth. I didn't approve of the idea.

I went through space toward Mars. I couldn't speak.

I could only feel voice-vibrations throughout my length. The voices of Hillary and Conrad arguing about their woman named Alice in York Port, and the captain snapping at the heels of his crew when we hit the asteroid-skirt, and then the subtle undercurrent of poison stirring in the midst of this—Larian and Belloc—their voices touched my hull:

"You're familiar with the plan, Belloc; I don't want you turning silly at the crisis."

"I know what to do. Don't worry. What the hell."

"All right, I'm just explaining. Now—as far as killing Captain Lamb, that's out. We're only two against twenty-four others. I want to be alive to collect that money we're guaranteed, for this—work."

"Logically, then—the engines...."

"I'm in favor of it, if you are. This is a war-rocket; spare parts, excess cargo, all that's eliminated for speed. Timebombs should work miracles with the main jet-engines. And when it happens we can be out and away in space in plenty of time?"

"When?"

"During the next shift of crew relief. There's a certain amount of inescapable confusion then. Half the crew's too tired to worry, the other half is just turning out, groggy."

"Sounds okay. Huh. It seems a damn shame though, in a way."

"What?"

"Nice new rocket, never tested before. Revolutionary design. I never enjoyed working on engines before, until I got my station with this jalopy. She's sweet. Those engines—sweet as the guts of a flower. And it all goes to hell before it has a chance to prove itself."

"You'll get paid for it. What else do you want?"

"Yeah, I'll get paid, won't I? Yeah."

"Shut up, then. Come on."

The routine circulation of crew-blood through the arteries of the ship took Larian and Belloc below to their stations in the fuel and engine cubicles. The poison was in my heart, waiting.

What went on inside my metal is not to be described. There are no similes, comparatives for the hard, imprisoned, frustrated vibrations that surge through tongueless *durasteel*. The rest of the blood in me was still good, still untouched and untainted and tireless.

"Captain." A salute.

"Belloc." Lamb returned the salute. "Larian."

"Captain."

"Going below?" said the captain. "Yes, sir."

"I'll be down in—" Lamb eyed his wristwatch. "Make it thirty minutes. We'll check the auxiliaries together, Belloc."

"Right, sir."

"Go on down, then."

Belloc and Larian descended.

LAMB WALKED QUICKLY into the computation cube and struck up a rapid word exchange with young Ayres. Ayres, who looked like he was barely out of blushing and floppy hair and semantics school, and still not shaving as often as the others. His pink face glowed when the captain was around. They got on like grandfather and grandson.

They probed charts together. When they finished, Lamb walked off the yardage in the computation room, scowling, examining his boots. Ayres computated.

Lamb paused, looked out the visual-port concernedly. After a moment he said, "When I was a very little kid I stood on the edge of the Grand Canyon, and I thought I'd seen everything there was to see—" A pause, "And now I've got my first captaincy, and—" he patted the hull of my body quietly "—a fine first-rate lady of a ship." Quick, to Ayres: "What are you, Ayres?"

Startled, Ayres blinked. "Me, sir?"

The captain stood with his strong, small back to Ayres, inspecting the stars as if they were a celestial regiment under his personal say-so. "Yes. I mean religion," he explained.

"Oh." Ayres pulled his right earlobe with finger and thumb, musing. "I was a first-class agnostic. Graduated, or should I say demoted? From an Atheist academy."

The captain kept looking at the stars. "You use the word *was*, Ayres. You emphasize that word."

Ayres half-smiled. "Sure. I mean—yes, sir. But this is my first trip, sir, so that changes things."

"Does it?"

"Yes, it does, sir."

The captain rocked casually on his heels. "How's that, Ayres?"

"You know the tale as well as I, sir. It's an old tale. And a good one, I might add. To put it one way: 'A Baptist is an atheist who took a trip to the Moon.'"

"That holds true for Methodists, Episcopalians and Holy Rollers, doesn't it?"

"It does, sir."

The captain made a noise that sounded like laughter. "We're all the same. Every damned one of us, Ayres. Hard-shelled God-fighters, good and true, when we're home in Brooklyn and Waushawkee. Take away land and gravity, though, and we're babes, undiapered and crying in a long dark night. Hell, there's not a man rocketing today who isn't religious, Ayres!"

"Are you religious, Captain?"

Lamb closed his mouth, looked out the port straight ahead. He raised one small-boned hand, spreading it in a measured movement. "It's always the same, Ayres. The first trip converts us. The very first trip. All you have to do is stand here for fifteen minutes or half an hour looking at space, feeling how insignificant you are flying around like a gnat in the middle of it, looking at those damned wonderful stars, and first thing you know you're down on your knees, crying your eyes out, with a hot stomach, a wild head and a humble attitude forever after."

Lamb pulled back from himself suddenly, snapped around, stalked to a down-ladder, grabbed a rung and glared at Ayres. "And so," he pointed out, "you'll notice that I never look at the stars too long! I've a ship to run—no time for it. And in case you believe all I tell you—go to hell! I should demerit you for questioning a superior!"

Lamb dropped down the rungs like a weight.

Ayres sat there a moment, trying to computate. After a while he looked up at the starport. His eyes dilated very dark and wide. He stood up. He walked across the computation room and stood there, staring out. He looked like he was listening to music. His lips moved.

"What did the Cap say? Stand here fifteen minutes or half an hour? Why, hell—" He bent his knees until they touched the deck. "I got the Cap's time beat all hollow!"

Good blood. Good leucocyte. Good Ayres.

• • •

MARS CAME UP AHEAD, the first really intense gravity I had felt since leaving earth and moon behind. It came up like a ruddy drop of dried blood on the void. Mass is the sexual drive of space, and gravity the intensified yearning of that mass, the gravitic libido of one tremendous body for the love, the following of any and all smaller bodies who transgress its void boundaries. I have heard the simple men within me speak of a planet as one speaks of a queen bee. The ultimate gravity toward which all smaller gravities and bodies yearn. Merciless harlot, mating with all, leading all on to destruction. Queen bee followed by the swarms. And now I was part of a swarm, the first of many yet to follow, answering the urge of one gravity, refusing another.

But still the poison was in me. And no way possible for Captain Lamb's crew to know of it. Time ticked on my console-chronometers and swung by, imperceptibly majestic in the moves of stars.

Captain Lamb went down to the engine rooms, examined my heart and my auxiliaries. Bitingly, he commented and instructed, interspersing that with vituperative barks. Then he hopped up the rungs to the galley for something to eat.

Belloc and Larian stayed below. "First now, Belloc, you checked the lifeboats?"

"I did. Number Three boat's ready. I fixed it an hour ago."

"Good. Now...."

THE SLOP PUT OUT a bowl of soup for Captain Lamb. Lamb pursed his lips to a spoon of it, and smacked them in appreciation. "Slop?"

"Yes, sir?" Slop wiped greasy hands on a large towel.

"Did you invent the gravity soup-bowl and gravity spoon?"

Slop looked at his feet. "I did, sir."

"An admirable invention, Slop. I recall the day when all rocket liquids were swilled by suction from a nippled bottle. Made me feel like a god-damned baby doing it."

Slop chuckled deep, as he returned to cleaning the mess-plates. "Ship gravity wasn't strong enough to hold soup down, so I thunk up the gravity spoon in my spare time. It helped."

The captain ate in silence. After a moment he said, "I must be getting old, Slop. I think I'm sick."

"Captain!"

Lamb waved his spoon, irritated. "Oh, nothing as bad as all that. I mean I'm getting soft-headed. Today, I feel—how should I put it? Dammit to hell, it's hard finding words. Why did you come along on this war-rocket, Slop?"

Slop twisted his towel tight. "I had a little job to do with some Martians who killed my parents three years ago."

"Yes," said the captain.

Belloc and Larian were down below.

Slop looked at his chief. At the tight little brown face that could have been thirty-five as easily as forty or fifty.

Lamb glared up at him, quick. Slop gulped. "Pardon me."

"Uh?"

"I was just wondering...?"

"About...?"

Belloc. Larian. Belloc down below. Larian climbing rungs, on his way to get the time-bombs. Mars looming ahead. Time getting shorter, shorter.

In a dozen parts of my body things were going on at an oblivious, unsuspecting norm. Computators, gunners, engineers, pilots performed their duties as Lamb and Slop talked casual talk in the galley. While Larian muscled it up the rungs toward his secreted time-explosives.

Slop said, "About why you became captain on a war-rocket, yourself, sir?"

"Me?" Lamb snorted, filled his mouth half a dozen times before answering very slowly. "Five years ago I was in a Blue Canal liquor dive on Mars. I met a Martian girl there...."

"Oh, yes...."

"Yes, *nothing*, you biscuit-burner! Damn but she was sweet. With a temper like a very fine cat-animal, and morals to match. Hair like glossy black spider-silk, eyes like that deep cold blue canal water. I wanted to bring her back to Earth with me. The war came, I was recalled and—"

"And someday," finished Slop, "when you've helped get the war over, you'll go looking for her. And being at Deimos-Phobos Base, maybe you can sneak down and kidnap her sometime."

Lamb ate awhile, making motions. "Pretty childish, isn't it?"

"No, I guess it's all right if she's still waiting."

"She is—if I know Yrela, she is."

Ayres in Computation.

Mars off in space, blood-red and growing.

Lamb in the galley.

Hillary and Conrad in control room One!

And down below, where all of my power grew and expanded and burst out into space, I felt the vibration of Belloc. And coming up the ladder to the supply room—Larian.

Larian passed through the galley. "Sir."

Lamb nodded without looking up from his meal.

Larian proceeded up to Computation, passed through Computation, whistling, and lingered in Supply AC.

Space vibrated with my message.

MY GUNS WERE BEING trimmed, oiled and ready. Ammunition passed up long powered tracks from Locker Five to Blister Fourteen. Scarlet ammunition. Men sweated and showed their teeth and swore. Belloc waited down below, his face twitching its nerves, in the engine room. The captain ate his meal. I drove through space. Ayres computated. Belloc waited. Captain, eating. Space. Larian. Time-bombs. Captain. Belloc. Guns. Waiting. Waiting. Driving.

The metal of my structure was sickened, stressing, striving inward, trying to shout, trying to tell all that I knew in my positive-negative poles, in my subatomic awareness, in my neutronic vibrations.

But the blood of my body moved with a mind of its own, pulsing from chamber to chamber in their sweating, greasy togs, with their waiting, tightened faces. Pulsing nervously. Pulsing, pulsing, pulsing, not knowing that soon poison might spread through every and all of my compartments.

And there was a girl named Alice waiting in York Port. And the memory of two parents dead. And on Mars a cool-eyed Martian dancing girl, still dancing, perhaps, with silver bells on her thumbs, tinkling. Mars was close. I made an angry jolt and swerve in space. I leaped with metal frustration!

Around and around and around went my coggery, the flashing, glinting muscles of my soul's heart. Oil surged through my metal veins. And Belloc was down below, smoking one cigarette after another.

I thought about Ayres, about Captain Lamb and the way he barked, about Ayres and the way he kneeled and felt what he had to feel. About Hillary and Conrad thinking about a woman's lips. About The Slop troubling to invent a gravity soup plate.

I thought about Belloc waiting.

And Mars getting near. And about the war I had never seen but always heard about. I wanted to be part of it. I wanted to get there with Lamb and Hillary and The Slop!

The Slop took away the plate the captain had cleaned with his spoon. "More?"

Lamb shook his head. "No. just a hunk of fruit now. An apple or something." He wiped his small mouth with the back of his hand.

"Okay," said The Slop.

At that moment there was a hiss, an explosion.

Somebody screamed, somewhere.

I knew who it was and where it was.

The captain didn't. "Dammit to hell!" he barked, and was out of the galley in three bounds. Slop dropped a soup kettle, following.

WARNING BELLS CLAMORED through me. Ayres, in Computation, grinding out a parabolic problem, jerked his young, pink face, and fear came into it instantly. He arose and tried walking toward the drop-rungs, but he couldn't do it. He didn't have legs for the job.

Conrad scuttled down the rungs, yelling. He vanished toward the engine room; the floor ate him up.

Hillary grabbed the ship-controls and froze to them, listening and waiting. He said one word. "Alice—"

Slop and the captain got there first in Section C.

"Cut that feed valve!" yelled Lamb. The Slop grasped a valve-wheel glinting on the wall in chubby fingers, twisted it, grunting.

The loud, gushing noise stopped. Steam-clouds billowed in my heart, wrapping Captain Lamb and The Slop tight and coughing. Conrad fell the rest of the way down the ladder into my heart, and the steam began to clear away as my vacuum ventilators began humming.

When the steam cleared they saw Belloc.

The Slop said, "Gahh. That's bad. That's *very* bad."

Conrad said, "How'd it happen? Looks like he died quick."

Lamb's leather-brown face scowled. "Quick is the word. That oil-tube burst, caught him like a steel whip across the bridge of his nose. If that hadn't killed him, scalding oil would have." Crumpled there, Belloc said not a word to anybody. He just bled where the oil pipe had caught him on the nose and cheek and plunged on back into his subconscious. That was all there was to him now.

Captain Lamb cursed. Conrad rubbed his cheek with the trembling flat of his hand. "I checked those oil-lines this morning. They were okay. I don't see—"

Footsteps on the rungs. Larian came down, feet first, quick, and turned to face them. "What happened...?" He looked as if somebody had kicked him in the stomach when he saw Belloc lying there, his face sucked bone-white, staring. His jaw dropped down and he said, emptily, "You—killed him. You—found out what we were going to do—and you killed him...."

The Slop's voice was blank. "What?"

"You killed him," repeated Larian. He began to laugh. He opened his mouth and let the laughter come out in the steam-laden room. He darted about suddenly and leaped up the rungs. "I'll show you!"

"Stop him!" said Lamb.

Conrad scuttled up at Larian's heels. Larian stopped and kicked. Conrad fell, heavy, roaring. Larian vanished. Conrad got up, yelling, and pursued. Captain Lamb watched him go, not doing anything himself, just watching. He just listened to the fading feet on the rungs, going up and up.

The deck and hull quivered under Lamb's feet.

Somebody shouted.

Conrad cried, from far off, "Watch it!"

There was a thumping noise.

Five minutes later Conrad came down the ladder lugging a time-bomb. "It's a good thing that oil-pipe burst, Cap. I found this in Supply AC. That's where Larian was hiding it. Him and Belloc—"

"What about Larian?"

"He tried to escape through an emergency lifeboat airlock. He opened the inner door, slammed it, and a moment later when I opened that same inner door, I almost got killed the same way—"

"Killed?"

"Yeah. The damned fool must have opened the outer door while he was still standing in the middle of the airlock. Space suction yanked him right outside. He's gone for good."

The Slop swallowed thickly. "That's funny, he'd do that. He knew how those airlocks work, how dangerous they are. Must've been some mistake, an accident, or something...."

"Yeah," said Captain Lamb. "Yeah."

They held Belloc's funeral a few hours later. They thrust him overboard, following Larian into space.

My body was cleansed. The organic poison was eliminated.

Mars was very close now. Red. Bright red.

In another six hours we would be engaged in conflict.

I HAD MY TASTE OF WAR. We drove down, Captain Lamb and his men inside me, and I put out my arms for the first time, and I closed fingers of power around Martian ships and tore them apart, fifteen of them—who tried to prevent our landing at Deimos-Phobos Base. I received only minor damage to my section F Plates.

Scarlet ammunition went across space, born out of myself. Child out of metal and exploding with blazing force, wounding the stratas of emptiness in the void. I exhilarated in my new-found arms of strength. I screamed with it. I talked rocket talk to the stars. I shook Deimos Base with my ambitious drive. Cap I dissected Martian ships with quick calm strokes of my ray-arms, and spunky little Lamb guided my vitals, swearing at the top of his lungs!

I had come into my own. I was fully grown, fully matured. War and more war, plunging on for month after month.

And young Ayres collapsed upon the computation deck one day, just like he was going to say a prayer, with a shard of shrapnel webbed in his lungs, blood dropping from his parted lips instead of a prayer. It reminded me of that day when first he had kneeled there and whispered, "Hell, I got the captain's time beat all hollow!"

Ayres died.

They killed Conrad, too. And it was Hillary who took the news back to York Port to the girl they had both loved.

After fourteen months we headed home. We landed in York Port, recruited men to fill our vacancies, and shot out again. We knocked holes in the vacuum. We got what we wanted out of war, and then, quite suddenly one day space was silent. The Martians retreated, Captain Lamb shrugged his fine-boned little shoulders and commanded his men down to the computation room:

"Well, men, it's all over. The war's over. This is your last trip in this damned nice little war-rocket. You'll have your release as soon as we take gravity in York Port. Any of you want to stay on—this ship is being converted into cargo-freighting. You'll have good berths."

The crew muttered, shifting their feet, blinking their eyes. Cap said: "It's been good. I won't deny it. I had a fine crew and a sweet ship. We worked hard, we did what we had to do. And now it's all over and we have peace. Peace."

The way he said that word, it meant something.

"Know what that means?" said Lamb. "It means getting drunk again, as often as you like; it means living on earth again, forgetting how religious you ever were out in space, how you were converted the first trip out. It means forgetting how non-gravity feels on your guts. It means a lot. It means losing friends, and the hard good times brawling at Phobos-Deimos Base.

"It means leaving this rocket."

The men were silent.

"I want to thank you. You, Hillary. And you, Slop. And you, Ayres, for sining on after your brother died. And you, Thompson, and McDonald and Priory. And that's about all.

"Stand by to land!"

We landed without fanfare.

The crew packed their duffles and left ship. Cap lingered behind awhile, walking through me with his short, brisk strides. He swore under his breath, twisted his small brown face. After a while he walked away, too.

I wasn't a war-rocket anymore. They crammed me with cargo and shipped me back and forth to Mars and Venus for the next five years. Five long years of nothing but spider-silk, hemp and mineral-ore, a skeleton crew and a quiet voyage with nothing happening. Five years.

I had a new captain, a new, strange crew, and a strange peaceful routine going and coming across the stars.

Nothing important happened until July 17th, 2243.

That was the day I cracked up on this wild pebbled little planetoid where the wind whined and the rain poured and the silence was too damned silent.

The crew was crushed to death inside me, and I just lay here in the hot sun and the cold night wind, waiting for rescue that never seemed to come.

My life blood was gone, dead, crushed, killed. A rocket thinks in itself, but it lives through its crew and its captain. I had been living on borrowed time since Captain Lamb went away and never came back.

I lay here, thinking about it all. Glorious months of war, savage force and power of it. The wild insanity of it. I waited. I realized how out of place I was here, how helpless, like a gigantic metal child, an idiot who needs control, who needs pulsing human life blood.

Until very early one morning, after the rain, I saw a silver speck on the sky. It came down fast—a one-man Patrol inspector, used for darting about in the asteroid belt.

The ship came down, landing about one hundred yards away from my silent hulk. A small man climbed out of it.

He came walking up the pebbled hill very slowly, almost like a blind man.

He stood at my airlock door. I heard him say, "Hello—"

And I knew who it was. Standing there, not looking much older than when first he had clipped aboard me, little and lean and made of copper wire and brown leather.

Captain Lamb.

After all these years. Dressed in a black patrol uniform. An inspector of asteroids. No cargo job for him. A dangerous one instead. Inspector.

His lips moved.

"I heard you were lost four months ago," he said to me, quiet-like. "I asked for an appointment to Inspector. I thought—I thought I'd like to hunt for you myself. Just—just for old time's sake." His wiry neck muscles stood out, and tightened. He made his little hands into fists.

He opened my airlock, laughing quietly, and walked inside me with his quick, short strides. It felt good to have him touch me again, to hear his clipped voice ring against my hull again. He climbed the rungs to my control room and stood there, swaying, remembering all the old times we had fought together.

"Ayres!"

"Aye, sir!"

"Hillary!"

"Aye, sir!"

"Slop!"

"Aye, sir!"

"Conrad!"

"Aye, sir!"

"Where in hell is everybody? Where in hell is everybody?" raged Lamb, staring about the control room. "Where in the damned hell—!"

Silence.

He quit yelling for people who couldn't answer him, who would never answer him again, and he sat down in the control chair and talked to me. He told me what he'd been doing all these years. Hard work, long hours, good pay.

"But it's not like it used to be," he told me. "Not by a stretched length. I think though—I think there'll be another war soon. Yes, I do." He nodded briskly. "And how'd you like to be in on it, huh? You can, you know."

I said nothing. My beams stretched and whined in the hot sun. That was all. I waited.

"Things are turning bad on Venus. Colonials revolting. You're old-fashioned, but you're proud and tall, and a fighter. You can fight again."

He didn't stay much longer, except to tell me what would happen. "I have to go back to Earth, get a rescue crew and try to lift you under your own power next week. And so help me God, I'll be captain of you again and we'll beat the bloody marrow out of those Venerians!"

He walked back through my compartments, climbed down into my heart. The galley. The computation. The Slop. Ayres. Larian. Belloc. Memories. And he walked out of the airlock with eyes that were anything but dry. He patted my hull.

"After all, now—I guess you were the only thing I ever really loved…."

He went away into the sky, then.

And so I'm lying here for a few more days, waiting with a stirring of my old anticipation and wonder and excitement. I've been dead a while. And Cap has showed up again to slap me back to life. Next week he'll be here with the repair crew and I'll sail home to Earth and they'll go over me from seam to seam, from dorsal to ventral.

And someday soon Cap Lamb'll stomp into my airlock, cry, "Rap her tight!" and we'll be off to war again! Off to war! Living and breathing and moving again. Captain Lamb and I and maybe Hillary and Slop if we can find them after all this time. Next week. In the meantime, I can think.

I've often wondered about that blue-eyed Martian dancing girl with the silver bells on her fingers.

I guess I could read it in Captain Lamb's eyes, how that turned out.

I wish I could ask him.

But at least I won't have to lie here forever. *I'll be moving on—next week!*

"I, Rocket" first appeared in the May 1944 issue of Amazing Stories. *In July 2020, at the 78th World Science Fiction Convention, the tale won the 1945 Retrospective Hugo Award for Best Short Story.*

Author and screenwriter Ray Bradbury (1920–2012) sold his first story in 1938, when he was 19, to Forrest J. Ackerman's fanzine, Imagination! *Later that year, Bradbury launched his own fanzine,* Futuria Fantasia, *which ran for four issues, each with a print run of less than 100 copies. Bradbury wrote most of the fanzine's content. It's from these humble beginnings that the 20th century's greatest and best-loved fantasist started on his literary journey.*

CONTINUED ON PAGE 116

ROCKET SUMMER

BY RAY BRADBURY

ART BY H. VESTAL

THE CROWD GATHERED TO MAKE A CURIOUS NOISE THIS COLD GREY MORNING BEFORE THE SCHEDULED BIRTH. They arrived in gleaming scarlet tumble-bugs and yellow plastic beetles, yawning and singing and ready. The Birth was a big thing for them.

He stood alone up in his high office tower window, watching them with a sad impatience in his grey eyes. His name was William Stanley, president of the company that owned this building and all those other work-hangars down on the tarmac, and all that landing field stretching two miles off into the Jersey mists. William Stanley was thinking about the Birth.

The Birth of *what*? Stanley's large, finely sculptured head felt heavier, older. Science, with a scalpel of intense flame would slash wide the skulls of engineers, chemists, mechanics in a titanic Caesarian, and out would come the Rocket!

"Yezzir! Yezzir!" he heard the far-off, faint and raucous declarations of the vendors and hawkers. "Buy ya Rocket Toys! Buy ya Rocket Games! Rocket Pictures! Rocket soap! Rocket teethers for the tiny-tot! Rocket, Rocket, Rocket! *Hey!*"

Shutting the open glassite frame before him, his thin lips drew tight. Morning after morning America sent her pilgrims to this shrine. They peered in over the translucent restraint barrier as if the Rocket were a caged beast.

He saw one small girl drop her Rocket toy. It shattered, and was folded under by the moving crowd's feet.

"Mr. Stanley?"

"Uh? Oh, Captain Greenwald. Sorry. Forgot you were here." Stanley measured his slow, thoughtful steps to his clean-topped desk. "Captain," he sighed wearily, "you're looking at the unhappiest man alive." He looked at Greenwald across the desk. "That Rocket is the gift of a too-generous science to a civilization of adult-children who've fiddled with dynamite ever since Nobel invented it. They—"

He got no further. The office door burst inward. A tall, work-grimed man strode swiftly in—all oil, all heat, all sunburnt, wrinkled leather skin. Rocket flame burnt in his dark, glaring eyes. He stopped short at Stanley's desk, breathing heavily, leaning against it.

Stanley noticed the wrench in the man's fist. "Hello, Simpson."

Simpson swore bitterly. "What's all this guff about you stopping the Rocket tomorrow?" he demanded.

Stanley nodded. "This isn't a good time for it to go up."

Simpson snorted. "This isn't a good time," he mimicked. Then he swore again. "By George, it's like telling a woman her baby's been still-born!"

"I know it's hard to understand—"

"Hard, *hell!*" shouted the man. "I'm Head Mechanic! I've worked two years! The others have worked, too! And the Rocket'll travel tomorrow or we'll know why!"

Stanley crushed out his cigar, inside his fist. The room swayed imperceptibly in his vision. Sometimes, one wanted to use a gun—he shook away the thought. He kept his tongue.

Simpson raged on. "Mr. Stanley, you have until three this afternoon to change your mind. We'll pull strings and you'll be out of your job by the weekend! If not—" and he said the next words very slowly, "how would your wife look with her head bashed in *Mister* Stanley?"

"You can't threaten me!"

The door slammed in Stanley's face. Simpson was gone.

CAPTAIN GREENWALD put out a manicured hand. On one slender finger shone a diamond ring. His wrist was circled by an expensive watch. His shiny brown eyes were invisibly cupped by contact lenses. Greenwald was past fifty inside; outside he seemed barely thirty. "I advise you to forget it, Stanley. Man's waited a million years for tomorrow."

Stanley's hand shook, lighting a cigarette. "Look here, Captain, where *are* you going?"

"To the stars, of course."

Stanley snapped out the alcohol match. "In the name of heaven, stop the melodrama and inferior semantics. What kind of thing is this you're handing the people? What'll it do to races, morals, men and women?"

Greenwald laughed. "I'm only interested in reaching the Moon. Then I'll come back to earth, and retire happily, and die."

Stanley stood there, tall and very grey. "Does the effect of the introduction of the crossbow to English and French history interest you?"

"Can't say I know much about it."

"Do you recall what gunpowder's invention did to civilization?"

"That's irrelevant!"

"You must admit if there'd been some subjective planning with the auto and airplane, millions of lives would've been saved, and many wars prevented. An ethical code should've been written for all such inventions and strictly observed, or else the invention forfeited."

Greenwald shook his head, grinning. "I'll let you handle that half of it. I'll do the traveling. I'm willing to abide by any such rules, if you'll draw them up and enforce them. All I want is to reach the Moon first. I've got to get downstairs now. We're still loading the ship, you know, in spite of your decree. We expect to get around you somehow. I'm sympathetic, of course, to your beliefs. I'll do anything you say except ground the Rocket. I won't get violent, but I can't vouch for Simpson. He's a tough man, with strong notions."

They walked from the office to the dropper. Compression slid them down to ground level, where they stepped out, Stanley still re-emphasizing his beliefs. "—for centuries science has given humanity play-toys, ships, machines, guns, cars, and now a Rocket, all with supreme disregard for man's needs."

"Science," announced Greenwald as they emerged onto the tarmac, "has produced, via private enterprise, greater amounts of goods than ever in history! Why, consider the medical developments!"

"Yes," said Stanley doggedly, "we cure man's cancer and preserve his greed in a special serum. They used to say 'Starve a cold, stuff a fever.' Today's fever is materialism. All the things science has produced only touch the *Body*. When Science invents something to touch the Mind, I'll give it its due. No.

"You cloak your voyage with romantic terminology. Outward to the stars! you cry! Words! What's the *fact*? Why, *why* this rocket? Greater production? We have *that*! Adventure? Poor excuse to uproot Earth. Exploration? It *could* wait a few years. Lebensraum? Hardly. *Why*, then, Captain?"

"Eh?" murmured Greenwald distractedly. "Ah. Here's the Rocket, now."

They walked in the incredible Rocket shadow. Stanley looked at the crowd beyond the barrier. "*Look* at them. Their sex still a mixture of Victorian voodoo and clabbered Freud. With education needing reorientation, with wars threatening, with religion and philosophy confused, you want to jump off into space!"

Stanley shook his head. "Oh, I don't doubt your sincerity, Captain. I just say your timing's poor. If we give them a Rocket toy to play with, do you honestly think they'll solve war, education, unity, thought? Why, they'd propel themselves away from it so quickly your head'd swim! Wars would be fought between worlds. But if we want more wars, let's have them *here*, where we can get at their sources, before we leap to the asteroids seeking our lost pride of race.

"What little unity we *do* have would be broken by countries and individuals clamoring and cut-throating for planets and satellites!"

Pausing, Stanley saw the mechanics standing in the Rocket shadow, hating him. Outside the barrier, the crowd recognized him; their murmur grew to a roar of disapproval.

Greenwald indicated them. "They're wondering why you waited so long before deciding to stop the Rocket."

"Tell them I thought there'd be laws controlling it. Tell them the corporations played along, smiling and bobbing to me, until the Rocket was completed. Then they threw off their false faces and withdrew the legislation only this morning. Tell them that, Captain. And tell them the legislation I planned would've meant a slow, intelligent Rocket expansion over an era of three centuries. Then ask them if they think any business man could wait even five *minutes*."

Captain Greenwald scowled. "All I want to do is prove it can be done. After I come back down, if I can help in any way to control the Rocket, I'm your man, Stanley. After I *prove* it's possible, I don't care what in hell happens...."

Stanley slid into his 'copter, waved morosely at the captain. The crowd shouted, waved its fists at him over the barrier. He sat watching their distorted, sullen faces. They detested him. The Rocket balloon man, the Rocket soap man, the tourists detested him.

What was more, when his son Tommy found out, Tommy would hate him, too.

HE TOOK HIS TIME, heading home. He let the green hills slide under. He set the automatic pilot and sank back into the sponge-softness, suspended in a humming, blissful dream. Music played. Cigarettes and whiskey were in reach if he desired them. Soft music. He could lapse back into the dreaming tide, dissolve worry, smoke, drink, chortle luxuriously, sleep, forget, pull a shell of synthetic, hypnotizing objects in about himself.

And wake ten years from today with his wife disintegrating swiftly in his arms. And one day see his son's skull shattered against a plastic wall.

And his own heart whirled and burst by some vast atom power of a starship passing Earth far out in space!

He dumped the whiskey over the side, followed it with the cigarettes. Finally, he clicked off the soft music.

There was his home. His eyes kindled. It lay out upon a green meadow, far from the villages and towns, salt-white and surrounded by tapered sycamores. As he watched, lowering his 'copter, he saw the blonde streak across the lawn; that was his daughter, Alyce. Somewhere else on the premises his son gamboled. Neither of them feared the dark.

Angrily, Stanley poured on full speed. The landscape jerked and vanished behind him. He wanted to be alone. He couldn't face them yet. Speed was the answer. Wind whistled, roared, rushed by the hurtling 'copter. He rammed it on. Color rose in his cheeks.

THERE WAS MUSIC in the garden as he parked his 'copter in the fine blue plastic garage. Oh, beautiful garage, he thought, you contribute to my peacefulness. Oh, wonderful garage, in moments of torment, I think of you, and I am glad I own you.

Like hell.

In the kitchen, Althea was whipping food with mechanisms. Her mother sat with one withered ear to the latest audio drama. They glanced up, pleased.

"Darling, so early!" she cried, kissing him. "How's the Rocket?" piped mother-in-law. "My, I bet you're proud!"

Stanley said nothing.

"Just imagine." The old woman's eyes glowed like little bulbs. "Soon we'll breakfast in New York and supper on Mars!"

Stanley watched her for a long moment, then turned hopefully to Althea. "What do *you* think?"

She sensed a trap. "Well, it would be different, wouldn't it, vacationing our summers on Venus, winters on Mars—wouldn't it?"

"Oh, good Lord," he groaned. He shut his eyes and pounded the table, softly. "Good Lord."

"*Now* what's wrong. What did *I* say?" demanded Althea, bewildered.

He told them about his order preventing the flight.

Althea stared at him. Mother reached and snapped off the audio. "*What* did you say, young man?"

He repeated it.

Into the waiting silence came a distant "psssheeew!" rushing in from the dining room, flinging the kitchen door wide, his son ran in, waving a bright red Rocket in one grimy fist. "Psssheeew! I'm a Rocket! Gangway! Hi, Dad!" He swung the ship in a quick arc. "Gonna be a pilot when I'm sixteen! Hey." He stopped. "What's everybody standing around for?" He looked at Grandma. "Grammy?" He looked at his mother. "Mom?" And finally at his father. "Dad...?" His hands sank slowly. He read the look in his father's eyes. "Oh, gosh."

BY THREE O'CLOCK that afternoon, he had showered and dressed in clean clothes. The house was very silent. Althea came and sat down in the living room and looked at him with hurt, stricken eyes.

He thought of quoting a few figures at her. Five million people killed in auto accidents since the year 1920. Fifty thousand people killed every year, *now*, in 'copters and jet-planes. But it wasn't in the figures, it was in a feeling he had to make her *feel*. Maybe he could illustrate it to her. He picked up the hand-audio, dialed a number. "Hello, Smitty?"

The voice on the other end said, clearly, "Oh, Mr. Stanley?"

"Smitty, you're a good average man, a pleasant neighbor, a fine farmer. I'd like your opinion. Smitty, if you knew a war was coming, would you help prevent it?"

Althea was watching and listening.

Smitty said, "Hell, yes. Sure."

"Thanks, Smitty. One more thing. What's your opinion of the Rocket?"

"Greatest thing in history. Say, I heard you were going to—"

Stanley did not want to get involved. He hurriedly excused himself and hung up. He looked directly at his wife. "Did you notice the separation of means from end? Smitty thinks two things. He thinks he can prevent war; that's one. He thinks the Rocket is a great thing; that's number two. But they don't match, unfortunately.

"The Rocket isn't a means to happiness the way it'll be used. It's the wrong means. And with a wrong means you invariably wind up with a wrong end. A criminal seeks wealth. Does he get it? Temporarily. In the end, he suffers. All because he took the wrong *means*." Stanley held his hands out, uselessly. "How can I make you understand."

Tears were in her eyes. "I understand *nothing*, and don't need to understand! Your job, they'll take it away from you and fly the Rocket anyway!"

"I'll work on the legislation again, then!"

"And perhaps be killed? No, please, Will."

Killed. He looked at his watch. Exactly three.

He answered the audio when it buzzed. "Stanley talking."

"Stanley, this is Cross, at Cal-Tech."

"Cross! Good Lord, it's good to hear you!"

"I just heard the news-flash," said Cross. He had the same clipped, exact voice he'd had years ago, Stanley realized. "You're really on the spot this time, aren't you, Will? That's why I called. I like your ideas on machinery. I've always thought of machines, myself, as nothing but extensions of man's frustrations and emotions, his losses and compensations in life. We agree. But you're wrong this time, Will. You made a mistake today."

"Now, don't *you* start on me! You're my last friend," retorted Stanley tiredly. "What else could I do—destroy the rocket?"

"That would be negative. No good. Give them something positive. Tell them to go ahead," advised Cross, pleasantly enough. "Warn them, like a kindly father, of the consequences. Then, when their fingers are burnt—"

"Humanity might go down the drain," finished Stanley abruptly.

"Not if you play your cards right, control the variables. There must be some way around them without getting yourself mangled. I'm ready to help when you have a plan. Think it over."

"I still think blowing the damn thing up would be—"

"They'd build a bigger one. And they'd persecute you and your family the rest of your life," explained Cross logically. "You and I may know that science hasn't contributed one whit to man's *mental* progress, but Mr. Everyman likes his babies diapered in disposable tissues and likes to travel from Siberia to Johnstown like an infuriated bullet. You can't stop them, you can only divert them a bit."

Stanley grasped the hand-audio, tightly. He listened.

A GREAT ROAR OF 'copters sounded out in the afternoon sky, directly overhead. The house shook. Althea sprang up lithely and ran to look out. "I can't talk any more, Cross. I'll call you back. *They're* outside, waiting for me, now...."

Cross' voice faded like a dream. "Remember what I tell you. Let them go ahead."

Stanley walked to the door, opened it, stepped half through.

A radio voice boomed out of the bright blue sky.

"STANLEY!" it shouted. It was Simpson's voice.

"STANLEY! COME OUT AND TALK! COME OUT AND TELL US, STANLEY! STANLEY!"

Althea would not stay in. She walked with him out onto the moist green lawn, in the open.

The heavens were flooded with 'copters whirling. The sun shook in its place. 'Copters hung everywhere, like huge hummingbirds, swiveling, whirring. Five hundred of them, at least, shadowing the lawns and shaking the housetops.

"OH, *THERE* YOU ARE, STANLEY!"

Stanley shaded his eyes. His lips drew away from his teeth in a grimace, as he stared upward, tense and afraid.

"IT'S AFTER THREE O'CLOCK, STANLEY!" came the dull boom of words.

In this moment, with the spiraling 'copters suspended over his lawn, over his wife and children and house, over himself and his beliefs, Stanley swallowed, stepped back, put his hands down and let the idea grow within him. Yes, he would give them their rocket. He would give it to them. You cannot fight the children, he thought. They must have their green apples. If you refuse them, they will find a way around you. Go along with their illogical tide and make logic of it. Let the children eat their full of green apples, many, many green apples to swell their vast stomach into sickness. Yes. A slow smile touched the corners of his mouth, vanished. The plan was complete.

The voice from the sky fell on him like an iron fist! "STANLEY! WHAT IS YOUR WORD NOW? HOW WILL YOU SPEAK NOW? WITH A THOUSAND POUNDS OF NITROGLYCERINE OVER YOUR HOME, HOW WILL YOU TALK?"

The 'copters sank, malignantly. Thunder swept the lawn. Althea's brilliant amber skirt flared in the wash of it.

"WILL THE ROCKET FLY, STANLEY?"

From the corners of his aching, straining eyes, Stanley saw his son poised in the window, watching him.

"RAISE YOUR RIGHT HAND AND WAVE IT," thundered the sky-voice. "IF THE ANSWER IS YES!"

Stanley made them wait for it. He wetted his lips with a slow tongue, then, gradually, very casually, he raised his right hand, palm up, and waved it to the thundering sky.

A torrent of exultation poured in a Niagara from the heavens. Five hundred audios blasted, cheered, exulted! The trees ripped and tore in the cyclone of energy and explosion! The noise continued as Stanley turned, took Althea's elbow, and steered her blindly back to the door.

•••

THE LITTLE BLACK-JET-PLANE dropped out of the midnight stars. Moments later, Cross was getting out of it, crossing the dark lawn, grasping Stanley's hand warmly. "Made good time, eh?"

Inside, they downed their glasses of brandy first, then got to business. Stanley outlined his plan, his contacts, his psychology. He was pleased and excited to see an extraordinary smile of approval come to Cross's pink, round face. "Excellent! Now you're talking!" cried Cross.

"I like your plan, Stanley. It places the blame right back on the people. They won't be able to persecute you."

Stanley refilled the glasses. "I'll see to it you're on the Rocket tomorrow. Greenwald—he's the captain—will cooperate, I'm certain, when the trip is over. It's up to you and Greenwald then."

They raised their glasses. "And when it's all over," observed Cross slowly. "We'll have the long, hard struggle to revise our educational system. To begin to apply the scientific method to man's thinking, instead of just to his machines. And when we've built a logical subjective world, then it'll be safe to make machines of all and any kinds. Here's to our plan, may it be completed." They drank.

The next day two million people spread over the rolling hills, through the tiny Jersey towns, sitting atop bugs and plastic beetles. An excitement pervaded the day. The sky was a blue vacuum, the 'copters grounded by law. The Rocket lay gleaming and monstrous and silent.

At noon, the crew ambled across the tarmac, Captain Greenwald leading. Cross walked among them. The huge metal doors slammed, and with a blast of Gargantuan flame, the Rocket heaved upward and vanished.

People cheered and laughed and cried.

Stanley watched his son and daughter and mother-in-law do likewise. He was deeply pleased to see that Althea did not join them. Hand in hand they watched the sky dazzlement fade. The first Rocket to the moon was gone. The world was drunkenly happy in its delirium.

Two weeks passed slowly. Astronomers were unable to keep an eye on the Rocket. It was so small and unaccountable in the void between earth and lunar surface.

Stanley slept little in the passing of the fourteen days. He was constantly attacked by fears and confusions of thought. He dreamed of the Rocket going up. He had seen men month on month walking in the metal shadow of their wonderful Rocket, patting it with their greasy, calloused hands, loving it with their quick, appreciative eyes.

If for one moment you let yourself think of it, you loved it, too, for even though it symbolized wars and destruction, you had to admire its balance and slenderness of structure. With it, you could rub away the fog cosmetic of Venus, re-delineate its prehistorically shy face. And there was Mars, too. Man had been imprisoned a million years. Why not freedom now, at last?

Then he labeled all these fantasies by their correct name, ESCAPE, and settled back, to wait the return of the Rocket.

"THE MOON ROCKET is returning! It will land this morning at nine o'clock!" Everybody's audio was blatting.

Like a yellow seed, the Rocket dropped down the sky, to sprout roots of flame on which to cushion itself. It fried the tarmac and a vast deluge of warm air rushed across the country for miles. People sweltered amidst a sudden rocket summer.

In his tower room, William Stanley watched, solemn and wordless.

The Rocket shimmered. Across the cooling tarmac, the crowd rioted, bursting through the barrier, sweeping the police aside in elation.

The tide halted and boiled and changed form, layer upon layer. A vast hush came upon it.

Now the round airlock door of the Rocket jetted out air in a compressed sigh.

The thick door, sandwiched into the ship-hull, took two minutes to come outward and pull aside on its oiled hingework. The crowd

pressed closer, flesh to flesh, eyes widened. The door was now open completely. A great cheer went up. The crew of the Moon Rocket stood in the airlock. The cheer faded, almost instantly.

The crew of the Rocket were not exactly standing. They were hunched over.

The captain stepped forward. Well, he didn't exactly *step*. He sort of dragged his feet and shambled. He made a speech.

But all it sounded like, coming from his twisted, swollen lips, was, "Uns—rrrr—oh—god—disss—ease—unh—rrr—nnn—"

He held out his grey-green fingers, raw, bleeding, for all to see. He lifted his face. Those red things, were they actually eyes? That depression, that fallen socket, had it been a nose? And where were the teeth in that gagging, hissing mouth? His hair was thin and grey and infected. He stank.

The hypnotic silence was shattered. The first line of people turned and clawed at the second line. The second turned instinctively to claw the third, and so on. The television cameras caught it all.

Screams, yelling, shouting. Many fell and were trampled, crushed under. The captain and his crew came out, gesturing, calling them to come back. But who would heed their rotting movements? The ridiculous souvenir seekers trampled each other, ripping the clothes from one another's backs!

A souvenir? A scab of crawling flesh, a drop of yellow fluid from their gaping wounds? Souvenirs for earth, buy them right here, get them while they last! We mail anywhere in the United States!

The characters in order of appearance: The Captain, the astrogator, held sagging between two astronomers, who were followed by sixteen mathematicians, technicians, chemists, biologists, radio men, geographers and machinists. Shamble forth, gentlemen, and bring the brave new future with you!

The balloon vendor, in flight, jettisoned his entire stock. Rubber rockets floated wildly, crazily bobbling, bouncing the river of rioting heads until they were devoured, exploded and crumpled underfoot.

Sirens sounded. Police beetles rushed to the field exits. Ten minutes later the tarmac was empty. No sign of captain or crew. A few shreds of their fetid clothing were found, partially disintegrated. An audio-report five minutes later stated simply, "The captain and crew were destroyed on orders of the health bureau! An epidemic was feared—"

The sounds of riot faded. The door to Stanley's office opened, someone entered and stood behind him, and closed the door.

STANLEY DID NOT TURN from the window for a moment. "Fifty people injured, five of them critically. I'm sorry for that. But it was a small price for the world's security." He turned, slowly.

A horrible creature stood, diseased and swollen, before him. A captain's uniform, filthy and torn, hung tattered from the disgusting flesh. The creature opened its bleeding mouth.

"How was it?" asked the creature, muffledly.

"Fine," said Stanley. "Did you reach the moon?"

"Yes," replied the creature. "Captain Greenwald sends his regards to you. He says he knows we can do it again and again, any time we want, now, and that's all he wanted to know. He wishes you luck and tells you to go ahead. We landed the rocket on the way back from the moon, first of all, up at Fairbanks, Alaska, outside the settlement, naturally, during the night. Things worked as you planned them. We changed crews there. There was a minor fight. Simpson and the original crew, including Captain Greenwald, are still up there, under psycho-hypnosis. They'll live out their lives happily, unaware, with new names. They won't remember anything. We took off from Fairbanks again this morning with the new crew and our act all rehearsed, I think we did all right."

"Where's the substitute crew now?" inquired Stanley.

"Downstairs," said the creature. "Getting psychoed themselves. Getting mental blocs inserted, so they'll forget they ever fooled the world today. Then we'll send them back to their regular jobs. Can I use your shower?"

Stanley pressed a button, a panel slid aside. "Go ahead."

The creature pulled its face around the edges until it shed off into its hands, a green-grey pallid mask of plastic rubber. The sweating pink face of Cross appeared. He wriggled his fingers next, until the green-gray, chemically bleeding horror gloves sucked off. He tossed these into a wall-incinerator.

"The day of the Rocket is over," he said, quietly. "They'll be putting your bill up before the World Legislature tomorrow, or I miss my guess. Carefulness, thought and intellect will now get a start. Humanity is saved from itself."

Stanley watched Cross walk into the shower-cube, peel, and switch on the spray.

He turned to the window again. Two billion people were thinking tonight. He knew what they were thinking. Outside, he heard the explosion as the health department blew up the great Rocket.

That was all. The sound of water on the shower-tiles was a good clean sound.

> *"Rocket Summer" first appeared in the Spring 1947 issue of* Planet Stories, *and should not be confused with the short, similarly titled narrative bridge "January 1999: Rocket Summer" which Bradbury wrote in 1950 for his classic fix-up novel* The Martian Chronicles.
>
> *Ray Bradbury wrote habitually, rarely missing a day. Early in his career, he often tapped out pages on borrowed or rented typewriters, in local libraries or at the YMCA. Over the next 70-plus years, he produced about 600 stories and over two dozen novels and collections, as well as scores of film and television scripts. His work has been adapted for radio and comics, translated into over 36 languages, and has sold over 8 million copies. His most famous and critically praised work is* Fahrenheit 451, *a cautionary novel depicting the perils of censorship.*
>
> *Bradbury once described his avocation as "a God-given thing, and I'm so grateful, so, so grateful. The best description of my career as a writer is 'at play in the fields of the Lord.'"*
>
> *In 2005, Bradbury was awarded an honorary degree of Doctor of Laws, by the National University of Ireland. In 2007, he was made a Commander of the Order of the Arts and Letters, by the French government. And in 2009 he was awarded an Honorary Doctorate by Columbia College, Chicago. Not bad for a self-taught writer who never attended a single day of college, let alone earned a degree. But then, Bradbury never obtained a driver's license, either. Hence, for most of his life, he bicycled or relied on public transportation.*

CONTINUED ON PAGE 123

MORGUE SHIP

By RAY BRADBURY   Illustration by JOSEPH DOOLIN

H E HEARD THE STAR-PORT GRIND OPEN, AND THE MOVEMENT OF THE METAL CLAWS GROPING INTO SPACE, AND THEN THE STAR-PORT CLOSED.

There was another dead man aboard the *Constellation*.

Sam Burnett shook his long head, trying to think clearly. Pallid and quiet, three bodies lay on the cold transparent tables around him; machines stirred, revolved, hummed. He didn't see them. He didn't see anything but a red haze over his mind. It blotted out the far wall of the laboratory where the shelves went up and down, numbered in scarlet, keeping the bodies of soldiers from all further harm.

Burnett didn't move. He stood there in his rumpled white surgical gown, staring at his fingers gloved in bone-white rubber; feeling all tight and wild inside himself. It went on for days. Moving the ship. Opening the star-port. Extending the retriever claw. Plucking some poor warrior's body out of the void.

He didn't like it any more. Ten years is too long to go back and forth from Earth to nowhere. You came out empty and you went back full-cargoed with a lot of warriors who didn't laugh or talk or smoke, who just lay on their shelves, all one hundred of them, waiting for a decent burial.

"Number ninety-eight." Coming matter of fact and slow, Rice's voice from the ceiling radio hit Burnett.

"Number ninety-eight," Burnett repeated. "Working on ninety-five, ninety-six and ninety-seven now. Blood-pumps, preservative, slight surgery." Off a million miles away his voice was talking. It sounded deep. It didn't belong to him anymore.

Rice said:

"Boyohbody! Two more pick-ups and back to New York. Me for a ten-day drunk!"

Burnett peeled the gloves off his huge, red, soft hands, slapped them into a floor incinerator mouth. Back to Earth. Then spin around and shoot right out again in the trail of the war-rockets that blasted one another in galactic fury, to sidle up behind gutted wrecks of ships, salvaging any bodies still intact after the conflict.

Two men. Rice and himself. Sharing a cozy morgue ship with a hundred other men who had forgotten, quite suddenly, however, to talk again.

Ten years of it. Every hour of those ten years eating like maggots inside, working out to the surface of Burnett's face, working under the husk of his starved eyes and starved limbs. Starved for life. Starved for action.

This would be his last trip, or he'd know the reason why!

"Sam!"

Burnett jerked. Rice's voice clipped through the drainage-preservative lab, bounded against glassite retorts, echoed from the refrigerator shelves. Burnett stared at the tabled bodies as if they would leap to life, even while preservative was being pumped into their veins.

"Sam! On the double! Up the rungs!"

Burnett closed his eyes and said a couple of words, firmly. Nothing was worth running for anymore. Another body. There had been one hundred thousand bodies preceding it. Nothing unusual about a body with blood cooling in it.

SHAKING HIS HEAD, he walked unsteadily toward the rungs that gleamed up into the airlock, control-room sector of the rocket.

He climbed without making any noise on the rungs.

He kept thinking the one thing he couldn't forget.

You never catch up with the war.

All the color is ahead of you. The drive of orange rocket traces across stars, the whamming of steel-nosed bombs into elusive targets, the titanic explosions and breathless pursuits, the flags and the excited glory are always a million miles ahead.

He bit his teeth together.

You never catch up with the war.

You come along when space has settled back, when the vacuum has stopped trembling from unleashed forces between worlds. You come along in the dark quiet of death to find the wreckage plunging with all the fury of its original acceleration in no particular direction. You can only see it; you don't hear anything in space but your own heart kicking your ribs.

You see bodies, each in its own terrific orbit, given impetus by grinding collisions, tossed from mother ships and dancing head over feet forever and forever with no goal. Bits of flesh in ruptured spacesuits, mouths open for air that had never been there in a hundred billion centuries. And they kept dancing without music until you extended the retriever-claw and culled them into the airlock.

That was all the war-glory he got. Nothing but the stunned, shivering silence, the memory of rockets long gone, and the shelves filling up all too quickly with men who had once loved laughing.

You wondered who all the men were; and who the next ones would be. After ten years you made yourself blind to them. You went around doing your job with mechanical hands.

But even a machine breaks down....

"SAM!" Rice turned swiftly as Burnett dragged himself up the ladder. Red and warm, Rice's face hovered over the body of a sprawled enemy official. "Take a look at this!"

Burnett caught his breath. His eyes narrowed. There was something wrong with the body; his experienced glance knew that. He didn't know what it was.

Maybe it was because the body looked a little *too* dead.

Burnett didn't say anything, but he climbed the rest of the way, stood quietly in the grey-metal airlock. The enemy official was as delicately made as a fine white spider. Eyelids, closed, were faintly blue. The hair was thin silken strands of pale gold, waved and pressed close to a veined skull. Where the thin-lipped mouth fell open a cluster of needle-tipped teeth glittered. The fragile body was enclosed completely in milk-pale syntha-silk, a holstered gun at the middle.

Burnett rubbed his jaw. "Well?"

Rice exploded. His eyes were hot in his young, sharp-cut face, hot and black. "Good Lord, Sam, do you know who this is?"

Burnett scowled uneasily and said no.

"It's Lethla!" Rice retorted.

Burnett said, "Lethla?" And then: "Oh, yes! Kriere's majordomo. That right?"

"Don't say it calm, Sam. Say it big. Say it big! If Lethla is here in space, then Kriere's not far away from him!"

Burnett shrugged. More bodies, more people, more war. What the hell. What the hell. He was tired. Talk about bodies and rulers to someone else.

Rice grabbed him by the shoulders. "Snap out of it, Sam. Think! Kriere—The All-Mighty—in our territory. His right-hand man dead. That means Kriere was in an accident, too!"

Sam opened his thin lips and the words fell out all by themselves. "Look, Rice, you're new at this game. I've been at it ever since the Venus-Earth mess started. It's been see-sawing back and forth since the day you played hookey in the tenth grade, and I've been in the thick of it. When there's nothing left but seared memories, I'll be prowling through the void picking up warriors and taking them back to the good green Earth. Grisly, yes, but it's routine.

"As for Kriere—if he's anywhere around, he's smart. Every precaution is taken to protect that one."

"But Lethla! His body must mean something!"

"And if it does? Have we got guns aboard this morgue-ship? Are we a battlecruiser to go against him?"

"We'll radio for help?"

"Yeah? If there's a warship within our radio range, seven hundred thousand miles, we'll get it. Unfortunately, the tide of battle has swept out past Earth in a new war concerning Io. That's out, Rice."

Rice stood about three inches below Sam Burnett's six-foot-one. Jaw hard and determined, he stared at Sam, a funny light in his eyes. His fingers twitched all by themselves at his sides. His mouth twisted, "You're one hell of a patriot, Sam Burnett!"

Burnett reached out with one long finger, tapped it quietly on Rice's barrel-chest. "Haul a cargo of corpses for three thousand nights and days and see how patriotic you feel. All those fine muscled lads bloated and crushed by space pressures and heat-blasts. Fine lads who start out smiling and get the smile burned off down to the bone—"

Burnett swallowed and didn't say anything more, but he closed his eyes. He stood there, smelling the death-odor in the hot air of the ship, hearing the chug-chug-chug of the blood pumps down below, and his own heart waiting warm and heavy at the base of his throat.

"This is my last cargo, Rice. I can't take it any longer. And I don't care much how I go back to earth. This Venusian here—what's his name? Lethla. He's number ninety-eight. Shove me into shelf ninety-nine beside him and get the hell home. That's how I feel!"

Rice was going to say something, but he didn't have time.

Lethla was alive.

He rose from the floor with slow, easy movements, almost like a dream. He didn't say anything. The heat-blaster in his white fingers did all the necessary talking. It didn't say anything either, but Burnett knew what language it would use if it had to.

Burnett swallowed hard. The body had looked funny. Too dead. Now he knew why. Involuntarily, Burnett moved forward. Lethla moved like a pale spider, flicking his fragile arm to cover Burnett, the gun in it like a dead, cold star.

Rice sucked in his breath. Burnett forced himself to take it easy. From the corners of his eyes he saw Rice's expression go deep and tight, biting lines into his sharp face.

Rice got it out, finally. "How'd you do it?" he demanded, bitterly. "How'd you live in the void? It's impossible!"

A crazy thought came ramming down and exploded in Burnett's head. *You never catch up with the war!*

But what if the war catches up with you?

What in hell would Lethla be wanting aboard a morgue ship?

LETHLA HALF-CROUCHED in the midst of the smell of death and the chugging of blood-pumps below. In the silence, he reached up with quick fingers, tapped a tiny crystal stud upon the back of his head, and the halves of a microscopically thin chrysalis parted transparently off of his face. He shucked it off, trailing air-tendrils that had been inserted, hidden in the uniform, ending in thin globules of oxygen.

He spoke. Triumph warmed his crystal-thin voice. "That's how I did it, Earthman."

"Glassite!" said Rice. "A face-molded mask of glassite!"

Lethla nodded. His milk-blue eyes dilated. "Very marvelously pared to an unbreakable thickness of one-thirtieth of an inch; worn only on the head. You have to look quickly to notice it, and, unfortunately, viewed as you saw it, outside the ship, floating in the void, not discernible at all."

Prickles of sweat appeared on Rice's face. He swore at the Venusian and the Venusian laughed like some sort of stringed instrument, high and quick.

Burnett laughed, too. Ironically. "First time in years a man ever came aboard the *Constellation* alive. It's a welcome change."

Lethla showed his needle-like teeth. "I thought it might be. Where's your radio?"

"Go find it!" snapped Rice, hotly.

"I will." One hand, blue-veined, on the ladder-rungs, Lethla paused. "I know you're weaponless; Purple Cross regulations. And this airlock is safe. Don't move." Whispering, his naked feet padded white up the ladder. Two long breaths later something crashed; metal and glass and coils. The radio.

Burnett put his shoulder blades against the wall-metal, looking at his feet. When he glanced up, Rice's fresh, animated face was spoiled by the new bitterness in it.

Lethla came down. Like a breath of air on the rungs. He smiled. "That's better. Now. We can talk—"

Rice said it, slow: "Interplanetary law declares it straight, Lethla! Get out! Only dead men belong here."

Lethla's gun grip tightened. "More talk of that nature, and only dead men there will be." He blinked. "But first—we must rescue Kriere...."

"Kriere!" Rice acted as if he had been hit in the jaw.

Burnett moved his tongue back and forth on his lips silently, his eyes lidded, listening to the two of them as if they were a radio drama. Lethla's voice came next:

"Rather unfortunately, yes. He's still alive, heading toward Venus at an orbital velocity of two thousand m.p.h., wearing one of these air-chrysali. Enough air for two more hours. Our flag ship was attacked unexpectedly yesterday near Mars. We were forced to take to the lifeboats, scattering, Kriere and I in one, the others sacrificing their lives to cover our escape. We were lucky. We got through the Earth cordon unseen. But luck can't last forever.

"We saw your morgue ship an hour ago. It's a long, long way to Venus. We were running out of fuel, food, water. Radio was broken. Capture was certain. You were coming our way; we took the chance. We set a small time-bomb to destroy the life-rocket, and cast off, wearing our chrysali-helmets. It was the first time we had ever tried using them to trick anyone. We knew you wouldn't know we were alive until it was too late and we controlled your ship. We knew you picked up all bodies for brief exams, returning alien corpses to space later."

Rice's voice was sullen. "A setup for you, huh? Traveling under the protection of the Purple Cross you can get your damned All-Mighty safe to Venus."

Lethla bowed slightly. "Who would suspect a Morgue Rocket of providing safe hiding for precious Venusian cargo?"

"Precious is the word for you, brother!" said Rice.

"Enough!" Lethla moved his gun several inches.

"Accelerate toward Venus, mote-detectors wide open. Kriere must be picked up—*now*!"

Rice didn't move. Burnett moved first, feeling alive for the first time in years. "Sure," said Sam, smiling. "We'll pick him up."

"No tricks," said Lethla.

Burnett scowled and smiled together. "No tricks. You'll have Kriere onboard the *Constellation* in half an hour or I'm no coroner."

"Follow me up the ladder." Lethla danced up, turned, waved his gun. "Come on."

Burnett went up, quick. Almost as if he enjoyed doing Lethla a favor. Rice grumbled and cursed after him.

On the way up, Burnett thought about it. About Lethla poised like a white feather at the top, holding death in his hand. You never knew whose body would come in through the star-port next. Number ninety-eight was Lethla. Number ninety-nine would be Kriere.

There were two shelves numbered and empty. They should be filled. And what more proper than that Kriere and Lethla should fill them? But, he chewed his lip, that would need a bit of doing. And even then the cargo wouldn't be full. Still one more body to get; one hundred. And you never knew who it would be.

He came out of the quick thoughts when he looped his long leg over the hole-rim, stepped up, faced Lethla in a cramped control room that was one glittering swirl of silver levers, audio-plates and visuals. Chronometers, clicking, told of the steady dropping toward the sun at a slow pace.

Burnett set his teeth together, bone against bone. Help Kriere escape? See him safely to Venus, and then be freed? Sounded easy, wouldn't be hard. Venusians weren't blind with malice. Rice and he could come out alive; if they cooperated.

But there were a lot of warriors sleeping on a lot of numbered shelves in the dim corridors of the long years. And their dead lips were stirring to life in Burnett's ears. Not so easily could they be ignored.

You may never catch up with the war again. The last trip!

Yes, this could be it. Capture Kriere and end the war. But what ridiculous fantasy was it made him believe he could actually do it?

Two muscles moved on Burnett, one in each long cheek. The sag in his body vanished as he tautened his spine, flexed his lean-sinewed arms, wet thin lips.

"Now, where do you want this crate?" he asked Lethla easily.

Lethla exhaled softly. "Cooperation. I like it. You're wise, Earthman."

"Very," said Burnett. He was thinking about three thousand eternal nights of young bodies being ripped, slaughtered, flung to the vacuum tides. Ten years of hating a job and hoping that someday there would be a last trip and it would all be over.

Burnett laughed through his nose. Controls moved under his fingers like fluid; loved, caressed, tended by his familiar touching. Looking ahead, he squinted.

"There's your Ruler now, Lethla. Doing somersaults. Looks dead. A good trick."

"Cut power! We don't want to burn him!"

BURNETT CUT. Kriere's milky face floated dreamily into a visual-screen, eyes sealed, lips gaping, hands sagging, clutching emptily at the stars.

"We're about fifty miles from him, catching up." Burnett turned to Lethla with an intent scowl. Funny. This was the first and the last time anybody would ever board the *Constellation* alive. His stomach went flat, tautened with sudden weakening fear.

If Kriere could be captured, that meant the end of the war, the end of shelves stacked with sleeping warriors, the end of this blind searching. Kriere, then, had to be taken aboard. After that—

Kriere, the All-Mighty. At whose behest all space had quivered like a smitten gong for part of a century. Kriere, revolving in his neat, water-blue uniform, emblems shining gold, heat-gun tucked in glossy jet holster. With Kriere aboard, chances of overcoming him would be eliminated. Now: Rice and Burnett against Lethla. Lethla favored because of his gun.

Kriere would make odds impossible.

Something had to be done before Kriere came in. Lethla had to be yanked off guard. Shocked, bewildered, fooled—somehow. But—how?

Burnett's jaw froze tight. He could feel a spot on his shoulder-blade where Lethla would send a bullet crashing into rib, sinew, artery—heart.

There was a way. And there was a weapon. And the war would be over and this would be the last trip.

Sweat covered his palms in a nervous smear.

"Steady, Rice," he said, matter of factly. With the rockets cut, there was too much silence, and his voice sounded guilty standing up alone in the center of that silence. "Take controls, Rice. I'll manipulate the star-port."

Burnett slipped from the control console. Rice replaced him grimly. Burnett strode to the next console of levers. That spot on his back kept aching like it was sear-branded X. For the place where the bullet sings and rips. And if you turn quick, catching it in the arm first, why—

Kriere loomed bigger, a white spider delicately dancing on a web of stars. His eyes flicked open behind the glassite sheath, and saw the *Constellation*. Kriere smiled. His hands came up. He knew he was about to be rescued.

Burnett smiled right back at him. What Kriere didn't know was that he was about to end a ten-years' war.

There was only *one* way of drawing Lethla off guard, and it had to be fast.

Burnett jabbed a purple-topped stud. The star-port clashed open as it had done a thousand times before; but for the first time it was a good sound. And out of the star-port, at Sam Burnett's easily fingered directions, slid the long claw-like mechanism that picked up bodies from space.

Lethla watched, intent and cold and quiet. The gun was cold and quiet, too.

The claw glided toward Kriere without a sound, now dream-like in its slowness.

It reached Kriere.

Burnett inhaled a deep breath.

The metal claw cuddled Kriere in its shiny palm.

Lethla watched.

He watched while Burnett exhaled, touched another lever and said: "You know, Lethla, there's an old saying that only dead men come aboard the *Constellation*. I believe it."

And the claw closed as Burnett spoke, closed slowly and certainly, all around Kriere, crushing him into a ridiculous posture of silence. There was blood running on the claw, and the only recognizable part was the head, which was carefully preserved for identification.

That was the only way to draw Lethla off guard.

Burnett spun about and leaped.

The horror on Lethla's face didn't go away as he fired his gun.

Rice came in fighting, too, but not before something like a red-hot ramrod stabbed Sam Burnett, catching him in the ribs, spinning him back like a drunken idiot to fall in a corner.

Fists made blunt flesh noises. Lethla went down, weaponless and screaming. Rice kicked. After a while Lethla quit screaming, and the room swam around in Burnett's eyes, and he closed them tight and started laughing.

He didn't finish laughing for maybe ten minutes. He heard the retriever claws come inside, and the star-port grind shut.

Out of the red darkness, Rice's voice came and then he could see Rice's young face over him. Burnett groaned.

Rice said, "Sam, you shouldn't have done it. You shouldn't have, Sam."

"To hell with it." Burnett winced, and fought to keep his eyes open. Something wet and sticky covered his chest. "I said this was my last trip and I meant it. One way or the other, I'd have quit!"

"This is the hard way—"

"Maybe. I dunno. Kind of nice to think of all those kids who'll never have to come aboard the *Constellation*, though, Rice." His voice trailed off. "You watch the shelves fill up and you never know who'll be next. Who'd have thought, four days ago—"

Something happened to his tongue so it felt like hard ice blocking his mouth. He had a lot more words to say, but only time to get a few of them out:

"Rice?"

"Yeah, Sam?"

"We haven't got a full cargo, boy."

"Full enough for me, sir."

"But still not full. If we went back to Center Base without filling the shelves, it wouldn't be right. Look there—number ninety-eight is Lethla—number ninety-nine is Kriere. Three thousand days of rolling this rocket, and not once come back without a bunch of the kids who want to sleep easy on the good green earth. Not right to be going back any way—but—the way—we used to—"

His voice got all full of fog. As thick as the fists of a dozen warriors. Rice was going away from him. Rice was standing still, and Burnett was lying down, not moving, but somehow Rice was going away a million miles.

"Ain't I one hell of a patriot, Rice?"

Then everything got dark except Rice's face. And that was starting to dissolve.

Ninety-eight: Lethla. Ninety-nine: Kriere.

RAY BRADBURY RETURNS IN OUR NEXT GREAT ISSUE: FIRST CONTACT

He could still see Rice standing over him for a long time, breathing out and in. Down under the tables the blood-pumps pulsed and pulsed, thick and slow. Rice looked down at Burnett and then at the empty shelf at the far end of the room, and then back at Burnett again.

And then he said softly: "*One hundred.*"

👽 👽 👽

"Morgue Ship" first appeared in the Summer 1944 issue of Planet Stories.

The New York Times *once described Ray Bradbury as "the writer most responsible for bringing modern science fiction into the literary mainstream." Bradbury was aided in this endeavor, no doubt, by a finicky editor who rejected the author's story "Homecoming" for publication in* Weird Tales. *Bradbury then took a long shot and submitted the tale to the mainstream magazine* Mademoiselle, *where a young editorial assistant named Truman Capote pulled the manuscript from the slush pile. "Homecoming" was published in a special Halloween edition of* Mademoiselle, *with illustrations by Bradbury's friend Charles Addams, for the October, 1946 issue, and later was honored with an O'Henry Award as one of the best American short stories of the year. Many similar honors would follow: a Prometheus Award (for* Fahrenheit 451*), an Emmy (for* The Halloween Tree*), two Retro Hugos, and both the Bram Stoker and the World Fantasy Awards for Lifetime Achievement. He was named the 10th SFWA Grand Master in 1989, had an asteroid discovered in 1992 named "9766 Bradbury" in his honor, and received a star on the Hollywood Walk of Fame in 2002. In 2004, President George W. Bush presented Bradbury with the National Medal of Arts.*

Ray Bradbury had the ability "to write lyrically and evocatively of lands an imagination away," wrote The L.A. Times, *"...anchored in the here and now with a sense of visual clarity and small-town familiarity." The Pulitzer Prize jury awarded a special citation to Bradbury in 2007, "for his distinguished, prolific, and deeply influential career as an unmatched author of science fiction and fantasy."*

RETINA SCAN COMPLETE. YOUR IDENTITY HAS BEEN CONFIRMED. WELCOME TO ...

Matt Cowan's Threat Watch

YOU MAY NOW ACCESS THE FILES. THESE FILES CONTAIN DATA MODULES COMPILED FROM EVIDENCE PRESENTED IN CLASSIC MOVIES. EACH MODULE FOCUSES ON A SPECIFIC THREAT: DEADLY PLANETS, HOSTILE ALIENS, RENEGADE ROBOTS, OR THE DANGERS ENCOUNTERED WHILE EMPLOYING ...

ACCESSING ... ACCESSING.... OPENING MODULE 8:

ROCKETSHIPS AND SPACESUITS

MANNED ROCKET SHIPS AND PRESSURIZED SPACESUITS—MINIATURIZED ENCASEMENTS OF LIVABLE ATMOSPHERE DESIGNED TO ENABLE FRAGILE HUMAN ORGANISMS TO EXIST AMIDST INHERENTLY HOSTILE ENVIRONMENTS. These innovations are amazing feats of human engineering that certainly deserve the acclaim they have been afforded. Even so, how daring must one be to board such a ship, or don such a suit, to venture forth into deep space or set foot upon some inhospitable planet when the slightest occurrence of malfunction or incident resulting in damage could render their occupants dead within a matter of seconds. Our relentless drive to push past our borders, to scale any obstacle, to unearth every unrevealed secret has perpetually brought forth stalwart individuals willing to accept all imaginable risks to further the collective goal.

Arguments can be made regarding what, if any, tangible treasures have ever been brought back from our missions into the cosmos, but what cannot be disputed is the vast array of rewards we've reaped as a result of our headstrong attempts to make it happen. The very existence of artificial limbs, cochlear implants, anti-icing aircraft technology, freeze drying, ventricular assist devices, LASIK, and many more such advances can be traced directly to the efforts of NASA scientists and engineers in their search for solutions to problems posed by the enigmas of space. The universe is a brutal, unforgiving landscape teeming with incalculable mysteries, but that will never stop mankind from plunging forward with both eyes open. It's an unending puzzle begging to be solved, and thanks to the marvels of technology we have devised, it's one we will continue to tackle relentlessly.

Several of the rockets and spacesuits featured in each of the films listed below employ advances we have not yet attained, but ones which I have no doubt are achievable in this lifetime or the next. Most importantly, however, is the fact that each movie makes substantial use of either rocket ships, spacesuits, or both.

IT! THE TERROR FROM BEYOND SPACE
(United Artists, 1958)

Ship Designation: Unnamed
Location: Travel between Earth and Mars
Owner: United States Space Command
Method of Exterior Travel: Pressurized spacesuits
Mission Statement: The exploration of Mars
Specializations: Space travel between Earth and Mars
Anomalous Threat: A massively strong, invulnerable alien creature
Inherent Threats: Deep space travel
Favorite Scene: When the hideous alien creature forces its way deeper into the ship and is able to resist the armed crew's best defenses in a display of ferocious, raw power

Synopsis: The United States Space Command's first attempt to send a rocket ship to Mars goes

Crash site of the first Mars rocket. (United Artists/MGM)

awry when it breaks apart and crash lands on the planet's surface. Six months have passed by the time a rescue ship arrives at the crash site to find Col. Edward Carruthers (Marshall Thompson) as the sole survivor of his crew. Carruthers is taken into custody aboard the rescue ship to be returned to Earth to face a court-martial. Although the bodies of his former crew mates haven't been found, he's accused of having murdered them in the days following the crash. Carruthers claims a mysterious creature was the cause of their deaths.

When something begins killing the rescue ship's crew members as well, Carruther's story suddenly becomes more plausible. Soon a monstrous alien creature makes itself known to them, pitting the survivors against a powerful, murderous beast which seems immune to everything they throw at it. If they can't discover some means of stopping it, they will all die at its menacing, three-fingered hands.

My Take: This film is set in a 1958 vision of a futuristic 1973, and demonstrates just how much slower we've progressed from the pace the filmmakers had anticipated. Despite our failure to reach the advances in technology they foresaw, we appear to have done better than their version of gender equality, considering the only two women onboard the ship are relegated primarily to maid duty; but the 50's were a much different time with different societal outlooks.

Since we are discussing some of the characters involved, now seems a good time to look at the cast. It's very strong, with each member of the ensemble playing their part well—lending the sort of gravitas to their roles necessary for us to believe their situation is indeed dire—and most are given some share of the limelight before the end credits roll. Marshall Thompson in the lead role does an excellent job portraying the tortured Col. Carruthers who's just survived one

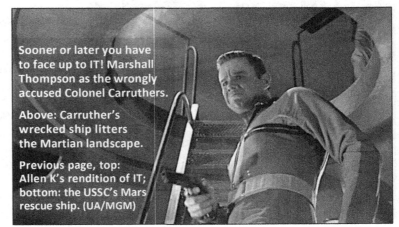

Sooner or later you have to face up to IT! Marshall Thompson as the wrongly accused Colonel Carruthers.

Above: Carruther's wrecked ship litters the Martian landscape.

Previous page, top: Allen K's rendition of IT; bottom: the USSC's Mars rescue ship. (UA/MGM)

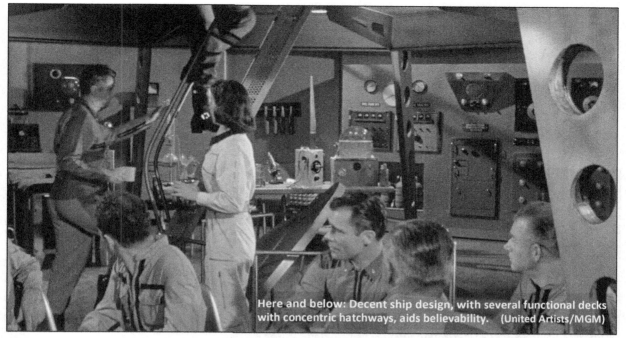

Here and below: Decent ship design, with several functional decks with concentric hatchways, aids believability. (United Artists/MGM)

traumatic experience to be thrust up against it once again. Other standout performances are given by Kim Spalding as the stubborn, unbelieving Col. Van Heusen; Shirley Patterson as the peacemaking female lead Ann Anderson; and Dabbs Greer as the friendly, resourceful Eric Royce.

While the acting shines, the special effects are a bit of a mixed bag. The creature effects aren't great; the suit appears too bulky and cumbersome at times, but in many scenes, it manages to be effective due to optimal uses of shadow and fog to obscure its flaws. I think the creature comes off much better than the weak attempts to show the rocket ship's journey through space or the brief glimpses we get of the Martian surface. These are very basic but can be forgiven considering the technology available to the filmmakers. The interior of the ship looks to have received far more consideration and budgetary allowance, which was probably a wise chose given that it's where the vast majority of the movie takes place.

This is a fun, creature-feature kind of film. The alien comes off as a terrifying, unstoppable force intent on killing them, and seems incapable of, or uninterested in, listening to reason. While there's no deep involved plot here, the film does a good job keeping you interested throughout, and as its run-time is just a little over an hour, it's a pretty fast-paced ride. It's also been cited as an inspiration for Ridley Scott's 1979 space-monster masterpiece *Alien*. **Rating: 7 out of 10**

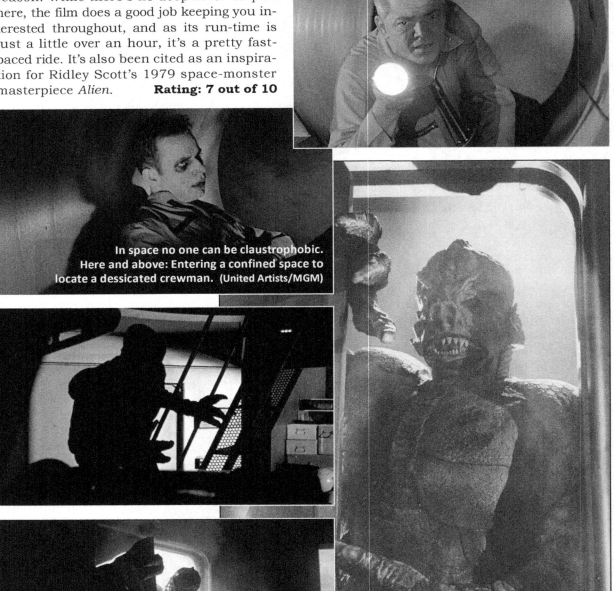

In space no one can be claustrophobic. Here and above: Entering a confined space to locate a dessicated crewman. (United Artists/MGM)

"Here's Johnny!" (All images © United Artists/MGM) With apologies to Stanley Kubrick's *The Shining*.

Get IT before IT gets us!
Crewmen nervously search each compartment for IT.

Suited-up to exit the ship in order to reach a deck unoccupied by IT. (United Artists/MGM)

CAPRICORN ONE
(Warner Bros, 1978)

Designation: *Capricorn One* (Rocket Ship)
Location: Earth
Owner: NASA
Method of Exterior Travel: Standard Astronaut Suits
Mission Statement: Transporting a three-man crew to the planet Mars
Specializations: Space travel
Primary Threat: Shadowy government agency
Favorite Scene: When Robert Caulfield (Elliott Gould) returns to the pool table in the bar where he just left his friend (a whistleblowing NASA technician) moments before, to find he's disappeared; It's subtle, but it makes you instantly aware of how high the stakes are from that moment forward.

Synopsis: The launch of the first manned mission to Mars is presented to the world as a momentous event, but much to their surprise, the rocket's three astronauts, Charles Brubaker (James Brolin), Peter Willis (Sam Waterston) and John Walker (O. J. Simpson), are secretly taken off the rocket and whisked away to a military base. There they are informed by high ranking

NASA official Dr. James Kelloway (Hal Holbrook) that they were taken from the ship because a defect in the craft had been discovered which would have resulted in all their deaths, and that such a national tragedy would have caused the project to lose its funding. To prevent this, a plan has been put in place to fake the mission as successful, by having the astronauts record from a soundstage made to appear as the red planet. Initially the astronauts want no part in the scheme, but when they are informed their families' lives may be in jeopardy if they refuse, they reluctantly agree.

The secret begins to unravel after a technician at the command station notices an anomaly in the transmissions, but when he

CAPRICORN ONE publicity art. (ITC/Warners)

NASA's Finest!
L to r: Peter Willis (Sam Waterston), Charles Brubaker (James Brolin), and John Walker (O. J. Simpson)

Publicity shots: Three alone, escaping through the desert.

Vaccaro, Karen Black, David Doyle, Telly Savalas and David Huddleston combine to create a very impressive roster of stars from that era, and they're all good in their respective roles. The nightmarish path O. J. Simpson's life would eventually go down casts a long shadow on his presence in the film, but he isn't given a lot to do here anyway. A highlight for me was Telly Savalas as a cantankerous, mercenary airplane pilot. Even though it's a pretty small role which appears late in the film, I really enjoyed its inclusion as the film's only real instance of comic relief.

There aren't many special effects of note to be found in this one, but none were really necessary given the sort of story being told. Everything looks adequately believable, so in that sense the filmmakers succeeded.

The focus of this movie is as an espionage thriller with a few minor science fiction trappings, but it's good at what it does, keeping the tension high as regular people are drawn into a dangerous game of cat and mouse against a shadowy, covert government organization.

Rating: 6 out of 10

mentions it to his superiors they dismiss his concerns and say it's a malfunction. Shortly afterward, when this technician tells his friend, journalist Robert Caulfield (Elliott Gould), what he discovered, he mysteriously disappears. This sends Caulfield on an investigation into the NASA mission, risking losing his life to powerful government forces who don't want the truth revealed. He isn't the only one in their crosshairs, however, after the rocket the world believes contains the three astronauts is very publicly destroyed upon re-entry to Earth—thus insuring they would never be allowed to leave without exposing the entire deception.

My Take: First off, this is a stacked cast! James Brolin, Elliott Gould, Hal Holbrook, Brenda

Cantankerous crop duster Albain (Telly Savalas) takes journalist Caulfield (Elliot Gould) over the desert floor in search of the three missing astronauts. (CAPRICORN ONE © ITC/Warner Bros.)

OUTLAND
(Warner Bros, 1981)

Designation: Con-Am 27 (Basestation on surface of Io)
Location: The Jovian Moon Io
Owner: Con-Amalgamate
Method of Exterior Travel: Heavy Space Suit
Mission Statement: To mine as much titanium as possible
Specializations: Titanium Ore Mining
Inherent Threats: Io's surface has no breathable atmosphere and a gravity only 1/6th that of Earth
Anomalous Threat: Secret, underhanded dealing, and individuals who don't want their schemes revealed
Favorite Scene: When hitmen arrive on the base to assassinate O'Niel and he's forced to use his resourcefulness to combat them.

Synopsis: Federal Marshall William O'Niel (Sean Connery) struggles with his recent one-year assignment to a base on Io, one of Jupiter's moons. His wife, who finds she can't deal with the conditions on the base, takes their son and swiftly leaves to the space station with plans to continue on to Earth, telling her husband about the decision via video message. O'Niel's boss, general manager Mark Sheppard (played by a young Peter Boyle), is also a problem, seeming intent on controlling him and ensuring nothing prevents the record-breaking productivity trend they've established of late. Recently, multiple workers have died under unusual circumstances (exposing themselves unprotected to zero-level atmosphere, or becoming homicidally violent, resulting in their being shot). Marshall O'Niel isn't so sure these apparent suicides and bouts of madness are as they initially appear, however, and wants to investigate further. O'Niel gains a reluctant ally in Dr. Lazarus (Frances Sternhagen), the ship's doctor. After analyzing the blood of the most recent victim, she makes a startling discovery. The investigation puts O'Niel at odds with people who hold superior political power to him, and who don't want their secrets uncovered. Despite all this, O'Niel proceeds anyway.

When hired guns arrive at the mining base on Jupiter's moon Io, Federal Marshall O'Niel (Sean Connery) is forced to face them alone, in an outer space version of HIGH NOON. (Warner Bros.)

My Take: This film is all about a man who refuses to set aside his principles in order to do the right thing when virtually everyone is against him. Sean Connery is always superb in everything, and this role is no exception. Frances Sternhagen is good as his lone, cynical but loyal friend on Con-Am 27. The special effects on screen are nothing exceptional, but it isn't really a drawback as they weren't necessary here. There aren't any alien life-forms or space battles which would necessitate big budget effects. The look of Con-Am 27 has that gritty feel a mining station should have. (Incidentally, as a fan of the board game *Terraforming Mars*, I loved that the Jovian moon was the site of a titanium mining base). The costume designer on this film was Oscar-winner John Mollo, and I liked the subtle but distinctive look of the uniforms throughout.

All in all, this is an enjoyable, if fairly basic film from a plotting standpoint. It's definitely worth a watch! **Rating: 7 out of 10**

to terraform Mars in order to create a new home capable of supporting human life. Issues arise when oxygen levels keep inexplicably dropping there, however. To combat this, a spacecraft christened *Mars 1* is sent into its orbit to investigate. Led by Commander Kate Bowman (Carrie-Ann Moss), her crew consists of egotistical geneticist Quinn Burchenal (Tom Sizemore), mechanical systems engineer Robby Gallagher (Van Kilmer, one of my favorite actors), philosopher and medic Bud Chantilas (played by the always excellent Terence Stamp), pilot Ted Santen (Benjamin Bratt), terraforming expert Chip Pettengill (Simon Baker) and *AMEE* (Autonomous Mapping Exploration and Evasion) a robotic navigator. When *Mars 1* is disabled by a gamma burst from a solar flare, Commander Bowman is forced to send everyone else to the surface in search of a safe location to hold up while she attempts to return the ship to functionality.

Once the away team lands on the surface of Mars, *AMEE* goes missing and Chantilas suffers

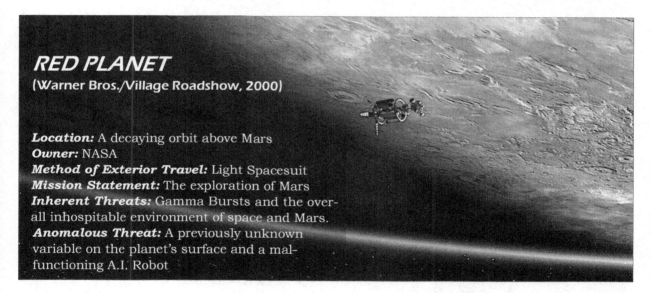

RED PLANET
(Warner Bros./Village Roadshow, 2000)

Location: A decaying orbit above Mars
Owner: NASA
Method of Exterior Travel: Light Spacesuit
Mission Statement: The exploration of Mars
Inherent Threats: Gamma Bursts and the overall inhospitable environment of space and Mars.
Anomalous Threat: A previously unknown variable on the planet's surface and a malfunctioning A.I. Robot

Favorite Scene: When the initial discovery of the reason they can breathe on the surface of the planet is revealed, and the illuminating sparks which spring forth from it soon afterwards.

Synopsis: After pollution and over-population threaten to overwhelm Earth, an effort is put forth

a ruptured spleen. Chantilas insists they leave him behind while the others continue their search for a habitable location. With *Mars 1* in a decaying orbit and the surface team concerned their suits may run out of oxygen, the stakes are high. When the surface team comes across a previously constructed base known as

Commander Kate Bowman (Carrie-Ann Moss) works to save her ship from a decaying orbit around Mars. (Village Roadshow/Warner Bros.)

HAB 1 (a place which had been designed to produce food and oxygen) that has been destroyed, they worry they are doomed to die in the planet's hostile environment. In the process of suffocating in his spacesuit, Gallagher opens his visor expecting a swift death, only to discover he's able to somehow breath the planet's thin atmosphere. With the ground crew attempting to scavenge what limited resources they can muster to try and survive, communicate, and fashion an escape from Mars, Commander Bowman remains in contact with Houston, updating the situation as best she can.

What is allowing the ground crew to breathe on Mars? Can they alert anyone that they are still alive? Can Bowman bring them all home safely? These questions are all in play as the film moves toward its finale.

Forced to evacuate *Mars I*, the away team face numerous problems on the planet surface. Unfortunately, their troubles are far from over.

AMEE stalks the crew after going rogue.

Hey there, you!

My Take: In regards to this issue's theme, the spacesuits here look a bit scaled down and less restrictive than the modern-day astronaut suit. The spaceship *Mars 1* on the other hand gets its share of the limelight throughout. The primary focus, however, involves the crew members who are trapped on Mars attempting to survive while facing threats posed by its unforgiving environment, its limited resources, as well as the powerful A.I. robot *AMEE*, which has gone murderously rogue. Val Kilmer is essentially our hero, as his skills, sense of humor and morality make him the person for whom we're most rooting. Carrie-Ann Moss does a suitable job as Captain Bowman, an effective leader capable of making hard decisions but one who also cares deeply for her crew. Tom Sizemore's Quinn Burchenal is another highlight, as the scientist who can't rest until he's unraveled whatever mystery is unfolding before him (in this case, finding themselves able to breath on Mars). I enjoyed the survival elements and the resourceful solutions that were employed along the way to solve them.

Things look bad, but Bowman has one last trick up her sleeve.

While they aren't exactly anything exceptional, this film probably has the best special effects of any of the four featured in this column, particularly in regards to several of the scenes which take place on the surface of Mars. This is a fun, popcorn-movie style of a watch which doesn't require too intense of an investment to follow along with the plot, and the actors do a good job investing you in the characters they are portraying.

Rating: 7 out of 10

HANGING VINES

By JAMES DORR
Art by ED EMSHWILLER

THE SHIP WAS LIKE A MOTHER TO HIM. A MOTHER TO ALL OF THEM. EVEN IN THIS, he thought as he swung just out of the way of another volley of bullet-fast seeds from the planet's surface. He watched as two of the seeds adhered to a bare patch of hull, then glanced up again to the top of the ship with its optical sensor turning almost immeasurably slowly to track the sun. Even in this, despite the fact it was trying to kill him.

Another volley—far enough away from him this time that he had no need to try to avoid it. Another *click* as the sensor moved one more minute of arc, as the sun's light advanced a tiny bit farther down the slope below, waking a new set of dormant pods into a frenzy of firing their seeds off. A *thump* as another seed stuck to the ship's side, immediately sprouting, burning its substance into a new, downward growing vine.

And him, afraid of heights....

"Ship?" he called out from his position twenty-five meters up its side, clinging to one of the earliest, most mature of the vines that grew in the morning sun. "This is Roger again. Planetologist Roger Borski. Are you sure you won't reconsider?"

He heard a metallic-sounding sigh—the ship, if nothing else, was compassionate—then a voice very much like a woman's.

"You know I'd like to, Roger. Really. Except that the captain told me you'd be outside all day. And he makes the rules, not me, Roger. We have to obey them."

"I understand, Ship. But the captain's dying—if you don't let me in, right now, it'll kill the whole crew. Can you understand *that*?"

"If you could just have *him* tell me that, Roger...."

He sighed himself, then laboriously climbed another five meters up the vine, hearing the hiss as clean air fed itself into his helmet. The planet had air too, but air that included caustic gases that could kill him if he breathed too much of it. That was part of the problem he had—he had just one air tank attached to his spacesuit, good for four Earth hours, but the planet's daytime would last for more than thirty. And both Captain Merrick and Linda had been hurt when he'd crashed the rover—no, when the planet's damn plant life had caused the crash—rupturing both of the vehicle's reservoirs, smashing its radio, leaving them just with emergency tanks too.

He counted the hours. He had already used one-and-a-half crossing the distance back on foot to beg the ship to let him in. Once inside, he could take the second rover, knowing this time what to avoid, or, better still, send it out on automatic to where he had crashed, guiding it from the ship's control room. But, when he had asked the ship to unroll its gangplank for him, the ship had said no.

"The captain ordered me to stay buttoned up until sundown," the ship had told him. "You know the routine, Roger. Even though I've detected no signs of hostile life forms, I have to stay closed for security's sake. You *depend* on this, Roger—my following orders. Suppose something happened…?"

"But something *has* happened," Roger had shouted. "And, as for life forms, what about these stinking vines?"

"Well … one can hardly call plant life hostile"—the ship had sounded miffed when it said that—"and, anyway, when we approached the planet, there weren't any signs of life at all."

Because it was still night, Roger had added under his breath. And the plants, apparently, died at sundown, leaving their seed pods to burst the next morning. To stick to the highest thing they could find and then grow like lightning, taking nourishment from the thick air, until they, in turn, could bury their tips in the ground below to deposit new seed pods.

One-and-a-half hours. He'd looked at his watch, confirming the time. One-and-three-quarters. If he had a rover, it would take only a half hour to get back. Plenty of time to rescue the others except, before he could get a rover, he had, somehow, to get the ship to let him inside.

That's when he'd looked up and seen how the vines trailed down the spaceship's sun-facing side, from the optical sensors way up at the top, past the forward viewports, down past the main hatch, still halfway up….

Like the tree he remembered when he had been young. The tree in the garden, covered with some kind of weed-like vine that made it easy for a boy like him to climb. Till his mother forbade him….

He'd found out later how much he'd feared heights since, when he had *had* to climb the tree. Now, though, he looked up—a vine-covered spaceship. A hatch, halfway up, like the tree-houses some of his braver friends had continued to play in. And, fear or not, he had started to climb.

Ten meters more—be sure not to look down—then rest again. Fifteen minutes more taken. But now he was at the hatchway's level. He eased to his left, toward the ship's shadow-side where the hatch and its lip were still free of obstruction, inching his way from vine to vine. Trying his best not to think of falling.

Two hours taken. Two-and-a-quarter. The hatch had a manual override lever, used for emergencies in space when one or more crew members had to go outside.

He reached—the vines here were thin and slippery, but more were already growing down toward him as the sun continued to rise in the planet's sky. His fingertips touched … now he had the lever. Bracing one foot on the lip of the hatchway, he pulled it downward.

"Roger!" the ship said. "Let go of that lever."

The hatch remained shut tight.

"What?" Roger shouted. "Look, Ship, I have to get inside. I'm overriding your orders—you understand? That's what this goddamn lever is *for*."

"Only in space, Roger," the ship said. Its voice took on a tone of scolding. "You know the manual. Once we're on planetside, captain's orders take precedence. Always."

"The captain is *dying*!"

"*He* has to tell me that. You know that, Roger. Or else he has to personally appoint you the new captain. If you can have him tell me *that*, Roger...."

He thought of the rover—the captain hurt badly. Linda, their astrogator, hurt too. The seeds smashing into it, just as he'd climbed up a ridge into sunlight, spewing their tendrils over the windscreen, jamming its treads, and then, when they'd rolled, the radio's external antenna snapping....

Damn cheap equipment.

He looked up the ship's side—looking *up* somehow wasn't frightening. The ship had been cheap, too. As well as its central controlling computer, a model no longer in manufacture, and now he had a good idea why. But then the whole setup had been on the cheap, as three-member, independent exploring trips so often were. Land on the planet, without even taking time to orbit first. Time was money for an exploring team. Get out the rover, drive in an outward extending spiral to cover as much as you could in a planet-day, with all hands working to set detectors. Then let the ship's calculator crunch numbers while you blasted off to a new star system—if anything showed up, minerals, artifacts, you could come back—to cover your sector before supplies ran out.

"Roger?" the ship said. "I want you to move away from the hatch now. Since you're not the captain, you have no business there. And anyway, since you're not *supposed* to be back until nightfall, I have to warn you I'm starting to find your behavior suspicious."

"Suspicious of *what*?" he started to ask. He thought of the manual that it had cited—he hadn't read it. No one read manuals, especially for obsolete equipment, but now he wondered. He tried to remember. The ship *had* been military surplus....

"Roger, I'm warning you—if you *are* Roger. If you don't move away from that hatch, I *will* be suspicious. Can you hear me, Roger?"

"Yes, Ship," he muttered, then said it again in a louder voice, making sure it could hear him. "Just give me a moment." He looked above him, then grasped the largest vine he could find, using it to steady himself as he eased himself back to the vine he'd been climbing. He inched farther upward, afraid to look down. Afraid to look sideways, even, for fear the ship might have some way to back up its warning.

Suspicious of what? he wondered as he continued to climb. That he was an enemy boarding party? Or maybe a saboteur?

That was just what he needed—a paranoid spaceship.

But....

He looked up, seeing the curve where the ship's side sloped in toward its nose cone. The forward view-ports. He had an idea.

Ten, fifteen meters more, he thought. Fifteen more minutes—an hour-and-a-half left. He thought again of the tree in the garden. The one time, no matter what his mother told him, he'd *had* to climb it. He'd had a pet then, a cat-like lizard his father had brought back from one of *his* voyages. Needless to say, his mother had not approved of the creature, but he had loved it.

Then one morning, cat like, it had climbed the tree and couldn't get back down. It had been raining. He remembered. His mother was not at home—he *had* to save it.

Like now. With Linda. And Captain Merrick. He'd gripped the vines that hung down the tree's trunk, slippery with rain, and, in desperation, he'd climbed higher than he'd ever climbed before to reach it.

Like now, he thought, though where he was now at least it was sunny. A little *too* sunny. He'd frozen once on the slippery tree—one time, when he'd looked down—but he'd cleared his head and continued upward, learning the trick of always looking up, never around him. In desperation.

He reached the nearest of the view-ports and looked inside, then checked his watch—not much more than an hour left. But, if the ship were going to be suspicious, by God, perhaps he could give it a *reason*.

He tapped the plexiglass of the port, then, gripping vines with both of his hands to steady himself, he raised himself to a half standing position. Planting one foot on the ship's metal hull, he lifted the other—the glass was tough, sure, but, even in slightly less than Earth gravity, his steel-soled boot should at least be able to make a crack in it. And then the ship would *have* to open up, if only to repair the damage.

He brought his foot down. Hard. In desperation. He thought of his pet—how in daytime it stayed out, but then, at night, it had been his job to let it back inside. He laughed as he kicked again. Like Captain Merrick had made it the ship's job not to let *him* in until it was nighttime.

"Roger!" the ship screamed.

He just laughed louder.

"Stop it, Roger!"

He raised his foot to kick a third time—then nearly fell as a jolt of electricity crackled through him.

"I'm warning you, Roger," the ship said, more calmly. "I don't mind you climbing all over my hull, if that's what your captain wants you to do. But, if you make one more attempt to damage me...."

"I-I understand, Ship," Roger whispered. His feet dangled free, the left one, which had been clamped to the ship's hull, only now starting to lose its numbness. The vines—thank God he had gripped them so tightly. At least they, apparently, hadn't been hurt.

He looked up—he thought of the tree and his lizard. How he had reached it, always looking up, but then discovered *he* had no way of getting down either. Above him, twenty meters higher, where the ship's nose curved to almost level, the optical sensor clicked another beat.

One more minute of arc. How many more would it be until nightfall? How many more Earth-standard hours and minutes?

He checked his watch again—how much more air in his tank? In the tanks of the others?

Less than an hour left.

"I'm warning you, Roger. Considering what you tried to do, I don't want you hanging so close to my windows."

"Yes, mother," he muttered, under his breath, then planted his feet—*away* from the view-port—and went back to climbing.

Another click. The sun had advanced another minute of arc above him. Another thump as another seed pod fired.

He reached the near-level of the ship's nose cone—not even noon by the time the planet kept.

This time he *did* look down, down to the main hatch directly below him. The curve, starting gently, then getting steeper, the vines trailing down it past the stub of the ship's rolled-up gangplank.

His mother had come back just before noon with him still in the tree, clutching his pet. She'd screamed and yelled at him until he was crying for her to stop, then she'd run inside to call men with ladders to help get him down. He'd waited until he'd seen the red trucks come, humiliated, soaked in the rain....

Huddling the lizard-cat to him as the sky darkened....

But it was still morning.

The optical sensor clicked. It had been morning, but, because of the clouds and the rain, it had *seemed* as dark to him as the darkest night.

He looked above him—the optical sensor on its round platform, maybe as thick as a man's head and shoulders. He didn't dare touch it—the ship had warned him what would happen if it thought he was trying to damage it further—but....

If he could trick it. So it couldn't see the sun.

He checked his watch. Maybe forty minutes more. Then, with his air gone, he was dead anyway. Maybe five or ten minutes more than that in the planet's air, breathing shallowly, if he opened his helmet to it.

But, if he could somehow convince the ship it was night already, then when Linda and the captain didn't come in like they were supposed to, it might at least send the second rover out to search for them.

He turned his head and looked at the sun, squinting his eyes for the moment it took for his visor to darken—to keep its direct rays from burning his eyes. Then looked back at where the sensor continued its own slow turning, noting again that the sensor was head-sized....

The tree. He remembered. When the trucks came, he'd refused to depend on his mother to save him. *He'd thrust the lizard into his jacket and, closing his eyes, clutched the thickest vine, launched himself into space, letting himself slide....*

He took the deepest breath he could, then unshipped his helmet. He lifted it, carefully, over the sensor, making sure it touched only the platform...

...heard clicking and whirring. A *thump* beneath him, but louder than those the seeds made on the ship's side...

...and, shutting his eyes tight, he gripped the vine he knew trailed to the hatchway, launched himself downward, shinnying, sliding, until—another thump. His feet struck hardness. The gangplank was rolled out, the main hatch open as he scrambled inside, into the airlock, slapping the CLOSE lever, hearing the outer door hiss shut behind him.

And breathed. Gasping. Choking. But filling his lungs back up with ship's air.

He rolled to his feet, running, to the control room, ignoring whatever the ship was saying until he'd punched the computer sequence to send out the rover with extra air tanks. With splints and medicines and a new radio.

Looked at his watch.

Exactly a half hour....

And sank, exhausted, into the big control-room chair, only now hearing as the ship's voice continued on in its gentle chiding...

"...rules are rules, Roger. I hope you've learned by now—after all, that's what we depend on. But now that it's evening, I want to welcome you back again, and express my sincere hope that you and your friends had a very *nice* outing."

"Hanging Vines" *first appeared in the* ConAdian Souvenir Book *(for the 52nd World Science Fiction Convention, September 1994).*

Indiana author James Dorr's most recent book is a novel-in-stories from Elder Signs Press, Tombs: A Chronicle of Latter-Day Times of Earth. *Working mostly in dark fantasy/horror with some forays into science fiction and mystery, his* The Tears of Isis *was a 2013 Bram Stoker Award® finalist for Superior Achievement in a Fiction Collection, while other books include* Strange Mistresses: Tales of Wonder and Romance, Darker Loves: Tales of Mystery and Regret, *and his all-poetry* Vamps (A Retrospective). *He has also been a technical writer, an editor on a regional magazine, a full-time non-fiction freelancer, and a semi-professional musician, and currently harbors a Goth cat named Triana. An Active Member of SFWA and HWA, Dorr invites readers to visit his blog at:* jamesdorrwriter.wordpress.com

THE ROCKETEERS HAVE SHAGGY EARS

★★★ STORY BY ★★★
KEITH BENNETT

★★★ ART BY ★★★
ALDEN McWILLIAMS

THE COMMANDER'S VOICE WENT DRONING ON, BUT HAGUE'S FATIGUED BRAIN REGISTERED IT AS MERE SOUND WITH NO WORDS OR MEANING. He'd been dazed since the crash. Like a cracked phonograph, his brain kept playing back the ripping roar of jet chambers blowing out with a sickening lurch that had thrown every man in the control room to the floor. The lights had flickered out, and a sickening elevator glide began as Patrol Rocket One smashed down through the Venusian rainforest roof, and crashed in a clearing blasted by its own hurtling passage.

Hague blinked hard and tried to focus his brain on what hard-faced Commander Devlin was saying, something about the Base and *Odysseus*, the mother ship.

"We've five hundred miles before we'll be in their vicinity, and every yard of it we walk. Hunting parties will shoot food animals. All water is to be boiled and treated with ultra-violet by my section. The photographers will march with the science section, which will continue classifying and writing reports. No actual specimens will be taken. We can't afford the weight."

To Hague, the other five men seated around the little charting table appeared cool, confidently ready to march through five hundred or a thousand miles of dark, unexplored, steaming Hell that is Venusian rainforest. Their faces tight-set, icily calm, they nodded in turn as the Commander looked at each one of them; but Hague wondered if his own face wasn't betraying the fear lurking within him. Suddenly Commander Devlin grinned, and pulled a brandy bottle from his pocket, uncorking it as he spoke: "Well, Rocketeers, a short life and a merry one. I never did give a damn for riding in these tin cans."

The tension broke, they were all smiling, and saying they'd walk into the base camp with some kind of a Venusian female under each arm for the edification of Officers' Mess.

Leaden doubt of his own untried abilities and nerve lay icy in Hague's innards, and he left after one drink. The others streamed from the brightly lighted hatch a moment later. The Commander made a short speech to the entire party. Then Navigator Clark, a smiling, wiry little man, marched out of the clearing with his advance guard. Their voices muffled suddenly as they vanished down a forest corridor that lay gloomy between giant tree boles.

Commander Devlin slapped Hague cheerfully on the shoulder as he moved past; and the second section, spruce and trim in blue-black uniforms, with silver piping, followed him. Crewmen Didrickson and Davis followed with rifles and sagging bandoliers of explosive bullets crossing their chests; and then Arndt, the lean craggy geologist, his arm in a sling; and marching beside him was rotund, be-goggled Gault, the botanist. The little whippet tank clattered by next with Technician Whittaker grinning down at Hague from the turret.

"It pains me somethin' awful to see you walkin' when I'm ridin'," Whittaker piped over the whippet's clanking growl.

Hague grinned back, then pinched his nose between two fingers in the ageless dumb show of disgust, pointed at the tank, and shook his head sadly. The two carts the whippet towed swayed by, and the rest of the column followed; Bachmann, the doctor and Sewell, his beefy crotchety assistant. The two photographers staggered past under high-piled equipment packs, and Hague wondered how long they would keep all of it. Lenkranz, Johnston, Harker, Szachek, Hirooka, Ellis— each carried a pack full of equipment. The rest filed by until finally Swenson, the big Swede technician, passed and the clearing was empty.

Hague turned to look over his own party. In his mind's eye bobbed the neatly typed "Equipment, march-order, light field artillery" lists he'd memorized along with what seemed a thousand other neatly typed lists at Gunnery School.

The list faded, and Hague watched his five-man gun-section lounge against their rifles, leaning slightly forward to ease the heavy webbing that supported their marching packs and the sectioned pneumatic gun.

"All right," Hague said brusquely. He dredged his brain desperately then for an encouraging speech, something that would show the crew he liked them, something the Commander might say, but he couldn't think of anything that sounded witty or rang with stirring words. He finally muttered a disgusted curse at his own blank-headedness, and said harshly, "All right, let's go."

The six men filed silently out of the clearing battered in the forest by Patrol Rocket One, and into damp gloom between gargantuan trunks that rose smoothly out of sight into darkness. Behind them a little rat-like animal scurried into the deserted slot of blasted trees, its beady black eyes studying curiously the silver ship that lay smashed and half-buried in the forest floor.

BASE COMMANDER CHAPMAN shuffled hopelessly through the thick sheaf of onionskin papers, and sank back sighing. Ammunition reports, supply reports, medical reports, strength reports, reconnaissance reports, radio logs, radar logs, sonar logs, bulging dossiers of reports, files full of them, were there; and elsewhere in the ship efficient clerks were rapping out fresh, crisp battalions of new reports, neatly typed in triplicate on onion-skin paper.

He stared across his crowded desk at the quiet executive officer.

"Yes, Blake, it's a good picture of local conditions, but it isn't exploration. Until the Patrol Rocket gets in, we can send only this local stuff, and it just isn't enough."

Blake shrugged.

"It's all we've got. We can send parties out on foot from the base here, even if we do lose men, but the dope they'd get would still be on a localized area."

The Commander left his desk, and stared through a viewport at the plateau, and beyond that at the jungled belt fringing an endless expanse of rainforest lying sullenly quiet under the roof of racing grey clouds.

"The point is we've got to have more extensive material than this when we fire our robot-courier back to earth. This wonderful mountain of papers—what do they do, what do they tell? They describe beautifully the physical condition of this Base and its complement. They describe very well a ten-mile area around the Base—but beyond that area they tell nothing. It's wonderful as far as it goes, but it only goes ten miles, and that isn't enough."

Blake eyed the snowy pile of papers abstractedly. Then he jumped up nervously as another bundle shot into a receiving tray from the pneumatic message tube. He began pacing the floor.

"Well, what can we do? Suppose we send the stuff we have here, get it microfilmed and get it off—what then?"

The Commander swore bitterly, and turned to face his executive.

"What then?" he demanded savagely. "Are we going into that again? Why, the minute every other branch of the services realize that we haven't got any kind of thorough preliminary report on this section of Venus, they'll start pounding the war drums. The battleship admirals and the bayonet generals will get to work and stir up enough public opinion to have the United States Rocket Service absorbed by other branches—the old, old game of military politics."

Blake nodded jerkily. "Yes, I know. We'd get the leftovers after the battleships had been built, or new infantry regiments activated, or something else. Anyway, we wouldn't get enough money to carry on rocket research for space explorations."

"Exactly," the Commander cut in harshly. "These rockets would be grounded on earth. The generals or admirals would swear that the international situation demanded that they be kept there as weapons of defense; and that would be the end of our work."

"We've got to send back a good, thorough report, something to prove that the Rocket Service can do the job, and that it is worth the doing. And, until the patrol rocket gets back, we can't do it."

"Okay, Commander," Blake called as he went through the steel passage opening onto the mother ship's upper corridor, "I'll be holding the Courier Rocket until we get word."

SEVEN HOURS LATER it lightened a little, and day had come. Hague and the Sergeant had pulled the early morning guard shift, and began rolling the other four from their tiny individual tents.

Bormann staggered erect, yawned lustily, and swore that this was worse than spring maneuvers in Carolina.

"Shake it," Brian snarled savagely. "That whistle will blow in a minute."

When it did sound, they buckled each other into pack harness and swung off smartly, but groaning and muttering as the mud dragged at their heavy boots.

At midday, four hours later, there was no halt, and they marched steadily forward through steaming veils of oppressive heat, eating compressed ration as they walked. They splashed through a tiny creek that was solidly slimed, and hurried ahead when crawling things wriggled in the green mass. Perspiration ran in streams from each face filing past on the trail, soaked through pack harness and packs; and wiry Hurd began to complain that his pack straps had cut through his shoulders as far as his navel. They stopped for a five-minute break at 1400, when Hurd stopped fussing with his back straps and signaled for silence, though the other five had been too wrapped in their own discomfort to be talking.

"Listen! Do you hear it, Lieutenant? Like a horn?" Hurd's wizened rat face knotted in concentration. "Way off, like."

Hague listened blankly a moment, attempted an expression he fondly hoped was at once intelligent and reassuring, then said, "I don't hear anything. You may have taken too much fever dope, and it's causing a ringing in your ears."

"Naw," with heavy disgust. "Listen! There it goes again!"

"I heard it." That was Sergeant Brian's voice, hard and incisive, and Hague wished he sounded like that, or that would have heard the sound before his second in command. All of the six were hunched forward, listening raptly, when the Lieutenant stood up.

"Yes, Hurd. Now I hear it."

The whistle blew then, and they moved forward. Hague noticed the Sergeant had taken a post at the rear of the little file, and watched their back trail warily as they marched.

"What do you think it was, sir?" Bucci inquired in the piping voice that sounded strange coming from his deep chest.

"The Lord knows," Hague answered, and wondered how many times he'd be using that phrase in the days to come. "Might have been some animal. They hadn't found any traces of intelligent life when we left the Base Camp."

BUT IN THE DAYS that followed there was a new air of expectancy in the marchers, as if their suspicions had solidified into a waiting for attack. They'd been moving forward for several days.

Hague saw the pack before any of his men did, and thanked his guiding star that for once he had been a little more alert than his gun-section members.

The canvas carrier had been set neatly against one of the buttressing roots of a giant tree bole and, from the collecting bottles strapped in efficient rows outside, Hague deduced that it belonged to Bernstein, the entomologist. The gunnery officer halted and peered back into the gloom off the trail, called Bernstein's name; and when there was no reply moved cautiously into the hushed shadows with his carbine ready. He sensed that Sergeant Brian was catfooting behind him.

Then he saw the ghostly white bundle suspended six feet above the forest floor, and moved closer, calling Bernstein's name softly. The dim bundle vibrated gently, and Hague saw that it hung from a giant white lattice radiating wheel-like from the green gloom above. He raised his hand to touch the cocoon thing, noted it was shaped like a man well-wrapped in some woolly material; and on a sudden hunch pulled his belt knife and cut the fibers from what would be the head.

It was Bernstein suspended there, his snug, silken shroud bobbing gently in the dimness. His dark face was pallid in the gloom, sunken and flaccid of feature, as though the juices had been sucked from his corpse, leaving it a limp mummy.

The lattice's thick white strands vibrated—something moved across it overhead, and Hague flashed his lightpak up into the darkness. Crouched twenty feet above him, two giant legs delicately testing the strands of its lattice-like web, Hague saw the spider, its bulbous furred body fully four feet across, the monster's myriad eyes glittering fire-like in the glow of Hague's lightpak, as it gathered the great legs slightly in the manner of a tarantula ready to leap.

BRIAN'S SHARP YELL broke Hague from his frozen trance. He threw himself down as Brian's rifle crashed, and the giant arachnid was bathed in a blue-white flash of explosive light, its body tumbling down across the web onto Hague where he lay in the mud. The officer's hoarse yells rang insanely while he pulled himself clear of the dead spider-beast, but he forced himself to quiet at the sound of the Sergeant's cool voice.

"All clear, Lieutenant. It's dead."

"Okay, Brian. I'll be all right now." Hague's voice shook, and he cursed the weakness of his fear, forcing himself to walk calmly without a

glance over his shoulder until they were back on the trail. He led the other four gunners back to the spider and Bernstein's body, as a grim object lesson, warned them to leave the trail only in pairs. They returned their weary footslogging pace down the muddy creek marked by Clark's crew. When miles had sweated by at the same steady pace, Hague could still feel in the men's stiff silence their horror of the thing Brian had killed.

HOURS, AND THEN DAYS, rolled past, drudging nightmares through which they plowed in mud and steamy heat, with punctually once every sixteen hours a breathtaking, pounding torrent of rain. Giant drops turned the air into an aqueous mixture that was almost unbreathable, and smashed against their faces until the skin was numb. When the rain stopped abruptly the heat came back and water vapor rose steaming from the mud they walked through; but always they walked, shoving one aching foot ahead of the other through sucking black glue. Sometimes Bormann's harmonica would wheedle reedy airs, and they would sing and talk for a time, but mostly they swung forward in silence, faces drawn with fatigue and pale in the forest half-light. Hague looked down at his hands, swollen, bloody with insect bites, and painfully stiff; and wondered if he'd be able to bend them round his ration pan at the evening halt.

Hague was somnambulating at the rear of his little column, listening to an ardent account from Bormann of what his girl might expect when he saw her again. Bucci, slowing occasionally to ease the pneumatic gun's barrel assembly across his shoulder, chimed in with an ecstatic description of his little Wilma. The two had been married just before the Expedition blasted Venus-ward out of an Arizona desert. Crosse was at the front end, and his voice came back nasally.

"Hey, Lieutenant, there's somebody sitting beside the trail."

"Okay. Halt." The Lieutenant swore tiredly and trotted up to Crosse's side. "Where?"

"There. Against the big root."

Hague moved forward, carbine at ready, and knew without looking that Sergeant Brian was at his shoulder, cool and self-sufficient as always.

"Who's there?" the officer croaked.

"It's me, Bachmann."

Hague motioned his party forward, and they gathered in a small circle about the Doctor, seated calmly beside the trail, with his back against a root flange.

"What's the matter, Doc? Did you want to see us?"

"No. Sewell seems to think you're all healthy. Too bad the main party isn't as well off. Quite a bit of trouble with fever. And, Bernstein gone, of course."

Hague nodded, and remembered he'd reported Bernstein's death to the Commander three nights before.

"How's the Commander?" he inquired.

The Doctor's cherubic face darkened. "Not good. He's not a young man, and this heat and walking are wrecking his heart. And he won't ride the tank."

"Well, let's go, Doc." It was Brian's voice, cutting like a knife into Hague's consciousness. The Doctor looked tired, and drawn.

"Go ahead, lads. I'm just going to sit here for a while." He looked up and smiled weakly at the astonished faces, but his eyes were bleakly determined.

"This is as far as I go. Snake bite. We've no anti-venom that seems to work. All they can do is to amputate, and we can't afford another sick man." He pulled a nylon wrapper from one leg that sprawled at an awkward angle beneath him. The bared flesh was black, swollen, and had a gangrenous smell. Young Crosse turned away, and Hague heard his retching.

"What did the Commander say?"

"He agreed this was best. I am going to die anyway."

"Will—will you be all right here? Don't you want us to wait with you?"

The Doctor's smile was weaker, and he mopped at the rivulets of perspiration streaking his mud-spattered face.

"No. I have an X-lethal dosage and a hypodermic. I'll be fine here. Sewell knows what to do." His round face contorted, "Now, for God's sake, get on, and let me take that tablet. The pain is driving me crazy."

Hague gave a curt order, and they got under way. A little further on the trail, he turned to wave at Doctor Bachmann, but the little man was already invisible in forest shadows.

THE TENTH DAY after the crash of Patrol Rocket One, unofficially known as the Ration Can, glimpses of skylight opened over the trail Clark's crew were marking; and Hague and his men found themselves suddenly in an opening where low, thick vines, and luxuriant, thick-leaved shrubs struggled viciously for life. Balistierri, the zoologist, slight wisp of a dark man always and almost a shadow now, stood wearily beside the trail waiting as they drew up. Their shade-blinded eyes picked out details in the open ground dimly. Hague groaned inwardly when he saw that this was a mere slit in the forest, and the great trees loomed again a hundred yards ahead. Balistierri seized Hague by the shoulder and pointed into the thick mat of green, smiling.

"Watch, all of you."

He blew a shrill blast on his whistle and waited, while Hague's gunners wondered and watched. There was a wild, silvery call, a threshing of wings, and two huge birds rose into the gold tinted air. They flapped up, locked their wings, and glided, soared, and wheeled over the earth-stained knot of men—two great white birds, with crests of fire-gold, plumage snowy save where it was dusted with rosy overtones. Their call was bell-like as they floated across the clearing in a golden haze of sunlight filtered through clouds.

"They're—they're like angels." It was Bormann, the tough young sentimentalist.

"You've named them, soldier," Balistierri grinned. "I've been trying for a name; and that's the best I've heard. Bormann's angels they'll be. In Latin, of course."

Unfolding vistas of eternal zoological glory left Bormann speechless and red-faced. Sergeant Brian broke in.

"I guess they would have made those horn sounds. Right, Lieutenant?" His voice, dry and a little patronizing, suggested that this was a poor waste of valuable marching time.

"I wouldn't know, Sergeant," Hague answered, trying to keep dislike out of his voice, but the momentary thrill was broken and, with Balistierri beside him, Gunnery Officer Hague struck out on the trail that had been blasted and hacked through the clearing's wanton extravagance of greedy plant life.

As they crossed the clearing, Bucci tripped and sprawled full length in the mud. When he tried to get up, the vine over which he'd stumbled clutched with a woody tendril that wound snakelike tightly about his ankle; and, white-faced, the rest of the men chopped him free of the serpentine thing with belt knives, bandaged the thorn wounds in his leg, and went on.

The clearing had one more secret to divulge, however. A movement in the forest edge caught Brian's eye and he motioned to Hague, who followed him questioningly as the Sergeant led him off trail. Brian pointed silently and Hague saw Didrickson, Sergeant in charge of Supplies, seated in the lemon-colored sunlight at the forest edge, an open food pack between his knees, from which he snatched things and swallowed them voraciously, feeding like a wild dog.

"Didrickson! Sergeant Didrickson!" the Lieutenant yelled. "What are you doing?"

The supply man stared back, and Hague knew from the man's face what had happened. He crouched warily, eyes wild with panic and jaw hanging foolishly slack. This was Didrickson, the steady, efficient man who'd sat at the chart table the night they began this march. He had been the only man Devlin thought competent and nerveless enough to handle the food. This was the same Didrickson, and madder now than a March hare, Hague concluded grimly. The enlisted man snatched up the food pack, staring at them in wild fear, and began to run back down the trail, back the way they'd come.

"Come back, Didrickson. We've got to have that food, you fool!"

The madman laughed crazily at the sound of the officer's voice, glanced back for a moment, then spun and ran.

Sergeant Brian, as always, was ready. His rifle cracked, and the explosive missile blew the running man nearly in half. Sergeant Brian silently retrieved the food pack and brought it back to Hague.

"Do you want it here, Lieutenant, or shall I take it up to the main party?"

"We'll keep it here, Sergeant. Sewell can take it back tonight after our medical check." Hague's voice shook, and he wished savagely that he could have had the nerve to pass that swift death sentence. Didrickson's crime was dangerous to every member of the party, and the Sergeant had been right to shoot. But when the time came—when perhaps the Sergeant wasn't with him—would he, Hague, react swiftly and coolly as an officer should, he wondered despairingly?

"All right, lads, let's pull," he said, and the tight-lipped gun crew filed again into the hushed, somber forest corridors.

II

COMMUNICATIONS TECHNICIAN HARKER took a deep pull at his mug of steaming coffee, blinked his eyes hard at the swimming dials before him, and lit a cigarette. *Odysseus* warning center was never quiet, even now in the graveyard watch when all other lights were turned low through the great ship's hull. Here in the neat grey room, murmuring, softly-clicking signal equipment was banked against every wall in a gleaming array of dials and meters, heavy power leads, black panels, and intricate sheaves of colored wire. The sonar kept up a sleepy drone, and radar scopes glowed fitfully with interference patterns, and the warning buzzer beeped softly as the radar echoed back to its receivers the rumor of strange planetary forces that radar hadn't been built to filter through. What made the interference, base technicians couldn't tell, but it practically paralyzed radio communication on all bands, and blanketed out even radar warnings.

The cigarette burned his fingertips, and Harker jerked awake and tried to concentrate on the letter he was writing home. It would be microfilmed, and go on the next courier rocket. A movement at the Warnings Room door brought Harker's head up, and he saw Commander Chapman, lean and grey, standing there.

"Good evening, sir. Come on in. I've got coffee on." The Communications Technician took a pot from the glow heater at his elbow, and set out another cup.

The Commander smiled tiredly, pulled out a stubby metal stool, and sat across the low table from Harker, sipping the scalding coffee cautiously. He looked up after a moment.

"What's the good word, Harker? Picked up anything?"

Harker ran his fingers through his mop of black hair, and grimaced.

"Not a squeak, sir. No radio, no radar. Of course, the interference may be blanketing those. Creates a lot of false signals, too, on the radar screens. But we can't even pick 'em up with long-range sonar. That should get through. We're pretty sure they crashed, all right."

"How about our signals, Harker? Do you think we're getting through to them?"

Harker leaned back expansively, happy to expound his specialty.

"Well, we've been sending radio signals every hour on the hour, and radio voice messages every hour on the half hour. We're sending a continuous sonar beam for their direction-finder. That's about all we can do. As for their picking it up, assuming the rocket has crashed and been totally knocked out, they still have a radio in the whippet tank. It's a transreceiver. And they have a portable sonar set, one of those little twenty-pound armored detection units. They'll use it as a direction finder."

Chapman swirled the coffee around in the bottom of his cup and stared thoughtfully into it.

"If they can get sonar, why can't we send them messages down the sonar beam? You know, flick it on and off in Morse code?"

"It won't work with a small detector like they have, sir. With our big set here, we could send them a message, but that outfit they have might burn out. It has a limited sealed motor supply that must break down an initial current resistance on the grids before the rectifiers can convert it to audible sound. With the set operating continuously, power drainage is small, but begin changing your signal beam and the power has to break down the grid resistance several hundred times for every short signal sent. It would burn out their set in a matter of hours.

"It works like a slide trombone, sort of. Run your slide way out, and you get a slowly vibrating column of air, and that is heard as a low note, only on sonar it would be a short note. Run your slide way up, and the vibrations are progressively faster and higher in pitch. The sonar set, at peak, is vibrating so rapidly that it's almost static, and the power flow is actually continuous. But, starting and stopping the set continuously, the vibrators never have a chance to reach a normal peak, and the power flow is broken at each vibration in the receiver—and a few hours later your sonar receptor is a hunk of junk."

"All right, Harker. Your discussion is vague, but I get the general idea that my suggestion wasn't too hot. Well, have whoever is on duty call me if any signals come through." The Commander set down his cup, said goodnight, and moved off down the hushed corridor. Harker returned to his letter and a chewed stub of pencil, while he scowled in a fevered agony of composition. It was a letter to his girl, and it had to be good.

NIGHT HAD BEGUN to fall over the forest roof, and stole thickening down the muddy cathedral aisles of great trees, and Hague listened hopefully for the halt signal from the whippet tank, which should come soon. He was worried about Bucci who was laughing and talking volubly, and the officer decided he must have a touch of fever. The dark, muscular gunner kept talking about his young wife in what was almost a babble. Once he staggered and nearly fell, until Hurd took the pneumatic gun barrel assembly and carried it on his own shoulders. They were all listening expectantly for the tank's klaxon, when a brassy scream ripped the evening to echoing shreds and a flurry of shots broke out ahead.

The scream came again, metallic, and shrill as a locomotive gone amok; yells, explosive-bullet reports, and the sound of hammering blows drifted back.

"Take over, Brian," Hague snapped. "Crosse, Hurd—let's go!"

The three men ran at a stagger through the dragging mud around a turn in the trail, and dropped the pneumatic gun swiftly into place, Hurd at firing position, Crosse on the charger, and Hague prone in the slime snapping an ammunition belt into the loader.

Two emergency flares someone had thrown lit the trail ahead in a garish photographic fantasy of bright, white light and ink-black shadow, a scene out of *Inferno*. A cart lay on its side, men were running clear, the whippet tank lay squirming on its side, and above it towered the screaming thing. A lizard, or dinosaur, rearing up thirty feet, scaly grey, a man clutched in its two hand-like claws, while its armored tail smashed and smashed at the tank with pile-driver blows. Explosive bullets cracked around the thing's chest in blue-white flares of light, but it continued to rip at the man twisting pygmy-like in its claws—white teeth glinting like sabers as its blindly malevolent screams went on.

"On target," Hurd's voice came strained and low.

"Charge on," from Crosse.

"Let her go!" Hague yelled, and fed APX cartridges as the gun coughed a burst of armor-piercing, explosive shells into the rearing beast. Hague saw the tank turret swing up as Whittaker tried to get his gun in action, but a slashing slap of the monster's tail spun it back brokenly. The cluster of pneumatic shells hit then and burst within that body, and the great grey-skinned trunk was hurled off the trail, the head slapping against a tree trunk on the other side as the reptile was halved.

"Good shooting, Crosse," Hague grunted. "Get back with Brian. Keep the gun ready. That thing might have a mate." He ran toward the main party, and into the glare of the two flares.

"Where's Devlin?"

Clark, the navigation officer, was standing with a small huddle of men near the smashed supply cart.

"Here, Hague," he called. His eyes were sunken, his face older in the days since Hague had last seen him. "Devlin's dead, smashed between the cart and a tree trunk. We've lost two men, Commander Devlin and Ellis, the soils man. He's the one it was eating." He grimaced.

"That leaves twenty-three of us?" Hague inquired, and tried to sound casual.

"That's right. You'll continue to cover the rear. Those horn sounds you reported had Devlin worried about an attack from your direction. I'll be with the tank."

SERGEANT BRIAN was stoically heating ration stew over the cook unit when Hague returned, while the crew sat in a close circle, alternately eying nervously the forest at their backs, and the savory steam that rose from Brian's mixture. There wasn't much for each of them, but it was hot and highly nutritious, and after a cigarette and coffee they would feel comfort for a while.

Crosse, seated on the grey metal charger tube he'd carried all day, fingered the helmet in his lap, and looked inquiringly at the Lieutenant.

"Well, sir, anybody hurt? Was the tank smashed?"

Hague squatted in the circle, sniffed the stew with loud enthusiasm, and looked about the circle.

"Commander Devlin's dead, and Ellis. One supply cart smashed, but the tank'll be all right. The lizard charged the tank. Balistierri thinks it was the lizard's mating season, and he figured the tank was another male and he tried to fight it. Then he stayed—to—lunch, and we got him. Lieutenant Clark is in command now."

The orange glow of Brian's cook unit painted queer shadows on the strained faces around him, and Hague tried to brighten them up.

"Will you favor us with one of your inimitable harmonica arrangements, Maestro Bormann?"

"I can't right now. I'm bandaging Helen's wing." He held out something in the palm of his hand, and the heater's glow glittered on liquid black eyes. "She's like a little bird, but without her feathers. See?" He placed the warm lump in Hague's hand. "For wings, she's just got skin, like a bat, except she's built like a bird."

"You ought to show this to Balistierri, and maybe he'll name this for you too."

Bormann's homely face creased into a grin. "I did, sir. At the noon halt when I found it. It's named after my girl. 'Bormann's Helen', only in Latin. Helen's got a broken wing."

As they ate, they heard the horn note again. Bucci's black eyes were feverishly bright, his skin hot and dry, and the vine scratches on his leg badly inflamed; and when the rest began to sing he was quiet. The reedy song of Bormann's harmonica piped down the quiet forest passages, and echoed back from the great trees; and somewhere, as Hague dozed off in his little tent, he heard the horn note again, sandwiched into mouth organ melody.

TWO DAYS OF slogging through the slimy green mud, and at a noon halt Sewell brought back word to be careful, that a man had failed to report at roll call that morning. The gun crew divided Bucci's equipment between them, and he limped in the middle of the file on crutches fashioned from ration cart wreckage. Crosse, who'd been glancing off continually, like a wizened, curious rat, flung up his arm in a silent signal to halt, and Hague moved in to investigate, the ever-present Brian moving carefully and with a jungle beast's silent poise just behind him. Crumpled like a sack of damp laundry, in the murk of two root buttresses, lay Romano, one of the two photographers. His Hasselblad camera lay beneath his body crushing a small plant he must have been photographing.

From the back of Romano's neck protruded a gleaming nine-inch arrow shaft, a lovely thing of gleaming bronze-like metal, delicately thin of shaft and with fragile hammered bronze vanes. Brian moved up behind Hague, bent over the body and cut the arrow free.

They examined the thing, and when Brian spoke Hague was surprised that this time even the rock-steady Sergeant spoke in a hushed voice, the kind boys use when they walk by a graveyard at night and don't wish to attract unwelcome attention.

"Looks like it came from a blowgun, Lieutenant. See the plug at the back. It must be poisoned; it's not big enough to kill him otherwise."

Hague grunted assent, and the two moved back trailward.

"Brian, take over. Crosse, come on. We'll report this to Clark. Remember, from now on wear your body armor and go in pairs when you leave the trail. Get Bucci's plates on to him."

Bormann and Hurd set down their loads, and were buckling the weakly protesting Bucci into his chest and back plates, as Hague left them.

COMMANDER CHAPMAN stared at the circle of faces. His section commanders lounged about his tiny square office. "Well, then, what are their chances?"

Bjornson, executive for the technical section, stared at Chapman levelly.

"I can vouch for Devlin. He's not precisely a rule-book officer, but that's why I recommended him for this expedition. He's at his best in an unusual situation, one where he has to depend on his own wits. He'll bring them through."

Artilleryman Branch spoke in turn. "I don't know about Hague. He's young, untried. Seemed a little unsure. He might grow panicky and be useless. I sent him because there was no one else, unless I went myself."

The Commander cleared his throat brusquely. "I know you wanted to go, Branch, but we can't send out our executive officers. Not yet, anyway. What about Clark? Could he take over Devlin's job?"

"Clark can handle it," Captain Rindell of the Science Section, was saying. "He likes to follow the rule-book, but he's sturdy stuff. He'll bring them through if something happens to Devlin."

"Hmmmm—that leaves Hague as the one questionable link in their chain of command. Young man, untried. Of course, he's only the junior officer. There's no use stewing over this; but I'll tell you frankly, that if those men can't get their records through to us before we send the next courier rocket to earth, I think the U.S. Rocket Service is finished. This attempt will be chalked up as a failure. The project will be abandoned entirely, and we'll be ordered back to Earth to serve as a fighter arm there."

Bjornson peered from the spaceport window and looked out over the cinder-packed parade a hundred feet below. "What makes you so sure the Rocket Service is in immediate danger of being scrapped?"

"The last courier rocket contained a confidential memo from Secretary Dougherty. There is considerable war talk, and the other Service Arms are plunging for larger armaments. They want their appropriations of money and stock pile materials expanded at our expense. We've got to show that we are doing a good job, show the Government a concrete return in the form of adequate reports on the surface of Venus, and its soils and raw materials."

"What about the 'copters!" Rindell inquired. "They brought in some good stuff for the reports."

"Yes, but with a crew of only four men, they can't do enough."

Branch cut in dryly. "About all I can see is to look hopeful. The Rocket would have exhausted its fuel long ago. It's been over ten weeks since they left Base."

"Assuming they're marching overland, God forbid, they'll have only sonar and radio, right?" Bjornson was saying. "Why not keep our klaxon going? It's a pretty faint hope, but we'll have to try everything. My section is keeping the listeners manned continually, we've got a sonar beam out, radio messages every thirty minutes, and with the klaxon we're doing all we can. I doubt if anything living could approach within a twenty-five-mile range without hearing that klaxon, or without us hearing them with the listeners."

"All right." Commander Chapman stared hopelessly at a fresh batch of reports burdening his desk. "Send out ground parties within the ten-mile limit, but remember we can't afford to lose men. When the 'copters are back in, send them both West." West meant merely in a direction west from Meridian 0, as the mother rocket's landing place had been designated. "They can't do much searching over that rainforest, but it's a try. They might pick up a radio message."

Chapman returned grumpily to his reports, and the others filed out.

III

AT NIGHT, ON GUARD, Hague saw a thousand horrors peopling the Stygian forest murk; but when he flashed his lightpak into darkness there was nothing. He wondered how long he could stand the waiting, when he would crack as Supply Sergeant Didrickson had, and his comrades would blast him down with explosive bullets. He should be like Brian, hard and sure, and always doing the right thing, he decided. He'd come out of OCS Gunnery School, trained briefly in the newly-formed U.S. Rocket Service. Then the expedition to Venus—it was a fifty-fifty chance they said, and out of all the volunteers he'd been picked. And when the first expedition was ready to blast off from the Base Camp on Venus, he'd been picked again. Why, he cursed despairingly? Sure, he wanted to come, but how could his commanders have had faith in him, when he didn't know himself if he could continue to hold out.

Sounds on the trail sent his carbine automatically to ready, and he called a strained, "Halt."

"Okay, Hague. It's Clark and Arndt."

The wiry little navigation officer, and lean, scraggy Geologist Arndt, the latter's arm still in a sling, came into the glow of Hague's lightpak.

"Any more horns or arrows?" Clark's voice sounded tight, and repressed; Hague reflected that perhaps the strain was getting him too.

"No, but Bucci is getting worse. Can't you carry him on the cart?"

"Hague, I've told you twenty times. That cart is full and breaking down now. Get it through your head that it's no longer individual men we can think of now, but the entire party. If they can't march, they must be left, or all of us may die!" His voice was savage, and when he tried to light a cigarette his hand shook. "All right. It's murder, and I don't like it any better than you do."

"How are we doing? What's the overall picture?" Both of the officers tried to smile a little at the memory of that pompous little phrase, favorite of a windbag they'd served under.

"Not good. Twenty-two of us now."

"Hirooka thinks we may be within radio range of Base soon," he continued more hopefully. "With this interference, we can't tell, though."

They talked a little longer, Arndt gave the gunnery officer a food-and-medical supply packet, and Hague's visitors became two bobbing glows of light that vanished down the trail.

A SOUL CRUSHING WEIGHT of days passed while they strained forward through mud and green gloom, like men walking on a forest sea bottom. Then it was a cool dawn, and a tugging at his boot awoke the Lieutenant. Hurd, his face a strained mask, was peering into the officer's small shelter tent and jerking at his leg.

"Get awake, Lieutenant. I think they're here."

Hague struggled hard to blink off the exhausted sleep he'd been in.

"Listen, Lieutenant, one of them horns has been blowing. It's right here. Between us and the main party."

"Okay." Hague rolled swiftly from the tent as Hurd awoke the men. Hague moved swiftly to each.

"Brian, you handle the gun. Bucci, loader. Crosse, charger. Bormann, cover our right; Hurd the left. I'll watch the trail ahead."

Brian and Crosse worked swiftly and quietly with the lethal efficiency that had made them crack gunners at Fort Fisher, North Carolina. Bucci lay motionless at the ammunition box, but his eyes were bright, and he didn't seem to mind his feverish, swollen leg. The Sergeant and Crosse slewed the pneumatic gun to cover their back trail, and fell into position beside the gleaming grey tube. Hague, Bormann and Hurd moved quickly at striking tents and rolling packs, their rifles ready at hand.

Hague had forgotten his fears and the self-doubt, the feeling that he had no business ordering men like Sergeant Brian, and Hurd and Bormann. They were swallowed in intense expectancy as he lay watching the dawn fog that obscured like thick smoke the trail that led to Clark's party and the whippet tank.

He peered back over his shoulder for a moment. Brian, Bucci, and Crosse, mud-stained backs toward him, were checking the gun and murmuring soft comments. Bormann looked at the officer, grinned tightly, and pointed at Helen perched on his shoulder. His lips carefully framed the words, "Be a pushover, Helen brings luck."

The little bird peered up into Bormann's old-young face, and Hague, trying to grin back, hoped he looked confident. Hurd lay on the other side of the trail, his back to Bormann, peering over his rifle barrel, bearded jaws rhythmically working a cud of tobacco he'd salvaged somewhere, and Hague suddenly thought he must have been saving it for the finish.

Hague looked back into the green light beginning to penetrate the trail fog, changing it into a glowing mass—then thought he saw a movement. Up the trail, the whippet tank's motor caught with a roar, and he heard Whittaker traversing the battered tank's turret. The turret gun boomed flatly, and a shell burst somewhere in the forest darkness to Hague's right.

Then there was a gobbling yell and gray man-like figures poured out onto the trail. Hague set his sights on them, the black sight-blade silhouetting sharply in the glowing fog. He set them on a running figure, and squeezed his trigger, then again, and again, as new targets came. Sharp reports ran crackling among the great trees. Sharp screams came, and a whistling sound overhead that he knew were blowgun arrows. The pneumatic gun sputtered behind him, and Bormann's and Hurd's rifles thudded in the growing roar.

Blue flashes and explosive bullets made fantastic flares back in the forest shadows; and suddenly a knot of man-shapes were running toward him through the fog. Hague picked out one in the glowing mist, fired, another, fired. Gobbling yells were around him, and he shot toward them through the fog, at point-blank range. A thing rose up beside him, and Hague yelled with murderous fury, and drove his belt knife up into grey leather skin. Something burned his shoulder as he rolled aside and fired at the dark form standing over him with a poised, barbed spear. The blue-white flash was blinding, and he cursed and leaped up.

There was nothing more. Scattered shots, and the forest lay quiet again. After that shot at point-blank range, Hague's vision had blacked out.

"Anyone else need first aid?" he called, and tried to keep his voice firm. When there was silence, he said, "Hurd, lead me to the tank."

He heard the rat-faced man choke, "My God, he's blind."

"Just flash blindness, Hurd. Only temporary." Hague kept his face stiff, and hoped frantically that he was right, that it was just temporary blindness, temporary optic shock.

Sergeant Brian's icy voice cut in. "Gun's all right, Lieutenant. Nobody hurt. We fired twenty-eight rounds of H.E. No A.P.X. Get going with him, Hurd."

He felt Hurd's tug at his elbow, and they made their way up the trail.

"What do they look like, Hurd?"

"These men-things? They're grey, about my size, skin looks like leather, and their heads are flattish. Eyes on the side of their heads, like a lizard. Not a stitch of clothes. Just a belt with a knife and arrow holder. And they got webbed claws for feet. They're ugly-looking things, sir. Here's the tank."

Clark's voice came, hard and clear. "That you, Hague?" Silence for a moment. "What's wrong? You're not blinded?"

Sewell had dropped his irascibility, and his voice was steady and kindly.

"Just flash blindness, isn't it, sir? This salve will fix you up. You've got a cut on your shoulder. I'll take care of that too."

"How are your men, Hague?" Clark sounded as though he were standing beside Hague.

"Not a scratch. We're ready to march."

"Five hurt here, three with the advance party, and two at the tank. We got 'em good, though. They hit the trail between our units and got fire from both sides. Must be twenty of them dead."

Hague grimaced at the sting of something Sewell had squeezed into his eyes. "Who was hurt?"

"Arndt, the geologist; his buddy, Gault, the botanist; lab technician Harker, Crewman Harker, and Szachek, the meteorologist man. How's your pneumatic ammunition?"

"We fired twenty-eight rounds of H.E."

Cartographer Hirooka's voice burst in excitedly.

"That gun crew of yours! Your gun crew got twenty-one of these—these lizard-men. A bunch came up our back trail, and the pneumatic cut them to pieces."

"Good going, Hague. We'll leave you extended back there. I'm pulling in the advance party, and there'll be just two groups. We'll be at point, and you continue at afterguard." Clark was silent for a moment, then his voice came bitterly, "We're down to seventeen men, you know."

He cursed, and Hague heard the wiry little navigator slosh away through the mud and begin shouting orders. He and Hurd started back with Whittaker and Sergeant Sample yelling wild instructions from the tank as to what the rear guard might do with the next batch of lizard-men who came sneaking up.

Hague's vision was clearing, and he saw Balistierri and the photographer Whitcomb through a milky haze, measuring, photographing, and even dissecting several of the lizard-men. The back trail, swept by pneumatic gunfire was a wreck of wood splinters and smashed trees, smashed bodies, and cratered earth.

They broke down the gun, harnessed the equipment, and swung off at the sound of Clark's whistle. Bucci had to be supported between two of the others, and they took turnabout at the job, sloshing through the water and mud, with Bucci's one swollen leg dragging uselessly between them. It was punishing work as the heat veils shimmered and thickened, but no one seemed to consider leaving him behind, Hague noticed; and he determined to say nothing about Clark's orders that the sick must be abandoned.

Days and nights flashed by in a dreary monotony of mud, heat, insects and thinning rations. Then one morning the giant trees began to thin, and they passed from rainforest into jungle.

The change was too late for Bucci. They carved a neat marker beside the trail, and set the dead youth's helmet atop it. Lieutenant Hague carried ahead a smudged letter in his shirt, with instructions to forward it to Wilma, the gunner's young wife.

Hague and his four gunners followed the rattling whippet tank's trail higher, the jungle fell behind, and their protesting legs carried them over the rim of a high, cloud-swept plateau, that swept on to the limit of vision on both sides and ahead.

THE CITY'S BLACK WALLS squatted secretively; foursquare, black, glassy walls with a blocky tower set sturdily at each of the four corners, enclosing what appeared to be a square mile of low buildings. Grey fog whipped coldly across the flat bleakness and rustled through dark grass.

Balistierri, plodding beside Hague at the rear, stared at it warily, muttering, "And Childe Roland to the dark tower came."

Sampler's tank ground along the base of the twelve-foot wall, turned at a sharp right angle, and the party filed through a square cut opening that once had been a gate. The black city looked tenantless. There was dark-hued grass growing in the misted streets and squares, and across the lintels of cube-shaped, neatly aligned dwellings, fashioned of thick, black blocks. Hague could hear nothing but whipping wind, the tank's clatter, and the quiet clink of equipment as men shuffled ahead through the knee-high grass, peering watchfully into dark doorways.

Clark's whistle shrilled, the tank motor died, and they waited.

"Hague, come ahead."

The gunnery officer nodded at Sergeant Brian, and walked swiftly to Clark, who was leaning against the tank's mud-caked side.

"Sampler says we've got to make repairs on the tank. We'll shelter here. Set your gun on a roof top commanding the street—or, better yet, set it on the wall. I'll want two of your gunners to go hunting food animals."

"What do you think this place is, Bob?"

"Beats me," and the navigator's wind-burned face twisted in a perplexed expression. "Lenkranz knows more about metals, but he thinks this stone is volcanic, like obsidian. Those lizard-men couldn't have built it."

"We passed some kind of bas-relief or murals inside the gate."

"Whitcomb is going to photograph them. Blake, Lenkranz, Johnston, and Hirooka are going to explore the place. Your two gunners, and Crewman Swenson and Balistierri will form the two hunting parties."

For five days, Hague and Crosse walked over the sullen plateau beneath scudding, leaden clouds, hunting little lizards that resembled dinosaurs and ran in coveys like grey chickens. The meat was good, and Sewell dropped his role of medical technician to achieve glowing accolades as an expert cook. Balistierri was in a zoologist's paradise, and he hunted over the windy plain with Swenson, the big white-haired Swede, for ten and twelve hours at a stretch. Balistierri would sit in the cook's unit glow at night, his thin face ecstatic as he described the weird life forms he and Swenson had tracked down during the day; or alternately he'd bemoan the necessity of eating what were to him priceless zoological specimens.

Whittaker and Sampler hammered in the recalcitrant tank's bowels and shouted ribald remarks to any one nearby, until they emerged the third day, grease-stained and perspiring, to announce that "She's ready to roll her g—— d—— cleats off."

Whittaker had been nursing the tank's radio transreceiver beside the forward hatch this grey afternoon, when his wild yell brought Hague erect. The officer carefully handed Bormann's skin bird back to the gunner, swung down from the city wall's edge, and ran to Whittaker's side. Clark was already there when Hague reached the tank.

"Listen! I've got 'em!" Whittaker yelped and extended the crackling earphones to Clark.

A tinny voice penetrated the interference.

"Base.... Peter One.... Do you hear... to George Easy Peter One ... hear me ... out."

Whittaker snapped on his throat microphone.

"George Easy Peter One to Base. George Easy Peter One to Base. We hear you. We hear you. Rocket crashed. Rocket crashed. Returning overland. Returning overland. Present strength sixteen men. Can you drop us supplies? Can you drop us supplies?"

The earphones sputtered, but no more voices came through. Clark's excited face fell into tired lines.

"We've lost them. Keep trying, Whittaker. Hague, we'll march-order tomorrow at dawn. You'll take the rear again."

GREY, WINDY, dawn light brought them out to the sound of Clark's call. Strapping on equipment and plates, they assembled around the tank. They were rested, and full fed.

"Walk, you poor devils," Whittaker was yelling from his tank turret. "And, if you get tired, run awhile," he snorted, grinning heartlessly, as he leaned back in pretended luxury against the gunner's seat, a thinly padded metal strip.

Balistierri and the blond Swenson shouldered their rifles and shuffled out. They would move well in advance as scouts.

"I wouldn't ride in that armored alarm-clock if it had a built-in harem," Hurd was screaming at Whittaker, and hurled a well-placed mudball at the tankman's head as the tank motor caught, and the metal vehicle lumbered ahead toward the gate, with Whittaker sneering, but with most of his head safely below the turret rim. Beside it marched Clark, his ragged uniform carefully scraped clean of mud, and with him Lenkranz, the metals man. Both carried rifles and wore half empty bandoliers of blast cartridges.

The supply cart jerked behind the tank, and behind it filed Whitcomb with his cameras; Sewell, the big, laconic medical technician; Johnston; cartographer Hirooka perusing absorbedly the clip board that held his strip map; Blake, the lean and spectacled bacteriologist, brought up the rear. Hague waited until they had disappeared through the gate cut sharply in the city's black wall, then he turned to his gun crew.

Sergeant Brian, saturnine as always, swung past carrying the pneumatic barrel assembly, Crosse with the charger a pace behind. Next, Bormann, whispering to Helen who rode his shoulder piping throaty calls. Last came Hurd, swaggering past with jaws grinding steadily at that mysterious cud. Hague cast a glance over his shoulder at the deserted street of black cubes, wondered at the dank loneness of the place, and followed Hurd.

The hours wore on as they swung across dark grass, through damp tendrils of cloud, and faced into whipping, cold wind, eyes narrowed against its sting. Helen, squawking unhappily, crawled inside Bormann's shirt and rode with just her brown bird-head protruding.

"Look at the big hole, Lieutenant," Hurd called above the wind.

Hurd had dropped behind, and Hague called a halt to investigate Hurd's find, but as he hiked rapidly back, the wiry little man yelled and pitched out of sight. Brian came running, and he and Hague peered over the edge of a funnel shaped pit, from which Hurd was trying to crawl. Each time he'd get a third of the way up the eighteen-foot slope, gravelly soil would slide and he'd again be carried to the bottom.

"Throw me a line."

Brian pulled a hank of nylon line from his belt, shook out the snarls, and tossed an end into Hurd's clawing hands. Hague and the Sergeant anchored themselves to the upper end and were preparing to haul, when Hague saw something move in the gravel beneath Hurd's feet, at the funnel bottom, and saw a giant-pincers emerging from loose, black gravel.

"Hurd look out!" he screamed.

The little man, white-faced, threw himself aside as a giant beetle head erupted through the funnel bottom. The great pincers jaws fastened around Hurd's waist as he struggled frantically up the pit's side. He began screaming when the beetle monster dragged him relentlessly down, his distorted face flung up at them appealingly. Hague snatched at his rifle and brought it up. When the gun cracked, the pincers tightened on Hurd's middle, and the little man was snipped in half. The blue-white flash and report of the explosive bullet blended with Hurd's choked yells, the beetle rolled over on its back, and the two bodies lay entangled at the pit bottom. Brian and Hague looked at each other in silent, blanched horror, then turned from the pit's edge and loped back to the others.

Bormann and Crosse peered fearfully across the wind-whipped grass, and inquired in shouts what Hurd was doing.

"He's dead, gone," Hague yelled savagely over the wind's whine. "Keep moving. We can't do anything. Keep going."

IV

AT 1630 HOURS Commander Technician Harker slipped on the earset, threw over a transmitting switch, and monotoned the routine verbal message.

"Base to George Easy Peter One.... Base to George Easy Peter One.... Do you hear me George Easy Peter One?... Do you hear me George Easy Peter One?... reply please ... reply please." Nothing came from his earphones, but bursts of crackling interference, until he tried the 'copters next, and "George Easy Peter Two" and "George Easy Peter Three" reported in. They were operating near the base.

He tried "One" again, just in case.

"Base to George Easy Peter One.... Base to George Easy Peter One.... Do you hear me?... Do you hear me?... out."

A scratching whisper resolved over the interference. Harker's face wore a stunned look, but he quickly flung over a second switch and the scratching voice blared over the mother ship's entire address system. Men dropped their work throughout the great hull, and clustered around the speakers.

"George One.... Base ... hear you ... rocket crashed ... overland ... present strength ... supplies ... drop supplies."

Interference surged back and drowned the whispering voice, while through *Odysseus'* hull a ragged cheer grew and gathered volume. Harker shut off the address system and strained over his crackling earphones, but nothing more came in response to his radio calls.

He glanced up and found the Warning Room jammed with technicians, science section members, officers, men in laboratory smocks, or greasy overalls, or spotless Rocket Service uniforms, watching intently his own strained face as he tried to get through. Commander Chapman looked haggard, and Harker remembered that someone had once said that Chapman's young sister was the wife of the medical technician who'd gone out with Patrol Rocket One.

Harker finally pulled off the earphones reluctantly and set them on the table before him. "That's all. You heard everything they said over the P.A. system. Nothing more is coming through."

NIGHT CAME, another day, night again, and they came finally to the plateau's end, and stood staring from a windy escarpment across an endless roof of rainforest far below, grey green under the continuous roof of lead-colored clouds. Hague, standing back a little, watched them. A thin line of ragged men along the rim peering mournfully out across that endless expanse for a gleam that might be the distant hull of *Odysseus*, the mother ship. A damp wind fluttered their rags and plastered them against gaunt bodies.

Clark and Sampler were conferring in shouts.

"Will the tank make it down this grade?" Clark wanted to know.

For once, Sergeant Sampler's mobile, merry face was grim.

"I don't know, but we'll sure try. Be ready to cut that cart loose if the tank starts to slip."

Drag ropes were fastened to the cart, a man stationed at the tank hitch, and Sampler sent his tank lurching forward over the edge, and it slanted down at a sharp angle.

Hague, holding a drag rope, set his heels and allowed the tank's weight to pull him forward over the rim; and the tank, cart, and muddy figures hanging to drag ropes began descending the steep gradient. Bormann, just ahead of the Lieutenant, strained back at the rope and turned a tight face over his shoulder.

"She's slipping faster!"

The tank was picking up speed, and Hague heard the clash of gears as Sampler tried to fight the downward pull of gravity. Gears ground, and Sampler forced the whippet straight again, but the downward slide was increasing. Hague was flattened under Bormann, heels digging, and behind him he could hear Sergeant Brian cursing, struggling to keep flat against the downward pull.

The tank careened sideways again, slipped, and Whittaker's white face popped from her turret.

"She's going," he screamed.

A drag rope parted. Clark sprang like a madman between tank and cart, and cut the hitch. The tank, with no longer sufficient restraining weight, tipped with slow majesty outward, then rolled out and down, bouncing, smashing as if in a slow-motion film, shedding parts at each crushing contact. It looked like a toy below them, still rolling and gathering speed, when Hague saw Whittaker's body fly free, a tiny ragdoll at that distance, and the tank was lost to view when it bounced off a ledge and went floating down through space.

Clark signaled them forward, and they inched the supply cart downward on the drag ropes, legs trembling with strain, and their nerves twitching at the memory of Whittaker's chalky face peering from the falling turret. It was eight hours before they reached the bottom, reeling with exhaustion, set a guard, and tumbled into their shelter tents.

OUTSIDE, HAGUE could hear Clark pacing restlessly, trying to assure himself that he'd been right to cut the tank free, that there'd been no chance to save Whittaker and Sampler when the tank began to slide.

Hague lay in his little tent listening to the footsteps splash past in muddy Venusian soil, and was thankful that he hadn't had to make the decision. He'd been saving three cigarettes in an oilskin packet, and he drew one carefully from the wrapping now, lit it, and inhaled deeply. Could he have done what Clark did—break that hitch? He still didn't know when he took a last lung-filling pull at the tiny stub of cigarette and crushed it out carefully.

As dawn filtered through the cloud layer, they were rolling shelter tents and buckling on equipment. Clark's face was a worn mask when he talked with Hague, and his fingers shook over his pack buckles.

"There are thirteen of us. Six men will pull the supply cart, and six guard, in four-hour shifts. You and I will alternate command at guard."

He was silent for a moment, then watched Hague's face intently as he spoke again.

"It'll be a first-grade miracle if any of us get through. Hague, you—you know I had to cut that tank free." His voice rose nervously. "You know that! You're an officer."

"Yeah, I guess you did." Hague couldn't say it any better, and he turned away and fussed busily with the bars holding the portable Sonar detection unit to the supply cart.

They moved off with Hague leaning into harness pulling the supply cart bumpily ahead. Clark stumbled jerkily at the head, with Blake, a lean, silent ghost beside him, rifle in hand. The cart came next with Hague, Bormann, Sergeant Brian, Crosse, Lenkranz and Sewell leaning in single file against its weight. At the rear marched photographer Whitcomb, Hirooka with his maps, and Balistierri, each carrying a rifle. The big Swede Swenson was last in line, peering warily back into the rainforest shadows. The thirteen men wound Indian file from sight of the flat-headed reptilian thing, clutching a sheaf of bronze arrows, that watched them.

HAGUE HAD LOST COUNT of days again when he looked up into the shadowy forest roof, his feet finding their way unconsciously through the thin mud, his ears registering automatically the murmurs of talk behind him, the supply cart's tortured creaking, and the continuous Sonar drone. The air felt different, warmer than its usual steam bath heat, close and charged with expectancy, and the forest seemed to crouch in waiting with the repressed silence of a hunting cat.

Crosse yelled thinly from the rear of the file, and they all halted to listen, the hauling crew dropping their harness thankfully. Hague turned back and saw Crosse's thin arm waving a rifle overhead, then pointing down the trail. The Lieutenant listened carefully until he caught the sound, a thin call, the sound of a horn mellowed by distance.

The men unthinkingly moved in close and threw wary looks into the forest ways around them.

"Move further ahead, Hague. Must be more lizard-men." Clark swore, with tired despair. "All right, let's get moving and make it fast."

The cart creaked ahead again, moving faster this time, and the snicking of rifle bolts came to Hague. He moved swiftly ahead on the trail and glanced up again, saw breaks in the forest roof, and realized that the huge trees were pitching wildly far above.

"Look up," he yelled, "wind coming!"

The wind came suddenly, striking with stone wall solidity. Hague sprinted to the cart, and the struggling body of men worked it off the trail, and into a buttress angle of two great tree roots, lashing it there with nylon ropes. The wind velocity increased, smashing torn branches overhead, and ripping at the men who lay with their heads well down in the mud. Tiny animals were blown hurtling past, and once a great spider came flailing in cartwheel fashion, then smashed brokenly against a tree.

The wind drone rose in volume, the air darkened, and Hague lost sight of the other men from behind his huddled shelter against a wall like root. The great trees twisted with groaning protest, and thunderous crashes came downward through the forest, with sometimes the faint squeak of a dying or frightened animal. The wind halted for a breathless, hushed moment of utter stillness, broken only by the dropping of limbs and the scurry of small life forms—then came the screaming fury from the opposite direction.

For a moment, the gunnery officer thought he'd be torn from the root to which his clawing fingers clung. Its brutal force smashed breath from Hague's lungs and held him pinned in his corner until he struggled choking for air as a drowning man does. It seemed that he couldn't draw breath, that the air was a solid mass from which he could no longer get life. Then the wind stopped as suddenly as it had come, leaving dazed quiet. As he stumbled back to the cart, Hague saw crushed beneath a thigh-sized limb a feebly moving reptilian head; and the dying eyes of the lizard-man were still able to stare at him in cold malevolence.

The supply cart was still intact, roped between buttressing roots to belt knives driven into the tough wood. Hague and Clark freed it, called a hasty roll, and the march was resumed at a fast pace through cooled, cleaner air. They could no longer hear horn sounds; but the grim knowledge that lizard-men were near them lent strength, and Hague led as rapidly as he dared, listening carefully to the Sonar's drone behind him, altering his course when the sound faded, and straightening out when it grew in volume.

A day slipped by and another, and the cart rolled ahead through thin greasy mud on the forest floor, with the Sonar's drone mingled with murmuring men's voices talking of food. It was the universal topic, and they carefully worked out prolonged menus each would engorge when they reached home. They forgot heat, insect bites, the sapping humidity, and talked of food—steaming roasts, flanked by crystal goblets of iced wine, oily roasted nuts, and lush, crisp green salads.

V

HAGUE, AGAIN marching ahead with Balistierri, broke into the comparatively bright clearing, and was blinded for a moment by the sudden, cloud-strained light after days of forest darkness. As their eyes accommodated to the lemon-colored glare, he and Balistierri sighted the animals squatting beneath low bushes that grew thickly in the clearing. They were monkey-like primates with golden tawny coats, a cockatoo crest of white flaring above dog faces. The monkeys stared a moment, the great white crests rising doubtfully, ivory canine teeth fully three inches long bared.

They'd been feeding on fruit that dotted the shrub-filled clearing; but now one screamed a warning, and they sprang into vines that made a matted wall on every side. The two rifles cracked together again, and three fantastically colored bodies lay quiet, while the rest of the troop fled screaming into tree tops and disappeared. At the blast of sound, a fluttering kaleidoscope of color swept up about the startled rocketeers, and they stood blinded, while mad whorls of color whirled around them in a miniature storm.

"Giant butterflies," Balistierri was screaming in ecstasy. "Look at them! Big as a dove!"

Hague watched the bright insects coalesce into one agitated mass of vermillion, azure, metallic green, and sulphur yellow twenty feet overhead. The pulsating mass of hues resolved itself into single insects, with wings large as dinnerplates, and they streamed out of sight over the forest roof.

"What were they?" he grinned at Balistierri. "Going to name them after Bormann?"

The slight zoologist still watched the spot where they'd vanished.

"Does it matter much what I call them? Do you really believe any one will ever be able to read this logbook I'm making?" He eyed the gunnery officer bleakly, then, "Well, come on. We'd better skin these monks. They're food anyway."

Hague followed Balistierri, and they stood looking down at the golden furred primates. The zoologist knelt, fingered a bedraggled white crest, and remarked, "These blast cartridges don't leave much meat, do they? Hardly enough for the whole party." He pulled a tiny metal block, with a hook and dial, from his pocket, looped the hook through a tendon in the monkey's leg and lifted the dead animal.

"Hmmm. Forty-seven pounds. Not bad." He weighed each in turn, made measurements, and entered these in his pocket notebook.

The circle around Sewell, who presided over the cook unit, was merry that night. The men's eyes were bright in the heater glow as they stuffed their shrunken stomachs with monkey meat and the fruits the monkeys had been eating when Hague and Balistierri surprised them. Swenson and Crosse and Whitcomb, the photographer, overate and were violently sick; but the others sat picking their teeth contentedly in a close circle. Bormann pulled his harmonica from his shirt pocket, and the hard, silvery torrent of music set them to singing softly. Hague and Blake, the bacteriologist, stood guard among the trees.

At dawn, they were marching again, stepping more briskly over tiny creeks, through green-tinted mud, and the wet heat. At noon, they heard the horn again, and Clark ordered silence and a faster pace. They swung swiftly, eating iron rations as they marched. Hague leaned into his cart harness and watched perspiration staining through Bormann's shirted back just ahead of him. Behind, Sergeant Brian tugged manfully, and growled under his breath at buzzing insects, slapping occasionally with a low howl of muted anguish. Helen, the skin bird, rode on Bormann's shoulder, staring back into Hague's face with questioning chirps; and Hague was whistling softly between his teeth at her, when Bormann stopped suddenly and Hague slammed into him. Helen took flight with a startled squawk, and Clark came loping back to demand quiet. Bormann stared at the two officers, his young-old face blank with surprise.

"I'm, I'm shot," he stuttered, and stared wonderingly at the thing thrusting from the side opening in his chest armor. It was one of the fragile bronze arrows, gleaming metallically in the forest gloom.

Hague cursed, and jerked free of the cart harness. "Here, I'll get it free." He tugged at the shaft, and Bormann's face twisted. Hague stepped back. "Where's Sewell? This thing must be barbed."

"Back off the trail! Form a wide circle around the cart, but stay under cover! Fight 'em on their own ground!" Clark was yelling, and the men clustered about the cart faded into forest corridors.

Hague and Sewell, left alone, dragged Bormann's limp length beneath the metal cart. Hague leaped erect again, man-handled the pneumatic gun off the cart and onto the trail, spun the charger crank, and lay down in firing position. Behind him, Sewell grunted, "He's gone. Arrow poison must have paralyzed his diaphragm and chest muscles."

"Okay. Get up here and handle the ammunition." Hague's face was savage as the medical technician crawled into position beside him and opened an ammunition carrier.

"Watch the trail behind me," Hague continued, slamming up the top cover plate and jerking a belt through the pneumatic breech. "When I yell charge, spin the charger crank; and when I yell off a number, set the meter arrow at that number." He snapped the cover plate shut and locked it.

"The other way! They're coming the other way!" Sewell lumbered to his knees, and the two heaved the gun around. A blowgun arrow rattled off the cart body above them, and gobbling yells filtered among the trees with an answering crack of explosive cartridges. A screaming knot of grey figures came sprinting down on the cart. Hague squeezed the pneumatic's trigger, the gun coughed, and blue-fire-limned lizard-men crumpled in the trail mud.

"Okay, give 'em a few the other way."

The two men horsed the gun around and sent a buzzing flock of explosive loads down the forest corridor opening ahead of the cart. They began firing carefully down other corridors opening off the trail, aiming delicately lest their missiles explode too close and the concussion kill their own men; but they worked a blasting circle of destruction that smashed the great trees back in the forest and made openings in the forest roof. Blue fire flashed in the shadows and froze weird tableaus of screaming lizard-men and hurtling mud, branches, and great splinters of wood.

An exulting yell burst behind them. Hague saw Sewell stare over his shoulder, face contorted, then the big medical technician sprang to his feet. Hague rolled hard, pulling his belt knife, and saw Sewell and a grey man-shape locked in combat above him, saw leathery grey claws drive a bronze knife into the medic's unarmored throat; and then the gunnery officer was on his feet, knife slashing, and the lizard-man fell across the prone Sewell. An almost audible silence fell over the forest, and Hague saw Rocketeers filtering back onto the cart trail, rifles cautiously extended at ready.

"Where's Clark?" he asked Lenkranz. The grey-haired metals man gazed back dully.

"I haven't seen him since we left the trail. I was with Swenson."

The others moved in, and Hague listed the casualties. Sewell, Bormann, and Lieutenant Clark. Gunnery Officer Clarence Hague was now in command. That the Junior Lieutenant now commanded Ground Expeditionary Patrol Number One trickled into his still numb brain; and he wondered for a moment what the Base Commander would think of their chances if he knew. Then he took stock of his little command.

There was young Crosse, his face twitching nervously. There was Blake, the tall, quiet bacteriologist; Lenkranz, the metals man; Hirooka, the Nisei; Balistierri; Whitcomb, the photographer, with a battered Hasselblad still dangling by its neck cord against his armored chest. Swenson was still there, the big Swede crewman; and imperturbable Sergeant Brian, who was now calmly cleaning the pneumatic gun's loading mechanism. And, Helen, Bormann's skin bird, fluttering over the ration cart, beneath which Bormann and Sewell lay in the mud.

"Crosse, Lenkranz, burial detail. Get going." It was Hague's first order as Commander. He thought the two looked most woebegone of the party, and figured digging might loosen their nerves.

Crosse stared at him, and then sat suddenly against a tree bole.

"I'm not going to dig. I'm not going to march. This is crazy. We're going to get killed. I'll wait for it right here. Why do we keep walking and walking when we're going to die anyway?" His rising voice cracked, and he burst into hysterical laughter. Sergeant Brian rose quietly from his gun cleaning, jerked Crosse to his feet, and slapped him into quiet. Then he turned to Hague.

"Shall I take charge of the burial detail, sir?"

Hague nodded; and suddenly his long dislike of the iron-hard Sergeant melted into warm liking and admiration. Brian was the man who'd get them all through.

The Sergeant knotted his dark brows truculently at Hague. "And I don't believe Crosse meant what he said. He's a very brave man. We all get a little jumpy. But he's a good man, a good Rocketeer."

THREE MARKERS beside the trail, and a pile of dumped equipment marked the battle ground when the cart swung forward again. Hague had dropped all the recording instruments, saving only Whitcomb's exposed films, the rations, rifle ammunition, and logbooks that had been kept by different members of the science section. At his command, Sergeant Brian reluctantly smashed the pneumatic gun's firing mechanism, and left the gun squatting on its tripod beside charger and shell belts. With the lightened load, Hague figured three men could handle the cart, and he took his place with Brian and Crosse in the harness. The others no longer walked in the trail, but filtered between great root-flanges and tree boles on either side, guiding themselves by the Sonar's hum.

They left no more trail markers, and Hague cautioned them against making any unnecessary noise.

"No trail markers behind us. This mud is watery enough to hide footprints in a few minutes. We're making no noise, and we'll drop no more refuse. All they can hear will be the Sonar, and that won't carry far."

On the seventy-first day of the march, Hague squatted, fell almost to the ground, and grunted, "Take ten."

He stared at the stained, ragged scarecrows hunkered about him in forest mud.

"Why do we do it?" he asked no one in particular. "Why do we keep going, and going, and going? Why don't we just lie down and die? That would be the easiest thing I could think of right now." He knew that Rocket Service officers didn't talk that way, but he didn't feel like an officer, just a tired, feverish, bone-weary man.

"Have we got a great glowing tradition to inspire us?" he snarled. "No, we're just the lousy rocketeers that every other service arm plans to absorb. We haven't a Grant or a John Paul Jones to provide an example in a tough spot. The U.S. Rocket Service has nothing but the memory of some ships that went out and never came back; and you can't make a legend out of men who just plain vanish."

There was silence, and it looked as if the muddy figures were too exhausted to reply. Then Sergeant Brian spoke.

"The Rocketeers have a legend, sir."

"What legend, Brian?" Hague snorted.

"Here is the legend, sir. 'George Easy Peter One'."

Hague laughed hollowly, but the Sergeant continued as if he hadn't heard.

"Ground Expeditionary Patrol One—the outfit a planet couldn't lick. Venus threw her grab bag at us, animals, swamps, poison plants, starvation, fever, and we kept right on coming. She just made us smarter, and tougher, and harder to beat. And we'll blast through these lizard-men and the jungle, and march into Base like the whole U.S. Armed Forces on review."

"Let's go," Hague called, and they staggered up again, nine gaunt bundles of sodden, muddy rags, capped in trim black steel helmets with cheek guards down. The others slipped off the trail, and Hague, Brian, and Crosse pulled on the cart harness and lurched forward. The cart wheel hub jammed against a tree bole, and as they strained blindly ahead to free it, a horn note drifted from afar.

"Here they come again," Crosse groaned.

"They—won't be—up—with us—for days," Hague grunted, while he threw his weight in jerks against the tow line. The cart lurched free with a lunge, and all three shot forward and sprawled raging in the muddy trail.

They sat wiping mud from their faces, when Brian stopped suddenly, ripped off his helmet and threw it aside, then sat tensely forward in an attitude of strained listening. Hague had time to wonder dully if the man's brain had snapped, before he crawled to his feet.

"Shut up, and listen," Brian was snarling. "Hear it! Hear it! It's a klaxon! Way off, about every two seconds!"

Hague tugged off his heavy helmet, and strained every nerve to listen. Over the forest silence it came with pulse-like regularity, a tiny whisper of sound.

He and Brian stared bright-eyed at each other, not quite daring to say what they were thinking. Crosse got up and leaned like an empty sack against the cartwheel with an inane questioning look.

"What is it?" When they stared at him without speaking, still listening intently, "It's the Base. That's it, it's the Base!"

Something choked Hague's throat, then he was yelling and firing his rifle. The rest came scuttling out of the forest shadow, faces breaking into wild grins, and they joined Hague, the forest rocking with gunfire. They moved forward, and Hirooka took up a thin chant:

"Oooooooh, the Rocketeers have shaggy ears. They're dirty——"

The rest of their lyrics wouldn't look well in print; but where the Rocketeers have gone, on every frontier of space, the ribald song is sung. The little file moved down the trail toward the klaxon sound. Behind them, something moved in the gloom, resolved itself into a reptile-headed, man-like thing, that reared a small wooden trumpet to fit its mouth, a soft horn note floated clear; and other shapes became visible, sprinting forward, flitting through the gloom....

WHEN A RED LIGHT flashed over Chapman's desk, he flung down a sheaf of papers and hurried down steel-walled corridors to the number one shaft. A tiny elevator swept him to *Odysseus'* upper side, where a shallow pit had been set in the ship's scarred skin, and a pneumatic gun installed. Chapman hurried past the gun and crew to stand beside a listening device. The four huge cones loomed dark against the clouds, the operator in their center was a blob of shadow in the dawn light, where he huddled listening to a chanting murmur that came from his headset. Blake came running onto the gundeck; Bjornson, and the staff officers were all there.

"Cut it into the Address system," Chapman told the Listener operator excitedly; and the faint sounds were amplified through the whole ship. From humming Address amplifiers, the ribald words broke in a hoarse melody.

"The rocketeers have shaggy ears,
They're dirty——"

The rest described in vivid detail the prowess of rocketeers in general.

"How far are they?" Chapman demanded.

The operator pointed at a dial, fingered a knob that altered his receiving cones split-seconds of angle. "They're about twenty-five miles, sir."

Chapman turned to the officers gathered in an exultant circle behind him. "Branch, here's your chance for action. Take thirty men, our whippet tank, and go out to them. Bjornson, get the 'copters aloft for air cover."

Twenty minutes later, Chapman watched a column assemble beneath the *Odysseus'* gleaming side, and march into the jungle, with the 'copters buzzing west a moment later, like vindictive dragon flies.

Breakfast was brought to the men clustered at Warnings equipment, and to Chapman at his post on the gundeck. The day ticked away, the parade ground vanished in thickening clots of night; and a second dawn found the watchers still at their posts, listening to queer sounds that trickled from the speakers. The singing had stopped; but once they heard a note that a horn might make, and several times gobbling yells that didn't sound human. George One was fighting, they knew now. The listeners picked up crackling of rifle fire, and when that died there was silence.

The watchers heard a short cheer that died suddenly, as the relief column and George One met; and they waited and watched. Branch, who headed the relief column communicated with the mother ship by the simple expedient of yelling, the sound being picked up by the listeners.

"They're coming in, Chapman. I'm coming behind to guard their rear. They've been attacked by some kind of lizard-men. I'm not saying a thing—see for yourself when they arrive."

Hours rolled past, while they speculated in low tones, the hush that held the ship growing taut and strained.

"Surely Branch would have told us if anything was wrong, or if the records were lost," Chapman barked angrily. "Why did he have to be so damned melodramatic?"

"Look, there—through the trees. A helmet glinted!" The laconic Bjornson had thrown dignity to the winds, and capered like a drunken goat, as Rindell described it later.

Chapman stared down at the jungle edging the parade ground and caught a movement.

A man with a rifle came through the fringe and stood eying the ship in silence, and then came walking forward across the long, cindered expanse. From this height, he looked to Chapman like a child's lead soldier, a ragged, muddy, midget scarecrow. Another stir in the trees, and one more man, skulking like an infantry-flanker with rifle at ready. He, too, straightened and came walking quietly forward. A file of three men came next, leaning into the harness of a little metal cart that bumped drunkenly as they dragged it forward. An instant of waiting, and two more men stole from the jungle, more like attacking infantry than returning heroes. Chapman waited, and no more came. This was all.

"My God, no wonder Branch wouldn't tell us. There were thirty-two of them." Rindell's voice was choked.

"Yes, only seven." Chapman remembered his field glasses and focused them on the seven approaching men. "Lieutenant Hague is the only officer. And they're handing us the future of the U.S. Rocket Service on that little metal cart."

The quiet shattered and a yelling horde of men poured from *Odysseus*' hull and engulfed the tattered seven, sweeping around them, yelling, cheering, and carrying them toward the mother ship.

Chapman looked a little awed as he turned to the officers behind him. "Well they did it. We forward these records, and we've proven that we can do the job." He broke into a grin. "What am I talking about? Of course we did the job. We'll always do the job. We're the Rocketeers, aren't we?"

👽 👽 👽

> "The Rocketeers Have Shaggy Ears" first appeared in the Spring 1950 issue of Planet Stories, and is arguably the earliest example of gritty, realistic Military SF.
>
> Little is known about American writer and editor Keith Bennett, but based on situations and circumstances presented in "The Rocketeers Have Shaggy Ears," SF novelist and Vietnam War veteran David Drake reasons that "Bennett had been a junior officer in an Army infantry division which fought on the jungle-covered islands of the Pacific. I suspect he commanded a battery of 75 mm pack howitzers."

MOONBASE ALPHA: MANKIND'S GREATEST ACHIEVEMENT. The sprawling lunar city, home to 311 mission specialists from an international scientific pool, had been constructed to further humanity's forward-reaching efforts to explore space as well as oversee solutions for its darkest mistakes of the recent past on home soil—namely, the removal and storage of atomic waste from Earth. That ticking time bomb, buried deep beneath the moon's surface, was heating up, changing. And when it reached flashpoint in a spectacular explosion that launched the moon out of Earth orbit, the courageous women and men of Moonbase Alpha were hurled into an unexplored and often hostile universe to search for a new home while coming to understand mankind's greater destiny, thus setting the stage for Gerry and Sylvia Anderson's outer space adventure series, *Space:1999*.

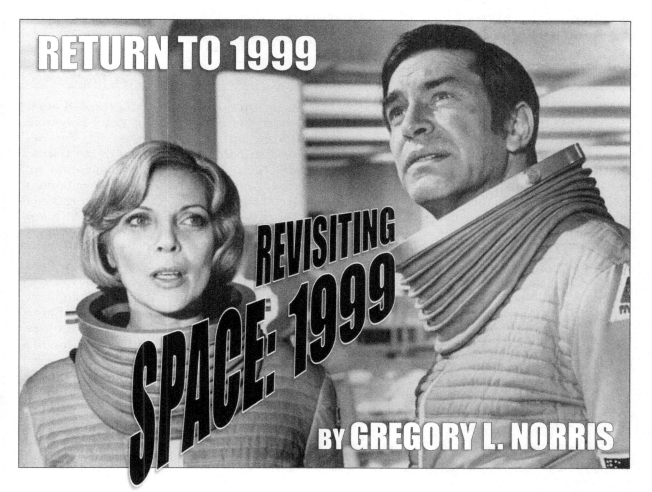

RETURN TO 1999
REVISITING SPACE: 1999
BY GREGORY L. NORRIS

BREAKAWAY

I WAS TEN-YEARS-OLD on that early September night in 1975, seated cross-legged on the living room floor before the big, boxy TV connected to rabbit ears and eagerly awaiting the premiere of a small screen television series with big screen production values and an epic story-line that would, frankly, steal my breath. The year 1999 seemed impossibly distant at the time. Transfixed, I had never been so astonished and, over the course of that first hour, forgot how

to blink. My life, after that night, was forever changed. As the residents of Moonbase Alpha began their odyssey, I, too, took my first step into a much larger and unexplored universe. On the following morning, I put pen to page and wrote my very first short story, a *1999* fan fiction still archived to this day in my filing cabinets filled with longhand drafts. *Space:1999* put that pen in my hand.

Martin Landau assumed leadership duties in the role of Commander John Koenig. Then real-life wife Barbara Bain played the base's brilliant and layered CMO, Doctor Helena Russell. On board as the wisest mind of all was Barry Morse as Professor Victor Bergman. Rounding out the cast were Nick Tate as Australian-born spaceship pilot Alan Carter, Prentis Hancock as second-in-command Paul Morrow, Zienia Merton as data analyst Sandra Benes, Clifton Jones as computer expert David Kano, Suzanne Roquette as Main Mission operative Tanya Alexander, and Anton Phillips as Doctor Bob Mathias.

"I met with the Andersons and liked their vision for the show, which was set in the not-too-distant future. I liked the concept of a group of people being forced into a situation they weren't either emotionally or technically prepared for," Landau told me during our sit-down conversation in 1998 when he starred in *The X-Files: Fight the Future*. "They couldn't have gone into deep space with the technology they had and survived. So this accident caused them to face perils and the unknown and all sorts of things. And not being in control—the moon's trajectory—added a wonderful element, whereas on

Season One Command crew. Below: Filming on the Main Mission set. Opposite: Moonbase Alpha, still in orbit around Earth. (Anderson Entertainment)

Star Trek they could go where they wanted. They were in control of their destiny. I felt that was a great idea in terms of testing human capabilities, strengths, and weaknesses."

Peripheral but unforgettable characters also included the base's nerve center, the cavernous and elegant Main Mission Tower set, Alpha's fleet of workhorse Eagle spacecraft, a hybrid rock/classic soundtrack composed by Barry Gray, and Alpha itself, spread in breathtaking detail across the heart of Crater Plato according to the *Moonbase Alpha Technical Notebook* published by Starlog Press in 1977. Dazzling special effects were created by Brian Johnson, who'd done the same for *2001: A Space Odyssey* and would go on to craft similar stunning work on *Alien* and its sequel *Aliens* and *The Empire Strikes Back*. The color-coded departmental Moon City regulation uniforms were designed by fashion icon Rudi Gernreich.

"I was so impressed, shocked," Landau added when asked about first impressions upon stepping onto the Main Mission set. "And there was one thing I contributed to. In the commander's office was this giant globe, which was a real globe of the Earth painted in real colors. I made the suggestion that they

BLACK INFINITY • 171

Throughout the initial run of twenty-four episodes, the Alphans encountered planets of mystery and danger. They got involved in interstellar wars, brought back life to dead worlds, and experienced the wondrous and terrifying. Of the latter, several of the First Season's episodes evoked a gory, gothic horror tone. In "The Troubled Spirit," one Alphan's vengeful ghost stalks the corridors of the moon base. "Force of Life" sees guest artist Ian McShane taken

Koenig's private office. (Anderson Entertainment)

paint it the same color as the rest of the set because I felt it was out of place. And so they painted that globe in the same shades of beige and gray. That was done the day we started shooting the pilot episode. I thought that colorful globe in the middle of all this was a reminder of the Earth and what they lost. It just looked wrong. So they heeded my advice and that was literally done with quick-drying paint the day we started shooting."

A sliding bulkhead allows Koenig quick access to Main Mission.

An Eagle spacecraft transports atomic waste over the lunar surface.

over by a heat-sucking alien vampire. The Alphans release an imprisoned alien from confinement on an asteroid, at first not suspecting he's an immortal murderer in "End of Eternity." And few children of the time to this day forget the white-knuckle chills of "Dragon's Domain," an episode told mostly in flashbacks about an Alphan pilot who captained a doomed deep space mission before the moon broke out of orbit, and encountered a one-eyed, tentacled Lovecraftian monster with an appetite for human flesh in a spaceship graveyard.

Eagles moniter the atomic-waste storage site. Below: A chain reaction detonates the waste, blasting the moon from Earth orbit. The resultant G-force briefly pins Dr. Russell (Barbara Bain) and crew to the deck. Bottom: Koenig is determined to bravely face the unknown. Alpha can and will survive.

1999's guest stars added another level of pedigree to the journey. Among them were Christopher Lee as Captain Zantor in the episode "Earthbound," Peter Cushing as an alien scientist in "Missing Link," Margaret Leighton as Queen Arra in "Collision Course," Leo McKern in "The Infernal Machine," and Bond girl Catherine Schell as an android that seduces the Alphans into feeding

BLACK INFINITY • 173

their life energy to maintain the needs of a powerful master machine in "The Guardian of Piri," long before The Matrix films.

The series embraced a dark tone that would, decades later, be appreciated by fans in such efforts as the *Battlestar Galactica* reboot, but was shocking and unexpected for the 1970s.

"I think we were given a bad rap at the time," Landau recalled. "The U.S.

Hammer Horror Heroes in Space: Christopher Lee in "Earthbound." Left: Peter Cushing in "Missing Link."

critics weren't particularly excited about it. They were and weren't. I found out that the *Star Trek* fans and our show's took sides. We weren't really in competition with *Star Trek*—ours was a different show. We never intended to invade territory as such. The fact that people started comparing them is logical, I suppose, but the texture of both shows was very different. We certainly never expected *Space* to be a rival but an extension of the genre. *Space* tried to create a reality as set on an actual moon base. The Eagles were framework machines—they weren't *Buck Rogers*. They were an extension of the technology at the time. And then there was the question of if there could be explosions in outer space. But there's nothing quite as dull as a silent fireball. Obviously, licenses were taken to create a cinematic element. It was a question of creating a show that was interesting and watchable. I think if you'd just followed astronauts around twenty-four hours a day in outer space the results would be rather mundane."

The series launched a deluge of merchandise, including games, models, and a line of books that novelized established episodes and original adventures. But a pickup for a second season was long in forthcoming. When it did at the eleventh hour, the series would undergo

Koenig tries to shake Kano (Clifton Jones) from a hypnotic state induced by an alien android (Catherine Schell), in "The Guardian of Piri."

CONTINUED AFTER NEXT PAGE

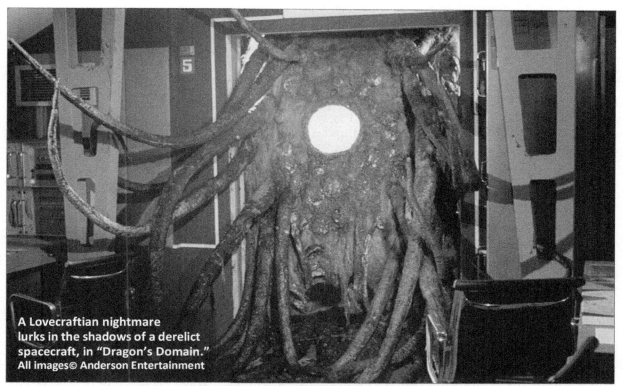

A Lovecraftian nightmare lurks in the shadows of a derelict spacecraft, in "Dragon's Domain."
All images © Anderson Entertainment

Helena recoils from the touch of a scientist's rapidly-decaying corpse, in "Death's Other Dominion."

shocking changes under new producer Fred Freiberger, who coaxed the renewal by agreeing to make certain course corrections, the biggest of which was to introduce a new character, the resident alien Maya who would join the moon base team in the Second Season opener, "The Metamorph." Maya, born on the planet Psychon, had the ability to transform her shape at will into any form of life.

Hers would not be the only transformation regarding the new season of Space:1999.

METAMORPHOSIS

AMONG THE NUMEROUS changes were, most notably, the absence of Morse's beloved Victor Bergman as well as the characters of Paul Morrow, David Kano, and Tanya Alexander, all of whom vanished from the canvas in a mass cast purge, their absences never explained. Ian Phillips' Bob Mathias only appeared in the first two episodes of the reimagined 1999 and was mentioned in the third. Though she received star billing alongside Tate and newcomer Tony Anholt as security chief Tony Verdeschi in the first act's opening credits, Zienia Merton, too, found her character in a diminished role. This set the stage for a revolving door of communications officers and doctors to round out the cast—Yasuko Nagazumi as

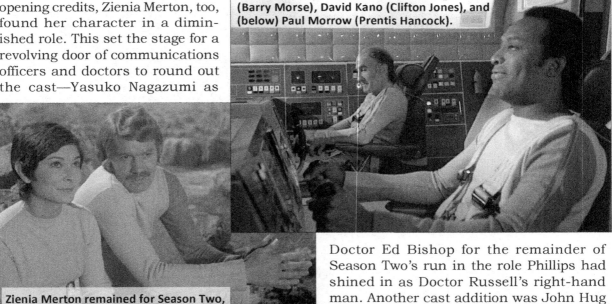

Catherine Schell as the alien Maya.

Yasko Nugami and Alibe Parsons later in the season in the role of Alibe Kurand as Sandra's replacements, and Jeffrey Kissoon as Doctor Ben Vincent, Raul Newey for one episode as Doctor Raul Nunez, and Sam Dastor as

Season Two's painful losses: Prof. Bergman (Barry Morse), David Kano (Clifton Jones), and (below) Paul Morrow (Prentis Hancock).

Zienia Merton remained for Season Two, but her role as Sandra Benes diminished.

Doctor Ed Bishop for the remainder of Season Two's run in the role Phillips had shined in as Doctor Russell's right-hand man. Another cast addition was John Hug as likeable Eagle pilot Bill Fraser.

a more claustrophobic tightness, including the removal of an entire section of the Eagle's storage lockers in the passenger module. Almost as big a challenge for viewers to accept as Morse's absence was the loss of the vast Main Mission set. Though never explained outright in the Second Season, the Alphans had moved operations underground to a bunker located at the very base of the Main Mission Tower within the very narrow confines of Command Center. Gone was Barry Gray's elegant soundtrack. The new score for *1999* was created by Derek Wadsworth and skewed toward trilling jazz and disco. The result was a sophomore shock to the system for fans, of an intensity that would repeat in 1994 with the Second Season premiere of NBC's retooled, inferior *seaQuest DSV*.

The new kids on the S2 block: Catherine Schell as Maya and Tony Anholt as Tony Verdeschi

But the shock didn't end there. The clean, color-coded Moon City uniforms were altered with new I.D. badges, collars, and jackets, and those jackets were then covered with a plethora of symbols. Alpha's women, when not visiting alien worlds, were given the option of uniform skirts. Sets were reconfigured in Freiberger's vision to lend the base environs

Alpha grows cold and things look black, but Victor remains optimistic, in the Season One episode "The Black Sun."

Given the pressure to produce twenty-four episodes in an abbreviated shooting schedule, Freiberger employed a two-for-one approach to much of the Second Season, which meant the leads were often separated during the runaway moon's adventures so that Landau could feature heavily in one story while Bain helmed another. Script

BLACK INFINITY • 177

quality also suffered under Freiberger's vision for the series. Gone was the metaphysical and deep philosophy of such gorgeous efforts as "The Testament of Arkadia" and "The Black Sun," which, along with "Collision Course," revealed destinies and designs behind Alpha's odyssey through the cosmos. The new offerings fell back on Science Fiction clichés that were tired even in 1976, like living rocks ("All That Glisters") and plant kingdom uprisings ("The Rules of Luton"), which had already gained notoriety in the *Lost in Space* episode "The Great

An Eagle approaches a desolate world that may hold the key to the origin of life on Earth, in the Season One episode "The Testament of Arkadia."

Below: Victor and Helena make a startling discovery on the planet Arkadia.

Vegetable Rebellion." A common complaint about the First Season of *Space:1999* was that it wasn't enough like its predecessor *Star Trek*. The opposite complaint is often made against the second run of twenty-four episodes.

But there were some very bright spots in Season Two, notably Catherine Schell's Maya, who remains one of the most human aliens in all of Science Fiction. Wadsworth's score often proved engaging, and episodes at the start and conclusion of Season Two's run like "The Metamorph," "The Exiles," "Journey to Where,"

Maya learns her father, Mentor (Brian Blessed), has been luring pilots to the planet Psychon to fuel his biological computer, in the Season Two premiere, "The Metamorph."

Above: Psychon's graveyard of abandoned ships.

"The Immunity Syndrome," and "The Dorcons" could have worked nicely in a Year One setting. The two-part "The Bringers of Wonder," in which aliens disguised as loved ones from home seek to detonate the remaining nuclear waste in order to feed their energy needs and Koenig is the only member of the base able to see through their deception, is filled with misdirection, gothic suspense, and adventure, and was, in 1978, repackaged as a movie. Parsons and Dastor shined despite limited screen time, and some of the gorgeous philosophical moments from Year One prevailed. In "The Rules of Luton," one of the least popular among fans, Koenig and Maya, forced to engage in combat against three alien criminals, have a heart-to-heart about the wars of Earth's past and the cost of such foolishness, and Maya shares insights into her family and the loss of the great love that broke her father, leading to the planet Psychon's destruction. The scene, like others in "The Immunity Syndrome" and the Green Sickness subplot in "The Séance Specter," in which the desire to live in open air once more drives a handful of Alphans to commit mutiny, are gorgeous in their presentation and respect for all that came before.

A Superswift reaches the Moon to rescue the Alphans, in the S2 adventure "The Bringers of Wonder." Among the crew and passengers: Tony's brother and many of the Alphan's oldest friends and colleagues. Are things too good to be true?

HUMAN DECISION REQUIRED

PLANS FOR A THIRD SEASON of *Space:1999* were in the works when the series was cancelled in 1977. What form that next chapter would have

180 • REVISITING SPACE: 1999

taken remains unclear, though a rumored spin-off starring Catherine Schell's Maya was reportedly in the earliest planning stages. Apart from the retooled *Destination: Moonbase Alpha* redux of "The Bringers of Wonder" and other feature film versions of episodes from both seasons, fans would have to wait another twenty-two years for the story of *Space:1999* to continue with new canon.

I, along with those in attendance at the big Breakaway convention held in Los Angeles on that pivotal September 13th weekend in the year 1999, never suspected that series writer Johnny Byrne had penned a forty-ninth episode and denouement for the show called "Message From Moonbase Alpha." Actress Zienia Merton reprised her role as Sandra Benes to give an outstanding and emotional conclusion to the original story-line in which the Alphans have settled their new home planet, Terra Alpha, and are about to abandon the moon base for the final phase of Operation: Exodus. The short film also left the door open for a return, as the moon's course was predicted to swing it around to within range of Terra Alpha in twenty-five years.

But the story of *Space:1999* was far from concluded. Not long after the convention, publisher Powys Media obtained the official rights to continue the adventure in a series of novels, and in 2020, Big Finish launched new audio books. In 2012, Jace Hall (who'd re-imagined the 1980s classic *V* for ABC TV) was tapped to helm *Space 2099*. The project never advanced beyond early production art and was one of two attempts to either reboot or

What really arrived in that Superswift? Alan Carter (Nick Tate) and Maya are among those unable to see the true form of these alien invaders, in "The Bringers of Wonder."

BLACK INFINITY • 181

continue the legacy of Moonbase Alpha and its citizens, the other from Space Opera Studios in Canada.

Before his death in 2017, Landau maintained contact with many of the actors he became friends with on the *1999* set.

"Obviously, I'm in contact with Barbara, who is my ex-wife, because we have two daughters," Landau said. "Nick Tate lives here in Los Angeles. He does all kinds of acting work, including a lot of voice-overs. Clifton Jones used to come here from time to time and I would see him when he was in town. Barry Morse, too. Catherine is married to a guy I know and for a number of years

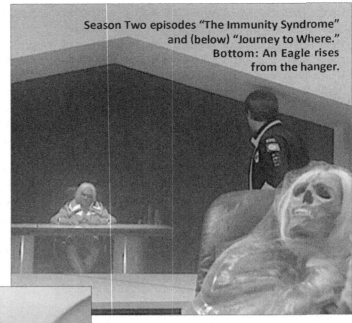

Season Two episodes "The Immunity Syndrome" and (below) "Journey to Where." Bottom: An Eagle rises from the hanger.

we would get together at least once a year. I mean, it's hard to believe we finished the show over twenty-some years ago!"

Though *Space:1999* concluded its run in 1977, its influence continued. The 1981 Second Season *Buck Rogers in the 25th Century* episode "Mark of the Saurians," in which the titular character claims visiting dignitaries

The WOW FACTOR: ships and suits! A detailed Eagle cockpit, some cool spacesuits, and a great Moon set.

are ruthless aliens in disguise but no one believes him, follows the plot of "The Bringers of Wonder" neck-in-neck. It can be argued that the blockbuster *Alien* owes mightily to the unforgettable "Dragon's Domain" about doomed crew members being devoured by the acid-blooded horror brought back from a derelict alien spacecraft. Episodes of *Star Trek: The Next Generation* blatantly borrowed from the *1999* experience: "The Arsenal of Freedom" has Doctor Crusher referencing

The superb special effects of *Space:1999* often rivaled those of big-budget films such as *2001: A Space Odyssey*.

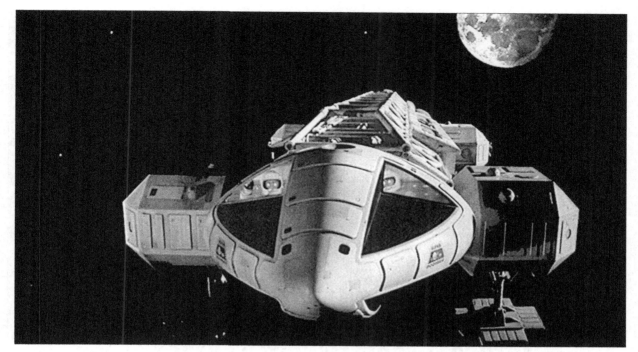

the healing powers of fungus when she and Captain Picard are injured and stranded in a crevice—a mirror image of the cave scene where Doctor Russell explains the same medical facts to Commander Koenig in "Journey to Where"; Counselor Troi's rapid-growing alien baby story-line in "The Child" is the *1999* episode "Alpha Child" in which the first baby born on Alpha rapidly grows from newborn to five-year-old; and "The Most Toys," which involves the kidnapping of Lt. Data by a collector of rarities could be "The Taybor," in which Maya is kidnapped by a collector who only deals in one-of-a-kind originals. *Star Trek: Deep Space Nine* featured a shape shifter among its central cast in the form of Constable Odo, but *Space: 1999* was the first, with Maya. One of *Trek*'s most glaring nods to *1999* comes in the famous "Resistance is futile" line that's a mantra for *Trek* baddies the Borg, but that dialog was delivered in an icy warning by Consul Varda (guest star Ann Firbank) from the command deck of a battle cruiser to Koenig as powerful aliens readied to invade Alpha in "The Dorcons." And Executive Producer Ronald D. Moore freely admits to cribbing the "This Episode" opening preview from the First Season of *Space:1999* for his reimagined *Battlestar Galactica*.

The year 1999 was a long time ago. So, too, was 1975. We still don't have manned bases on Earth's moon, but the enduring power of the story of Moonbase Alpha and its odyssey across the wilderness of space continues. Will there be a new version or continuation of *Space:1999* down the pike? Time will tell.

FROM **AUTHOR** AND **SCREENWRITER GREGORY L. NORRIS** AND **PRODUCER GERRY ANDERSON**, THE **CREATOR** OF **SPACE:1999**

Don't miss the AUTHORIZED novelization of Gerry Anderson's classic Made-for-TV movie or the stunning sequel INTO INFINITY: PLANETFALL

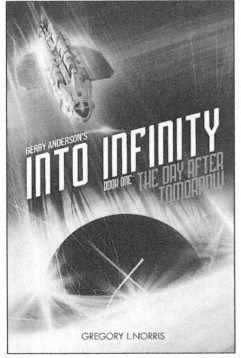

BOOK ONE
INTO INFINITY: THE DAY AFTER TOMORROW

BOOK TWO
INTO INFINITY: PLANETFALL

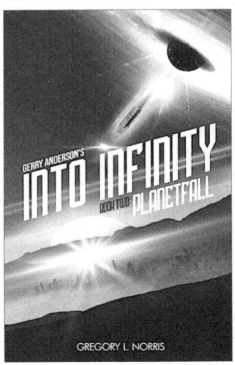

ANDERSON ENTERTAINMENT

SEA LEGS

by Frank Quattrocchi
art by Ed Emshwiller

FLIGHT OFFICER ROBERT CRAIG SURRENDERED THE TUBE CONTAINING HIS SERVICE RECORD TAPES AND STOOD WAITING WHILE THE BORED PROCESS CLERK EXAMINED THE SEAL.

"Your clearance," said the clerk.

Craig handed him a battered punch card and watched the man insert it in the reproducer. He felt anxiety as the much-handled card refused for a time to match the instrument's metal contact points. The line of men behind Craig fidgeted.

"You got to get this punched by Territorial," said the clerk. "Take it back to your unit's clearance office."

"Look again, Sergeant," Craig said, repressing his irritation.

"It ain't notched."

"The hell it isn't."

The man examined the card with squinting care and nodded finally. "It's so damn notched," he complained. "You ought to take care of that card; can't get on without one."

Craig hesitated before moving.

"Next," said the clerk, "What you waiting for?"

"Don't I take my 201 file?"

"We send it on ahead. Go to Grav 1 desk."

A murmur greeted the order. Craig experienced the thrill of knowing the envy of the others. Grav 1—that meant Terra. He crossed the long, dreary room, knowing the eyes of the other men were upon him.

"Your service tapes," the next noncom said. "Where you going?"

"Grav 1—Terra," fumbled Craig. "Los Angeles."

"Los Angeles, eh? Where in Los Angeles?"

"I—I—" Craig muttered, fumbling in his pockets.

"No specific destination," supplied the man

as he punched a key on a small instrument, "Airlock ahead and to your right. Strip and follow the robot's orders. Any metal?"

"Metal?" asked Craig.

"You know, *metal*."

"Well, my identification key."

"Here," commanded the clerk, extending a plastic envelope.

Craig moved in the direction indicated. He fought the irrational fear that he had missed an important step in the complicated clerical process. He cursed the grudging attitude of the headquarters satellite personnel and felt the impotence of a spaceman who had long forgotten the bureaucracy of a rear area base. The knowledge that much of it was motivated by envy soothed him as he clumsily let himself into the lock.

"Place your clothing in the receptacle provided and assume a stationary position on the raised podium in the center of the lock."

Craig obeyed the robot voice and began reluctantly to remove his flight jacket. Its incredibly fine-grained leather would carry none of the strange, foreign associations for the base station clerk who would appropriate it. He would never know the beautiful, gentle beast that supplied this skin.

"You are retarding the progress of others. Please respond more quickly to your orders."

Craig quickly removed the last of his clothing. It was impossible to hate a robot, but one could certainly hate those who set it into operation.

"You will find a red button at your feet. Lower your head and depress that button."

Stepping on the button with his bare foot produced an instant of brilliant blue illumination. A small scratch on his arm stung briefly and he was somewhat blinded by the flash even through his eyelids, but that was all there was to the sterilizing process.

"Your clothing and effects will be in the dressing room immediately beyond the locked door."

He found his clothing cleanly and neatly hung on plastic hangers just inside the door to the dressing room. The few personal items he carried in his pockets were still there. The Schtann flight jacket was actually there, looking like new, its space-blue unfaded and as wonderfully pliant as before.

"Insert your right arm into the instrument on the central table," commanded the same voice he had heard before. "Turn your arm until the scratch is in contact with the metal plate. There will be a slight pain, but it is necessary to treat the small injury you have been disregarding."

Craig obeyed and clenched his teeth against a sharp stinging. His respect for the robot-controlled equipment of bases had risen. When he withdrew his arm, the scratch was neatly coated with a layer of flesh-colored plastic material.

He dressed quickly and was on the verge of asking the robot for instructions, when a man appeared in the open doorway.

"I am Captain Wyandotte," said the man in a pleasant voice.

"Well, what's next?" asked Craig somewhat more belligerently than he had intended.

The man smiled. "Your reaction is quite natural. You are somewhat aggressive after Clerical, eh?"

"I'm a little anxious to get home, I suppose," said Craig defensively.

"By 'home' you mean Terra. But you've never been there, have you?"

"No, but my father—"

"Your parents left Terra during the Second Colonization of Cassiopeia II, didn't they?"

"Yes," Craig said. He was uncomfortable; Wyandotte seemed to know all about him.

"We might say you've been away quite a while, eh?"

"I was entered as a spaceman when I was 16," Craig said. "I've never been down for any period as yet."

"You mean you haven't been in a gravity system?"

"Oh, I've landed a few times, even walked around for a while...."

"With the help of paraoxylnebutal,"

supplied the captain.

"Well, sure."

"Mr. Craig, I suppose you've guessed that the next step in our little torture system here is psych."

"So I gathered."

The captain laughed reassuringly. "No, don't put up your guard again. The worst is over. Short of Gravitational conditioning, there is nothing to stop you from going to Terra."

"Sorry, I guess I'm a little touchy. This is my first time...."

"Quite natural. But it being your first time —in quite a number of ways, I might add—it will be necessary for you to undergo some conditioning."

"Conditioning?" asked Craig.

"Yes. You have spent eleven years in space. Your body is conditioned to a normal state of free fall, or at best to a state of acceleration."

"Yeah, I know. Once on Gerymeade...."

"You were ill, couldn't keep your balance, felt dizzy. That is why all spacemen carry PON, paraoxylnebutal, with them. It helps suppress certain physiological reactions to an entirely new set of conditions. Channels of the ear, for example. They play an important part in our awareness of balance. They operate on a simple gravity principle. Without gravity they act up for a time, then gradually lose function. Returning to gravity is rather frightening at first."

"I know all about this, Captain."

"You've undoubtedly read popularizations in tapezines. But you have experienced it briefly."

"I expect to have some trouble at first." Craig was disturbed by the wordy psychologist. What was the man actually saying?

"Do you know what sailors of ancient times meant by 'sea legs?'" asked Wyandotte. "Men on a rolling ocean acclimated themselves to a rolling horizontal. They had trouble when they went ashore and the horizontal didn't roll any more."

"It meant more than that. There were excellent psychological reasons for the old stereotype, the 'drunken sailor.' A port city was a frightening thing to an old sailor—but let's begin our little job at the beginning. I'll turn you over to psychometry for the usual tests and pick you up tomorrow morning at, say, 0900."

DURING THE DAYS that followed, the psychologist seemed to Craig to become progressively more didactic. He would deliver long speeches about the "freedom of open space." He spoke repetitiously of the "growing complexity of Terran society." And yet the man could not be pinned down to any specific condition the spaceman would find intolerable.

Craig began to hate the delay that kept him from Terra. Through the ports of the headquarters base satellite, he scanned the constellations for the scores of worlds he had visited during his eleven years in space. They were incredibly varied, even those that supported life. He had weathered difficult landings on worlds with riptide gravities, had felt the pull of the incredible star-tides imparted by twin and even triple star systems. He had been on Einstein IV, the planet of eight moons, and had felt the pulse of all eight of the satellites at once that no PON could completely nullify.

But even if he could accept the psychologist's authority for the cumulative effect of a gravity system, he could not understand the unspoken warning he felt underlying all that the man said.

"Of course it has changed," Craig was protesting. "Anyway, I never really knew very much about Terra. So what? I know it won't be as it was in tapezines either."

"Yet you are so completely sure you will want to live out your life there, that you are willing to give up space service for it."

"We've gone through this time and time again," Craig said wearily. "I gave you my reasons for quitting space. We analyzed them. You agreed that you could not decide that for me and that my decision is logical. You tell me spacemen don't settle down on Terra. Yet you won't—or can't—tell me why. I've got a damned good job there—"

"You may find that 'damned good jobs' become boring."

"So I'll transfer. I don't know what you're trying to get at, Captain, but you're not talking me out of going back. If the service needs men so badly, let them get somebody else. I've put in *my* time."

"Do you really think that's my reason?"

"Sure. What else can it be?"

"Mr. Craig," the psychologist said slowly, "you have my authorization for you to return to Terra as a private citizen of that planet. You will be given a very liberal supply of PON —which you will definitely need. Good luck. You'll need that too."

ON THE EIGHTH DAY, two attendants, who showed the effects of massive doses of PON to protect themselves from the centrifugal force, had to carry a man out of the tank. Many others asked to be removed, begged to be allowed to withdraw their resignations.

"The twelfth day is the worst," a grizzled spaceman told Craig. "That's when the best of 'em want out."

Craig clenched the iron rung of his bed and struggled to bring the old man's face into focus.

"How ... how do they know when you ought ... to come out?" he asked between waves of nausea.

"Blood pressure. They get you just before you go into shock."

"How can they tell?" Craig fought down his growing panic. "I can't."

"That strap around your belly. You mean you ain't noticed it?"

"Haven't noticed much of anything."

"Well, it's keyed to give them some kind of signal."

The old man lapsed into silence. Craig wished him to continue. He desperately wanted something to distract his mind from the ghastly conditioning process.

Slowly at first, the lines formed by seams in the metal ceiling began to bend. Here it came again!

"Old man!" shouted Craig.

"Yeah, son. They've dropped it down a notch."

"Dropped ... it ... down?"

"Maybe that ain't scientific, but it's the way I always think of it."

"Can't they ... drop it down continuously?"

"They tried that a few times—once when I was aboard. You wouldn't like it, kid. You wouldn't like it at all."

"How ... many times ... do they drop it?"

"Four times during the day, three at night. Twenty days."

A nightmare of visual sensations ebbed into Craig's mind. He was vaguely aware of the moans of other men in the vault-like room. Wave upon wave of nausea swept him as he watched the seam lines bend and warp fantastically. He snapped his eyelids shut, only to begin feeling the nightmarish bodily sensations once more. He felt the cot slowly rise longitudinally, felt himself upside down, then the snap of turning right side up once more—and he knew that neither he nor the cot had moved so much as an inch.

Craig heard the voices around him, muffled, as though talking through wadding.

"... got it bad."

"We better take him out."

"... pretty bad."

"He'll go into shock."

"... never make it the twelfth."

"We better yank him."

"I'm ... all right," Craig mumbled at the voices. He struggled with the bonds of his cot. With terrible effort he forced his eyes open. Two white-clad figures, ridiculously out of proportion, hovered wraithlike over him. Four elongated eyes peered at him.

Attendants coming for to take me home....

"Touch me and I'll kick your teeth in!" he yelled. "I'm going to Terra. Wish you were going to Terra?"

Then it was better. Oddly, he passed the twelfth day easily. By the fourteenth day, Craig knew he could stand Grav 1. The whine of the centrifuge's motors had diminished to a low hum. Either that or they had begun to produce ultrasonic waves. Craig was not sure.

Most of the men had passed through the torments of gravitational conditioning. The huge headquarters base centrifuge aboard the man-made satellite had gradually caused their bodies to respond once more to a single source of pull. They were now ready to become inhabitants of planets again, instead of free-falling ships.

On the eighteenth day, automatic machinery freed them from their imprisoning cots. Clumsily and awkwardly at first, the men began to walk, to hold their heads and arms in proper attitudes. They laughed and joked about it and kidded those who were slow at adjusting. Then they again began taking paraoxylnebutal in preparation for the free-fall flight to Terra.

Only one of the score of men in the centrifuge tank remained voluntarily in his cot.

"Space article violator," the old man informed Craig. "Psycho, I think. Went amuck with some extraterritorials. Killed a dozen."

"What will they do, exile him?"

"Not to Chociante, if that's what you mean. They just jerked his space card and gave him a one-way ticket to Terra."

"For twelve murders?" asked Craig incredulously.

"That's enough, son." The old man eyed Craig for an instant before looking away. "Pick something to talk about. What do you figure on doing when you get to Terra, for instance?"

"I'm going into Import. My father was in it for twenty years."

"Sure," said the old spaceman, watching a group of young crewmen engaged in an animated conversation.

"It's a good job. There's a future to it."

"Yeah."

Why did he have to explain anything at all to the old space tramp?

"Once I get set up, I'll probably try to open my own business."

"And spend your weekends on Luna."

Craig half rose from his cot, jarred into anger.

But the old spaceman turned, smiling wryly. "Don't get hot, kid. I guess I spent too long in Zone V." He paused to examine his wrinkled hands. They were indelibly marked with lever callouses. "You get to thinking anyone who stays closer'n eighty light-years from Terra is a land-lubber."

Craig relaxed, realizing he had acted childishly. "Used to think the same. Then I took the exam and got this job."

"Whereabouts?"

"Los Angeles."

The old man looked up at Craig. "You don't know much about Terra, do you, son?"

"Not much."

"Yeah. Well, I hope you ain't disappointed."

"My father was born there, but I never saw it. Never hit the Solar System, matter of fact. Never saw much of anything close up. I stood it a long time, old man, this hitting atmospheres all over the Universe."

But the spaceman seemed to have lost interest. He was unpacking some personal belongings from a kit.

"What are you doing in Grav 1?" Craig asked.

The old man's face clouded for an instant. "In the old days, they used to say us old-timers acted like clocks. They used to say we just ran down. Now they got some fancy psychology name for it."

Craig regretted his question. He would have muttered some word of apology, but the old man continued.

"Maybe you've read some of the old sea stories, or more'n likely had 'em read to you. Sailors could go to sea until they just sort of dried up. The sea tanned their skins and stiffened their bones, but it never stiffened their hearts. When they got old, it just pulled them in.

"But space is different. Space is raw and new. It tugs at your guts. It sends the blood rushing through your veins. It's like loving. You don't become a part of space the way you do the old sea, though. It leaves you strictly alone. Except that it sucks you dry, takes all the soup out of you, leaves you brittle and old —old as a dehydrated piece of split leather.

"Then one day it shoots a spurt of blood around in one of your old veins. Something gives. Space is through with you then. And if you can stand this whirligig conditioning, you're through with space."

"You can't figure it. Some of 'em urp all over and turn six shades of green."

"You got to watch the ones that don't."

"Yeah, you got to watch the ones that don't. Especially the old ones."

"He's old. You think it was his heart?"

"Who knows?"

"They'll dump him, won't they?"

"After a tracer is sent through. But it won't do any good."

"He probably outlived everybody that ever knew him."

"Wouldn't be surprised. Here, grab his leg."

Robert Craig folded the flight jacket tightly and stuffed it into the cylindrical carton. A sleeve unwound just as he did so, making it difficult to fit into the place he had made for it. Exasperated, he refolded it and jammed it in place. Smaller rolls of underclothing were then fitted in. When he was satisfied with the layer, he tossed in a small handful of crystals and began to fill the next layer. After the carton was completely filled, he ignited the sealing strip and watched as the plastic melted into a single, seamless whole. It was ready for irradiation. Probably in another ten years his son-to-be would put it on and play spaceman. But Craig swore he'd make sure that the kid knew what a stinking life it was.

At 1300 hours, the ferry bumped heavily alongside the starboard lock. It was the signal for relief in the passengers' quarters; many were beginning to feel a reaction to the short free-fall flight from the headquarters satellite.

The audio called out: "Flight Officer Robert Craig. Flight Officer Robert Craig. Report to Orderly 12. Report to Orderly 12 through the aft door."

With pangs of anxiety he could not completely suppress, Craig obeyed.

Orderly 12 handed him a message container.

"Who's it from? Somebody on Terra?"

"From a private spaceman named Morgan Brockman."

"Brockman?"

"He was with you in the grav tank."

"The old man!"

The message container produced a battered punch card. Craig straightened it and was about to reach into his pocket for a hand transcriber. But then he noticed the card bore only a few irregular punches and was covered with rough hand printing.

Son, when the flunkies get around to giving you this, they'll have shot me out the tube. How do I know? Same way you know when your turbos are going to throw a blade. It's good this way.

There's something you can do for me if you want to. Way back, some fifty years ago, there was a woman. She was my wife. It's a long story I won't bother you with. Anyway, I left her. Wanted to take her along with me, but she wouldn't go.

Earth was a lot different then than it is now. They don't have to tell me; I know. I saw it coming and so did Ethel. We talked about it and I knew I had to go. She wouldn't or couldn't go. Wanted me to stay, but I couldn't.

I tried to send her some units once in a while. Don't know if she ever got them. Sometimes I forgot to send them at all. You know, you're way out across the Galaxy, while she's home.

Go see her if you can, son. Will you? Make sure she gets the unit transfer I made out. It isn't much out of seventy years of living, but she may need it. And maybe you can tell her a little bit about what it means to be out there. Tell her it's open and free and when you got hold of those levers and you're trying for an orbit on something big and new and green.... Hell, you remember. You know how to tell her.

Her name is Ethel Brockman. I know she'll still use my name. Her address is or was East 71, North 101, Number 4. You can trace her easy if she moved. Women don't generally shove off and not leave a forwarding address. Not Ethel, at least.

Craig put the battered card in his pocket and walked back through the door to the passenger room. How did you explain to an old woman why her husband deserted her fifty years before? Some kind of story about one's duty to the Universe? No, the old man had not been in Intergalactic. He had been a tramp spaceman. Well, why *had* he left?

Fifty years in space. *Fifty* years! Zone V had been beyond anybody's imagination that long ago. He must have been in on the first Cetusian flights and shot the early landings in Cetus II. God only knew how many times he had battled Zone 111b pirates....

Damn the old man! How did one explain?

CRAIG DESCENDED the ramp from the huge jet and concentrated on his impressions. One day he would recall this moment, his first on the planet Terra. He tried to recall his first thrill at seeing Los Angeles, 1500 square miles of it, from the ship as it entered the atmosphere.

He was about to step off the last step when a man appeared hurriedly. A rather plump man, he displayed a toothy smile on his puffy red face.

"A moment, sir. Just a little greeting from the Terra. You understand, of course. Purely routine."

Craig remained on the final step of the ramp, puzzled. The man turned to a companion at his right.

"We can see that this gentleman has come from a long, long way off, can't we?"

The other man did not look up. He was peering into what seemed to Craig to be a kind of camera.

"We can allow the gentlemen to continue now, can't we? It wasn't that we believed for a minute, you understand ... purely routine."

Both men were gone in an instant, leaving Craig completely bewildered.

"You goin' to move on, buddy, or you want to go back?"

Craig turned to face a line of his fellow passengers up the ramp behind him.

"Who was that?" Craig asked.

"Customs. Bet you never got such a smooth screening before, eh?"

"You mean he *screened* me? What for?"

"Hard to say," the other passenger said. "You'll get used to this. They get it over with quick."

Craig made his way toward the spaceport administration building. His first physical contact with Terra had passed unnoticed.

"Sir! Sir!" cried a voice behind him.

He wheeled to see a man walking briskly toward him.

"You dropped this, sir. Quite by accident, of course."

Craig examined the small object the man had given him before rushing off toward an exit.

It was an empty PON tube he had just discarded. He couldn't understand why the man had bothered until he realized that the plastaloid floor of the lobby displayed not the faintest scrap of paper nor trace of dirt.

THE IMPORT PERSONNEL MAN was toying with a small chip of gleaming metal. He did not look directly at Craig for more than an instant at a time, and commented on Craig's description of his trip through the city only very briefly between questions.

"It's a good deal bigger than I imagined," Craig was saying. "Haven't seen much of it, of course. Thought I'd check in here with you first."

"Yes, naturally."

"Thought you could give me some idea of conditions...."

"Conditions?"

"For instance, what part of the city I should live in. That is, what part is closest to where I'll work."

"I see," said the man noncommittally. It seemed to Craig that he was about to add something. He did not, however, but instead rose from his chair and walked to the large window overlooking an enormous section of the city far below. He stared out the window for a time, leaving Craig seated uncomfortably in the silent room. There was a distracted quality about him, Craig thought.

"You are the first man we have had from the Intergalactic Service," the personnel man said finally.

"That so?"

"Yes." He turned to face Craig briefly before continuing. "You must find it very strange here."

"Well, I've never seen a city so big."

"Yes, so big. And also...." He seemed to consider many words before completing the sentence. "And also different."

"I haven't been here very long," said Craig. "Matter of fact, I haven't been anywhere very long. This is my first real experience with life on a planet. As an adult, anyway."

The personnel man seated himself once more and pressed a button on a small instrument. A secretary entered the office from a door to Craig's left.

"Miss Wendel, this is Mr. Craig. Mr. Craig, my secretary. Mr. Craig will enter Minerals and Metals, Zone V."

They exchanged formal greetings. She was a moderately pretty girl of medium height and, to Craig, a pleasantly rounded figure. He would have attempted to catch her eye had she not immediately occupied herself with unfolding the legs of a small instrument she was carrying.

"This is Mr. Craig's first landing on Terra, Miss Wendel," the personnel man continued. "Actually, we shall have to consider him in much the same way we would an extraterrestrial."

The girl glanced at Craig, casting him a cool, impersonal smile.

"He was formerly a flight officer in the Intergalactic Space Service." The statement was delivered in an almost exaggeratedly casual tone.

The girl glanced at him once more, this time with a definite quizzical look in her brown eyes.

"Three complete tours of duty, I believe."

"Four," corrected Craig. "Four tours of three years each, minus a year's terminal leave."

"I take it you have no identification card?" the man asked.

"The one I held in the service. It's pretty comprehensive."

The other turned to the secretary. "You'll see that he is assisted in filing his application, won't you? A provisional Code II. That will enable you to enter all Import offices freely, Mr. Craig."

"Will he need a food and—clothing ration also?" asked the girl, without looking at Craig.

"Yes." The man laughed. "You'll excuse us, Mr. Craig. We realize that you couldn't be expected to be familiar with Terra's fashions. In your present outfit you would certainly be typed as a ... well, you'd be made uncomfortable."

Craig reddened in spite of himself. He had bought the suit on Ghandii.

"A hick," he supplied.

"I wouldn't go that far, but some people might."

CRAIG NOTED the pleasant way the girl filled her trim, rather severe business suit. He amused himself by calculating stress patterns in its plain, woven material as she assembled the forms for him.

"Here, Mr. Craig. I believe these are complete."

"They look pretty complicated."

"Not at all. The questions are quite explicit."

Craig looked them over quickly.

"I guess so. Say, Miss Wendel, I was wondering—I don't know the city at all. Maybe you could go with me to have dinner. It must be almost dinnertime now. You could sort of check me out on some...."

"I'm afraid that would be quite impossible. You couldn't gain admittance to any office you need to visit tonight. Therefore, it is impossible for me to be of any assistance to you."

"Oh, come now, Miss Wendel. There *are* women aboard spaceships. I'm not a starved wolf."

"Certainly you are not, Mr. Craig. But it is not possible for me...."

"You said that already, but you can have dinner with me. Just company."

"I'm afraid I don't understand."

THE GALACTIC HOTEL strove to preserve an archaic tone of hospitality. It advertised "a night's lodgings" and it possessed a bellboy. The bellboy actually carried Craig's plasticarton and large file of punch cards and forms to his room. Tired from the long, confusing day, Craig was not impressed. He vaguely wondered if the little drama of the hotel carried so far as a small fee to be paid the bellboy, and he hoped he would have the right size of Terran units in his wallet.

Outside the door to the room, the bellboy stopped and turned to Craig.

"For five I'll tell you where it is," he said in a subdued tone.

"Tell me where what is?"

"You know, the mike."

"Mike?"

"All right, mister, three units, then. I wasn't trying to hold you up."

"You mean a microphone?" asked Craig, mechanically fishing for his wallet.

"Sure, they don't put in screens here. Wanted to, but the boss convinced 'em there aren't any Freedomites ever stay here."

"Where is the microphone?" Craig asked as he found a ten unit note. He was too puzzled to wonder what he was expected to do with the information.

"It's in the bed illuminator. You can short it out with a razor blade. Or I'll do it for another two."

"Never mind," Craig said wearily. He waited while the bellboy inserted a key into the door and opened it for him.

"I can get you a sensatia-tape," whispered the boy when they had entered. He nudged Craig wickedly. "You know what they're like?"

"Yeah," Craig said disgustedly. Traffic in the illicit mental-image tapes was known as far into space as lonely men had penetrated. Intergalactic considered them as great a menace to mental and moral stability as the hectopiates. Craig wearily got the man out of the room, took a PON pill, and eased himself into the bed.

It had been a weird day and he had not liked it. There was no telling how long it would take him to shake his—sea legs, the psychologist had called it. One thing was sure: Terra aggressively went after its strangers.

USHERED INTO THE ROOM by a sullen and silent secretary, Craig found himself facing a semicircular table at which were seated five uniformed men. The center man, obviously their superior, rose to greet him. He wore the familiar smile Craig had come to know so well and hate so much. The man was somewhat over forty years old, short, stout, entirely unpleasant and puffy.

"Mr. Craig, I believe," he greeted Craig. Since it seemed to be more of a statement than a question, Craig did not answer. He took up a position of more or less military attention at the center of the curved table.

"You *are* Robert Craig," insisted the man.

"Yes, I'm Robert Craig," he answered, somewhat surprised.

The stout man seated himself with a sigh and began to sort through some papers on the table before him. The other four men continued to stare at Craig silently, until he began to feel uncomfortable and hostile. He stiffened his position of attention defiantly.

"You may relax, Mr. Craig," said the first man without looking up. "You aren't nervous, are you?"

"No," Craig said, trying to smile. "This is the first time I've been here and...." He let the sentence trail off, hoping for a sympathetic response. But he did not get it.

"Flight Officer, eh?" said the man. Then, looking up, he added, "Somewhat unusual to find a vigorous young man like yourself abandoning the space service for a Terran job, isn't it?"

"I don't know. Is it?"

"Leaving something behind out there, Mr. Craig?"

"No, nothing," Craig snapped.

The other man glared at him a full minute. Craig met the stare and realized the considerable power behind the weak face.

"You don't like this sort of affair, do you, Mr. Craig?"

Craig was forced to look away. "I'm afraid I don't see the necessity," he answered in a controlled voice. "I served the Intergalactic Service well. My records prove that."

"Granted," said his questioner bluntly. "You are a Terran, are you not, Mr. Craig?"

"I should think that would be obvious," Craig said, matching the blunt tone.

The man rapped the table. "That's enough of your impertinence! You may very well have served the Intergalactic Service, but you are on Terra now. Terra, greatest, first of all civilized systems. Intergalactic may very well have to piddle with incompetent savages and wild colonists, but we of Terra assert our supremacy. Remember those words. You may not always find Terra so submissive to Intergalactic as Intergalactic would desire."

"Where are your loyalties, Mr. Craig?" demanded one of the other men suddenly.

"I am a Terran...."

"But your first loyalty is to Intergalactic. Is that right?"

"Is there a distinction?" Craig shot back, thoroughly angry.

"Do you wish to be held in contempt of this committee?" asked the first man, leaning forward half out of his chair.

"Of course not."

"Then you will confine your responses to simple yes and no answers, if you please, *Mr. Craig*."

Craig glared at the men in impotent rage. His head was beginning to ache. He had been many hours without paraoxylnebutal.

"Now, Mr. Craig," the first man began in an overly mild tone, "we shall begin again. Please try to restrain your show of emotion. You are here in petition of an identity card of provisional Code II type. You maintain that you have never been on Terra before. Indeed, you state that you have never had a political affiliation."

"Yes."

"What are your reactions to the latest acts of the Liberty party?" a third man abruptly asked.

"I have none," Craig answered, after an instant of confusion.

"You do not condemn the Liberty party?"

"I ... I...."

"Then you must favor it."

"I don't know anything about any...."

"Now, then, Mr. Craig," interrupted the head of the group. "The Import service report shows that you passed your tests aboard your ship. You were enabled to accomplish this through night study."

"Yes."

"Yet you maintain in your application that you had considered the space service a career."

"I changed my mind."

"Oh. You changed your mind. I see...."

"WHAT DO YOU DO if they turn you down on your food ration?" Craig asked the man by his side on the bench. He had intended it as a vaguely humorous question.

"You don't eat."

"You mean they would actually let you starve?"

"If you could not eat, you would starve," the man said matter-of-factly.

"What's all this for, anyway? I mean the medical part."

"You are rationed fairly in accordance with your particular metabolism."

"You're kidding."

"One does not jest of such matters," said the man, getting up to take a seat on another bench.

"But I'd like to keep it as a souvenir."

"It is not permitted."

"Look, it isn't issue. I bought the hide, had it made. I can pull off the marks of insignia and it's just another jacket...."

"That is not the point, Mr. Craig. Your clothing ration is defined by law. There are no exceptions."

"These are your permanent quarters. You will occupy them immediately. Then, if you believe the location is wasteful of your time, you must petition the appropriate committee. This department cannot accept such a petition."

"Your petition to be permitted to purchase a private means of conveyance is hereby denied."

THE BIG MAN leaned far back in the battered desk chair. It creaked at worn joints, but touched the wall without sliding from under its enormous load. The man was silent through Craig's long, confused speech. By turns he examined his fingernails, picked at yellowed teeth, and stared above his head at the discolored ceiling.

"...but you can get all this from ISS, maybe even from Import, if they'll release my file," Craig argued.

"Uh-huh," the big man said between closed lips.

"I just made a mistake, that's all. You don't hear much about Terra out there. It was different in my father's day. It must have been different."

"Yeah."

"I haven't any character references on Terra, but I can post a good-sized bond if they'll release my ISS units."

The space-freight agent glanced up at Craig at the remark.

"Anyway, I can get my units anywhere ISS has a base," Craig continued. "I can handle anything up to 15 Gs acceleration without a new license. I can go heavier if I get a check ride."

The fat man leaned forward in the protesting chair. "You got everything, but you can't go. I can't hire you."

"Why not?"

"Look, kid—Craig, is it?—how long you been in?"

"Four days. I'm still working on my work clearances."

"Four days. You tried Intergalactic to see if they'd take you back?"

"Yes. Their hands are tied by my Terran contract."

"And ours aren't, eh?" The man rose from the desk and walked to a water tap. He popped a pill into his gaping mouth and drank from a tin cup. Then he returned to the inadequate chair. "So you're a spaceman. Flight officer—*ex*-flight officer. You know how to navigate through four star zones and the asteroid belt thrown in. You got a license for 15 Gs, could get five more. You got enough brains to pass Import's senior router's exam.

"Still, you ain't got enough sense to come in out of the rain!"

Craig sat upright in his chair.

"We get guys like you two, three a day. You're hot. You're big. You're rarin' to go. But you ain't goin' nowhere!"

Craig glared at the big man.

"I don't know how you got here, Craig. It ain't none of my business. Maybe you did quit honorable. Quit to follow your daddy's footsteps. Or maybe you went and burned up a colony somewhere!"

"That would be in my records, wouldn't it?" Craig challenged.

"It still don't make any difference. You're stuck here. Nobody leaves Terra without a permit. Nobody. You couldn't get a permit with a crowbar and a blaster. You got a problem, son. You asked for it. Maybe they told you beforehand, maybe they didn't. You got a problem of adjustment. Terra's moved a long, long way since your daddy left it. We're doing things here. We're going places. Big things and big places.

"You got to fit into that, kid. Fit in quick. Move with it. You don't like the red tape, the committees? I don't like 'em either. But I been here a while. I can cut red tape. Red tape is for guys like you, guys that don't know Terra, don't know where we're going.

"Stick around, kid. You still got sea legs. You're still hopped up on PON. You're going to like it here on Terra. You're going to like it great. You can make a quick dollar on Terra. You can spend a quick dollar here too. Smarten up or you'll finish scrubbing radioactive dust off girders!"

THE GIRL APPROACHED his table, her hard eyes scanning him. Wordlessly she slid into the booth opposite him and made a sign for the bartender.

"Have a drink?" Craig suggested, smiling.

"Yeah."

"Work here?"

"What you mean by that?"

"I mean if you get a percentage on the drinks, I can...."

"I don't get no percentage."

The bartender brought them a version of N'cadian taz. The girl slouched in the booth and sullenly tapped the glass. The lights in the bar had dimmed to simulate some kind of planetary night. The walls came alive with projected images of Terran constellations. On their table, a globe lamp began to glow. Tiny bright lights swung orbits around a miniature sun inside the lamp.

As a miniature Pluto swung on its slow arc, an image of it was projected on the girl's dusky face. She seemed to be staring at nothing.

"Why d'you call me over here? You a purist, or don't you like the brand of sensatiatapes they're peddlin' these days?"

"I don't understand," Craig said.

She smiled crookedly at him. Not a bad face, Craig decided, but hard, hard as the

gradual dimming of the lights, the suppression of sound in the bar. He watched the tiny lights of other globes appear around shadows, watched as the lights traced fiery trails across the dusky skin of the girl opposite him, watched as they crossed the warm, rounded flesh....

"I TELL YA, we didn't give him nothing but a coupla tazes."

"The pump will determine that. You might as well tell the truth."

"I am tellin' the truth. He drank, let's see ... two, three."

"Four, five, six. You let her pump him full."

"Hey, look, this guy's a spaceman, or was."

"I didn't know that. Honest I didn't. He never told us."

"All right, you didn't know. What you put in those tazes—ether?"

"We denature the polyester just like the law says."

"And you get it straight from M'cadii, eh?"

"We put in some syn. So what? That ain't against the law."

ceramiplate of a ship. She could not be very old. It was the kind of wild look in her eyes that gave her a false appearance of age.

"Maybe you're writing a book—you got me over here for something."

"I just got in," Craig answered.

"What am I supposed to do for this drink?"

"Nothing. Nothing at all. I suppose. I thought...just skip it. I'm lonesome, that's all."

"Lonely, huh?" said the girl. "Lonely and just in, huh? Just in from space." She turned away from him to signal the bartender. "What you need is drinks."

There were more drinks. Many more drinks. The girl kept them coming, kept talking to him about—what was it? Craig looked at the girl and then at the globe lamp. He watched as the tiny bright orbs of light projected their images on the girl opposite him. He was aware of the

"He's probably got grav trouble, Chief."

"Who was the girl?"

"Girl? What girl?"

"You know what girl!"

"Just a girl, like a million of 'em these days."

"Professional?"

"There ain't any anymore. You know, sensatia-tapes."

"Know her name?"

"I don't ask no names. How you going to know names? She's a girl. Just like ten million of 'em these days."

"What you think a guy like this is doing here, Chief?"

"Why not?"

"Well, look at his clothes. He's got units, too. Can't figure that out. She must've been after something else."

BLACK INFINITY • 199

"How about his clothing and food tickets?"
"Uh ... that's it. She got his tickets."
"Come on, give me a hand. Lug him into the hold."

THE HARD FACE of the Civil Control chief peered down at him. It was a thick, red face that displayed no trace of feeling except perhaps toughness. It was long yet full, and it contained the proper features; but it added nothing of expression to the harsh, rasping voice.

"First time in, eh? Or else Central's too damned lazy to check the file. Okay, I ain't going to cite you. Waste of time. But listen to me. You got problems, we got problems. You solve yours and don't come back here."

Craig was aware of officers glowering at his back as he fumbled with the door button. The door opened onto a city street. It was entirely foreign to Craig. It was not a clean, straight thoroughfare at the bottom of a canyon of towering white buildings and contrived but bright parks. It was an old street, a dirty street; an incredible welter of color and line, of big and little shops, of dirty human shapes in drab gray. A flood of tone and noise hit Craig as he emerged from the station and descended the long, broad steps.

Craig's head was in a whirl despite the strong dose of paraoxylnebutal he had taken in the station clinic. He felt closed in and befogged. He could remember almost nothing of the night in Civil Control. Even the clinic was fading from his memory. He was aware that he stank, that he was dirty, that his clothing clung to his body. He was miserable.

He must call Import. He was due to begin work this morning, his period of personal adjustment complete. Instead, Craig turned and began to walk. He could not carry on a coherent conversation in his present state. He could never find his way unassisted back to his apartment; he was not even sure he remembered the address. But the thought of returning to his quarters, to Import sickened him.

What *was* his address? East 71, North.... No, that would be old lady Brockman. The association irritated him. He had completely forgotten the unwanted assignment, had forgotten to inquire where the address could be found.

Craig became aware of the heavy flow of vehicular traffic that roared a scant eight feet away. Large surface carriers whistled in the nearest lane of the complex four-lane pattern. Then there were the private surface craft; they were of many sizes and shapes. He guessed that they were turbine-powered, but he could not identify the odor of their exhausts.

There was an odd, unreal quality about the busy thoroughfare. Even myriad sounds from it were sounds he had never heard before and could not break down into their component parts.

Craig became aware of other humans, many of them, on the sidewalk. Again they were of a class that he could not identify. They had none of the brisk, purposeful stride of those he had seen near Import. They lacked also the graceful, colorful dress. Their faces, so far as he could separate them from the blurring film over his eyes, were different.

They seemed somehow *looser* faces, though Craig did not know exactly what he meant by the term. They were not tight, pinched, set, as were the faces he had seen before on Terra. There were bulbous noses, large ears, squint eyes, disheveled hair, the men's and women's faces strangely similar. Some were young, some old, but few were hard or fixed. They seemed more plastic, more full of expression than those he had come to know elsewhere in the city. He felt an inexplicable craving to know someone of this strange street.

"You looking for something, mister?" asked a voice near him.

Craig turned to find a middle-aged man eyeing him from the doorway of an empty building.

"I got it," the man added.

"Got what?" Craig asked.

"Anything a guy just outa the can would want."

"What would a 'guy just outa the can'

want that you have?" Craig examined the weathered, sharp face. It was an unpleasant one, but it belonged to this street; it would do to tell him what he wanted to know of the place.

"Follow me." The man quickly inserted a magnikey into the door of the vacant store building.

"There's a station just up the street," Craig warned.

"Sure. So what?"

The empty room was dusty and dark and received little light through the grimy display windows that faced on the street. What kind of store it had been, Craig could not guess. The man led him through a kind of storage room which was piled high with moldy paper cartons and back to a rear door. With quick, dextrous movements, the man swung an ancient bar assembly and pushed open the rear door. It led to a litter-strewn yard enclosed by rough, eroded shacks and a wooden garage.

They entered the garage through a creaking hinged door. It was a dank, almost completely dark room. Craig stumbled over something on the floor and fell against a packing box of some kind.

"Just stand still," said the man. He was shuffling invisibly about in the darkness. Craig could hear him opening a kind of cabinet or drawer while saying in a steady monotone, "You got the right man, mister. My stuff is pure. You can test it. But you'd rather *drink* it, right?"

For the tenth time, Craig asked himself why he had accepted the furtive invitation. The thought of this man's kind of intoxicant—however 'pure'—nauseated him. Nevertheless, he felt himself compelled by a kind of insatiable curiosity to follow out the part he had accepted. Perhaps through this man, through this somehow fascinating street, he could....

"You got ten; I know that. Maybe you got more, huh?" the man interrupted his confused train of thought.

"What makes you think I got ten?" Craig asked. He did not know himself how many units his wallet contained—certainly not after the previous night.

"Don't get sore. I'm honest. But I know you got ten. Otherwise you wouldn't have got out of the station."

The lack of clearly defined objects by which to orient himself in the darkness of the garage made his head begin to swim once more. He wanted to leave.

"Don't get scared, buddy. They don't ever come in here."

Craig fumbled for support in the darkness. He was afraid he would be sick. Fulfillment for the half-formed plan that was beginning to take shape in his mind would not come with the bootlegger. It would come into being somehow in the tawdry street he had just left, only he did not know how.

"They don't really go after polyester. They don't want to stop the stuff. It makes their job easier. You don't have to worry, buddy. Come on, how much you want? You might have trouble finding more for a while."

Craig said nothing. He fumbled for a grip on a packing box.

"You're from Out, aren't you, buddy? You ain't used to us here yet. Most of my customers are from Out. What jam'd you get into?"

"I got ten units, I think," Craig evaded.

"It ain't none of my business what you done. Nobody around here is going to ask you any questions. Long as you got units, you get poly like the big shots that come over here all the way from Uptown."

"Yeah," said Craig. "Gimme what I get for ten units and let's beat it out of here."

"Myself, I never been Out. Not even Luna. Never wanted to. I stay here and have my little business—you can call it a business. You'll see, buddy, there are millions of guys like me. The controllers don't stop us. We're respectable. A damned sight more respectable than those...."

"All right," snapped Craig. "Let's get out of here."

"You got it bad, huh? This poly will fix that up. It's pure. You just come back to old Nave and get poly."

"How ... how you get out of here?" asked Craig, nauseated.

"Get lost pretty easy in the dark, huh?" The man was beginning to mock him.

Craig lashed out suddenly at the unseen face in the darkness. He caught the thin throat in his left hand. His right left the packing box and cocked to deliver a blow. But he began to fall and had to let go.

"Okay, buddy, okay," the other man said soothingly as Craig was forced to catch himself. "I *like* ex-spacemen. I know lots of you. I sell you poly. You don't want to get tough with me."

He shoved a block of ten small cubes into Craig's hand and, while Craig fished for his wallet, he produced a tiny, narrow-beamed flash. The transaction was quickly over. The cube was small enough to be forced without much difficulty into Craig's jacket pocket.

The man led him back across the littered yard, through the empty store building, and out the front door. When Craig emerged onto the street once more, a uniformed figure was standing nearby.

"He'll need two," whispered the man from behind him.

Craig reached into his pocket and mechanically fumbled two of the small cubes of waxlike substance from the loose package. He placed them on the outstretched hand of the Civil Control officer. The officer did not look in his direction at any time, but accepted the offer and walked slowly on toward the station.

Craig continued aimlessly down the long street. His head cleared as he walked and once more began to form a kind of vague plan. There was anonymity to a street such as this. There was also a kind of freedom. Everywhere in the universe, there were such streets. Neutralized streets, where a kind of compromise was reached between law and lawlessness. They were permitted because it was always necessary to provide such a place for those who were not permitted elsewhere. Those who would not fit, could not be "rehabilitated," could neither be jailed nor permitted complete freedom.

Controllers of one kind or another patrolled such streets, keeping them in a kind of check—or, more accurately, in a kind of containment. But no amount of control would ever completely stamp out the likes of Nave, the bootlegger.

Perhaps here, on this street, Craig could be "lost." Here he might find security for a time in anonymity, security and time to find a way ... to what? He did not know.

"Mister! Mister!" cried a thin, high voice from somewhere to his left. "Here, quick!"

It was a young boy of perhaps nine or ten. Craig caught sight of him as he motioned urgently. He wore a shabby, torn version of what appeared to be a space service uniform.

"I'm not buying anything, son," Craig said, pausing briefly.

"Come here, quick!" insisted the boy, his eyes large in a dirty face. "You already bought too much."

The boy was motioning him to follow. He had stepped between two buildings. Craig approached him with suspicion.

"What did you say?"

"Slip in here quick! You bought from Nave the peddler. You bought poly, didn't ya?"

"How did you...." Craig began.

"Tell you later. Slip through here quick or they'll send you to *Hardy*!"

The genuine fear of the youngster conveyed itself to Craig. With effort he forced his body through the space between the old buildings. At first he did not intend to follow the boy, but only to stop him for an explanation. The boy, however, continued down the tight corridor formed by the buildings.

"There's a window soon," he said from ahead of Craig. "Hurry. You lost time with that peddler."

Lost time? Cursing himself for becoming involved again in something he did not understand, Craig nevertheless followed as best he could. It was a tight squeeze and he found himself becoming breathless.

"Dive down!" shouted the boy, looking back with terror in his eyes.

Instinctively Craig did so. The rough walls tore at his suit.

"Stop!" shouted a voice from behind Craig. "Stop or we fire!"

Craig suddenly felt the sill of a window which opened into the building to his left. He quickly pulled himself into it. There was a sickening whine and a part of the window disintegrated in a cloud of splinters and plaster.

"Through here," said the boy from the semi-darkness. "They'll blast their way inside in a minute!"

Craig found himself in another empty building. He followed the boy through a doorway and felt his way as he half ran along the dark hall.

"Who are *they*?" he panted.

"Controllers."

"Civil Control?"

"Sure. You must be pretty important. I didn't get it all. But they say the controllers checked up on you after.... I'll explain later."

The hall ended in a dim room piled high with plasmolite packing boxes in great disarray. The boy chose a box and lifted a lid.

"Follow me. It's a passage."

"Where to?"

"No time now. Down here."

The passage, which seemed to be constructed of plasmolite boxes, seemed somehow lit by daylight, although Craig could not actually see the source of the light.

The tunnel ended in broad afternoon daylight. As he climbed out he saw a large clearing surrounded by ruins.

"We're just inside the old city," the boy said. "We're safe now—unless those controllers are willing to take more chances than I think."

"Wait a minute, son. You said 'old city.' You mean that this is a part of pre-war Los Angeles?"

"Well, sure."

"But that's supposed to be...."

"Radioactive? Most of it, anyway. Good thing, too. Otherwise we'd have no place to go."

"Look, kid, you better explain," said Craig. "You were right about somebody being after me, but I don't get the 'we' business. Or how you knew all about this."

"All right, mister, but let's get away from here. Those guys won't come through to here, even if they find a way—I don't think. But they're gettin' smarter and you're pretty hot right now."

The boy led the way to what appeared to be a completely demolished building.

"Used to be the old library," he said.

They circled the heap of plaster, brick, and twisted steel. On the other side Craig saw what appeared to be a window. The boy let himself down through it.

Craig was amazed to find a large, relatively clear area inside, probably part of an old room that had been spared by some freak of the blast.

"You *live* here?" Craig asked the youngster incredulously.

"Part of the time." The boy brought up an old crate and offered it to Craig as a chair. "Listen, mister, I don't know who you are. You're an ex-spaceman and that's enough for me." There was a slightly amusing attempt at adult hardness about him. "You shouldn't have wasted time with Nave. You should have got out of there."

"Why?"

"I don't know. What you done, anyway?"

"I don't remember. Passed out at a bar...."

The boy showed disgust. He glanced at the pocket which contained the polyester.

Craig smiled. "I don't use this stuff. At least not enough to deserve what you're thinking." He tossed the remaining cubes on the littered floor of the room.

The boy maintained his look of scorn for a time, but then softened. "I was afraid you got kicked out of the service for that."

"How did you know I was ever in it?"

"Easy. You don't know how to walk on a planet yet. Anybody can tell."

"I didn't get kicked out," Craig said. "I came here to take a civil service job."

"It'd almost be better if you had been."

"I didn't know about Terra. None of us had any idea."

"I know," said the boy sadly. "My father quit, too. *He* quit to marry my mother. That was before it was ... so bad."

"Where—" Craig began, then bit off the question.

"Oh, gee, mister, Terra's in an *awful* bad shape! They took ... my parents. They hunt us down. They...."

Craig approached the boy and put a hand on his shoulder. "What's your name, son?"

"Phil."

"Phil what?"

"I don't know exactly. My father had to use so many names toward the ... end. He once had only one name, but I guess even he forgot what it was."

THEY PREPARED to spend the night in the old library room, but first Phil left it and made his way into the wilderness of rubble. He returned dragging a packing box of plastic insulating material, out of which they fashioned a crude bed. Despite the thousands of questions that paraded across Craig's mind, he waited each time for the boy to speak.

"I can't take you any further until...."

"Until you know more about me?"

"In a way. *They'll* let me know."

Craig would have risked much to identify the "they" Phil referred to, but he did not ask the question. As he watched the boy preparing the dimly lit room for the night, he felt sure Phil could be trusted. He was almost frighteningly mature for his age.

The room was well hidden, for the once great library lay in a powdered ruin about it on all sides but a part of one. Only by accident or knowledge would a stranger recognize it in what was literally a world of rubble. During the moments of silence between the boy's volunteered statements, Craig tried to visualize the awful catastrophe that had befallen the old city. Piles of powdered masonry restricted his view greatly under the gathering night. He could see a scant city block through the window, but he knew the wreckage around them must extend for miles.

"You don't have to worry, mister...."

"Craig."

"Mr. Craig. They don't come in here at night."

"Radioactivity?"

"Yes. Not right here, but all around, everywhere."

"What?"

"It's all around us. You go through it to get here, but you can't *stay* anywhere but a few places like this."

"How do you know all of these things, Phil?"

"Oh, we know, all right. We had to find out."

"You must have ion counters," he said in what he hoped was a casual tone.

"We have lots of things."

Craig was thoughtful for a minute. The boy was obviously on his guard now.

"Those empty buildings?" Craig asked tentatively.

"They built them too close," said the boy. It seemed to be a safe subject. "They built them up as close as they thought was safe. Space is very valuable here. But they built them too close."

"Yet the 'we' you speak of live even closer?"

The boy bit his lip and eyed him suspiciously in silence.

"Look, kid," Craig said very deliberately, "I'm not a controller and I'm not interested in a bunch of petty thieves."

The effect was just what he had intended. "We're *not* thieves! And we're not traitors, either! We're...."

The boy was almost in tears. Craig waited a moment, then continued in a soft voice. "Phil, I'm just beginning to realize what a rotten place Terra is. From just what I've seen —it isn't very much—I can imagine such a system producing a great many 'we' groups like yours. I don't know who you are or what you are, but you can't be any worse than what I've already seen of Terran officials. Tell me, kid, what's it all about? And is there any way out of here? I mean—*way* out!"

"You may tell him, Philip," said a quiet voice from the window entrance. "Like us, Philip, Mr. Craig is an enemy of tyranny, though he doesn't realize it yet."

Craig instinctively jumped back to get out of range of the window, meanwhile feeling around for something that could be used as a weapon. But the boy ran to the silhouetted figure in the window.

"Mr. Sam!" he cried eagerly.

Craig relaxed his hold on a strip of heavy metal. When the man had entered, the boy pulled a ragged black cloth across the window once more. He then ignited a small oil burning lamp in a carved-out nook in the wall.

"It's all right, Philip, nobody is following me," the newcomer said.

Craig studied his face. It was an old face covered by a stained gray beard. With a shock Craig recognized the man as a tramp he had seen earlier on the street, napping, sprawled in a doorway. Now for the first time he saw the eyes. Sharp and clear, they caught up the yellow light of the oil lamp and glowed warmly as they turned to Craig.

"I am 'Mr. Sam,' Mr. Craig. You might know me by the full name, Samuel Cocteau, but I doubt it. Even the names of the infamous do not penetrate space."

"I guess not," Craig agreed. "But you said something about my being an enemy of tyranny."

"Whether you like it at once or not, you are temporarily one of us—one of the 'we' Philip has been speaking of. But all of that in due time. Right now, it is necessary for us to leave here."

"They're going to try to find us *tonight?*" asked Phil, startled.

"Yes, a tribute to Mr. Craig," said the old man. "A Geiger team is being readied at the station."

Craig started to protest as the boy began hurriedly to pick up his few possessions in the room.

"I'm sorry, Mr. Craig," the man said. "I must ask you to decide now whether to trust us and our judgment. There is grave danger for you if you are caught by the Civil Control. The report I have received is that you are largely unaware of the 'crimes against the state' you have committed. The Civil Control hoped to capture you before you find them out. But that, of course, is my word only. There is no time to give you proof, even if I had it."

Craig's mind whirled under the sudden onslaught of new facts. He had followed a peddler without knowing why he did it. He had bought polyester he had no use for. He had followed a boy who beckoned to him. Now—how much longer was he to move haphazardly through Terra like a cork on a windblown sea? Who were these strange fugitives who said he was one of them and who lived in the heart of a radioactive city?

"Well, Mr. Craig?" asked Cocteau quietly.

Craig glanced at the boy. The child's eyes were wide and pleading in the dim light of the oil lamp.

"Let's go," Craig said.

DARKNESS was swiftly falling on the wilderness of heaping ruin. The three made their way toward what Craig at first thought was an unbroken wall of rubble. The near-horizontal rays of the sun tipped the white mass of broken stone with brilliance, and gave the entire scene an unearthly quality. Below the towering rubble mountains, long black shadows were reaching toward what Craig knew to be the living city.

Cocteau took the lead and set a fast pace for a man of his age. He took a highly devious path through the "mountain," or what began to seem to Craig needlessly difficult and that outlined them against the bright western sky. At one point, Craig left the invisible path of the older man to avoid an exhaustingly steep rise.

"Follow me exactly," warned Cocteau in a sharp voice. "There is only one relatively safe path through here."

"They'll see us against the sky!"

"It cannot be helped."

But there was no indication that they were followed. They pushed onward, scurrying over heaps of weathered plaster and brick. The old man seemed to avoid with great care places where metal girders were visible.

The exertion, together with walking directly into the setting sun, made Craig begin to feel the old nausea return. He resisted it for a time, but it would not be repressed, particularly as he strove to maintain his balance on difficult climbs. Once he stumbled on a splintered building stone and fell. It was a long minute before he could regain his feet and mutter a feeble, "Sorry."

"We must push on, Mr. Craig," was Cocteau's only comment.

"It's safe here for a *minute*, isn't it?" Craig panted, dizzy and breathless.

"There is no safe place here, Mr. Craig."

They continued their winding way through the growing darkness. For Craig it became a nightmare of stumbling over the endless piles of sharp stones. His mind spun sickeningly and he retched as he half ran along the path Cocteau set for them.

"Please, mister," breathed the voice of Phil behind him. "It isn't so far now."

Doggedness carried Craig onward long after awareness left him.

HE BECAME conscious suddenly, as though by an injection of stimulant. He found himself surrounded by a number of figures, including Cocteau and a white garbed man, evidently a doctor.

"You are quite safe now, Mr. Craig," said Cocteau warmly. "Welcome to the *City of We*."

"Where are we?"

"Deep in the old city, in a place where the radioactivity is negligible," the man answered as the doctor took his pulse. "This is Dr. Grant and these others are members of the *Liberty party*."

"Liberty!"

"You've heard of it?"

"Yeah, you're pretty unpopular, aren't you?"

"Unpopular? Let us say that all of Terran *officialdom* is dedicated to exterminating us."

"The committee on something-or-other asked me about my attitudes toward the Liberty party," said Craig, rising to a sitting position on the cot.

"And at the time you had a lack of attitude, which most likely was unacceptable to them," supplied Cocteau, smiling. "Well, you may be interested to know that you are considered one of us by most of Terra just now."

"What?"

"That is correct," said another of the group. "It seems you were in a bar in—ah—in a somewhat less than fully conscious state...."

"But I didn't know anything about the Liberty party."

"No, nor is it alleged that you actually mentioned the party in so many words," continued the white-haired man, smiling. "But it seems that you did make certain statements in the presence of certain persons that did indicate a definite predilection...."

"That's crazy," said Craig angrily.

"Of course," Cocteau agreed.

"Furthermore," the other man said, "you are charged with willful abandonment of duty and 'acts indicative of your desire to shun the best utilization of your talents in behalf of the state of Terra.'"

"In other words," explained Cocteau, "you applied for a job on a private space freighter. Without permission to do so."

Craig was silent. He lay back down on the cot and tried to absorb the data he had just received.

"So I'm accused of belonging to something I don't know anything about?"

"Then I'll tell you briefly about us. You have a right to know the magnitude of the crime with which you are charged." Cocteau took a seat by Craig's cot. The others also found chairs.

"But first a brief bit of history—a history that you have never heard before. Not your fault. It is not allowed to penetrate Terra's atmosphere."

"I don't know much about Terra," Craig interjected. "I'm just finding out how much I don't know."

"God, I wish the rest of the Universe could find out with you!" said one of the group.

"Yes, the history of Terra is almost lost now. That is, the part of it that followed the Great Wars of seventy-five years ago. You know of those wars; you have just walked through one of the physical results of them. No nation or alliance of nations can be said to have won them, but the wars had a most profound effect upon Terra. More than anything else, they made men reach to the stars, if only to escape the deadly conflicts of Terra.

"Ideological issues were involved, naturally, but the underlying cause of the Great Wars was the struggle for power. The world was disunited. Peoples were divided from peoples by an almost inconceivable number of unimportant distinctions. These were ethnical, national, racial, cultural—name any brand of prejudice and you'll find it existed then.

"Incredibly enough, the destructiveness of the Great Wars accomplished a kind of unity. Gone were the once proud aggressive nations. Gone into oblivion. Gone, too, were the systems of economics and sociology of which men were once so sure. There was a kind of 'plague-on-both-your-houses' attitude among the peoples of the world. There was a large measure of anarchy following the Great Wars. Not a violent, active anarchy of hate and terror, but of apathy and weariness. Apathy at the outcome of false conflicts, and weariness of the self-defeating strife of man against man.

"At first men produced by the full extent of their labors barely enough on which to survive. Only gradually did they regain their ability to produce surpluses once more. Of course, surpluses mean exchanges—trade. And trade requires order and system.

"The first ten years following the Great Wars was a period of gradualism in all things. Peoples united in small groups. There were no political or racial divisions. The units were built upon functional lines. They were natural and free. Above all, they were cooperative.

"It was not communism. Men knew all too well the mental and physical slavery of that brutally rigid system. It was not rugged individualism either. Rugged individuals during this period either starved or were driven out by the starving.

"This natural, cooperative unity spread and became more complex. There came into being natural associations of units. Not exclusive but inclusive associations that linked all who would join and could produce surpluses. Productivity increased thereby. Men were intelligent enough to avoid many of the old abuses.

"Ways were found to harness the productivity of each man and woman. Genuine efforts were made to avoid misfits, to make those who produced fit. It was realized, Mr. Craig, that the unhappy man will infect others with his misery, and the trouble he will cause is much more difficult to undo than to prevent in the first place.

"There were, of course, mistakes, false starts. But the new-found system of worldwide unity proved flexible. It was multiple-based. To a very large degree, all men fitted into it logically and naturally. It was the first truly 'grass-roots' economic and social system in the history of man. And it was a great tribute to his ability to work out his destiny, particularly since it came after a tragedy that was so enormous and devastating.

"The list of its successes is incredible. For in a decade the age-old problem of poverty seemed to have disappeared. There were no significant outbreaks of disorder and lawlessness—indeed, there was comparatively little need for a written law. The principle of mutuality and cooperation was too strongly conditioned into the people.

"Scientifically, the first half of the new century, a scant twenty-five years after the last bomb was dropped, was the greatest in man's history. Man reached the stars. He began to know the molecule, the atom, the electron. He pushed the frontier of his knowledge deep into both microcosm and macrocosm.

"But a fatal flaw had long before developed in the structure, wonderful as it was. It was an age-old flaw. It was one that was disguised by the very nature of the new system. When it was recognized, that flaw had so weakened the system that its spread was all but inevitable. It is a flaw that will always plague man to a certain extent, but one that must keep us eternally vigilant.

"It is this: the greatest human good comes not in how well you learn to control man and keep him from harming himself. What determines it is how completely you learn to free him.

"Conversely, the law provides that no control system, however devised, will succeed in bringing happiness and security to man to any greater extent than it permits the fullest expression of his nature.

"Man is *inherently* good. He will *always* choose a moral path when free to do so. He strives for justice and truth both as an individual and in mass.

"Mr. Craig, democracy is man's greatest *a priori*. Yet based upon a law of restraint, it cannot escape the hopeless contradiction that leads to its own destruction. Man can democratically do the irrational and the insane. He can democratically limit and coerce the absolute highest nature of himself. Bad laws are forever passed to achieve good ends. But each new law produces new criminals while the cause of the new crime remains unsolved.

"Ergo, the world you have just seen. Ergo, the Liberty party. Mr. Craig, our world is ruled by a vast and horrible bureaucracy whose terrible weapon is conformity. You would find few laws even today written in books. Our assemblies pass few statutes. They determine dogma instead. They 'resolve' and 'move.' They fix a new 'position,' define a 'stand.' Our equivalent of judge and attorney is no student of law. He is a kind of moralist. He is sensitive to the 'trend' and appreciative of the 'proper.'

"Terra fits uncomfortably in the Intergalactic System. Like many of the undemocratic systems of the dark past, the Terran state must expand. It is based upon a self-limiting philosophy unless it can spread fast enough. You are charged with being 'unTerran,' Mr. Craig. A system that forever seeks 'unTerrans' must inevitably exile or kill itself!"

It had been a long speech. Craig had listened in awe, for it was a completely new story to him.

"And you propose to destroy this bureaucracy?" he said.

"In so far as it is a philosophical entity, yes."

"And you say I am one of you now?"

"You are considered one of us. Your employer and his secretary are also suspected."

"But I'm entitled to a trial, or at least a hearing."

"Not now, Mr. Craig. It would do you little good, anyway. The 'position' of the Assembly on subversion is that it 'rightly behooves every loyal Terran so to conduct his behavior that a suspicion of membership in the Liberty party is unthinkable.'"

Craig found himself regretting every minute of his stay on Terra. Old Brockman had been right—it was no place for a spaceman. Now it was probably too late. No Terran space freighter would accept him and Intergalactic could not. There was not even a way for him to recover his service records.

"Will you join us, Mr. Craig?" asked one of the men. "We can use your skills, particularly your knowledge of space."

"Look, how do I know you aren't a bunch of traitors? Maybe all this you've told me is true. I've seen plenty of that bureaucracy and there seems to be damned little freedom of action left on Terra. But how do I know you can do any better when you get in power?"

"Liberty will never be 'in power,' Mr. Craig," Cocteau said quietly. "Liberty will attempt to reach the minds of the people with our message of hope, of freedom in true democracy."

Another of the group joined Cocteau. "We are now hunted as criminals. We have only this small stronghold in the old city."

"We shall attempt only to gain entry to the minds of the people," said Cocteau. "Gain entry to tell them how they live, for most of them have had no contact with any other kind of life."

"It would mean killing a few people," Craig pointed out.

"One of the basic principles of Liberty is the inherent goodness of every man," Cocteau repeated. "We have never taken a life, even in self-defense. We shall never take one. Nor will it ever be necessary for a member of the Liberty party to hold public office, to own a weapon, to coerce a man in any physical way."

"But you will coerce them with ideas. Is that what you have in mind?" Craig protested.

"If a point of view, a promise, a goal is coercion, then the answer to your question is yes. But ideas are not dangerous when a man is free to argue and act against them."

"Look here, Cocteau," Craig said earnestly, "all you say may be true. I believe it is. But what can I do? I'm a spaceman, or at best an apprentice import clerk. I don't know anything about this sort of work."

"Come here a moment," invited a member of the group.

Through the window indicated by the man, Craig saw an incredible sight. The entire scene seemed to be on the inside of a vast underground cavern. There were other buildings and some kind of systematic work being done by many men and women. But the thing that caught Craig's eye seemed to be cradled in a kind of hangar.

"A spaceship!" exclaimed Craig.

"A very modest one, yet not so modest when you consider that it was necessary to carry in every single piece and part by hand."

"Good Lord!"

"*You*, Mr. Craig, might captain that ship. Very few Terrans have ever even flown in one. It will be necessary to establish contact with possible assistance outside of Terra. You can make that possible."

Craig was thoughtful. "I suppose, now that I've seen all this, you can't let me leave here unless I join you."

"No," denied Cocteau. "You may leave here any time you like."

"I'd be sure to get caught, of course...."

"Within limits, it might be possible to help you avoid capture." Cocteau reached into his beggar's coat and withdrew a wallet. "Identity card, food ration, clothing, work card, even a Government party card. It's all here, Mr. Craig. You could have a slightly altered physical appearance. Liberty accepts no unwilling members. You are given as nearly a free choice in this matter as is possible to give you."

"Suppose I talked?" asked Craig, nodding bluntly toward the port.

Cocteau smiled. "It was necessary to prepare for that. You were given a drug. It has not affected your thinking capacity in any way. But once it wears off, you will be unable to remember what took place while under its influence.

"When agents of the Liberty party are sent out of here, they go having had all experience with Liberty take place while under the drug. None of us could remember for more than a few hours the exact location of this headquarters. When it is necessary to leave for very long, we carry a small amount of the drug with us. Many of our agents have been caught and a few have resigned. But none has divulged enough information to harm us seriously."

Craig was postponing his decision to the last. "They must know you're somewhere in here. If the radioactivity keeps them out, why shouldn't they put a cordon around the entire old city?"

"Periodically, they try. But there are many, many other ways of leaving here than by the surface. Underground water conduits, ancient power and sewer lines, a number of tunnels we have dug...."

Craig was solemnly handed the wallet.

"If you will submit to sufficient plastic surgery to make you resemble this man, you may safely leave here no later than tomorrow night."

A long silence ensued. It was interrupted by a noise from outside the door of the room. It was the voice of Phil.

"Has he decided to stay? Did you see him? He looks like my daddy did.... Will he stay?"

"You mustn't interrupt, son. They're in conference now. We'll let you know."

"Tell him yes!" said Craig in a loud voice. "Tell him hell, yes, I'm staying!"

The men gathered around him to congratulate him on the decision.

Phil was allowed in the clinic to join them.

"Oh, Cocteau, one more thing," Craig said.

"Yes?"

Craig was fumbling for his own wallet. He extracted a folded card.

"Where would East 71, North 101, Number 4 be?"

"It *would* have been somewhere here in Old City."

"God! How did the old guy expect me to deliver this message? Old man named Brockman. He sent me a message just before he died in Gravitation. I was to visit his wife."

"Brockman?" asked Cocteau. "You mean Ethel Brockman?"

"Yeah. How'd you know?"

"Ethel Brockman was one of the organizers of the Liberty party. She served as its chairman until her death only a few years ago. Her husband must have felt your 'sea legs' would lead you to us eventually. And, of course, they did."

👽 👽 👽

"Sea Legs" first appeared in the November 1951 issue of Galaxy Science Fiction. *The story was adapted in 1956 for NBC's popular half-hour radio drama* X Minus One.

Little is known of Hollywood writer Frank Quattrocchi. During the first half of the 1950s, he published eight stories in SF pulps such as Astounding, Galaxy, *and* Fantasy and Science Fiction. *In 1966, producer Alex Gordon (*Day the World Ended, The Atomic Submarine, *etc.) discovered Quattrocchi's unproduced screenplay* The Projected Man, *and purchased the script directly from the writer. The British movie was quickly produced and released in the UK in 1966. The following year, Universal Studios released the movie in the U.S., as the second half of a double bill with* Island of Terror. *The plot of* The Projected Man *is noticeably similar to that of the classic 1958 feature film* The Fly.

MINUTEMEN

By Kurt Newton

"**IT WAS THE LAST WAR. A BARBAROUS UNDERTAKING THAT SPILLED YOUNG BLOOD ON DESERT SAND AND DEBRIS-STREWN CITY STREETS.** *No more!* the cry from mothers. *No more!* the chant from protesters. *No more!* the declaration from a generation of legislators who had seen their fathers, mothers, sons and daughters pay the ultimate price. There had to be a better way. And, so, the Minutemen were born...."

Harrison Burch sat with his three grandchildren—Janey, Marli and Ezra—on the living room sofa. Harrison had told this story many times over the years to his own children, and now his children's children.

"You mean made," said Ezra.

"What's that?" said Grandpa Burch.

"You mean made, not born. The Minutemen were built like robots. They weren't born." Ezra, in all his learned nine years on the planet was showing off in front of his younger sisters by pointing out this error in semantics.

"Why, yes, indeed, they were made," said Grandpa Burch, not missing a beat. "They were made to save us all." Harrison bopped little Janey on the nose with his bent index finger to accentuate this fact.

"But how, Grandpa? How did the robots save us?" said Marli.

"Well, first, the Minutemen were not robots. They were men who volunteered to take a ride inside a rocket and guide it toward its target. You see, back then, computers controlled everything. And, as we've learned, if a computer can control something, a person can break into that computer and control it just the same."

"They're called hackers."

"That's right, Ezra. But a person can't be hacked. It was the only way our missiles would not be sent into the ocean or, worse, turned against us. The Minutemen were special. They were the heroes who finally brought an end to not only the last war but to all war. Their sacrifice could not be defended against. They were the perfect weapon. And they brought peace."

"And you were one of them, right, Grandpa?"

"Yes, Janey, I was."

"But they died," said Ezra. "How come you lived?"

"Because the war ended before my missile was launched. I was lucky, I guess."

"Oh," said Ezra.

Harrison looked at his grandson. The boy would never understand the sacrifice fighting men and women had to make to secure freedom around the world. "But I was ready. I was ready to give my life for my country."

"Telling stories again, Dad?"

Harrison's daughter, Elise, placed her hands on Harrison's shoulders. He patted her hand. "Better to hear it from someone who lived it," he said.

"Okay, kids, wash up. Dinner's almost ready." Elise clapped her hands to get the children moving. Janey gave Harrison a hug before scrambling off the couch. Ezra lingered.

"Something on your mind, Ezra?"

"Yeah. Why'd they call them Minutemen? It takes more than a minute for a rocket to get across the ocean."

"You've been reading about us in school?"

The boy nodded.

"Well, in truth, it took about thirty minutes. At twenty we reached the point of no return. From there it was just gravity and inertia. You know what inertia is?"

"It's like momentum."

"Yes. They called us Minutemen because only minutes separated us from losing the war. If we hadn't launched when we did … we wouldn't be here."

Harrison's voice cracked as he looked at his grandson.

Ezra popped up. "I'm going to go wash up before Mom starts counting."

"Smart boy," said Harrison, clearing his throat.

Alone now, Harrison allowed his thoughts to transport him to that day. It was the most thrilling day of his life. He felt he was a part of something truly momentous. He remembered suiting up… participating in the ceremonial salute… the ladder climb to the top of the makeshift gantry… seeing the open, waiting door to the inside of the missile… and once inside, hearing that door shut with an irreversible finality. He was supposed to hear that countdown, feel his ears pop as the miniature cabin pressurized… feel the G-force push his organs to his feet as the missile launched. He was supposed to go join his buddies on one last amusement park ride into the stratosphere and light up the horizon with their sacrifice. But, no.

Harrison took a deep breath. He got up and walked over to the window. He pushed the button that retracted the protective shield.

Outside, beyond the yellowish tint of leaded glass, was a horrid landscape. The scientists were wrong. There was no nuclear winter to cover the sins of the past with an ice blue layer of forgetfulness. No, what resulted was an oily abstract painting of oozing, bubbling rivers of rust and luminescent fields of radioactive fungi.

He was supposed to not be here.

And sometimes he wished he wasn't. Sometimes he wished his moment in the sun hadn't been stolen by news of the enemy's surrender.

His daughter, Elise, called from the kitchen. "Dad? Your dinner's getting cold."

"Coming," he said.

Harrison closed the window and made his way to the dinner table. The children laughed and joked as they ate their meal. Harrison sat. "Pass the rolls, please." Ezra grabbed the basket of rolls and passed them down. Elise shot him a look of surprise. Harrison nodded to his daughter. "Thank you, Ezra," he said.

And there were times like these that Harrison thanked all the stars in heaven for allowing him to see this day, to have these moments with his children, and his children's children. When the time finally came to step back outside, they would be the ones who would set things right again. They would be the ones to mend what's been damaged, to adopt a better way of living and a better way of dying. They would be the ones to, at last, make peace with the planet.

"Minutemen" debuts in this issue of Black Infinity.

As a child, Kurt Newton was weaned on episodes of The Twilight Zone *and* The Outer Limits, *and* Chiller Theater *(which showed many of the classic sci-fi horror movies of the '50s and '60s), laying the groundwork for his fertile imagination. His stories have appeared in numerous publications over the last twenty years, including* Weird Tales, Weirdbook, Space and Time, Dark Discoveries, Daily Science Fiction, The Arcanist *and* Hinnom Magazine. *He lives in Connecticut.*

DUEL ON SYRTIS
Poul Anderson

THE NIGHT WHISPERED THE MESSAGE. OVER THE MANY MILES OF LONELINESS IT WAS BORNE, CARRIED ON THE WIND, RUSTLED BY THE HALF-SENTIENT LICHENS AND THE DWARFED TREES, MURMURED FROM ONE TO ANOTHER OF the little creatures that huddled under crags, in caves, by shadowy dunes. In no words, but in a dim pulsing of dread which echoed through Kreega's brain, the warning ran—

They are hunting again.

Kreega shuddered in a sudden blast of wind. The night was enormous around him, above him, from the iron bitterness of the hills to the wheeling, glittering constellations light-years over his head. He reached out with his trembling perceptions, tuning himself to the brush and the wind and the small burrowing things underfoot, letting the night speak to him.

Alone, alone. There was not another Martian for a hundred miles of emptiness. There were only the tiny animals and the shivering brush and the thin, sad blowing of the wind.

The voiceless scream of dying traveled through the brush, from plant to plant, echoed by the fear-pulses of the animals and the ringingly reflecting cliffs. They were curling, shriveling and blackening as the rocket poured the glowing death down on them, and the withering veins and nerves cried to the stars.

Kreega huddled against a tall gaunt crag. His eyes were like yellow moons in the darkness, cold with terror and hate and a slowly gathering resolution. Grimly, he estimated that the death was being sprayed in a circle some ten miles across. And he was trapped in it, and soon the hunter would come after him.

He looked up to the indifferent glitter of stars, and a shudder went along his body. Then he sat down and began to think.

IT HAD STARTED a few days before, in the private office of the trader Wisby.

"I came to Mars," said Riordan, "to get me an owlie."

Wisby had learned the value of a poker face. He peered across the rim of his glass at the other man, estimating him.

Even in godforsaken holes like Port Armstrong one had heard of Riordan. Heir to a million-dollar shipping firm which he himself had pyramided into a System-wide monster, he was equally well known as a big game hunter. From the firedrakes of Mercury to the ice crawlers of Pluto, he'd bagged them all. Except, of course, a Martian. That particular game was forbidden now.

He sprawled in his chair, big and strong and ruthless, still a young man. He dwarfed the unkempt room with his size and the hard-held dynamo strength in him, and his cold green gaze dominated the trader.

"It's illegal, you know," said Wisby. "It's a twenty-year sentence if you're caught at it."

"Bah! The Martian Commissioner is at Ares, halfway round the planet. If we go at it right, who's ever to know?" Riordan gulped at his drink. "I'm well aware that in another year or so they'll have tightened up enough to make it impossible. This is the last chance for any man to get an owlie. That's why I'm here."

Wisby hesitated, looking out the window. Port Armstrong was no more than a dusty huddle of domes, interconnected by tunnels, in a red waste of sand stretching to the near horizon. An Earthman in airsuit and transparent helmet was walking down the street and

BLACK INFINITY • 213

a couple of Martians were lounging against a wall. Otherwise nothing—a silent, deadly monotony brooding under the shrunken sun. Life on Mars was not especially pleasant for a human.

"You're not falling into this owlie-loving that's corrupted all Earth?" demanded Riordan contemptuously.

"Oh, no," said Wisby. "I keep them in their place around my post. But times are changing. It can't be helped."

"There was a time when they were slaves," said Riordan. "Now those old women on Earth want to give 'em the vote." He snorted.

"Well, times are changing," repeated Wisby mildly. "When the first humans landed on Mars a hundred years ago, Earth had just gone through the Hemispheric Wars. The worst wars man had ever known. They damned near wrecked the old ideas of liberty and equality. People were suspicious and tough—they'd had to be, to survive. They weren't able to—to empathize the Martians, or whatever you call it. Not able to think of them as anything but intelligent animals. And Martians made such useful slaves—they need so little food or heat or oxygen, they can even live fifteen minutes or so without breathing at all. And the wild Martians made fine sport—intelligent game, that could get away as often as not, or even manage to kill the hunter."

"I know," said Riordan. "That's why I want to hunt one. It's no fun if the game doesn't have a chance."

"It's different now," went on Wisby. "Earth has been at peace for a long time. The liberals have gotten the upper hand. Naturally, one of their first reforms was to end Martian slavery."

Riordan swore. The forced repatriation of Martians working on his spaceships had cost him plenty. "I haven't time for your philosophizing," he said. "If you can arrange for me to get a Martian, I'll make it worth your while."

"How much worth it?" asked Wisby.

They haggled for a while before settling on a figure. Riordan had brought guns and a small rocketboat, but Wisby would have to supply radioactive material, a "hawk," and a rockhound. Then he had to be paid for the risk of legal action, though that was small. The final price came high.

"Now, where do I get my Martian?" inquired Riordan. He gestured at the two in the street. "Catch one of them and release him in the desert?"

It was Wisby's turn to be contemptuous. "One of *them*? Hah! Town loungers! A city dweller from Earth would give you a better fight."

The Martians didn't look impressive. They stood only some four feet high on skinny, claw-footed legs, and the arms, ending in bony four-fingered hands, were stringy. The chests were broad and deep, but the waists were ridiculously narrow. They were viviparous, warm-blooded, and suckled their young, but gray feathers covered their hides. The round, hook-beaked heads, with huge amber eyes and tufted feather ears, showed the origin of the name "owlie." They wore only pouched belts and carried sheath knives; even the liberals of Earth weren't ready to allow the natives modern tools and weapons. There were too many old grudges.

"The Martians always were good fighters," said Riordan. "They wiped out quite a few Earth settlements in the old days."

"The wild ones," agreed Wisby. "But not these. They're just stupid laborers, as dependent on our civilization as we are. You want a real old timer, and I know where one's to be found."

He spread a map on the desk. "See, here in the Hraefnian Hills, about a hundred miles from here. These Martians live a long time, maybe two centuries, and this fellow Kreega has been around since the first Earthmen came. He led a lot of Martian raids in the early days, but since the general amnesty and peace he's lived all alone up there, in one of the old ruined towers. A real old-time warrior who hates Earthmen's guts. He comes here once in a while with furs and minerals to trade, so I know a little about him." Wisby's eyes gleamed savagely. "You'll be doing us all a favor by shooting the arrogant bastard. He struts around here as if the place belonged to him. And he'll give you a run for your money."

Riordan's massive dark head nodded in satisfaction.

THE MAN HAD A BIRD and a rockhound. That was bad. Without them, Kreega could lose himself in the labyrinth of caves and canyons and scrubby thickets—but the hound could follow his scent and the bird could spot him from above.

To make matters worse, the man had landed near Kreega's tower. The weapons were all there—now he was cut off, unarmed and alone save for what feeble help the desert life could give. Unless he could double back to the place somehow—but meanwhile he had to survive.

He sat in a cave, looking down past a tortured wilderness of sand and bush and wind-carved rock, miles in the thin clear air to the glitter of metal where the rocket lay. The man was a tiny speck in the huge barren landscape, a lonely insect crawling under the deep-blue sky. Even by day, the stars glistened in the tenuous atmosphere. Weak pallid sunlight spilled over rocks tawny and ocherous and rust-red, over the low dusty thorn-bushes and the gnarled little trees and the sand that blew faintly between them. Equatorial Mars!

Lonely or not, the man had a gun that could spang death clear to the horizon, and he had his beasts, and there would be a radio in the rocketboat for calling his fellows. And the glowing death ringed them in, a charmed circle which Kreega could not cross without bringing a worse death on himself than the rifle would give—

Or was there a worse death than that— to be shot by a monster and have his stuffed hide carried back as a trophy for fools to gape at? The old iron pride of his race rose in Kreega, hard and bitter and unrelenting. He didn't ask much of life these days—solitude in his tower to think the long thoughts of a Martian and create the small exquisite artworks which he loved; the company of his kind at the Gathering Season, grave ancient ceremony and acrid merriment and the chance to beget and rear sons; an occasional trip to the Earthling settling for the metal goods and the wine which were the only valuable things they had brought to Mars; a vague dream of raising his folk to a place where they could stand as equals before all the universe. No more. And now they would take even this from him!

He rasped a curse on the human and resumed his patient work, chipping a spearhead for what puny help it could give him. The brush rustled dryly in alarm, tiny hidden animals squeaked their terror, the desert shouted to him of the monster that strode toward his cave. But he didn't have to flee right away.

RIORDAN SPRAYED the heavy-metal isotope in a ten-mile circle around the old tower. He did that by night, just in case patrol craft might be snooping around. But once he had landed, he was safe—he could always claim to be peacefully exploring, hunting leapers or some such thing.

The radioactive had a half-life of about four days, which meant that it would be unsafe to approach for some three weeks—two at the minimum. That was time enough, when the Martian was boxed in so small an area.

There was no danger that he would try to cross it. The owlies had learned what radioactivity meant, back when they fought the humans. And their vision, extending well into the ultra-violet, made it directly visible to them through its fluorescence—to say nothing of the wholly unhuman extra senses they had. No, Kreega would try to hide, and perhaps to fight, and eventually he'd be cornered.

Still, there was no use taking chances. Riordan set a timer on the boat's radio. If he didn't come back within two weeks to turn it off, it would emit a signal which Wisby would hear, and he'd be rescued.

He checked his other equipment. He had an airsuit designed for Martian conditions, with a small pump operated by a power-beam from the boat to compress the atmosphere sufficiently for him to breathe it. The same unit recovered enough water from his breath so that the weight of supplies for several days was, in Martian gravity, not too great for him to bear. He had a .45 rifle built to shoot in Martian air, that was heavy enough for his purposes. And, of course, compass and binoculars and sleeping bag. Pretty light equipment, but he preferred a minimum anyway.

For ultimate emergencies there was the little tank of suspensine. By turning a valve, he could release it into his air system. The gas didn't exactly induce suspended animation, but it paralyzed efferent nerves and slowed the overall metabolism to a point where a man could live for weeks on one lungful of air. It was useful in surgery, and had saved the life of more than one interplanetary explorer whose oxygen system went awry. But Riordan didn't expect to have to use it. He certainly hoped he wouldn't. It would be tedious to lie fully conscious for days waiting for the automatic signal to call Wisby.

He stepped out of the boat and locked it. No danger that the owlie would break in if he should double back; it would take tordenite to crack that hull.

He whistled to his animals. They were native beasts, long ago domesticated by the Martians and later by man. The rockhound was like a gaunt wolf, but huge-breasted and feathered, a tracker as good as any Terrestrial bloodhound. The "hawk" had less resemblance to its counterpart of Earth: it was a bird of prey, but in the tenuous atmosphere it needed a six-foot wingspread to lift its small body. Riordan was pleased with their training.

The hound bayed, a low quavering note which would have been muffled almost to inaudibility by the thin air and the man's plastic helmet had the suit not included microphones and amplifiers. It circled, sniffing, while the hawk rose into the alien sky.

Riordan did not look closely at the tower. It was a crumbling stump atop a rusty hill, unhuman and grotesque. Once, perhaps ten thousand years ago, the Martians had had a civilization of sorts, cities and agriculture and a neolithic technology. But according to their own traditions they had achieved a union or symbiosis with the wild life of the planet and had abandoned such mechanical aids as unnecessary. Riordan snorted.

The hound bayed again. The noise seemed to hang eerily in the still, cold air; to shiver from cliff and crag and die reluctantly under the enormous silence. But it was a bugle call, a haughty challenge to a world grown old—stand aside, make way, here comes the conqueror!

The animal suddenly loped forward. He had a scent. Riordan swung into a long, easy low-gravity stride. His eyes gleamed like green ice. The hunt was begun!

BREATH SOBBED in Kreega's lungs, hard and quick and raw. His legs felt weak and heavy, and the thudding of his heart seemed to shake his whole body.

Still he ran, while the frightful clamor rose behind him and the padding of feet grew ever nearer. Leaping, twisting, bounding from crag to crag, sliding down shaly ravines and slipping through clumps of trees, Kreega fled.

The hound was behind him and the hawk soaring overhead. In a day and a night they had driven him to this, running like a crazed leaper with death baying at his heels—he had not imagined a human could move so fast or with such endurance.

The desert fought for him; the plants with their queer blind life that no Earthling would ever understand were on his side. Their thorny branches twisted away as he darted through and then came back to rake the flanks of the hound, slow him—but they could not stop his brutal rush. He ripped past their strengthless clutching fingers and yammered on the trail of the Martian.

The human was toiling a good mile behind, but showed no sign of tiring. Still Kreega ran. He had to reach the cliff edge before the hunter saw him through his rifle sights—had to, had to, and the hound was snarling a yard behind now.

Up the long slope he went. The hawk fluttered, striking at him, seeking to lay beak and talons in his head. He batted at the creature with his spear and dodged around a tree. The tree snaked out a branch from which the hound rebounded, yelling till the rocks rang.

The Martian burst onto the edge of the cliff. It fell sheer to the canyon floor, five hundred feet of iron-streaked rock tumbling into windy depths. Beyond, the lowering sun glared in his eyes. He paused only an instant, etched black against the sky, a perfect shot if the human should come into view, and then he sprang over the edge.

He had hoped the rockhound would go shooting past, but the animal braked itself barely in time. Kreega went down the cliff face, clawing into every tiny crevice, shuddering as the age-worn rock crumbled under his fingers. The hawk swept close, hacking at him and screaming for its master. He couldn't fight it, not with every finger and toe needed to hang against shattering death, but—

He slid along the face of the precipice into a gray-green clump of vines, and his nerves thrilled forth the appeal of the ancient symbiosis. The hawk swooped again and he lay unmoving, rigid as if dead, until it cried in shrill triumph and settled on his shoulder to pluck out his eyes.

Then the vines stirred. They weren't strong, but their thorns sank into the flesh and it couldn't pull loose. Kreega toiled on down into the canyon while the vines pulled the hawk apart.

Riordan loomed hugely against the darkening sky. He fired, once, twice, the bullets humming wickedly close, but as shadows swept up from the depths the Martian was covered.

The man turned up his speech amplifier and his voice rolled and boomed monstrously through the gathering night, thunder such as dry Mars had not heard for millennia: "Score one for you! But it isn't enough! I'll find you!"

The sun slipped below the horizon and night came down like a falling curtain. Through the darkness Kreega heard the man laughing. The old rocks trembled with his laughter.

RIORDAN WAS TIRED with the long chase and the niggling insufficiency of his oxygen supply. He wanted a smoke and hot food, and neither was to be had. Oh well, he'd appreciate the luxuries of life all the more when he got home —with the Martian's skin.

He grinned as he made camp. The little fellow was a worthwhile quarry, that was for damn sure. He'd held out for two days now, in a little ten-mile circle of ground, and he'd even killed the hawk. But Riordan was close enough to him now so that the hound could follow his spoor, for Mars had no watercourses to break a trail. So it didn't matter.

He lay watching the splendid night of stars. It would get cold before long, unmercifully cold, but his sleeping bag was a good-enough insulator to keep him warm with the help of solar energy stored during the day by its Gergen cells. Mars was dark at night, its moons of little help—Phobos a hurtling speck, Deimos merely a bright star. Dark and cold and empty. The rockhound had burrowed into the loose sand nearby, but it would raise the alarm if the Martian should come sneaking near the camp. Not that that was likely—he'd have to find shelter somewhere too, if he didn't want to freeze.

The bushes and the trees and the little furtive animals whispered a word he could not hear, chattered and gossiped on the wind about the Martian who kept himself warm with work. But he didn't understand that language which was no language.

Drowsily, Riordan thought of past hunts. The big game of Earth, lion and tiger and elephant and buffalo and sheep on the high sunblazing peaks of the Rockies. Rain forests of Venus and the coughing roar of a many-legged swamp monster crashing through the trees to the place where he stood waiting. Primitive throb of drums in a hot wet night, chant of beaters dancing around a fire—scramble along the hell-plains of Mercury with a swollen sun licking against his puny insulating suit—the grandeur and desolation of Neptune's liquid-gas swamps and the huge blind thing that screamed and blundered after him—

But this was the loneliest and strangest and perhaps most dangerous hunt of all, and on that account the best. He had no malice toward the Martian; he respected the little being's courage as he respected the bravery of the other animals he had fought. Whatever trophy he brought home from this chase would be well earned.

The fact that his success would have to be treated discreetly didn't matter. He hunted less for the glory of it—though he had to admit he didn't mind the publicity—than for love. His ancestors had fought under one name or another—viking, Crusader, mercenary, rebel, patriot, whatever was fashionable at the moment. Struggle was in his blood, and in these degenerate days there was little to struggle against save what he hunted.

Well—tomorrow—he drifted off to sleep.

HE WOKE in the short gray dawn, made a quick breakfast, and whistled his hound to heel. His nostrils dilated with excitement, a high keen drunkenness that sang wonderfully within him. Today—maybe today!

They had to take a roundabout way down into the canyon and the hound cast about for an hour before he picked up the scent. Then the deep-voiced cry rose again and they were off—more slowly now, for it was a cruel stony trail.

The sun climbed high as they worked along the ancient river-bed. Its pale chill light washed needle-sharp crags and fantastically painted cliffs, shale and sand and the wreck of geological ages. The low harsh brush crunched under the man's feet, writhing and crackling its impotent protest. Otherwise it was still, a deep and taut and somehow waiting stillness.

The hound shattered the quiet with an eager yelp and plunged forward. Hot scent! Riordan dashed after him, trampling through dense bush, panting and swearing and grinning with excitement.

Suddenly the brush opened underfoot. With a howl of dismay, the hound slid down the sloping wall of the pit it had covered. Riordan flung himself forward with tigerish swiftness, flat down on his belly with one hand barely catching the animal's tail. The shock almost pulled him into the hole, too. He wrapped one arm around a bush that clawed at his helmet and pulled the hound back.

Shaking, he peered into the trap. It had been well made—about twenty feet deep, with walls as straight and narrow as the sand would allow, and skillfully covered with brush. Planted in the bottom were three wicked-looking flint spears. Had he been a shade less quick in his reactions, he would have lost the hound and perhaps himself.

He skinned his teeth in a wolf-grin and looked around. The owlie must have worked all night on it. Then he couldn't be far away—and he'd be very tired—

As if to answer his thoughts, a boulder crashed down from the nearer cliff wall. It was a monster, but a falling object on Mars has less than half the acceleration it does on Earth. Riordan scrambled aside as it boomed onto the place where he had been lying.

"Come on!" he yelled, and plunged toward the cliff.

For an instant a gray form loomed over the edge, hurled a spear at him. Riordan snapped a shot at it, and it vanished. The spear glanced off the tough fabric of his suit and he scrambled up a narrow ledge to the top of the precipice.

The Martian was nowhere in sight, but a faint red trail led into the rugged hill country. *Winged him, by God!* The hound was slower in negotiating the shale-covered trail;

his own feet were bleeding when he came up. Riordan cursed him and they set out again.

They followed the trail for a mile or two and then it ended. Riordan looked around the wilderness of trees and needles which blocked view in any direction. Obviously the owlie had backtracked and climbed up one of those rocks, from which he could take a flying leap to some other point. But which one?

Sweat which he couldn't wipe off ran down the man's face and body. He itched intolerably, and his lungs were raw from gasping at his dole of air. But still he laughed in gusty delight. What a chase! What a chase!

KREEGA LAY in the shadow of a tall rock and shuddered with weariness. Beyond the shade, the sunlight danced in what to him was a blinding, intolerable dazzle, hot and cruel and life-hungry, hard and bright as the metal of the conquerors.

It had been a mistake to spend priceless hours when he might have been resting working on that trap. It hadn't worked, and he might have known that it wouldn't. And now he was hungry, and thirst was like a wild beast in his mouth and throat, and still they followed him.

They weren't far behind now. All this day they had been dogging him; he had never been more than half an hour ahead. No rest, no rest, a devil's hunt through a tormented wilderness of stone and sand, and now he could only wait for the battle with an iron burden of exhaustion laid on him.

The wound in his side burned. It wasn't deep, but it had cost him blood and pain and the few minutes of catnapping he might have snatched.

For a moment, the warrior Kreega was gone and a lonely, frightened infant sobbed in the desert silence. *Why can't they let me alone?*

A low, dusty-green bush rustled. A sand-runner piped in one of the ravines. They were getting close.

Wearily, Kreega scrambled up on top of the rock and crouched low. He had backtracked to it; they should by rights go past him toward his tower.

He could see it from here, a low yellow ruin worn by the winds of millennia. There had only been time to dart in, snatch a bow and a few arrows and an axe. Pitiful weapons—the arrows could not penetrate the Earthman's suit when there was only a Martian's thin grasp to draw the bow, and even with a steel head the axe was a small and feeble thing. But it was all he had, he and his few little allies of a desert which fought only to keep its solitude.

Repatriated slaves had told him of the Earthlings' power. Their roaring machines filled the silence of their own deserts, gouged the quiet face of their own moon, shook the planets with a senseless fury of meaningless energy. They were the conquerors, and it never occurred to them that an ancient peace and stillness could be worth preserving.

Well—he fitted an arrow to the string and crouched in the silent, flimmering sunlight, waiting.

The hound came first, yelping and howling. Kreega drew the bow as far as he could. But the human had to come near first—

There he came, running and bounding over the rocks, rifle in hand and restless eyes shining with taut green light, closing in for the death. Kreega swung softly around. The beast was beyond the rock now, the Earthman almost below it.

The bow twanged. With a savage thrill, Kreega saw the arrow go through the hound, saw the creature leap in the air and then roll over and over, howling and biting at the thing in its breast.

Like a gray thunderbolt, the Martian launched himself off the rock, down at the human. If his axe could shatter that helmet—

He struck the man and they went down together. Wildly, the Martian hewed. The axe glanced off the plastic—he hadn't had room for a swing. Riordan roared and lashed out with a fist. Retching, Kreega rolled backward.

Riordan snapped a shot at him. Kreega turned and fled. The man got to one knee, sighting carefully on the gray form that streaked up the nearest slope.

A little sandsnake darted up the man's leg and wrapped about his wrist. Its small strength was just enough to pull the gun aside. The bullet screamed past Kreega's ear as he vanished into a cleft.

He felt the thin death-agony of the snake as the man pulled it loose and crushed it underfoot. Somewhat later, he heard a dull boom echoing between the hills. The man had gotten explosives from his boat and blown up the tower.

He had lost axe and bow. Now he was utterly weaponless, without even a place to retire for a last stand. And the hunter would not give up. Even without his animals, he would follow, more slowly but as relentlessly as before.

Kreega collapsed on a shelf of rock. Dry sobbing racked his thin body, and the sunset wind cried with him.

Presently he looked up, across a red and yellow immensity to the low sun. Long shadows were creeping over the land, peace and stillness for a brief moment before the iron cold of night closed down. Somewhere the soft trill of a sandrunner echoed between low wind-worn cliffs, and the brush began to speak, whispering back and forth in its ancient wordless tongue.

The desert, the planet and its wind and sand under the high cold stars, the clean open land of silence and loneliness and a destiny which was not man's, spoke to him. The enormous oneness of life on Mars, drawn together against the cruel environment, stirred in his blood. As the sun went down and the stars blossomed forth in awesome frosty glory, Kreega began to think again.

He did not hate his persecutor, but the grimness of Mars was in him. He fought the war of all which was old and primitive and lost in its own dreams against the alien and the desecrator. It was as ancient and pitiless as life, that war, and each battle won or lost meant something even if no one ever heard of it.

You do not fight alone, whispered the desert. *You fight for all Mars, and we are with you.*

Something moved in the darkness, a tiny warm form running across his hand, a little feathered mouse-like thing that burrowed under the sand and lived its small fugitive life and was glad in its own way of living. But it was a part of a world, and Mars has no pity in its voice.

Still, a tenderness was within Kreega's heart, and he whispered gently in the language that was not a language, *You will do this for us? You will do it, little brother?*

* * *

RIORDAN WAS TOO TIRED to sleep well. He had lain awake for a long time, thinking, and that is not good for a man alone in the Martian hills.

So now the rockhound was dead too. It didn't matter, the owlie wouldn't escape. But somehow the incident brought home to him the immensity and the age and the loneliness of the desert.

It whispered to him. The brush rustled and something wailed in darkness and the wind blew with a wild mournful sound over faintly starlit cliffs, and it was as if they all somehow had voice, as if the whole world muttered and threatened him in the night. Dimly, he wondered if man would ever subdue Mars, if the human race had not finally run across something bigger than itself.

But that was nonsense. Mars was old and worn-out and barren, dreaming itself into slow death. The tramp of human feet, shouts of men and roar of sky-storming rockets, were waking it, but to a new destiny, to man's. When Ares lifted its hard spires above the hills of Syrtis, where then were the ancient gods of Mars?

It was cold, and the cold deepened as the night wore on. The stars were fire and ice, glittering diamonds in the deep crystal dark. Now and then he could hear a faint snapping borne through the earth as rock or tree split open. The wind laid itself to rest, sound froze to death, there was only the hard, clear starlight falling through space to shatter on the ground.

Once something stirred. He woke from a restless sleep and saw a small thing skittering toward him. He groped for the rifle beside his sleeping bag, then laughed harshly. It was only a sandmouse. But it proved that the

Martian had no chance of sneaking up on him while he rested.

He didn't laugh again. The sound had echoed too hollowly in his helmet.

With the clear bitter dawn he was up. He wanted to get the hunt over with. He was dirty and unshaven inside the unit, sick of iron rations pushed through the airlock, stiff and sore with exertion. Lacking the hound, which he'd had to shoot, tracking would be slow, but he didn't want to go back to Port Armstrong for another. No, hell take that Martian, he'd have the devil's skin soon!

Breakfast and a little moving made him feel better. He looked with a practiced eye for the Martian's trail. There was sand and brush over everything, even the rocks had a thin coating of their own erosion. The owlie couldn't cover his tracks perfectly—if he tried, it would slow him too much. Riordan fell into a steady jog.

Noon found him on higher ground, rough hills with gaunt needles of rock reaching yards into the sky. He kept going, confident of his own ability to wear down the quarry. He'd run deer to earth back home, day after day until the animal's heart broke and it waited quivering for him to come.

The trail looked clear and fresh now. He tensed with the knowledge that the Martian couldn't be far away.

Too clear! Could this be bait for another trap? He hefted the rifle and proceeded more warily. But no, there wouldn't have been time—

He mounted a high ridge and looked over the grim, fantastic landscape. Near the horizon he saw a blackened strip, the border of his radioactive barrier. The Martian couldn't go further, and if he doubled back Riordan would have an excellent chance of spotting him.

He tuned up his speaker and let his voice roar into the stillness: "Come out, owlie! I'm going to get you, you might as well come out now and be done with it!"

The echoes took it up, flying back and forth between the naked crags, trembling and shivering under the brassy arch of sky. *Come out, come out, come out—*

The Martian seemed to appear from thin air, a gray ghost rising out of the jumbled stones and standing poised not twenty feet away. For an instant, the shock of it was too much; Riordan gaped in disbelief. Kreega waited, quivering ever so faintly as if he were a mirage.

Then the man shouted and lifted his rifle. Still the Martian stood there as if carved in gray stone, and with a shock of disappointment Riordan thought that he had, after all, decided to give himself to an inevitable death.

Well, it had been a good hunt. "So long," whispered Riordan, and squeezed the trigger.

Since the sandmouse had crawled into the barrel, the gun exploded.

RIORDAN HEARD the roar and saw the barrel peel open like a rotten banana. He wasn't hurt, but as he staggered back from the shock Kreega lunged at him.

The Martian was four feet tall, and skinny and weaponless, but he hit the Earthling like a small tornado. His legs wrapped around the man's waist and his hands got to work on the airhose.

Riordan went down under the impact. He snarled, tigerishly, and fastened his hands on the Martian's narrow throat. Kreega snapped futilely at him with his beak. They rolled over in a cloud of dust. The brush began to chatter excitedly.

Riordan tried to break Kreega's neck—the Martian twisted away, bored in again.

With a shock of horror, the man heard the hiss of escaping air as Kreega's beak and fingers finally worried the airhose loose. An automatic valve clamped shut, but there was no connection with the pump now—

Riordan cursed, and got his hands about the Martian's throat again. Then he simply lay there, squeezing, and not all Kreega's writhing and twistings could break that grip.

Riordan smiled sleepily and held his hands in place. After five minutes or so Kreega was still. Riordan kept right on throttling him for another five minutes, just to make sure. Then he let go and fumbled at his back, trying to reach the pump.

The air in his suit was hot and foul. He couldn't quite reach around to connect the hose to the pump—

Poor design, he thought vaguely. *But then, these airsuits weren't meant for battle armor.*

He looked at the slight, silent form of the Martian. A faint breeze ruffled the gray feathers. What a fighter the little guy had been! He'd be the pride of the trophy room, back on Earth.

Let's see now—He unrolled his sleeping bag and spread it carefully out. He'd never make it to the rocket with what air he had, so it was necessary to let the suspensine into his suit. But he'd have to get inside the bag, lest the nights freeze his blood solid.

He crawled in, fastening the flaps carefully, and opened the valve on the suspensine tank. Lucky he had it—but then, a good hunter thinks of everything. He'd get awfully bored, lying here till Wisby caught the signal in ten days or so and came to find him, but he'd last. It would be an experience to remember. In this dry air, the Martian's skin would keep perfectly well.

He felt the paralysis creep up on him, the waning of heartbeat and lung action. His senses and mind were still alive, and he grew aware that complete relaxation has its unpleasant aspects. Oh, well—he'd won. He'd killed the wiliest game with his own hands.

Presently Kreega sat up. He felt himself gingerly. There seemed to be a rib broken—well, that could be fixed. He was still alive. He'd been choked for a good ten minutes, but a Martian can last fifteen without air.

He opened the sleeping bag and got Riordan's keys. Then he limped slowly back to the rocket. A day or two of experimentation taught him how to fly it. He'd go to his kinsmen near Syrtis. Now that they had an Earthly machine, and Earthly weapons to copy—

But there was other business first. He didn't hate Riordan, but Mars is a hard world. He went back and dragged the Earthling into a cave and hid him beyond all possibility of human search parties finding him.

For a while he looked into the man's eyes. Horror stared dumbly back at him. He spoke slowly, in halting English: "For those you killed, and for being a stranger on a world that does not want you, and against the day when Mars is free, I leave you."

Before departing, he got several oxygen tanks from the boat and hooked them into the man's air supply. That was quite a bit of air for one in suspended animation. Enough to keep him alive for a thousand years.

"Duel on Syrtis" first appeared in the March 1951 issue of Planet Stories, *with an illustration by Herman Vestal.*

Multiple award-winning American author Poul Anderson (1928 – 2001) enjoyed an amazingly prolific writing career that touched six decades and produced around six dozen novels and about two hundred short stories. Along the way, Anderson picked up seven Hugo Awards, five Prometheus Awards, three Nebulas, and an Inkpot, among many such honors. He was named the 16th SFWA Grand Master, in 1998, by the Science Fiction Writers of America.

Algis Budrys once stated, Anderson "has for some time been science fiction's best storyteller." In 2001, Anderson was further honored when Asteroid 7758, discovered in 1990 by American astronomer Eleanor Helin, was officially named (at the suggestion of SF author David Brin) as Poulanderson.

COMPLETE YOUR COLLECTION!

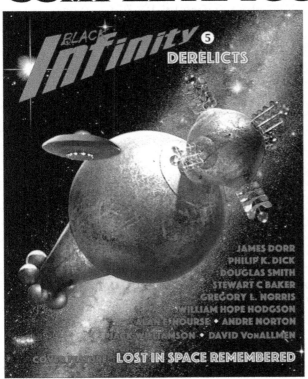

TEST ROCKET!
By Jack Douglas

CAPTAIN BAIRD STOOD AT THE WINDOW OF THE LABORATORY WHERE THE THOUSAND PARTS OF THE STRANGE ROCKET LAY STREWN IN CAREFUL ORDER. SMALL GROUPS WORKED SLOWLY OVER THE DISMANTLED PARTS. The captain wanted to ask but something stopped him. Behind him Doctor Johannsen sat at his desk, his gnarled old hand tight about a whiskey bottle, the bottle the doctor always had in his desk but never brought out except when he was alone, and waited for Captain Baird to ask his question. Captain Baird turned at last.

"They are our markings?" Captain Baird asked. It was not the question. Captain Baird knew the markings of the Rocket Testing Station as well as the doctor did.

"Yes," the doctor said, "they are our markings. Identical. But not our paint."

Captain Baird turned back to the window. Six months ago it had happened. Ten minutes after launching, the giant test rocket had been only a speck on the observation screen. Captain Baird had turned away in disgust.

"A mouse!" the captain had said, "unfortunate a mouse can't observe, build, report. My men are getting restless, Johannsen."

"When we are ready, Captain," the doctor had said.

It was twelve hours before the urgent call from Central Control brought the captain running back to the laboratory. The doctor was there before him. Professor Schultz wasted no time, he pointed to the instrument panel. "A sudden shift, see for yourself. We'll miss Mars by a million and a quarter at least."

Two hours later the shift in course of the test rocket was apparent to all of them and so was their disappointment.

* * *

"ACCORDING TO THE INSTRUMENTS the steering shifted a quarter of an inch. No reason shows up," Professor Schultz said.

"Flaw in the metal?" Doctor Johannsen said.

"How far can it go?" Captain Baird asked.

Professor Schultz shrugged. "Until the fuel runs out, which is probably as good as never, or until the landing mechanism is activated by a planet-sized body."

"Course? Did you plot it?" The doctor asked.

"Of course I did," Professor Schultz said, "as close as I can calculate it is headed for Alpha Centauri."

Captain Baird turned away. The doctor watched him.

"Perhaps you will not be quite so hasty with your men's lives in the future, Captain?" the doctor said.

Professor Schultz was spinning dials. "No contact," the professor said, "No contact at all."

That had been six months ago. Three more test rockets had been fired successfully before the urgent report came through from Alaskan Observation Post No. 4. A rocket was coming across the Pole.

BLACK INFINITY • 225

The strange rocket was tracked and escorted by atomic-armed fighters all the way to the Rocket Testing Station where it cut its own motors and gently landed. In the center of a division of atomic-armed infantry the captain, the doctor, and everyone else, waited impatiently. There was an air of uneasiness.

"You're sure it's not ours?" Captain Baird asked.

The doctor laughed. "Identical, yes, but three times the size of ours."

"Perhaps one of the Asian ones?"

"No, it's our design, but too large, much too large."

Professor Schultz put their thoughts into words. "Looks like someone copied ours. Someone, somewhere. It's hard to imagine, but true nevertheless."

They waited two weeks. Nothing happened. Then a radiation-shielded team went in to examine the rocket. Two more weeks and the strange rocket was dismantled and spread over the field of the testing station. The rocket was dismantled and the station had begun to talk to itself in whispers and look at the sky.

Captain Baird stood now at the window and looked out at the dismantled rocket. He looked but his mind was not on the parts of the rocket he could see from the window.

"The materials, they're not ours?" the captain asked.

"Unknown here," the doctor said.

The captain nodded. "Those were our instruments?"

"Yes." The doctor still held the whiskey bottle in a tight grip.

"They sent them back," the captain said.

* * *

THE DOCTOR CRASHED the bottle hard against the desk top. "Ask it, Captain, for God's sake!"

The captain turned to face the doctor directly. "It was a man, a full-grown man."

The doctor sighed as if letting the pent-up steam of his heart escape. "Yes, it is a man. It breathes, it eats, it has all the attributes of a man. But it is not of our planet."

"Its speech..." the captain began.

"That isn't speech, Captain," the doctor said, breaking in sharply, "It's only sound." The doctor stopped; he examined the label of his bottle of whiskey very carefully. A good brand of whiskey. "He seems quite happy in the storeroom. You know, Captain, what puzzled me at first? He can't read. He can't read anything, not even the instruments in that ship. In fact, he shows no interest in his rocket at all."

The captain sat down now. He sat at the desk and faced the doctor. "At least *they* had the courage to send a man, not a mouse. Doctor, a man."

The doctor stared at the captain, his hand squeezing and unsqueezing on the whiskey bottle. "A man who can't read his own instruments?" The doctor laughed. "Perhaps you too have failed to see the point? Like that stupid general who sits out there waiting for the men from somewhere to invade?"

"Don't you think it's a possibility?"

The doctor nodded. "A very good possibility, Captain, but they will not be men." The doctor seemed to pause and lean forward. "That rocket, Captain, is a test rocket. A test rocket *just like ours!*"

Then the doctor picked up his whiskey bottle at last and poured two glasses.

"Perhaps a drink, Captain?"

The captain was watching the sky outside the window.

👽 👽 👽

"Test Rocket!" first appeared in the April 1959 issue of Amazing Science Fiction Stories.

American author and comedy writer Jack Douglas (1908–1989) wrote material for Bob Hope, Jerry Lewis, Johnny Carson, Woody Allen and other stars, as well as scripts and sketches for several television shows, including The Adventures of Ozzie and Harriet. In 1967 Douglas took home the Emmy for Outstanding Writing Achievement in Comedy, for his work on Rowan & Martin's Laugh-In.

"Test Rocket!" is one of only three known SF stories by Douglas, all of which appeared in Amazing Stories in 1959 and 1960.

SPACE ANGEL

in "RESCUE MISSION"

"ALL SET, SKIPPER!"

AT AN EARTH LAUNCHING SITE WE FIND SCOTT McCLOUD, BETTER KNOWN AS *SPACE ANGEL*, AND TAURUS, HIS FLIGHT ENGINEER, LOADING AN UNTESTED AUXILIARY CRAFT, DART II, ABOARD THEIR GIANT SPACE SHIP, THE STARDUSTER.....

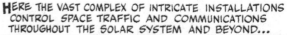

Story and art by Alex Toth
From *JACK and JILL* Magazine 1960

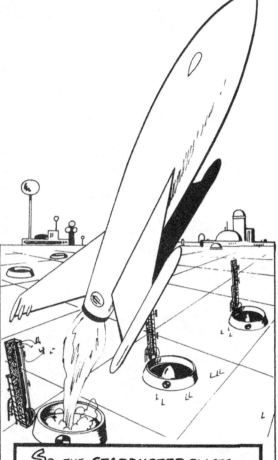

Made in the USA
Middletown, DE
05 March 2022